Over the following months, Rose saw her own image transformed, almost as though she herself had nothing to do with it. She was expected to pay for her own shoes and underwear, but she had some savings and it would have been a sin, she told herself, to wear the beautiful clothes handed down by the countess with her clumsy maid's footwear. So she allowed Rodwell to steer her into the shoe department at Harrods, where she paid a breathtaking £3 – almost three weeks' wages – for a pair of black and a pair of beige leather shoes, both with high Louis heels and fancy-cut instep straps. Still aghast at her own extravagance, she crowned the exercise by spending thirteen shillings on two pairs of silk stockings with fancy clocks up the sides, and four shillings on a pair of suede gloves.

After that they went up to the beauty salon to arrange her hairdressing and hair waving lessons, and a course of instruction in manicure. That would cost even more than her shoes, stockings and gloves, but at least Lady Clifton was paying . . . But Harrods was only the beginning.

Also by Merle Jones

Mademoiselle
Kingmaker
Lottie Casanova

For Annwen Williams
who sets the gold standard
for good neighbours

Prologue
New York, 1957

Nobody should be allowed to wear Balenciaga to the office, Alexandra Moncreiff reflected savagely — particularly a jumped-up former parlour-maid.

The woman across the desk eyed her with suppressed amusement and thought in her turn that no one should radiate such an air of hostile dissatisfaction — particularly the impoverished and under-qualified grand-daughter of an earl out seeking her first job.

'Hmm, not a very academic CV for someone applying for a teaching post,' she said neutrally.

Alexandra bridled. 'I attended the best schools in Europe and my languages are impeccable.'

'True. A pity, though, that you don't offer German in addition to French and Italian.' Her tone suddenly changed. '*Parliamo Italiano!*'

Alexandra's upper lip curled contemptuously. Really, was there no end to this woman's vulgarity? 'I beg your pardon,' she said, her tone making it clear that was the last thing she was asking.

Rose Rush tapped the table irritably with a silver pencil and said, still in Italian: 'I am not showing off, Miss Moncreiff — I am testing you. This *is* an interview, you know.'

Colour flared in Alexandra's cheeks. How dare she? She's humiliating me for the fun of it! She gritted her teeth and managed to force out an appropriate response.

The exchange ground on, and Alexandra gradually began to realise this was not the beggar on horseback she had confidently expected to encounter. She was grilled in impeccable Italian and French — and no nonsense about the pen of her aunt: incisive enquiries about the contents of obscure Parisian museums with which she had professed familiarity; questions about the train service in central Italy and the quickest way to travel between various cultural centres. As they progressed, Alexandra forced herself to remember this was the best staff agency on the Eastern seaboard. If one was accepted by Best of British, one was better paid and more highly respected than any other member of staff.

Any other member of staff . . . that was really the rub. The indignity of being cross-examined by this nobody was only a small part of it. That she should be reduced to looking for paid employment in a job of the sort for which she had once assumed she would engage her own household staff was the worst humiliation she could imagine. That the person directing the disaster should be a former servant of her family was almost too much to bear.

With a start she realised her attention had wandered from what Miss Rush had been discussing. Alexandra was infuriated again to see the woman eyeing her without anger but with cool speculation. She took a deep, sighing breath and said to Alexandra: 'I wonder if we really have anything to say to each other, Miss Moncreiff. I think perhaps too much has gone on between your family and me for there to be any easy business relationship now. What on earth brought you to me?'

'Where else could I go?' Alexandra almost spat the words.

Her hostility was so intense that Rose recoiled from her, then said: 'Don't be absurd! Manhattan is full of high-grade placement agencies. Why mine? It's obvious you knew of the connection. Your whole attitude has been shrieking it ever since you came in.'

Alexandra could not meet her eyes. 'Because you're the best,' she said sullenly. 'It was shaming enough to have come to this, but to have gone to one of those . . . those slave markets! At least your establishment gives the impression that some of its employees are working because they choose to do so rather than because they have to.'

Rose Rush's expression was ice cold. 'Make no mistake, Miss Moncreiff. No one takes on this type of work unless they have to, whatever they may say about it. It involves a certain loss of face, however glamorous the job, and none of us likes that, do we?' As she spoke the last words, she smiled. It was like a sliver of broken glass.

She went on: 'I'm about to offer you some sincere advice. I have to say before I start that I believe you will disregard it. Nevertheless, please try to remember it does not help me in any way to give it, and I believe it will save you a great deal of pain in future if you bear it in mind. If you feel unable to take any notice of what I say, I have one further suggestion: forget about working for a family and train as a secretary. At least in an office job you will retain some personal freedom.'

'Yes, in some Wall Street anthill along with hundreds of common little girls from Queens!'

'There are far worse companions — the rich, for instance. Now listen carefully, because I have no intention of repeating myself. No doubt you see me placing you with, say, an ambassadorial family in Washington, or some old-established southern aristocrats in Virginia, or even the sort of square-jawed New England protestants so beloved of the movies. Forget it. That was twenty years ago. Most of them are either as impoverished as your own family nowadays, or if they come from Europe they bring their own help with them.'

Rose did not fail to notice Alexandra wince as she used the graphic Americanism, 'help'. Hell, she thought, anyone would think a governess was less of a servant than a cook or a butler! She sighed. This was proving even harder than she had expected.

'Your potential employers are drawn from quite a different society. Currently my best posts are with a Greek shipping magnate, a Saudi-Arabian oil billionaire and an Australian newspaper proprietor. All are richer than any of your imaginary clients; all are far, far nastier. The Saudi will expect you to go veiled whenever you are in the Middle East, and to wear long dresses and headscarves even in Paris and New York. You will have no disciplinary authority over the male children, who will ride roughshod over you, and the women of the immediate family will feel quite free to slap and pummel you, as they do their household slaves, whenever they are so inclined. The salary is excellent and the governess lives in her own gorgeous apartment, with access to a chauffeur and air-conditioned limousine for personal use. I have yet to see an English or American girl last more than six months in the job.

'With the shipping tycoon it's a little different. He has a somewhat similar attitude about the children not being disciplined excessively, and in his case it extends to his daughters, as well as the boys. In addition, he has a large and omnivorous sexual appetite, and no scruples about forcing his tastes on the temporary objects of his affections. He is always present at the final interviews for senior female domestic staff, and always vetoes the ugly ones. You would be very much to his taste and I have a strong suspicion he would be not at all to yours. When that has happened in the past, the girl concerned has been known to be ejected from his Caribbean island in the small hours, badly bruised, wearing a torn dress and without luggage. Her possessions and a large severance payment invariably follow speedily enough, but never a professional reference. Unpleasant isn't it?'

Alexandra was for once at a loss for words. 'What about the newspaperman?' she said faintly.

'Mmm, well, if it were just him, not too bad. He's a little . . . er . . . racy, by your standards, but nothing to worry about. His wife is quite another matter. She drinks rather a lot, and even when sober is convinced every woman under forty who comes within two hundred yards of her man is going to steal him away. She apparently did just that to the first Mrs X and I can only ascribe her present behaviour to a guilty conscience. The husband no longer trusts her judgement because of her drinking, and prefers to select staff himself. This makes her instantly suspicious, and if the employee is female, it's only a matter of time — a very short and sometimes violent time. I take it that by now you are beginning to get the picture?'

Alexandra nodded, then posed what she thought an inevitable question. 'But you are reputed to be the best in the business. How can you take on such people and maintain that reputation?'

Rose Rush looked at her incredulously for a long moment, then said: 'My dear, who d'you think I work *for*? I'm not here to help the Alexandra Moncreiffs of this world. I exist to service the extremely expensive needs of all those terrible rich people we read about in the papers each day. I enjoy an unmatched reputation because I seldom fail. Such people know they are very difficult to please. Many of them take a pride in it. Any old agency could fling them a Cambridge graduate or a cordon bleu cook or the Duke of Devonshire's ex-butler. One only needs a big bank-roll for that. I take on the beasts, and I keep them happy. Of course, I also have lots of perfectly delightful clients, but they tend to be pleasant, modestly rich people who would never offer the sort of conditions you appear to believe you deserve. You would regard them as unforgivably middle-class and they are wealthy enough not to have to put up with that.

'Normally I would not dream of discussing clients as intimately as I just have. Perhaps it's my version of *noblesse oblige*, to indicate I have not quite forgotten our shared past. I only hope you take full advantage of the wisdom I've passed on and get yourself some commercial training instead of persevering in such an unrewarding field. Now, I don't think we have anything else to say to each other, and I have a very important luncheon appointment.'

She stood up and moved towards the door. Alexandra cursed silently at the thought that she had been upstaged even in dismissal. She forced herself to shake hands with the older woman at the office door, then walked off down the corridor, fighting an urge to kick and scream in temper.

* * *

Rose had not worn the Balenciaga that morning for Alexandra Moncreiff's benefit — well, only a little bit, anyway, she told herself, smiling wryly, as the elevator descended. Its main purpose was to impress Jim Austerlitz. He looked like the sort of man who could distinguish Balenciaga from American pie at a range of fifty yards in poor light.

Now she made her way to the hotel where they were to lunch. She wanted half an hour to contemplate her strategy with him. In the cocktail bar, she sat down and ordered a large gin and tonic. Jim Austerlitz . . . California . . . the commercial instead of the domestic employment field. It was all challenging stuff, so why was her attention wandering? Rose took a long pull at her gin and lit a thin black Burmese cheroot from the elegant tortoiseshell case in her bag. Stop playing games with yourself — you know exactly why! It's that girl . . . that confounded, long-necked, arrogant, aristo-bloody-cratic girl! In spite of herself, Rose smiled. I should feel mad, she thought, but I don't. In a way, I admire the little cow's arrogance. And I did throw her my worst three. She leaned back against the banquette seat and gently exhaled the smoke from her cheroot. It took me such a long time to learn a little arrogance. Such a long, long time . . .

Chapter One
London, Autumn, 1923

I'm not going back there, Rose told herself as she moved briskly along the pavement to fend off the evening chill. She never thought of Ladysmith Court as home. It was always 'there' or 'that place', just as her father was never anything but 'him' or 'that rotten pig'.

Which was all very well, but it didn't help solve her problem. It was early October and it had not been a warm year. A mean wind whipped round the corner, reminding her with every eddy of cold, dusty air that her jacket was worn out and her cotton stockings full of holes.

Rose had not been back to Ladysmith Court for almost two weeks. When it was possible to stay away, she did. Since mid-September she had been doing everything from returning old mineral water bottles to shops for the deposit money, and running errands for street stallholders, to begging in the Underground. Now, though, she was close to defeat. She could feel a sniffling cold starting in her nose and throat, and her bones ached from constantly resting on park benches and the hard ground. She would have given anything at that moment for a cup of tea. All she had drunk recently was cheap bottled lemonade; and a couple of pieces of overdone fried fish reduced by the shop man had been her only hot food for more than a week. She was beaten and she knew it. It looked as if she had no choice about going back to her detested father. Wearily, Rose headed eastward up Ludgate Hill, oblivious of the majestic outline of St Paul's Cathedral ahead of her.

'Ah, so yer've decided to come back, yer slut!' Joe Rush

was not angry. He seldom addressed anyone in more courteous terms.

Rose gave him a glance compounded almost equally of hatred and contempt. 'Didn't 'ave a lotta choice, did I?' she retorted. 'Any tea 'ere?'

Rush shrugged. 'How should I know? Never been my tipple.' He gave a raucous chortle. 'Fair bitta pale ale over there, though, if yer fancy some a that. Not every day me only child comes 'ome!'

Rose flashed him a suspicious look. He had some scheme in mind – must do. He never offered her any of his precious booze unless he was hoping to persuade her to do something unpleasant. She tried to keep her face impassive and merely shook her head. 'Tea, if there is any,' she said.

There was a scattering of tea leaves in the bottom of a grubby old caddy at the back of a cupboard. It was what she had left when she slammed out of the flat after their last row. She might have known he'd have no use for it. To her delight, she discovered there was also a small tin of condensed milk. God alone knew where that could have come from, but at least it would colour and sweeten her tea.

There her luck ended. The cracked tea-cup she had been using for months had disappeared. Two fly-blown glass jam jars were the only containers she could find. Rose sighed. She might have known. Still, she'd drunk from worse. At least it was going to be hot and sweet. At least afterwards she could curl up in some sort of bedding and get a bit of sleep . . .

It must be colder outside than she had realised. Perhaps her longish spell sleeping rough had toughened her. Rush had taken the trouble to light the filthy little kitchen range – something he only did when he was feeling the cold. Relieved that she might yet get her hot drink, Rose took the kettle and went to fill it at the communal cold water tap on the landing, then wedged it on the fire to boil.

Her father was sitting in the ruined armchair beside the fireplace, watching her with a sly grin on his face. As she bent to take the boiling water from the fire, he said: 'You'm lookin' a bit peaky, girl. 'ope you ain't gone and made yerself ill messing abaht around town when you coulda been back here wiv me.'

She did not even bother to look at him. 'Sorta clothes I gotta wear, how d'you expect me to look?' she said. 'The wind cuts through that old jacket like a knife. I gotta bad cold coming on if you must know. It's the only reason I'm back in this fleapit, I can tell you.'

'Charmin'! Not a word a concern for yer poor old father!'

'My poor old father looks a bloody sight more comfortable than me, and if yer've gotta crate a pale ale tucked away somewhere, yer can't be all that down and out. You just leave me be and I won't bovver yer. You know I always works my passage when I'm 'ere.'

For some unaccountable reason that brought back the secretive grin she had seen on his face when he offered her a drink earlier, and Rose shivered. The old sod was planning something, she was sure of that, and it was something that involved her. But what it was she had no idea.

The tea had brewed in an old earthenware jug — the teapot had broken a year or more ago — and now Rose filled a jam jar with the thick brown liquid, taking care to pour it down the stem of the metal teaspoon to prevent the heat from cracking the glass. She stirred in a generous spoonful of condensed milk and wrapped a piece of rag around the hot jar so that it would not burn her fingers. 'You still sleeping out here?' she asked Joe.

His eyes slid away from hers. 'Y-yeah. Yer know I never 'ave liked the other room since yer ma went.'

Too right, she thought. Who'd be surprised at that, seeing that you beat her to a pulp and left me to watch her die slowly in there? If I had on my conscience what you got on yours, I wouldn't sleep in there either. Aloud, she said: 'I'm off to bed, then. Don't bovver ter come an' wake me. I'll get meself up in the morning and get out early to look for some food an' stuff. I'll pay me way, don't you worry about that.'

'Oh, I know yer'll do that, Rosie love. Don't you worry

abaht a fing. Nice to 'ave yer 'ome, girl. I'll be off out in a bit. Back late, I shouldn' wonder . . .' He was talking to empty air. Rose had gone into the bedroom and closed the door firmly behind her.

The cramped flat at Ladysmith Court was indescribably filthy. The flickering gaslight in the bedroom revealed a broken-down bed covered in rags and a couple of old coats, probably undisturbed since Rose's last departure. She kept it as clean as she could, but with the bugs lodged behind the wallpaper it was a losing battle. There was a tiny fireplace, but Rose could not remember ever having seen a fire in it. Apart from the bed, a battered chest of drawers was the only furniture.

Rose was grateful for that. At least the combination of sparse furnishings and her father's bad conscience meant that this room remained relatively habitable — more than could be said for the kitchen-living room. There Joe presided over a scene of ever-increasing squalor, surrounded by empty tin cans and fried-fish wrappings, beneath which were submerged countless beer bottles. His bed was an appalling structure over in the corner, where another old army greatcoat partially concealed filthy, worn-out bedlinen and ancient items of clothing which he occasionally exchanged for some of the equally disreputable garments he was already wearing.

The range was cleared of ash and cinders only when it grew too blocked to light a fresh fire, and when he stopped needing the heat in summer, it remained piled chimney-high until the first autumn chill moved him to clear it again. As the main entrance to the flat opened directly into the room from a draughty landing, this ensured that swirls of ash were wafted around the room every time someone entered or left. Joe was drunk so often that he never noticed the mess. As long as he got plenty of beer and enough food to keep him going, he was indifferent to his surroundings.

It had not always been like this. Until four years ago, his wife Jean had battled against all odds to keep the place reasonably clean and tidy. In those days Joe and Jean had slept in the bedroom and Rose had shared the bed in the kitchen with her younger sister Louise. Their mother had taken on any work that was going in order to feed and clothe them decently — cleaning at a couple of the big West End theatres and some local offices, washing other people's clothes, even outwork from the factory that opened up along the street during the war.

Jean Rush had been a good domestic manager, and she would have kept them in passable comfort on her miserly wages, had it not been for Joe's drinking habits. Time and again he would raid the little store of housekeeping money to finance his drinking, and that week it would be bread and dripping for the girls and no fire in the grate. Jean had courage and frequently challenged him about it, but he was a bitter, violent man and merely knocked her about when she complained. In the end she took to hiding the cash away where she hoped he would not find it, although it meant standing up to extra beatings when he demanded to know where she kept it.

Joe had been a different man when she married him — swaggering, handsome, self-assured; a boisterous young East Ender with a high-earning trade, gasfitting and plumbing, that would ensure he was never short of work. But he came from a long line of drinkers and all too soon the weakness hit him as hard as it had his father and grandmother. Within five years of their marriage, he was losing contracts from the one-man business he had set up, and soon was forced to go back to working for someone else. He only lasted a few months before the foreman decided his skilful work could not make up for bad time-keeping. He was dismissed, and never held down a full-time job again. It was the start of his wife's descent to hell.

Jean kept telling herself there was nothing very unusual about their story. There were marriages all over East London just like hers, condemned from the start by cramped housing and too little money. She concentrated on bringing up her daughters to expect something better, and on providing the basic necessities for them all. There were no great material rewards ahead of her, only more sorrow.

At the end of the war, a vast influenza epidemic engulfed Europe and killed almost as many people as the fighting had done. Louise Rush, eight years old and her mother's favourite, died after two weeks' illness, in the course of which Jean could not even afford to consult a doctor on the child's behalf. She was buried in a pauper's grave and something in Jean seemed to die, too. Joe, of course, drowned what passed for his sorrow in the public bar of the Royal George, and neglected to come home for four days. Rose clung to her mother, whom she adored, and tried to comfort her. She even managed to persuade someone to pay her for scrubbing their floors until Jean found out about it and stopped her.

'I'll not have you wasting your youth to support that drunken swine,' she said. 'It's bad enough one of us has to do it.'

It was a hard existence and many other families lost sons and daughters to add to the list of casualties already caused by the war. Jean seemed to adjust to her grief and went back to the grinding routine of feeding and clothing them. Then Joe Rush began getting really violent.

He had always been prone to strike out at Jean when he wanted money, but that had been more in the nature of dealing with a nuisance than with any malicious intent behind it. Now all that changed. He began actively to resent his poverty and shabbiness, and as Jean and Rose were the only two people in his power, he punished them.

Jean was a respectable woman in spite of having fallen on hard times. It never crossed her mind to complain to the police about Joe's violence. Even if she had, the chances were that they would have done nothing. Wife-beating was practically a spectator sport in the slums of Britain's big cities and the best an abused wife could generally hope for was that a constable might scold her man back to temporary good behaviour.

Their last terrible fight, two years ago, was branded on Rose's soul. Even now, she still woke, sweating, and knew she must have been dreaming about it again. At first the dreams came almost every night, and she remembered them vividly all day at school. But gradually, only her waking memory retained the horror. Asleep, she relived it endlessly, but only knew this to have happened because of her terror on wakening.

Her father had come home very drunk and in a filthy temper because the money had run out. Her mother was furious, too, because what he had spent so carelessly was her week's pay for twelve hours of scrubbing steps and landings. It was to have financed their meals that week. Now all she had left was the proceeds of her other two cleaning jobs, hidden away where even he would never find them, ready to pay the rent and a repair bill for Rose's one pair of good boots.

Rush threw open the flat door with a deafening crash and clumped into the cramped living room. 'Where is it? Where's the rest of that bloody money you got?' he yelled.

Angrier than him but quiet as always, Jean said: 'There's nothing. You've already drunk our suppers for next week. What more d'you expect?'

He strode across to her and struck her two ringing blows, back and forth across the cheeks. She did not react in any way, merely letting the force of the slaps turn her face first to one side, then to the other. Afterwards she stared at him undaunted. 'There isn't any more,' she repeated.

'You lazy bitch! You been sitting around here on yer arse all week, using my light an' coal an' drinking my tea, when you shoulda been out earning? I could fucking kill yer for that!'

She sniffed. 'Wouldn't be the first time you'd tried would it? And while we're on the subject, where d'you get the idea it's *your* coal and light? You ain't paid a bill in this place since before the war.

His mood was changing rapidly. Now he was on the edge of blustering self-pity. 'You don't know what it's like, yer lucky cow . . . no woman ever does, protected by 'er menfolk and all. How d'yer fink it feels to be chucked on the scrap-heap at my age, eh? Eh? Tell me the answer ter that one if yer can!'

As he spoke he was leaning closer, bending over Jean as she sat in her rickety wooden armchair. She recoiled as his foul breath, a compound of beer and rotting teeth, washed over her. 'Gerraway from me, you pig! You weren't thrown on the scrap heap. You took a running jump at it and refused to get off it however many chances they gave you. You could be a skilled tradesman with his own business now, we could be comfortable an' respectable ... we might even have managed to keep our poor little Louise alive, an' all.' That thought brought tears to her eyes where nothing else could.

It also stirred some remnant of shame at his own bad behaviour in Joe Rush. He knew as well as Jean that the child would have had a better chance of recovery if she had been properly fed and they had sufficient money to consult a doctor. The shame bred fresh anger and he struck Jean again, thrusting aside any regrets about his dead daughter and revelling in his power over his wife.

'You *'ave* got money, 'aven't yer? You'd never go through a week without the rent and there wasn't enough to pay that in the first lot. Come on, you scheming bitch − where is it?' He grabbed the front of Jean's drab blouse and began shaking her like a terrier with a rat. As with the first blows, she rode the punishment impassively. There was undoubtedly worse to come. Better save the resistance for when it got really serious.

Rose had been in the bedroom when her father arrived. She had done as her mother always told her when Joe came home in this state, and stayed where she was. Now, as the sound of his mounting rage burst through the thin walls of the adjoining room, she began to fear for her mother's safety. For a while she paced back and forth on the bare floorboards, wrapping her arms around her upper body in a vain attempt to comfort herself. But when her mother started to cry out, she could endure no more and ran into the living room, bent on helping her.

One look made her realise she might have left it too late.

Joe had got really carried away this time, and as Jean rose from her chair to try and evade him, he had seized her and flung her against the wall. She had crashed into the wooden door frame, breaking her nose and laying open her cheek. That would normally have been enough to cool his temper, but he was still awash with righteous indignation at her openly expressed contempt for him. Renewing his grip on her arm, he hurled her back across the room and when she fell close to his feet, he began kicking her with his big hobnail boots. Jean was saved from instant major injury only by their advanced state of disrepair and the fact that drunkenness had made his aim inaccurate. Nevertheless, the damage her face had taken and the pain of the kicks which found their mark were sufficient to make her groan in agony. Now, as Rose came to her aid, she was trying to draw herself into a tight defensive ball to minimise the chances of further hurt. Rose's arrival added the fatal complication.

She flung herself on her father's back, screaming at him to stop attacking Jean. Momentarily taken by surprise, Rush straightened up, then, realising it was his daughter, uttered a roar of rage and threw her off. She bumped against the fireplace and gave a little cry as the mantelpiece struck her shoulder. But she was far more worried by what her intervention had done to her mother. Jean was struggling to get up, intent on preventing Joe from taking further revenge on their daughter.

As she staggered to her knees, then managed to put her weight on one foot, Joe seized her again and performed the appalling trick of wrenching her forward that he had used twice that evening to such horrific effect. This time the rickety kitchen table was in the way and Jean, still only three-quarters upright, crashed into it with a cry of pure animal agony. The edge of the table caught her lower ribs and the whole edifice collapsed around her. She fell forward into the pile of splintered wood and Joe stood over her for a few seconds, breathing heavily and staring down at the havoc he had wreaked. Even his violence had been abruptly stopped by the quality of that last scream.

Rose stood, petrified, where he had thrown her by the fireplace. She had forgotten the ache where the metal shelf had caught her, but was terrified to intervene again in case it made matters even worse for her mother. Joe might be drunk and unfit, but he could still handle both of them with little visible effort. Now, though, the fight seemed finally to have gone out of him. He stood where he was for a while, then turned and left the flat, slamming the door behind him. Rose, stifling fresh sobs, went to her mother.

It took Jean almost three days to die. She swooped between delirium and rationality at ever shorter intervals, and every time Rose implored her mother to let her go for help, she refused. 'I know it might kill me, love,' she croaked, 'but that'll be better than anyone knowing my own man did this to me. An' if I faints, just remember I ain't gonna change my mind about it.'

'But Mum, please — you know half the women in this building gets beaten up now an' then. You're too ill to get better without help!'

Jean had closed her eyes. Now they flickered open, pleading with Rose to respect her wishes. 'Don't matter about them, though I'd rather even they didn't see this . . . nah, they'd have to get someone in authority . . . this is too bad for Ada Biggs or anyone to handle. I could never let a proper doctor know Joe had done this to me.' Abruptly, the pain from her smashed ribs overwhelmed her and she fainted. When her consciousness fleetingly returned, she seemed only partially aware of her surroundings. Rose was desperate to find relief for her, but understood her mother's shame and therefore did nothing.

During one of her clearminded spells, Jean told Rose where the remaining money was, and she went to the street market and butcher's shop. She bought some cheap stewing meat and as many vegetables as she could carry, and back at the flat prepared a huge pot of soup, a broth her mother had always called beef tea with more optimism than accuracy. She strained it carefully and tried feeding small cups of it to Jean at regular intervals. But after the first day her mother could barely keep down even the sips of water she occasionally asked for.

Throughout the days of Jean's final torment, Joe Rush never returned to the flat. Rose prayed he would stay away. If he did come back, she knew he would do nothing to help, and she feared he might set upon her, too. But these fears, at least, were groundless. When Jean Rush coughed away her last breath just before dawn three days after her beating, they were still alone in the flat.

Sadie Lassiter, a neighbour from down the hall, had taken charge of the legal side of things. A long-term victim of domestic violence herself, she knew how to avoid too much attention from the police and she knew that was the way Jean Rush would have preferred matters. A constable was called. It was explained that Mrs Rush had slipped on some slimy refuse and lunged headfirst down two flights of stone tenement steps. The policeman accepted the tale with cynical tolerance. He had seen and heard it a hundred times before, and if the injuries of the deceased seemed a bit specialised for such a fall, it would do no one any good to have the matter pointed out. A compliant doctor duly signed a death certificate, and that was the end of Jean. By the time Joe finally reappeared, a Parish burial had taken place and it was as if Rose had never been part of a family at all. Joe had been a long time without beer money when he got back, so he was relatively sober. But his personality was only slightly different from that of the rampaging drunk who had killed her mother. The violence had burned itself out for the time being. Otherwise he was the same snivelling, idle, self-pitying object she had despised as long as she could remember.

He sidled into the flat, careful to avoid Rose's eyes. He knows exactly what's happened, she thought. One of the neighbours must have told him. He squatted on a rickety stool beside the window and peered down through the grimy panes. After a while, still not looking at her, he said: 'Aintcher going to get yer poor old dad a cuppa tea, then?'

Consciously forcing herself not to rush across and start

hitting him, Rose said: 'I'll never get you anything else again, you murdering bastard!' Then she picked up her skimpy coat and slammed out of the apartment, determined it was the last time she would see him.

It had not worked out that simply. Her hatred of the man burned as fiercely now, two years later, as it had that day, but she was penniless and lacked even decent clothes in which to go seeking work. She got by with a little small-scale theft, begging, running errands for shopkeepers and market traders who knew her from her mother's time, and sleeping rough or in Salvation Army hostels. Occasionally, though, she could stand no more, and would retreat to Ladysmith Court, half hoping to find Joe slumped dead in a corner, and that she might find a way of taking over the flat. But he seemed indestructible. She never learned where he managed to find the rent money, now there was no Jean to work for it. From time to time she would arrive, spend one or two nights there, and leave without his ever knowing she had been back. Presumably, then, he was out on another of his drunken progresses. More often of late, he would reappear at some point during her stay, and would either abuse her or whine at her, depending on which mood took him. This time, though, his behaviour had been subtly different. She wished she knew why. It made her feel nervous.

No point brooding about it now, she thought. If this rotten cold keeps up, I'll be here three or four days at least. Daren't go back on the streets till it's better, or I'll end up dying of pneumonia in some charity ward. She lay very still and listened carefully for sounds of movement in the room outside. There was nothing. He must be gone. Rose got up and went to get herself a jug of drinking water from the landing tap. She had no desire to pass through the room later on while he was there. After that she settled down and composed herself for sleep. At least her hard apprenticeship sleeping rough prevented her from suffering too much from the cold as long as she was indoors. There was precious little here to keep her warm, beyond the roof and four walls.

She must have drifted off to sleep then, and for a seemingly endless time was beset by feverish dreams. Then, in the small hours, her intuition snapped her awake. Something or someone was moving about stealthily outside. It took her a few seconds to grasp where she was, and she was about to try and settle down again, assuming the noise was merely Joe returning, when she realised something was not quite right. Drunk or sober, her father always thundered into the room, not caring if he woke the entire building. Why was he creeping about tonight? It must *be* Joe . . . no burglar would be stupid enough to break into Ladysmith Court. Nothing here was worth taking.

Then she heard a muffled oath, and it was clear the speaker was not talking to himself. She was still unable to distinguish what was said, but became convinced her father was out there with some crony, discussing something he wished to keep secret from her.

As quietly as she could, Rose eased herself off her bed and crept over to the door. She was about to lean forward and listen when it began to open very slowly. Her own sharp intake of breath warned the intruder of her presence close by, and the movement ceased momentarily. 'Don't worry, Rosie me love . . . only me . . . nothing to be scared of.' The door began to open further.

She was backing away now, casting about frantically for somewhere to hide, or from where she could defend herself. She knew that voice. It was Alf Dobson, probably the most repulsive of her father's string of unattractive drinking companions. Alf was a carter, and managed somehow to stay employed — it was said because drunk or sober he was a genius with draught horses — so he always had beer money in his pocket. He also had money for his other vices, and girls, young girls, were one of them. He had made no secret of his liking for Rose, and when Jean was alive she had always kept the child out of his way. Dimly, Rose began to understand where that crate of pale ale had come from, and what it represented. Reasoning that she would be back, if only briefly, when the weather worsened that autumn,

Dobson had probably bribed her father with it, and a promise of more when Rush delivered Rose to him.

There was a gap, barely two feet wide, between the end of the chest of drawers and the corner of the bedroom. Rose decided she had more chance of survival if she wedged herself in there and fought off Dobson's inevitable frontal attack. At least the chest was close to the door. If she could distract him for a moment, she might have the luck to make a dash for it. Yes, the water jug. That was on the top of the chest. If she threw the water in his face . . . with a fast sideways skittering movement, Rose reached the corner and turned to face her pursuer.

She had not seen him for more than a year, and now she wondered for a split second what possible chance she could have of holding him off. He was a giant — inches over six feet tall, with brawny shoulders, heavily muscled forearms and a huge paunch, fuelled by years of excessive drinking, which sagged over the lowslung leather belt he always wore. His great bulk filled the doorway, as he stooped slightly to enter the room, and then edged forward, wearing what he intended as an ingratiating grin.

'You keep away from me, you rotten swine,' shouted Rose, 'or I'll scream so loud everybody on the block will be in 'ere!'

Dobson bellowed with mirth. 'That'll be the bloody day! Remember where you are, Rosie. They hear noises o' that nature every night a the week. Why would they take any notice of you?'

He was right, and they both knew it. Rose burrowed further back into her corner, determined not to let him take her. She glanced wildly about her. At least he hadn't shut the door behind him. She might escape after all, if she could just catch him off balance.

'Come on, Rose, yer startin' ter make me nervous.' His ingratiating tone was fading fast, and irritation and excitement rasped close to the surface. 'Happens to everybody in the end. Yer might as well relax and enjoy it. What the bloody 'ell?' As Dobson came within range, she had taken up the jug and hurled about a quart of freezing water in his face. He reeled back momentarily and Rose was off across the room and through the door.

She had almost reached the landing and comparative safety when she was caught from behind. Biting, kicking and pushing, she gabbled: 'Lemme go, Alf — please — find someone willing . . . I ain't . . . nobody's done that to me, ever, don't you understand? Please?'

'Course he understands, you stupid bitch! Never a got him to part with a coupla weeks' supply o' pale ale else, would I?' Her heart sank as it dawned on her that it was her own father, not Alf Dobson, who had caught her. He had sold her for beer money and he had no intention of making a refund. The fight left her. There was no one to turn to, no one to help.

Joe dragged her back to the bedroom. 'Sorry abaht that, Alf. Thought the silly little cow 'ad more sense,' he said.

'Yeah, well you was wrong, wasn't you? I'll bloody show her. Chuck 'er dahn there.' Dobson, now in a towering rage, was mopping the water off his face and chest with a large, filthy handkerchief.

Rose lay inert on the bed where her father pushed her. Her eyes were open but she seemed to be looking at nothing. Dobson stood over her. 'Now, my lady, let's see how you like this,' he said, unbuckling his belt and opening his moleskin trousers. The sight of him, naked from the waist down, revived the fight in Rose. His hugely erect penis stuck out beneath the great belly like some hostile animal piercing the frizzy bush of his pubic hair. A line of hair continued up over his mountainous stomach as far as his navel, which was almost submerged in fat.

Rose began to sit up. 'Keep off me,' she shouted. 'Keep off me or I promise I'll cripple you!'

His laughter boomed out. 'What wiv? You've used up yer water. Can't see no other weapons, love!' With that he began to scramble on to the bed beside her, and she lashed out. Her untrimmed finger nails caught his cheek just below the eye, ripping the flesh open and making blood spurt.

Dobson hit her a big, open-handed slap, growling as he did so: 'I wantcha wide awake for this, or I'd knock you senseless, you cow! Here, Joe, she's your merchandise. Tie 'er up!' And holding Rose pinioned with one hand, he tossed Joe his trousers belt with the other.

'I-I don't understand, Alf. I'm off back aht there, ain't I? Can't stay here wiv you . . . you know . . .'

Alf gave Rose a hard shake to stop her renewed struggles. 'No, I don't bloody know, mate. If I don't get me oats, you don't get yer bevvies, so make up yer mind which it's to be. Tie that belt to 'er wrists and hold her hands above her head ahta my way.'

Rose thrashed about in a vain effort to prevent Joe from getting her wrists close enough to tie them. Alf was kneeling on her legs, so she could not kick out. She jerked her head up − if only she could get her jaws round the flesh of one of them, she'd bite him hard enough to put both men off; but it was futile. They were too strong for her.

Afterwards, the smell of him was what haunted her most. Much of the rest was blurred by pain and shame. But the smell . . . it was compounded of sour sweat, stale beer, the filthy old clothes she was lying on, and Dobson's foul breath on her face as his awful snaggle-toothed mouth enveloped hers in a travesty of a passionate kiss.

'Keep − her − *still*, damn you!' Alf ordered her father, and then she felt him force her legs apart and hard down on the bed. He began to heave himself against her and the huge member which had horrified her so much minutes before was driving into her body.

Oh God, no, no, no, no! she shrieked inwardly. But they heard nothing. Outwardly she was silent. Outwardly she was putting every ounce of energy into physical resistance. Only her spirit knew she had already lost. In a deep faraway place it cowered, vainly trying to escape acceptance of what was happening to her. But the rhythmic thrusting motion of the big body across her, the intensifying pain as Dobson penetrated her, the hideous pawing at her breasts and legs and throat, all conspired to force body and soul back together and confront her with the vileness of life. With one enormous terminal thrust, her assailant was right inside her, and with a shudder his hardness was extinguished. He slumped forward on Rose, almost smothering her, and her father rocked back on his heels, relief written large on his face. It was her last image as she cartwheeled down into unconsciousness.

Claude Hampson was the night desk sergeant at Shepherdess Walk nick. It was a quiet shift, especially for a Friday night. Well past two o'clock and all he had in the cells was two drunks and one brass. He yawned, stretched, and anticipated a strong cup of tea. The thought was instantly rewarded. A young police constable arrived with a steaming, overfilled mug, to which he gave his exclusive attention as he walked, in an effort to avoid spilling any.

'Good lad,' said Hampson. 'All the comforts of home. Remembered the three sugars, did you?' PC Johnson managed to nod without sticking out his tongue in concentration, and sighed with relief as he accomplished his mission and put down the cup on the desk.

The sergeant leaned forward to pick it up, then said, 'Oh, my Gawd!' changed his mind and came round the counter at a rush.

A young girl — still a child, really — had just staggered through the double doors. Her face had the look of a hunted animal, and although she was clutching her arms around her upper body, it was obvious her worn-out jumper had been torn apart at the front. A bruise was beginning to come up on her right temple. One of her stockings was crumpled down around the ankle and a long, dark streak of blood smeared the bare flesh between her skirt hem and the knitted cotton. She paused for a moment, leaning against the door jamb to support herself, then lurched forward towards them. After that the effort became too much for her and she folded, sliding to the ground in a faint.

Hampson was at her side in a moment, raising her slightly and brushing the wildly disordered hair back from her forehead. 'Dunno why, but after twenty years on the Force, I still can't get used to kids in this state,' he murmured to Johnson. 'Fetch us that tea, lad. Let's see if it'll bring her around.'

Half an hour later, Rose was sitting in the small, warm room behind the charge desk, her disordered clothing concealed by the thick blanket they had wrapped about her. She had just finished stammering out her story to Sergeant Hampson. 'I don't s'pose there's much any a you can do about it,' she said, 'but I couldn't stay there and I couldn't go back on the streets dressed like this, could I? Can either a you tell me what I ought to do?'

'You sit here and drink that other cuppa tea and have a nice rest, love,' Hampson told her. 'I'll step outside and have a word with the constable here, then we'll see what we can do. Of course you did the right thing.'

Outside, he turned a thunderous countenance on Johnson. 'I'd like to find those bastards and castrate the two a them!' he said. 'That a man could stand by and connive at doing that to his own daughter and for beer money at that!' His shoulders sagged and a look of despair replaced the fury for a moment. 'Trouble is, it's not even an uncommon story in these parts. Don't you ever listen to tales about how good the poor are to each other. They're as true as Santa Claus.'

'What're we gonna do with her, Sarge?' Johnson was troubled. 'You may be used to this sort of thing, but I've never run across it before and I know we don't act as a charity for the distressed. We might go after her old man and the other fellow, but how can we help her?'

'Well, we can't turn her loose like that, can we now? Normally, it'd be an orphanage for the younger girls or one of those places for kids in need of care and protection for the older ones. Reckon she'd have to go to the Care and Protection. She looks fourteen or fifteen to me – too old for the orphanage.

'Well then, shouldn't I get in touch with somebody?'

'Hold your horses a minute, Johnson. Are you afraid she'll remind you of the Old Adam in all of us if she stays here too long? I want to do what's best for the girl. She's suffered more than enough. Those places are tarted-up reformatories. They make the kids think they're the wrong-doers, although half of them are victims like little Miss Rush in there. Nah, I'd like to get her started a bit better than that. Think I'll give it a couple of hours until the world wakes up, then I'll try Fanny Macklin round St Luke's Workhouse.'

Johnson eyed him suspiciously. 'Won't put the kid in C and P but you'll hand her over to the workhouse matron? That don't sound very humane to me!'

'Just shows you still gotta lot ter learn, then, don't it? Fanny Macklin is not your general run of workhouse matron, as you'll have cause to discover if you stay in this nick any length of time. She's got a big heart behind that forbidding face, and I happen to know she's got contacts that may set Miss Rush off to a better start than you might expect.'

Hampson settled Rose down as comfortably as possible in an empty interview room that contained a battered but soft armchair. Exhausted by her ordeal, she drifted off to sleep almost immediately. As soon as he thought there was a chance of Mrs Macklin being on duty, he telephoned the workhouse, which was further along Shepherdess Walk from the police station. He briefly sketched the details of what had happened to the girl.

'No doubt I could get her in the local Care and Protection,' he said, 'but you can see why I don't want to. You know more about those places than I do. I wondered, is there a chance of you taking her in? She's in bad shape for an institution, anyway. She could do with a bit of minor medical attention, and I thought your sick bay . . . Another thing: she'll certainly need to be kitted out head to toe in clothes. Everything she's got on is wrecked. What I thought, Fanny, was you might be able to sweet talk some a your mates in the MABYS . . . Yeah, I know that strictly speaking she ain't one yet, but they take on orphans. Can't we pretend a bit for this kid?'

He was silent for some time as Fanny Macklin thought over his proposal, then beamed with relief at her answer. 'Half an hour? I'll bring her around meself when I come off shift. Fanny, I'd say you were a saint if I didn't have a feeling you got no time for religion!'

MABYS was the Metropolitan Association for Befriending Young Servants. From its original, Victorian brief to look after the moral welfare of young domestics in London, it had for a considerable time taken on orphans from the institutions of the capital, and placed them in domestic service. Fanny Macklin had been a volunteer member for years, and Hampson knew Rose would be safe in her hands once he had persuaded her to take the girl.

Within the hour, a sleepy Rose had been installed temporarily in the sick bay at St Luke's, where she stayed while Mrs Macklin tried to find a situation for her. The following week, her bruises gone, her cold cleared up, and dressed in second-hand but respectable clothes, Rose was enrolled in the Fulham residential training centre for domestics. Charity had repaired the outward signs of her violation. She herself was ready now to set to work to heal her spirit. She knew it would be hard, but she was determined to create a life for herself which had nothing to do with the slums of Shoreditch.

Chapter Two
Abercarn, South Wales

I won't cry, even if my legs hurt so much they fall right off, Jane Ellis told herself. It was only a wash . . .

In fact it had been what her mother called a *good* wash, and when it was carried out in a tin bath of tepid water on a chilly autumn morning, with the aid of a scrubbing brush and without consideration for the victim's chilblains, it was a painful process. Since then, Jane had been wandering about with her head corkscrewed into rag curlers wound so tightly through her long hair that it felt as if her eyebrows were about to be ripped off from above. The chilblains stung, her head ached, and now she had been banished to the icy-cold parlour where she sat, bored and shivering, on the grim black horsehair sofa, wondering what on earth was happening.

She glared at the stuffed ferret in its glass case on the sideboard. 'Ugly old bugger you are!' she told it. '*And* your back leg's falling off!' Her eldest brother Sam fancied himself as a taxidermist and had stuffed the beast after it failed to get the best of a fox. But by the look of the thing, he hadn't read the book right . . . still, Mam said it added a bit of tone to the room. She sighed, her inspection of the ferret having exhausted her resources. 'Mam! When can I come out? You'm never gonna leave me in yere all day, are you?' she yelled, as she heard her mother pass the parlour door.

Mrs Ellis looked in, her expression threatening. 'If you do move before I've finished in the other room, I'll flatten you! We gorra visitor coming after, and I want you looking your best. You stay there till I got time to undo your rags.'

Noticing her daughter's mutinous expression, she added in a more placatory tone: 'And then I'll let you wear our Maisie's lace frock. There, how about that?'

'Can I go out in it?'

'Don't be soft – you'd get it dirty. No, you can wear it when this lady do come to tea this afternoon.'

'What lady? You haven't never dressed me up before when we had visitors.' Jane was beginning to suspect her mother's motives.

'An old friend of Auntie Norrie's. Coming all the way from Cardiff, and Norrie have been bouncing you up to the skies, so I want you to look tidy.'

'Why would Auntie Norrie want to do that?'

Mari Ellis's face reddened and she looked away. 'Ask no questions and you'll be told no lies, my girl. Now you stay by there for half an hour and I'll come an' see to you. All right?'

'All right. But I want to know why this woman is coming.'

'You'll find out soon enough. You just make sure you'm polite to her and speak when you'm spoken to. Oh, and by the way . . . I've asked Eleri Jones to come in, an' all. She'll be around soon.'

Eleri? Exactly what was all this about? There was never enough food for the Ellises themselves at tea-time, let alone for Jane's friends. Now here was Mam inviting somebody in – and when a stranger was coming, too. Jane fought an impulse to creep out of the house and run off to hide somewhere for the rest of the afternoon. Only the thought of the ridiculous spectacle she would make in her rag curlers stopped her.

Jane cared a lot about her appearance, and longed for the day when she would be able to dress in the sort of clothes she saw on the cinema screen at Abercarn Hall. She was a bright girl, and knew such garments were not easily come by on a miner's wage, so she had decided long ago not to marry a miner. When she was not day-dreaming about slinky party frocks or hand-made shoes, she spent a lot of time speculating about the looks and temperament of the man who would one day waft her away from all this shabbiness.

Never for a moment did she question that it would happen; she could not afford to, because without that dream she had nothing worth anticipating. Sometimes the fantasy enabled her to escape the mining valleys without first finding the perfect man. In this version, she recovered a lost diamond ring and was handsomely rewarded, or won a fabulously well-endowed newspaper competition — anything which provided the necessary funds for her to float away from the humble hearth in Nant Pennar Terrace and land in more tempting surroundings.

At heart she was less of a dreamer. Constant sly peeps in the big wardrobe mirror upstairs told her she was an uncommonly attractive girl, with peachbloom skin, honey-blonde hair and brilliant blue eyes which had the trick of holding the gaze of men much older than she. That look already gave her mother endless sleepless nights as she tried to work out a strategy for keeping her youngest child away from the boys until a safe, respectable marriage was on the cards. Somehow, Mari Ellis invariably concluded, girls who looked like Jane never showed much keenness for a safe, respectable marriage.

At fourteen, Jane's body was lush and well-developed. She would never be very tall, but that merely added to her charms. She had always been one of those little girls whom people delighted in picking up and cuddling. Her worried mother was almost resigned to the idea that such cuddling was unlikely to stop when Jane reached womanhood. In fact, it would probably only get worse . . . This was the point at which Mrs Ellis normally heaved a deep sigh, turned over and composed herself for sleep. Tomorrow would undoubtedly be as long and hard as today, and Jane had the look of a girl who instinctively knew how to survive. That would have to do.

Two hours after Jane's banishment to the parlour, Mari Ellis opened the door to Eleri Jones. As she looked over the child, her face softened into an affectionate smile. Now here was one any mother would be happy to have! Eleri was less than a year younger than Jane, but at times they seemed separated by centuries. Eleri's hair was a mass of glossy sandy-brown curls, and her bright hazel eyes added to the impression that she was some attractive furry woodland animal, only down in the village for a visit. She was not pretty – the wide, full-lipped mouth and tip-tilted, freckled nose saw to that – but she came close to looking like every parent's ideal little girl.

'Come on in, love,' said Mari Ellis. 'Our Jane have been ready this long time – you know what she's like if you let her out of your sight for a minute. Little flibbertigibbet is gone for hours. You'm looking nice this afternoon.'

Like Jane, Eleri had been stuffed into a sister's best dress. The younger children in Valleys families seldom had new clothes of their own. Hand-me-downs had to be thoroughly worn out before new garments were bought, and economy dictated that these should be in sizes suitable for the biggest brothers and sisters. The others got their turn as they grew older. Eleri's dress was of dark blue worsted – less showy than the lace sported by Jane, but that was probably just as well, reflected Mrs Ellis, as the thing was a lot too big and the white would have shown it up. Otherwise, she could not have been neater, with calf-high white socks and ankle-strapped shoes which her father had polished to mirror brightness.

If today's plan comes off, it'll be the last time the poor kid do wear children's shoes and socks, thought Mari, fighting back an impulse to envelop the girl in a protective embrace. She pulled herself together. No use going soft on the idea now. Both Jane and Eleri had been lucky enough to stay at home until they were fourteen and thirteen. She had seen the last of her home even younger than that, when her aunt had consigned her to a kitchen-maid's job in one of the big houses in Cardiff. After a few years of that, marriage to Fred Ellis had seemed like paradise, even though it involved the constant war on coal dust and grime that every miner's wife waged each day.

She dragged her attention back to Eleri. 'Jane's in the

front room,' she said. 'You go in with her and stop her getting up to any mischief, all right? I'll call you when we'm ready for you.'

As she uttered the last word, she opened the door and ushered Eleri into the small parlour, pulling it shut behind her. 'When *who's* ready for us? What the bloody hell is going on round yere?' stormed Jane.

'You shouldn't swear. Not nice,' said Eleri, then caught the wicked look in Jane's eye and giggled. 'They'm all keeping it a bit close, ent they?' she added.

'Telling me. When have you ever come in yere to tea, particularly in your Ethel's frock? Bet she don't like that a bit.'

'I'm not sure I like it much, either. The dratted old thing is so long it's trailing along behind me like a robe. All right for the Queen, but not really me, is it?' Eleri studied her friend critically. 'You do look lovely, Jane, really lovely. Wish my hair would go like that.' Jane's mother had removed the rags half an hour earlier and now her hair hung in honey-coloured sausage-shaped ringlets as portrayed in all the best toilet soap advertisements.

Jane received the homage with modest pleasure. She had no intention of denying her own perfection. Eleri's next remark jolted her out of her satisfied self-contemplation however. 'Don't you think they might say it's a bit . . . well, you know . . . *fancy* for a servant though?'

'Servant? Wharra you on about?' Alarm rushed through Jane's body like an electric current.

Eleri seemed perplexed. 'Haven't they told you nothing about any a this?' Jane shook her head dumbly.

'Well, I don't know much, mind, but enough. When our mam and yours was talking things over yesterday, I was just out by the back kitchen and I could hear some a what they said. Your mam said she thought it was awful in this day and age that children like us had to leave their families and go miles away to work, keeping other people's houses clean and cooking their food, and our mam said it have always been the same and why did she think it would ever change?

Then she said Norrie Parker was a good soul and she wouldn't put us anywhere wrong. Then our Gerry come up the back way and saw me there and shouted out to me, so they stopped talking about it.'

'So Norrie Nosey Parker is coming to do a bitta slave trading, is she?' muttered Jane. 'We'll soon put a stop to that.'

'Wharra you gonna do?' Eleri was round-eyed with fright.

'Show the buggers that nobody in their right mind would want me as a skivvy, that's what! Shouldn't be too difficult . . .'

Abruptly, Eleri's pliable manner changed. 'You can stop that right this minute! What about our mams? What'll it do to them?'

'They don't seem to mind doing it to *us*.' Jane's tone was truculent but at least she was listening.

'You know that ent true. They do both feel rotten about it. That's why they'm acting so irritable and funny. But they both went away when they was even younger than us. They do know what it was like, Jane, and they wouldn't be sending us now if there was any way we could earn our keep yere.'

'The boys don't have to go away.'

'Don't talk soft! Would you go down the pit rather than work in somebody's kitchen, even if they'd let you? We'm still getting the better part.'

Jane reflected on that in silence, then heaved a vast sigh. 'Well,' she said, 'I spend enough time thinking what it'd be like to get away from yere. Now's my chance to find out. Didn't think I'd be doing it in a cap an' apron, though.'

Eleri reached over and squeezed her hand 'That's it, kidda. Don't never let them know they can get at you.'

Jane glanced up sharply, surprise in her face. 'You really mean that, don't you?'

'Course I do. When I'd had a think about all this, I promised myself one thing: whatever they try to do to me, I'll never let them see when they hurt me — whoever they turn out to be.' She finished on a note of triumph, but fear was strongly mixed with it and as she heard her mother hurry to answer Norrie Parker's knock on the front door, Jane wondered morosely how difficult it would prove to keep her own courage intact.

Norrie Parker was a big, bovine woman of uncertain years, with mournful washed-out blue eyes, red-veined cheeks and stringy brown hair. She worked as a cook-general in Cardiff, returning to her sister's house in nearby Newbridge on days off, and was a model of what the average middle-class employer required in an experienced senior domestic. Her diligence and industry had brought her to a relatively prosperous middle age, with an intermittent extra source of income that ensured her quietly respectable clothes were always matched by expensive shoes, gloves and handbags, and the occasional wildly inappropriate hat. Norrie used her time off to act as a go-between for well-off families seeking good junior servants, and received a commission for her efforts. Jane Ellis and Eleri Jones were earmarked as her latest pieces of merchandise.

Today's assignment was particularly important. No brief raid to snatch a tweeny for a Park Place basement, this. The two recruits were required for a nobleman's establishment, one for his London household and one for the country mansion in Wiltshire. Norrie's practised eye had been on Jane and Eleri for a year or more, with just such a special case in mind. The Ellis girl might be just a shade too cocky to make an ideal domestic, but they were an exceptionally personable pair, raised on good food so they still had their own teeth and straight, strong limbs. They were bright, and that meant they would learn quickly. Norrie's assessment was based on the sort of principles which had ensured sound choice of horses and dogs since time immemorial. It worked just as well on people.

The importance of today's mission was emphasised by the fact that Norrie was to be accompanied on her visit to Mari Ellis by the woman who would make the ultimate choice – Ada Bateman, once nanny to the Countess of Clifton and still a trusted retainer. The countess had grown up in South Wales as Venetia Haskins – she was the adored daughter of a millionaire Cardiff brewer and her brother still lived in the family home in the village of Lisvane. Nanny Bateman was semi-retired now, occupying her own cottage on the Lisvane estate, but the Haskins family still brought her all their minor domestic problems and the other servants regarded her as a sort of Shogun whom they dared not displease.

Now dear Miss Venetia, always her favourite, had written to her from Wiltshire to say she needed a personable, intelligent girl to be trained as second housemaid for London. Miss Venetia's smallest whim was Nanny Bateman's command, and now she threw herself into the search. Oh, and would it be possible to sort out a kitchen-maid too? the countess's letter had continued. She did so love the musical sound of a South Wales accent and one seldom heard anything except cockney or broad Wiltshire in either of their main houses.

That made even Nanny Bateman sigh with exasperation. When had Miss Venetia ever spent long enough below stairs to *see* one of the kitchen-maids, let alone converse with them? She did run off with some odd ideas! Still, it might not be a bad thought, for the housemaid at least. By the time the girl had risen to parlour-maid, the bumps would be ironed out of her speech, and what remained would sound much better than some of those hideous Midlands and North Country twangs you heard bandied about these days!

Next day, Nanny Bateman sent a note down to Norrie Parker at the Cathedral Road house where she worked. Parker had been very helpful in the past, particularly if she was well rewarded. This little errand would carry quite a sweetener with it. The Cliftons recruited for life. They didn't like fly-by-night servants. The terrible shortage of good domestics in London had prompted them to this extreme solution, and they would pay well to find suitable girls, knowing the appointments would be long-term.

Now Norrie's big day had come. Alan Haskins had lent

Nanny Bateman the Bentley for the day, and Norrie was ready to burst with happiness as the vast car whispered along Nant Pennar Terrace, silently stopping outside number eight to the slack-jawed wonder of every inhabitant.

Mari Ellis kept her nerve with difficulty. There was now a fire in the parlour grate, the table was covered by her one fine linen cloth, and the best china, usually used only for funerals and chapel socials, was disposed upon it, along with a selection of home-baked delicacies that normally appeared over six months of Sunday teas. This, though, was the Sunday tea to end them all. This might establish her girl in a secure household that would look after her for life. Covertly, Mari eyed Nanny Bateman's clothes. Nothing but the best there. The lace on that blouse was simple, but it was hand made. The cut of the suit was lovely, too, and the gloves the softest kid. If Jane could end up that well provided for, all this would be worthwhile.

Mari glanced at Eleri's mother, who had joined her at the last moment to greet the two visitors. Mrs Jones was scrutinising Nanny Bateman as closely as she herself had, and was evidently equally satisfied with what she saw. She half turned to Mari and gave a contented little nod. 'I think Mrs Ellis can speak for us both, Miss Bateman. I'll be happy to fall in with whatever she do decide.'

Mari uttered a flustered little giggle. 'I think it's more a case of what Miss Bateman thinks, don't you, Norrie?'

Norrie nodded, gratified that at last someone was deferring to her, too, if only indirectly. Before she had time to respond, Jane muttered: 'Isn't anybody going to ask us? We're the ones you'm after!'

'Jane! That's quite enough. It's your place to be polite and do what you're told.' Her daughter seemed about to launch into a stream of protest, but she loved her mother and the stricken expression on Mari's face stopped her. Miss Bateman frowned momentary disapproval but then returned to the discussion of the girls' merits.

After almost an hour of detailed cross-examination, the august visitor appeared to reach a decision. With the air of a headmaster presenting speech day prizes, she said: 'Your girls will need a lot of polishing, ladies — a lot of polishing. But by and large, they do you credit. I think we can place both of them with the family of the Earl of Clifton.' The title dripped off her tongue like unction, and she beamed with satisfaction at Jane's and Eleri's mothers.

'Wh-when would you want them?' said Mari faintly. Suddenly her certainty was deserting her. She remembered how much she loved her spirited daughter, and she did not want to lose her.

Nanny Bateman flapped a hand dismissively. 'Oh, today, of course! We can't have them trailing down to Cardiff and then on to London and Wiltshire without supervision, and I certainly shan't have time after today.'

'Norrie — what about Mrs Parker?' said Mrs Jones.

'Out of the question! Mrs Parker has given up a great deal of her free time as it is.' (And she'll be more than amply rewarded, Miss Bateman told herself. I'm not pushing even more unnecessary money her way.) 'I have the means to transport the girls back with me today. They can stay at Lisvane tonight and I shall arrange their onward journey in the morning. It's all been properly organised, I assure you.'

'But when will we see them? It's such a long way . . .' Mari Ellis was beginning to feel desperate.

Again the dismissive tone from the old nanny. 'Oh, that will have to wait a few months. Really, Mrs Ellis, you must see that at present the important thing for your daughter is a thorough training, not a lot of sentimental journeys back to the Valleys!'

Mari capitulated, crestfallen. She could think of no reasonable objections. When Norrie had first approached her, she had jumped at this chance of advancement for Jane. Now the doubt was growing with every second, but she felt powerless to argue against such a decisive personality and such obviously sensible views.

Nanny Bateman was speaking again. 'I shan't snatch them away from under your noses, you know. Chivers will take

me and Mrs Parker for a spin in the car and we sh...
in an hour or two. As long as the girls are packed and
by then, we shall make comfortable time back to Cardi...
Now, I'm sure you must have a great deal to do. Mrs
Parker . . .' She gestured at Norrie to indicate she was ready
to leave, and the two women went out to the car.

Jane rushed to the parlour window and peered into the street. What she saw disarmed her rebellious intentions. '*Duw*, Mam, is that the car we'm going in?' she asked.

Mari nodded listlessly. 'Can't imagine there'd be two chauffeur-driven jobs cruising up and down Nant Pennar Terrace this afternoon,' she said. 'Come on, kidda. We better sort out your things.'

Chapter Three
Fulham, West London

Eva Armstrong's despairing sigh was almost indistinguishable from a sob. She regarded the barren living room of her Fulham flat with tear-filled eyes and asked herself for the thousandth time why she had left all she knew in the North of England to chase some empty dream of prosperity in the South. Then she shrugged and muttered: 'Who am I trying to fool? It's bad here, but at least we're still alive.'

Eva had grown up in one of the Lancashire cotton towns, in a home made comfortable by a large family of healthy sons and daughters who all worked in the mills from the moment they were legally permitted to leave school. At twenty she had married Charlie Armstrong, a master weaver, and everyone told her what a good catch she had made. She produced three children within the first four years of their marriage, then disaster struck. England and Germany went to war and Charlie left hearth, home and responsibilities to join the Army. He never returned.

Earlier generations of Eva's family had managed in the face of similar tragedies, but times were changing. The war ended, the mill towns slumped into a depression, and Eva, once virtually guaranteed work as a skilled mill-hand, found herself permanently unemployed with two sons and a daughter to feed. It was 1922 and all the impoverished inhabitants of the Lancashire towns looked wistfully towards the South, where it was said there was plenty of work and good wages. Eva had already moved her family into the Manchester suburbs where she took lodgings with her sister. But Manchester offered no better prospects than her home town. Eva began to pay more attention to the talk about London and the rich pickings to be had there. What did she have to lose? She owned no property here, had no job.

She borrowed a little cash from her sister as a stake for the first few weeks, packed up the possessions she had accumulated over the years and moved South. Her sister Mary's husband was doing well as a travelling salesman with Far East imports of the very textiles which had displaced Lancashire cotton. Mary was glad enough to advance the money, secretly reasoning that otherwise Eva and her three brats might eventually expect to live on her charity.

Eva found no golden pavements in London. The metropolis had even less use than anyone else for a skilled mill-hand, and apart from her industrial experience, she was able to offer only a character reference from her local Methodist minister. Initially, that proved sufficient to keep body and soul together. London was already prey to the chronic servant shortage which was to preoccupy the upper and middle classes for ten years or more. Eva was considered unsuitable for engagement as parlour-maid or cook-general, but as a cleaner and laundry-maid she rapidly obtained work.

She hated it from the start. Mary's loan provided enough to rent a scruffy flat off the Fulham Road, which put her on a good West End bus route to get to and from her various jobs. But the family had virtually no bedding, no cooking pots or crockery, and for the first time in her life, Eva found herself feeding her children on fish and chips from the shop at the corner and serving them tea in old jam jars. And in between there was the drudgery; the endless, thankless, grey work at crack of dawn on someone's front step or hallway; the back-breaking hours over a Belfast sink or pounding sheets with a washtub dolly in some basement scullery unfit for anything beyond storing vegetables.

Somehow the money never added up to enough for more than their most basic needs. At first she had told the children they would only have to make do with the jam jar cups for a few weeks; that the smelly old Army greatcoats they used as blankets were a purely temporary measure; and that the fish and chips would swiftly give place to nourishing home-made stews and pies. She never managed to keep more than the last promise — with a stupendous effort she crammed one extra job into her third week, and spent the money on a baking tin, a stew pan and a couple of saucepans. Then she confronted the fact that her weekly workload usually left her too exhausted to cook the homely dishes her children needed. The blankets and teacups remained a dream. There never was any more surplus cash. Even a new pair of socks for one of the boys or a second-hand jumper for her daughter Margaret strained the budget almost to breaking point.

Margaret was the eldest child, tall, slender and dreamy-looking, with pale blonde hair and fine-drawn features that promised beauty. She was past her thirteenth birthday now, and the boys, Charlie and Victor, were nine and ten. Reluctantly, Eva decided there was no alternative to putting Margaret to work if the boys, at least, were to have a little more than any of them had enjoyed so far. When guilt threatened to swamp her she dismissed it impatiently, reasoning that it did not help Margaret, either, to share their poverty. With the right sort of position as a live-in-domestic, she would be well dressed and fed, and Eva's meagre earnings would in future have to support three rather than four. She began making enquiries among the housekeepers and head parlour-maids of the houses where she scrubbed floors and washed clothes.

She received little encouragement. The households where she worked were in the middle range, generally with fairly small live-in staffs. That was why Eva herself was employed in them as a daily. Only bigger establishments had the leeway to take on a complete novice like Margaret and train her from scratch. In 'her' families, everyone was far too busy with their regular tasks to take on more.

Eva was on the point of braving one of London's various domestic employment agencies, when the housekeeper at a Sloane Street mansion flat where she cleaned twice a week said she had something which might be of interest. A doctor she knew in North London was without servants at present: 'Their last girl was a treasure and she'd been with them for years, so now they're lost over where to start looking after all this time.' Would Mrs Armstrong like to send her daughter along to see them? They would train her but of course that meant the wages for the first few months would not amount to much more than bed and board.

Most of it sounded reasonable enough to Eva, except the part about not knowing where to start looking. Even with a shortage of skilled servants, there were plenty of honest but dispossessed women like herself around, of good character and able to run a modest household for a modest wage. Perhaps the conditions were not as reasonable as the housekeeper implied?

But Eva was desperate. Each week her money covered less and less. She needed fewer obligations, and so far this was the only offer which had materialised.

That was her first mistake. Her second was to let Margaret go alone to the interview in Finchley. Normally she would not have considered abandoning the girl thus, but their circumstances had been abnormal for some time, and to go with her, Eva would have needed time off from one of her endless jobs. That meant losing at least the cost of a family supper, and the price was too high. She made Margaret as neat and tidy as was possible in her hand-me-down clothes and patched shoes, gave her money for the fare out and back, and careful instructions on how to find the house. With that, and some firmly imparted views on how good domestics conducted themselves, she departed for her first job of the day.

From outside, the Bignall house looked neat and well-maintained. Inside it was showing signs of fatigue. The entrance hall needed sweeping, and the parlour in which Margaret was told to wait looked as if it had been a little too long without dusting. The woman who let her in said she would find the lady of the house, and disappeared. It was only days later when she encountered her at the tea table, that Margaret realised Elsie Shaw was a friend of her new employer, not a fellow-servant. Clearly Mrs Bignall thought it infra dig to open the front door personally to applicants for domestic work.

When she finally came in, Mrs Bignall circled Margaret warily as if the girl were some sort of slightly dangerous wild animal. Apparently deciding there was no immediate threat, she sat down beside a circular table. Clearly she expected Margaret to remain standing.

'Hmm, references are a bit thin, aren't they?' she finally asked.

'Th-this would be my first job, ma'am,' stammered Margaret.

'Well, I'm not at all sure I shall have time to train you from scratch, my girl. It's most inconvenient . . . most inconvenient . . . still, I need someone quickly and the qualified housekeeper I had in mind couldn't fill the vacancy for at least three months.'

Even an innocent like Margaret found that hard to believe. She had no experience of domestic service and had never lived in a house as big as this; but she knew it was modest compared with many other dwellings in the same neighbourhood, and if they all had their own housekeepers, there wouldn't be an unemployed domestic anywhere in London. There seemed no suitable response to Mrs Bignall's remarks, so she remained standing patiently before her, an expression of what she hoped was polite attentiveness on her face.

As Mrs Bignall spoke, she had drawn her hand across the surface of the table. Now she glanced down and winced at the sight of the track she had made in the patina of dust there. The sooner she found a replacement for Marion Withers the better, and at what she was offering this was the first applicant.

'I might be prepared to consider a beginner,' she said in a less carping voice. 'Of course, the wages would reflect your inexperience, and you would have to work very hard to catch up with all there is to learn.'

'Yes, ma'am. I'm willing to work hard, and as long as there's something coming to me on top of my bed and board, I can manage until you're satisfied I know the job.'

'Quite right — quite right.' Margot Bignall had a tendency to repeat phrases she wished to emphasise. It was a trait which had almost driven her doctor husband to drink many years ago. Now she was seized by optimism at the thought that this girl's lack of worldliness might suit her admirably. What she lacked in experience, she would make up for in cheapness — and Margot would see she got value for money from the child. A shy, hesitant cough roused her from her reverie. 'Yes, what is it?' she asked sharply.

'Uniform, ma'am. No doubt you'd be expecting me to wear one — you know, when I was working on this floor, letting in your visitors and such like.'

'Of course. In my experience a good maid usually provides her own.'

'Aye, well, that's it, you see. I've not done this work before, and I've no proper clothes to wear. I — I don't think I could accept a job, even if it was offered, if I had to find me own uniform.' She blushed furiously as she spoke, bitterly ashamed at the necessity for demonstrating such poverty.

Mrs Bignall expelled a silent breath of relief. She had almost overstepped the mark and lost the girl in her desire to get a bargain! Tempting though it was to tell her the uniform money would be stopped from her wages in instalments, Mrs Bignall knew the sum she was about to suggest was so derisory that it would have taken a year to clear the debt. True: the girl must have *something* in hand at the end of the month. She could always economise on Armstrong's food . . .

'The uniform will be my responsibility, Armstrong,' she announced graciously. 'Come, I'll show you the rest of the house and outline your duties. Then we can discuss terms of employment, and whether I feel able to offer you a position.' She rose and led the way out of the room. The back door clicked shut as Elsie Shaw, her duty as surrogate housekeeper discharged, slipped away to allow Margot to complete her confidence trick on the new servant girl.

Six weeks later, Margaret was wondering if anything could be as bad as the life of slavery she was forced to endure in the Bignall household. The only luxury in her life now was sleep — and she got precious little of that. Dr Bignall liked to be up and about by seven in the morning, so that meant she must rise before six to see that the morning room fire was laid and lit, the early tea delivered to his room, and a hot breakfast cooked to await his arrival at table.

At first the cooking had been the worst part of the job. Margaret had watched her mother prepare stews and hotpots, but had never done more herself than make tea. Now she was expected to meet the culinary needs of the Bignalls single-handed. At first Mrs Bignall had told her there was nothing to worry about; she would pass on the necessary cooking skills. Unfortunately, she was inept in the kitchen, and watching her, Margaret had to use her own judgement about the correct way of doing things. In the first month she managed, after a fashion, to master breakfast cookery, coffee-making, plain vegetable preparation and the basics of roasting meat. Now she was struggling to cope with pastry and boiled puddings. Margaret had no standard by which to evaluate her own intelligence and dexterity, so she was unaware that she had learned exceptionally quickly from an incompetent cook who was also a poor teacher. She herself would never be a cook of genius, but to have learned what she had from such patchy instruction in so short a time was little short of miraculous.

Many of the other tasks were easier to learn, though not necessarily less arduous to carry out. Dusting, polishing and scrubbing had their own obvious logic, which she followed after minimal instruction from the feather-brained Mrs Bignall. She was fortunate that the one really modern appliance in the basement kitchen was a gas cooker. At least she was not forced to rely on the vagaries of the solid fuel range, a massive edifice which dominated a whole wall of the kitchen. Her good luck continued when the chimney sweep arrived a few days after Margaret joined the Bignall household, and obligingly showed her how to clean the monstrous fireplace. It was quite beyond Mrs Bignall, but she did not hesitate to scold Margaret each time the chimney smoked or the fire burned too low to keep the bathroom water hot.

Margaret looked back on those first weeks and almost cried. What a sorry story! Use of a gas cooker and getting shown how to clean a range were the two best things to have happened to her in well over a month. Weariness and weakness swept over her in waves, and she had no need to ask why.

Her normal round, after the doctor had eaten his breakfast and departed, was to take Mrs Bignall a cup of tea in her room, then to start clearing grates and lighting fires in the dining room and sitting room. The drawing-room fire would have to be relaid if there had been company the previous evening. And as often as not, the sulky, inefficient kitchen range would have gone out and she would have to re-do that, too, so that Madam would have sufficient hot water for her ten o'clock bath.

Mrs Bignall seldom ate breakfast and went out for lunch twice or three times a week. But when she was home, Margaret had to prepare a midday meal, often for a guest as well as Mrs Bignall. When she was out for lunch, invariably she brought a woman friend home with her for tea. Tea was a ritual Margaret found very difficult. She had no talent for cutting either bread or cucumber into wafer-thin slices. She had yet to be taught how to make the little cakes and other sweet things which accompanied the meal, so she had to make time to hurry around to the nearest pastry shop and buy the goods. When she spent too much, Mrs Bignall snapped at her; when she economised, her employer complained at the sparseness of the spread. Margaret knew instinctively that the woman was only a step away from accusing her of incompetence for not knowing how to do the baking herself. She had escaped so far only because not even Mrs Bignall was quite mendacious enough to pretend she had not known of her maid's lack of skill.

Tea-time negotiated, Margaret started preparations for dinner. The Bignalls never dined before eight-thirty. When there were guests, it was more like nine-thirty. Margaret was forced to be in attendance throughout, and to wash up and tidy away after everyone had gone. Finally, there were the beds to turn down and hot water bottles to be put in. When Mrs Bignall was out during the day, she always left a list of jobs like washing her fine underclothes, or polishing the front door brassware, to keep Margaret occupied. In addition, she must clean and dust at least one of the house's eight main rooms in an unending rotation, like painting the Forth Bridge.

For her efforts, Margaret was paid five shillings a week, and so far it had not been convenient for Mrs Bignall to give her any time off. She sighed. Not that it mattered. She sent most of the money home to her mother, and she was invariably too impoverished and exhausted to want to do anything with her spare time except sleep. And eat. That was the worst thing of all.

Margaret was not a greedy girl, but she was still growing, and whatever else her mother had failed to provide, there was always some sort of filling food to keep the three children going. Not any more. The Bignalls were forced to eat fairly simply because Margaret was not yet highly skilled and Mrs Bignall herself was positively inept. Nevertheless they got through an apparently unending stream of roasts, bacon, ham, butter, eggs, sausages and vegetables. They liked hearty puddings and always made sure they were well-stocked with cakes and biscuits from the Austrian bakery up the road. But Mrs Bignall watched these food supplies with lynx-like care and it was made clear to Margaret from the beginning that she might eat only what was specifically designated for her. Invariably this turned out to be the soured remnant of a ham hock, a little piece of scrag-end that Mrs Bignall had asked the butcher to throw in as an afterthought to the saddle of lamb, or even a few slices of bread with a pot of dripping from the previous day's pork roast. As in many other houses undergoing the post-war struggle to keep up middle-class appearances, the Bignalls used every scrap of normal left-overs to eke out their own daily diet. The pieces of cold roast meat from Saturday's dinner party became Monday's lunchtime cottage pie. The vegetables uneaten at Sunday lunch were converted to bubble and squeak to accompany it. There was never any left for Margaret.

Now she slipped her hand through her belt. Never heavily fleshed, she was a good couple of inches thinner around the waist than she had been when Mrs Bignall bought her uniform six weeks before. For the tenth time, Margaret wondered what on earth she was going to do. She was already suffering frequent dizzy spells, and yesterday she had fainted briefly while she was cleaning the drawing-room windows. Next time, she might be carrying a tray full of Mrs Bignall's precious cut glass. Then the fat really would be in the fire!

She had time to brood today only because, out of the blue, she had been given some time off. Shortly after Dr Bignall departed for his surgery that morning, Madam had answered a telephone call from someone she called 'Dear Roy'. Since then she had been positively sweet-natured, presumably because she was going to see him for lunch.

Margaret had sighed when she overheard that. It meant she would be under pressure to cook something nice at the last minute, and she had no idea what to do. Then Mrs Bignall had astonished her by coming down to the basement and announcing that it was about time Armstrong had a little break. She could go off as soon as she liked, and there was no need to come back until, say, nine that evening, as she and Dr Bignall would be dining with friends.

This time, Margaret's sigh had been one of pure relief. 'I think, Madam, I'll just have a rest in my room then. I've got a lot of my own little jobs that need catching up with.' The prospect of a long, uninterrupted sleep was infinitely beguiling.

Alarm flared briefly in Margot Bignall's eyes. 'Nonsense — I won't hear of it! You've been looking positively peaky lately. I forbid you to stay here, my dear. You go off and get a good breath of fresh air. Go along now — leave what you're doing and go as soon as you like.'

Upstairs, Margaret looked at the tattered garments that were her only off-duty clothes. Where on earth could she go dressed like that? Then she thought: Of course, my wages! She had been sending her mother half-a-crown a week, but that had left her with half her earnings. She had received five weeks' money to date — not even Mrs Bignall had the nerve to pay her such a tiny sum quarterly or monthly — so there was twelve-and-six in the purse in her top drawer. She could have a slap-up plate of pie or fish and chips, then go off and buy herself some clothes. That would be something like an afternoon off! Then she could go and show her mother how well she was doing before it was time for her to return to Finchley. Margaret's weariness was fading fast. Now she took off her white cap and apron, and stood regarding the unadorned uniform dress, wondering if she could get away with wearing it as a going-out frock until she bought something. She could hardly go into a respectable department store in that ragged old sweater and skirt.

She began coming down to earth halfway through her second portion of apple tart and custard at a warm, brightly lit café along Finchley Road. She had already polished off the roast pork with stuffing, gravy, roast potatoes and two vegetables, and was drawing admiring glances from the ample woman who ran the establishment, who was wondering where such a little scrap of a thing put so much food. The feast had eroded just one and sixpence from Margaret's store of cash, but even so she was beginning to realise she lacked the money to outfit herself from a department store. For a start, she needed a coat. Luckily for her, today was unseasonably warm and she had come out in a frock. But it was early November; winter was almost here, and if she was ever to go out, she would need a topcoat.

Margot Bignall had seen no reason to supply one with the indoor uniform.

Margaret ordered and drank a cup of tea as she considered the problem. Her coatless state had been noticed, it seemed. A few minutes later the motherly proprietress ambled over to her and said confidentially: 'A little slip of a girl like you shouldn't be out without a coat, you know. Turns cold very early this time a year.' She was watching Margaret closely as she spoke. 'None a my business, a course, but I gotta feeling you don't own one. There's a nice little shop just round the corner — you know, nearly new stuff, all very high class — it's called the Mayfair Dress Agency. Bet they could fix you up lovely for a few bob. Don't mind me mentioning it, do you, love? Only you look as if you need a bitta looking after.'

Why didn't I think of that? Margaret wondered as she thanked the café owner. So used to them awful places Mam took us to, I forget there's respectable second-hand shops too.

Ten minutes later she was inside the Mayfair Dress Agency, a poky little shop which somehow managed to look jaunty thanks to a red-and-white striped awning outside. Ranks of dresses, all clean and well-pressed, hung on a rack down one side wall, and coats and suits occupied the back of the showroom. There were a couple of curtained fitting cubicles and a cheval mirror to permit customers to study their full-length appearance.

The manageress descended on Margaret with a gleam in her eye. She seldom got a chance to dress someone so slim, willowy and attractive. The girl could be a department store mannequin with a shape like that. She must starve herself to keep it that way. Enid Greaves wondered if the girl lived locally. If she did, there could be something in it for her.

'And what would you like to try, Miss — a winter suit, perhaps, or a coat?' Her eyes travelled meaningfully over Margaret's lightweight dress.

'I — I was wondering, that is . . . depending on the price, if I could manage a coat and a frock.'

'How much were you thinking of spending? Our clothes do run to an excellent quality.' She lowered her voice confidentially. 'In this sort of neighbourhood they like to change their whole wardrobe for the new season, so lots of our stuff's barely worn.'

'Oh, in that case, I don't suppose I could manage . . .'

'Now, now, we don't know till we try, do we? For a start, you're so slim you'll probably be able to get into clothes that very few of our ladies could wear, and there'd be a reduction if you were interested because of that. Of course, I'd want a little favour in return.'

'I don't think I'd have anything you wanted.'

Mrs Greaves uttered the tinkling little laugh her Bernard told her was so captivating. 'Let me worry about that, dear. All I'd want is that you mention my little establishment if people comment on your clothes. Nothing beats word-of-mouth recommendations when they come from someone as personable as you.'

Margaret blushed furiously. No one had ever praised her appearance. Until now she had no idea she was in any way remarkable.

'Now,' Mrs Greaves went on, 'had you any particular combination in mind – colour, style – you know?'

At that moment, Enid Greaves struck Margaret as the smartest, most sophisticated creature she had ever seen. Never having been inside even a good second-hand dress shop before, she had no idea that countless proprietresses looked much like Enid. 'I – I'd quite like to look like you,' said Margaret shyly.

What a nice little thing she is, Enid glowed to herself. I know I've got just the thing somewhere . . . 'And here we have it!' she finished aloud, triumphantly whipping out an ensemble from the coat and suit rack. It was a dress of fine, tan-coloured wool crepe, cut smooth and slinky to the lower hipline and then falling to calf length in a tumble of knife pleats, striped in tan, black and white. The coat that went with it was a slightly heavier worsted, warmly lined in silk satin, in plain tan. Margaret loved it on sight. She slipped it on in the fitting room, then strode out to look at herself in the cheval glass.

'Just as I thought — could be a mannequin,' breathed Enid Greaves. 'Half my friends would give a king's ransom to be built like that, you know. It's your height that does it.'

Margaret had barely heard. She was standing before the mirror, transfixed by the image that gazed back at her. She looked like a lady. A very fashionable lady . . . then she jolted back to reality. 'I can never afford this,' she said, 'never in a month of Sundays.'

The suit had been hanging on its rail for almost eight months. Enid's clients tended to be heavily built around bosom and hips and it had refused to fit any of them. It was a design from three seasons back, which dated it because it had been a high fashion ensemble, and she had only taken it because it came with a pile of other outfits which were far more like her normal stock. It had cost her pennies.

Now she smiled benignly and said: 'Remember what I told you about recommendations? Well, if you promised to do as much as you could there, I'd let you have that outfit for seven bob. You wouldn't find anything like it at four times the price.'

'Oh, I know, you needn't tell me!' Margaret was back in the clouds again. Seven shillings! She could afford it after all. 'I'll take it — and wrap my other clothes, please. I'll wear this out of the shop!' she said.

Afterwards she realised it had been at that moment that she decided she was never going back to Mrs Bignall. What if she *had* walked out in her uniform frock? The old cow had got enough work out of her to pay for six such dresses by now, and as she wouldn't get the week's pay that would be due her tomorrow, that could go towards it too. Looking at the tall, elegant girl in the cheval glass she decided her future did not lie in Margot Bignall's basement. Now her main desire was to get over to Fulham, show her mother the clothes and plan some other sort of future for herself. Why, with this outfit, she might persuade a shop to take her on!

Minutes later she was waiting at the Tube station for a train to West London. By the time she arrived, the early November dusk was already beginning to thicken, although it was barely three-thirty. Margaret got out at Parsons Green station and hurried around the corner towards Winchendon Road where her mother's flat was located. Then she realised it was early for her mother to be back on a Friday. She normally arrived at about half-past four, after doing a couple of hours in Sloane Street. Margaret went to get a cup of tea in the café opposite the end of the street, where she could intercept her mother as she arrived. She still had three shillings in her purse, and felt rich.

Somehow, the vigil on the barren edge of Fulham Road changed her mind about the nature of her welcome. The more she thought over what she had done, the more she came round to her mother's point of view. She had thrown up her first steady job, on the spur of the moment and with no financial backing, just because it was hard and she went hungry each day. What would her mother say to that? She certainly wouldn't greet it with pleasure. No more weekly half crowns coming in; instead at least the temporary presence of an extra mouth to feed. And what if this imagined shop job were not easily come by? She might find herself starting out afresh, under another Margot Bignall.

As she considered her plight, all Margaret's new-found confidence drained away and she sat staring morosely into her half-empty tea cup, wondering what on earth she would tell her mother. Then she saw Eva, outside, on the other side of Fulham Road, struggling along with a heavy bag over her arm. Mending, I'll bet, thought Margaret. She could never afford to buy that much in the way of food. For the first time she saw her mother objectively, prematurely aged by too much work and too little of everything else, bowed by taking the responsibility of two parents, isolated from all but her children, who were too young to understand.

Margaret fought back tears as she sat and watched. Eva put down the bag to rest for a moment at the corner, and in those few seconds Margaret realised she had not merely left the Bignalls forever. She was cutting loose from her family connections, too. She had no wish to go; she loved her mother and brothers. But she could be nothing but a burden to them at present. Best to disappear altogether, and maybe pop up again when she was prosperous and self-sufficient.

Margaret forced an optimistic smile to her lips and stared straight ahead, aware that Eva had now retrieved her burden and was shuffling off down Winchendon Road towards the flat. *Mam, I'm here, don't leave me!* the child within her cried out. But it was only a cry to her secret self. She waited until Eva had disappeared from view, then paid for her cup of tea and left, walking eastward along Fulham Road towards Walham Green. She could get a bed for the night at the YWCA branch there, and in the morning she could try for work on her own account. She could hardly make a worse job of it than others had so far.

Chapter Four

Nanny Bateman lived in a single-storey house within sight of the Haskins mansion in Lisvane. Jane and Eleri were to stay the night with her, and she was taking them to London by train the next day. The girls discovered they had been put in a bedroom which directly overlooked the drive to the big house.

By the time they arrived at Lisvane, it was after seven o'clock. The journey had passed like a dream for both girls. A limousine would have been impressive to anyone of their generation; to them it was little short of a fairy tale, as neither had been inside any sort of private car before. 'Pity it was dark most of the way,' whispered Jane as they swept along the Newport–Cardiff road. 'I'd have liked to wave at everybody as we passed by.'

Eleri glanced up nervously at Miss Bateman. 'Don't think she'd have let us,' she said. 'Bet she do think it's common to wave.'

'I most certainly do.' The stentorian voice made both girls start with fright. 'And I can assure you that thirty years spent looking after children have given me pin-sharp hearing, so if you have any secrets, I'd keep them to yourselves.' Having delivered her announcement, Nanny returned her attention to the dark road outside the window.

But Jane forgot she had missed anything when they were installed in their room at Lisvane. Nanny said: 'You two settle down, wash your hands and faces, and get ready to have supper with me at about half-past eight. We've got a very long day tomorrow and I want you both in bed early.'

'Yes, Nanny Bateman,' they chorused dutifully, departing for the room she had shown them. When they got inside, they discovered the delights that awaited them. The Haskins were giving a party that evening, and the first guests were beginning to arrive. Neither Eleri nor Jane had seen such expensive clothes, jewels and cars before. Ignoring the evening chill, they opened the big bedroom window and leaned out as far as they could to gape at the seemingly endless tapestry of beautiful and immaculate men's suiting.

'When I get rich,' said Jane dreamily, 'I'm going to have a dress like that orange one over there.'

'Fat chance either of us will ever get,' responded Eleri. 'We're gonna spend the rest of our lives close enough to see and touch them, but never to own one. How are you going to cope with that?'

Jane considered the question for a while, then said: 'Just you wait and see. I'm not spending the rest of my life in a cap and apron for anybody, but I think we'll have a better chance of getting somewhere if we start off like this than ever we would in the Valleys.'

Eleri sniffed. 'Since when have we had any choice? You know, Jane, I was really happy in school. I liked reading, and I liked painting. Didn't even mind sewing lessons, come to that. I'd a been happy to stay there another year.'

'And then what would you have done? You'd still have had to go into service in the end, and the only way you'd have managed to stay back in Abercarn woulda been if you went and skivvied for one a them schoolmarms or the bank manager up Pant-yr-esg Road. You've seen how they do treat their girls. Would you have put up with it for more than five minutes?'

'Not a chance!' Eleri's tone was vehement. 'You'm right, kidda. Better this, much better. And we seem to be doing better than most with this, an' all. They'm ever so much posher than the people some of the girls in our class have gone to.'

'Well, you'd better start watching your language, my lady, or you'll be back up that valley faster than you can say knife!' Unobserved, Miss Bateman had entered the room behind them. She had been watching their rapt scrutiny of the Haskins dinner guests with amusement for some minutes, but there was no trace of humour now in her tone or expression.

'Language?' Eleri was startled to see her there, but uncowed. 'I never said nothing wrong.'

'Not that sort of language, child! The *way* you talk — that's what I mean. You're going to work for a countess, remember. You're going to have to mind your Ps and Qs all the time from now on. You don't say "ent". You don't say "they'm". "They are" is the proper way to say it. Now, you can start practising on me this evening. It isn't difficult, as long as you think before you talk. Come along, quickly. If I know anything about girls, you won't even have washed yet. You'll have been gawping out of that window at Mrs Haskins's guests.' She turned and swept out of the room, gesturing to them to follow.

'Gawping?' Jane murmured rebelliously. 'If we're all being so bloody polite, what sorta word's gawping?'

Miss Bateman's bark proved much worse than her bite. Over supper she mixed admonitions about accent and table manners with reminiscences of her early years as a nurserymaid and later as a young nanny. 'You'll get lonely from time to time, and you'll have to put up with it,' she told them. 'But all work has its drawbacks, and service has more compensations than most.'

'I can't think of many just now,' chipped in Jane.

'Then you're a lot more stupid than I took you to be,' said Miss Bateman. 'You compare the pay, working conditions and prospects of the average young servant to a shop girl or factory hand, and then tell me if you can repeat that, hand on heart.'

'Well then, why do they all look down on servants?'

'Because they're ignorant and jealous, that's why! There's a lot more to life than being free to rush off around the pubs and dance halls every evening after work, and that's all they judge by.'

'I've never been in a dance hall.' Jane's voice was wistful.

'Good. You've missed nothing. Come along, eat up your supper. It's almost time for bed.'

Later, as they drifted towards sleep, the vibrant strains of a jazz tune drifted across the lawn from the big house, accompanied by fragments of laughter and chatter. 'One day,' said Jane with a long sigh, 'one day, it'll be me over there, dancing and drinking champagne, and some other little girl lying here listening and wishing it was happening to her.'

'Like I said, chance'd be a fine thing,' said Eleri.

'The sooner you get that new girl down to Fenton Parva, the better,' said Mrs Higgins, housekeeper at the Cliftons' London home. 'Cook is really coming to the boil about being short-handed. Trouble with that lot down there is they've always been spoiled for choice with staff. Not used to having to make do like in London.'

'Come along, Mrs H — we seldom have to cope with their numbers, do we now?' The butler, Watson, had always liked the cook at Fenton Parva, and thought Mrs Higgins's attitude unjustified.

'Well, one kitchen-maid — what difference does that make with an indoor staff the size of theirs?' she retorted. 'Probably just means the scullery-maid has to do the veg, that's all.'

'Even that can be a minor disaster when you consider Madam's high standards,' admonished Watson. 'Remember the ructions there were here the last time some carrots went to table badly prepared? Cook must be running herself ragged down at Fenton.'

Mrs Higgins, who harboured little affection for the Fenton Parva cook, sniffed her disdain. 'Ah, well, perhaps some people will have to use a bit of elbow grease for once.' Watson closed his eyes and gave a little shrug of impatience, then went about his business. No use trying to reason with Mrs Higgins when she was in one of her argumentative moods.

Eleri and Jane sat, ignored, beside the big deal kitchen table. Nanny Bates had dropped them off there before going off to have tea with the Clifton nanny. She had plenty of gossip to catch up with, and was curious about how successful Lady Clifton had been in staffing up the nursery properly. The two girls were waiting to be given their tea in the housekeeper's room, but Mrs Higgins was in no hurry. They still had only the vaguest idea of what was going to happen to them, and both were wide-eyed and slightly frightened at the sheer size of London and of the Clifton town house.

'My God, it's as big as County Hall!' Jane had exclaimed as they approached the huge house on the corner of Belgrave Square.

Nanny Bateman was too pleased by her charges' obvious awe to scold Jane for her coarse speech. 'The sort of establishment that befits an earl,' she said smugly. 'Wait until you see their place in Wiltshire.'

'Have you been there, too, Miss Bateman?' asked Eleri.

'Naturally. I worked there for six months, nursing the countess's first baby until the permanent nursery staff were up to scratch. Her Ladyship wanted to be completely sure they were trustworthy. It was the last full-time job I did before I moved into the cottage at Lisvane.'

Hell, thought Jane, imagine trying to start your first job as a senior nanny with this old bitch watching every move you made. She might be totally inexperienced so far, but she knew instinctively how uncomfortable such a situation must be.

Eleri was beyond such small thoughts. She was deeply involved in this adventurous new life, and wanted to know as much as possible about it. 'Tell us about the house, then.'

'It's the grounds you notice most of all — so big, you never saw anything like it. Bigger than Kensington Gardens and Hyde Park put together. They even call part of it the Park. Then there's the formal gardens, and a water garden, and terraces all along the southern and western sides of the main house to catch the best of the sun. You can see a little string of lakes down across the Park, and there's an island in the middle of one, with a dear little Chinese pagoda on it.' Even Nanny Bateman looked misty-eyed now. Eleri, watching the woman, wondered if she had ever been young enough to imagine herself the object of a lordly declaration of love in that little pagoda. It hardly seemed credible from this dried-up old stick, but something was obviously softening her as she talked of Fenton Parva.

'What's the house itself like, Nanny Bateman?' asked Jane, her mind as always on precious material goods rather than aesthetics.

Miss Bateman's expression reverted closer to its harsh normal lines, but she was still impressed by what she was remembering. 'Beyond your wildest dreams,' she said, her voice wistful. 'It was built over four centuries ago and bits have been added in every century since then. I'll tell you one thing, my girl: you've never seen anything like it back in the Valleys.'

With that, she had shepherded them into the basement area of the mansion and taken them through the kitchens to the servants' staircase and the housekeeper's room. Now, as they sipped cups of strong, sweet tea and ate chunks of Cook's Dundee cake, Miss Bateman bustled back to them.

'I hope you weren't setting too much store on Fenton Parva, Ellis,' she said to Jane. 'Mrs Higgins has decided you're just what she's looking for here. You start as underhousemaid tomorrow. Jones — you're the lucky one. You're off to Wiltshire in the morning. I've just been talking it over up in the nursery. They've taken on a couple of London girls. One will work here with you, Ellis, and the other is going to Fenton Parva as nursery-maid.'

'What about me?' said Eleri, her voice faint at the thought of losing touch with Jane, now the last remaining link with home.

'I just told you. Don't you ever listen? Oh, yes, I see, the job. Scullery-maid. Now, don't get disheartened. It gives you a chance to move up quickly if you've any talent. No girl worth her salt wants to stay among the pots and pans forever. You'll be a cook in next to no time if you listen and do what you're told.'

'But I didn't . . . don't . . .' Eleri's whisper faded to nothing.

'Speak up, speak up! What's wrong *now*?'

'I've never done any cooking or . . . or anything like that. I don't think I'd really want to.'

'Want to doesn't enter into it. You've been taken on and brought here at great expense. The least you can do is show a proper gratitude and get on with the tasks your betters decide on.'

Both Eleri and Jane realised that the subject was closed. Mrs Higgins had returned to the room as they spoke, and now she said: 'You can share the housemaids' room on the top floor tonight. The other girl comes in two days, so there's an empty bed at present.' She consulted her fob watch. 'My, it will be time for servants' supper soon and here are you two still having tea! You'll eat us out of house and home before you've done.'

The two girls followed a senior maid up flight after flight of stairs to the servants' attics, where they were shown a little spartan room with two narrow iron-framed beds and a sparse scattering of furniture. The minute the older girl had left them, Jane uttered a snort of contempt. 'Come to work for a grand family and live better, my foot! This doesn't look as good as that mansion in Lisvane to me — it's not even as cosy as the front bedroom back home!'

Eleri was more philosophical. 'Come on, kidda, you know our rooms at home was no better than this — damned sight more crowded, in fact. It's a bit bare, I know, but I don't think we'll be spending much time in our bedrooms.'

'No, I get that feeling, too. Poor old you! At least I'm up in London, and I don't have to wash pans in any rotten old kitchen!'

Eleri thrust aside her own misgivings about the job and said: 'Oh, I'm quite happy about going to the country. That house do sound lovely the way Nanny Bateman described it — and I may get a better room than this if they got more space down there.'

She could scarcely have been more wrong. Fenton Parva was all Nanny Bateman had said of it, and much more, but for her first months there, Eleri might have been living in a Seven Dials slum.

There was a small single room behind the scullery at Fenton Parva. This was always assigned to the most junior scullery- or kitchen-maid on the ground that they must be first up, at 6.30 in the morning, to light the range and take early tea to the housekeeper and the cook. For all the grandeur of the house above her, Eleri still lived in hutch-like conditions. Had she been less exhausted she would have cried herself to sleep each night for the first few weeks.

The mansion's kitchens lacked much of the modernity and big-city sophistication of the London establishment. With the exception of the refrigerators, everything seemed to have been installed in the previous century, including the vast cooking range which the second kitchen-maid had to clean and light each morning.

Mrs Stanley, the cook, was a decent sort who had started her own working life as a scullery-maid and was therefore inclined to gentleness with Eleri. 'Can't say I think you'll be pleased when I tell you your duties,' she said, 'but if you want my advice, the best way to handle it is do everything quick and thorough and you'll get quick promotion. That's what I did and I've never learned a better way of getting out of that scullery.'

By the end of her first, interminable, working day, Eleri was convinced Mrs Stanley was right. She was less sure of whether she could stand the pace. The most back-breaking, though by no means the most repulsive, job was washing up. The scullery was a long, narrow room with sash windows above eye level. It contained a range of vast sinks, half porcelain, half woodlined, the latter to protect fine china from breakage. Ridged wooden draining boards connected the sinks, and overhead plate racks were provided to drain wet crockery. Mountains of washing up were brought in even when only the family were at home. When there were guests in the house, the second kitchen-maid was drafted to help Eleri. Even so, it was a killing, unending task.

It was made harder by her small stature. Eleri was a sturdy girl — otherwise she would never have been taken on — but quite short. The sinks were so deep that she was unable to reach the bottom of the porcelain one, and had to stand on an upturned box. That put her in touch with the crockery, but did nothing to help her constant back-ache.

The washing up was only the beginning, though. A few days after she came to Fenton Parva, Eleri was hurrying between the sinks, transferring soaped breakfast plates to the rinser, when a shadow fell across her. She glanced up at the window and saw a man's gaitered legs and feet on the gravelled walk outside. As she watched, there was a soft thumping sound and a mass of fur and feathers was thrust through the open window, directly above the rinsing sink. She let out a squeal of dismay — more concerned about damage to the crockery than to the unknown bundle — and threw herself forward to catch whatever it was. She managed to save it, then dropped the lot on the floor when she discovered it comprised two brace of pheasant and a hare, all dead and extremely bloody.

'What be wrong wi' you, silly little lummox?' growled the man through the open window. 'Nearly ruined them birds, you did!'

Eleri was too startled and angry to restrain herself. 'Woulda been your fault if they *had* spoiled!' she snapped back. 'Why don't you warn people before you do a daft thing like that?'

'It's the maid's job to notice, not mine to warn 'er,' the man rumbled. She had no way of telling whether he was really angry with her or merely defending his own corner, because her view of him did not extend above his knees. Now he began to move away.

Eleri sighed, exasperated beyond words that she had no way of knowing the identity of this unfriendly new acquaintance. Reluctantly, she retrieved the pile of bloody game from the floor by the sink and took it over to the far corner of the scullery where she would not be forced to look at it. Then she noticed a trail of congealing blood across the tiles, and was delayed yet again while she rinsed it away. By the time she had caught up with her normal tasks, the kitchen-maid was at her elbow.

'Cook says have you gone to sleep in here? She was expecting that load of breakfast stuff back ready to put away half an hour ago.'

'Don't you start, too!' blurted Eleri. 'Everything's going wrong this morning and I've had about as much as I can stand.'

'What's going on now?' Mrs Stanley's voice boomed from the scullery door. 'Jones, unless you keep your mind on your work, you and I are going to fall out. Never could abide a lazy scullery-maid.'

Eleri could stand it no longer. The steam, the back-ache, the blood-soaked animal carcases all seemed to combine and crown her misery. Throwing down the wet cloth she had been holding, she crumpled on to the upturned box which had been her step-up to the sink, and began sobbing broken-heartedly. Abruptly the atmosphere changed, although she was too overcome to notice at first. She was vaguely aware of Cook saying something to the kitchen-maid, and after that, of being alone with Mrs Stanley, but it was some time before she even began to calm down. When she did, she let her hands fall back into her lap and looked up hopelessly, the tears still pouring down her cheeks. Mrs Stanley was standing over her, and to Eleri's confusion there was an expression of intense compassion on her face.

'If we was to go out into that kitchen this minute, I do believe we'd find it empty,' she said. 'And then you could come up to my sitting room for a few minutes and have a little talk over a cuppa tea.'

'B-but all the washing up. I'll never get on top of it . . .'

The cook cut her off with a single gesture. 'Nonsense. You've finished with the breakfast stuff, just about, and Mary can deal with anything that arrives in the next half hour. Others have done for her often enough. Come on now, I think it's time we sorted you out a bit.'

Over tea and fruitcake, Mrs Stanley pieced together Eleri's miserable first few days in service. When the girl came to the arrival of the gamekeeper's macabre bundle, she tutted in disapproval. 'That'll be Hadley. Always did make trouble for indoor servants when he could. I've tried and tried to stop him doing that and he never does. One day I shall tell the girl to let him drop the game in the sink. We'll see who comes out on top with the Master after *that*. Likes his hare and pheasant more than any man I ever saw. He'd be furious to have it spoiled.'

Eleri was feeling somewhat better, but not enough to enable her to contemplate her future with any enthusiasm. 'Did you really start in service the way I am, Cook?' she asked. Mrs Stanley nodded. 'How long did it take you to get out of that terrible scullery?'

'Too long by half. I was like you, fretting and worrying, missing my family. It was my first time away from home, an' all — and they were a long way off like your people, so there was no chance of the odd day off back with me mother. So I stayed in that scullery and snivelled to myself day after day. Of course, the more miserable I got, the slower I got, and the less work I did. Then I'd get into trouble and none a the other kitchen staff wanted much to do with me. Oh, it was 'orrible, I can tell you.'

'How could you bear to stay?'

Mrs Stanley's laugh was devoid of mirth. 'Lack of choice, love — sheer lack of choice. Now look, they'd skin me alive, senior staff though I am, if they thought I was skulking around up here this time a morning with a new scullery-maid. I'm only doing it 'cos I can see myself in you and I'd like it to be a bit easier for you than it was for me. I'm only gonna say all this once, so listen carefully. Took me nine months to work it out for myself and they was wasted. That sort of time never comes back. You knuckle down and make yourself go on with that rotten job. Don't admit to yourself how rotten it is — keep reminding yourself it's a path to being kitchen-maid. And kitchen-maid's a path to being Cook. Now that *is* worth having, you take it from me.

'I want you to stop worrying about the piddling little things, like that bugger Hadley and his game. I'll see you learn the job fast, and if you show any promise at all, I'll see you get quick promotion, too. I know it won't put you back with your family, but it's better than nothing, ennit?'

Eleri felt like smiling for the first time since she had started work in the scullery. 'A lot better, Cook.' Impulsively she stood up, went to the other woman and kissed her cheek. 'Thank you for taking so much trouble.'

Mrs Stanley made much of pushing her off, but it was obvious she was flustered and pleased by Eleri's demonstrative gratitude. 'Get along with you,' she said, 'back down that scullery before we're both ticked off. Quickly, girl! You'll have to put more speed into it if you're going to get on fast.'

After that, life was less bleak. Eleri went on feeling exhausted at the end of each day's work, but gradually the back-ache stopped as she adjusted to her new working stance. Hadley the gamekeeper gave a grudging tap on the scullery window now when he arrived with game, and the carcases were handed instead of being thrown in. She began to master small skills and to know her way around the house. Within a few weeks she was expert at plucking poultry and game birds and at skinning rabbits and hares, although she loathed the messiness of the tasks and her fingers were often raw from the rough little quills in the birds' plumage.

Mrs Stanley proved something of a guardian angel, keeping a strict but essentially kindly eye on her most junior maid, and quietly ensuring that the girl got some protection until she acquired sufficient emotional toughness to look after herself. She had never known any other system than the one which took girls from home at thirteen or fourteen and worked them like adults while treating them in all other respects like untrustworthy children, but she had always detested it. There was a softness and a charm in Eleri that deserved to survive, and if Mrs Stanley had any say in the matter it would not be smothered by years of browbeating and oppression.

Chapter Five

The training centre had started life as a public house, and many generations ago an enterprising landlord had attempted to add to its attractions by placing a large sculpted swan on the roof of the entrance porch. The inn had long ceased to serve ale to passing trade, but the graceful bird and the colonnaded porch remained as mute reminders of a more hospitable time. Nowadays The Swan in Parsons Green Lane trained young women to work as domestic servants in the grand houses of the West End. It was a gloomy establishment, staffed by irritable women who were sufficiently insecure about their own competence to be excessively strict with the young trainees. The girls worked on the lower floors of the house and slept in a connected warren of attic dormitories which had once been staff accommodation for the pub. It was cold and draughty up there under the roof, and the four bathrooms – they had four only because the trainees practised their cleaning skills there during the day – were on the lower floors.

None of this mattered to Rose. It was the first time she had lived in accommodation which had any sort of piped hot water supply or adequate provision of flush lavatories. The draughty roof space was safer than Ladysmith Court and a good deal warmer than the Embankment, and the lack-lustre stews and meat puddings which comprised their main meals were dietary perfection in comparison with stale fried fish. Within a few days, she was more content than at any time since her mother's death. Her gaunt frame started filling out pleasingly as the nourishing food took effect, and gradually the shadows which had once seemed permanently etched beneath her eyes faded and vanished. Without realising it, Rose was becoming a very good-looking girl. The change also remained unremarked among the other trainees and staff because she was so self-effacing that they seldom took a good look at her.

Rose was a natural observer. Bitter experience had taught her never to volunteer an opinion or to draw attention to herself. It always led to trouble. Now she watched the tinpot martinets at the training centre browbeating her fellow trainees when they made themselves conspicuous, and saw no reason to change tactics. She listened to what the instructors had to say, watched carefully while they demonstrated a cleaning or service technique, then set about doing it herself. When they criticised her, she endured in silence. When she was complimented for getting it right, she responded with a small smile, quickly gone, and a murmured word of thanks. She swiftly acquired a name for biddable efficiency among the staff. The other girls regarded her as a toady.

Rose did not care what they thought of her, so she felt no need to explain why she wanted to avoid trouble. Her sister Louise was little more than a dim memory now, and Rose had never known any other friendship beyond the fickle matiness of her adult neighbours around Ladysmith Court. It scarcely mattered that no one wished to gossip with her at the end of the day, or that none of them invited her to join them for an outing on their afternoons off. Life had always been solitary for Rose, apart from her closeness to her mother. If she ever encountered anyone she thought worthy of her love, she might even know how to give and accept affection, thanks to Jean Rush's endless warmth for her two daughters, but now she found no difficulty in cutting herself off from the rest of the world.

There was another reason for her willing acquiescence to the discipline imposed at the centre: it admitted no men, and while she was within its walls Rose felt wholly secure. Her nervousness in male company dated from a week or so after her father's connivance at her rape by Alf Dobson. At first, mercifully removed from Ladysmith Court, she had been too shocked to dwell on the incident, but as her physical condition improved, the full impact of the assault was borne home. She was determined such a thing would never happen again, and until she could find an adequate means of permanent protection, the training centre was the next best thing. Nothing would have persuaded her to do anything that might get her expelled before her period of training was over. She had already decided that even domestic service had something to be said for it. After all, the instructresses here kept emphasising the fact that their first employers would be morally responsible for them as long as they were under age. The other girls all made exasperated faces and sighed dramatically when the staff told them this. Clearly they were convinced they were going to work for middle-class kill-joys who locked them away from boys and made sure they were home early on their evenings off. It all sounded blissfully secure to Rose. They'll never have to worry about *me* flirting with the milkman or wasting time gossiping with the butcher's boy, she thought.

She had been at the training centre for almost a month when a late arrival joined the course. At first Rose barely noticed the other girl's presence. She was as quiet and self-effacing as Rose herself. Then the attitude of the other girls rapidly changed her mind, and for the first time Rose found herself thinking of someone else's interests.

The new trainee was Margaret Armstrong. She had impressed the Labour Exchange clerk with her elegant, if dated, appearance, and when he realised the training centre's course was already in progress this made him reluctant to refer the girl to an orphanage or young women's home, the logical destinations for destitute youngsters of Margaret's age when there was no work or benefit entitlement for them. That sort of thing was all very well when you saw some of the shabby little trollops who came along to register, but anyone with an eye for that sort of thing could see this girl was a cut above her own background. The clerk's instant rationalisation conveniently released him from further contemplation of the unwelcome thought that his own daughter Gillian was the same age as Margaret and bore a striking resemblance to her. But while Margaret stood before him homeless and penniless, asking for help his own child was still safely at school, with no prospect of her working for at least three or four more years.

He smiled cautiously at Margaret. Mustn't let the kid think he was giving out any preferential treatment. 'Let's see, perhaps if I telephoned the centre and told them you were willing to work harder to catch up . . . maybe that would persuade Miss Wilson, the supervisor. We can but ask!'

In fact he did a lot more than merely ask. Having sent Margaret to sit in the waiting area so that she could not overhear the conversation, he got hold of Mabel Wilson and provided the girl with what amounted to a glowing testimonial. Exceptionally quick on the uptake . . . good reader and writer . . . the best turned-out young unemployed person he'd seen for a long time, and quite clearly doing it on a shoestring. He was sure, he told Mabel, that the girl could read up one of those household management manuals they used to mug up part of what she had missed. And should Miss Wilson want to give Armstrong any extra jobs just to bring her up level with the rest, no one would complain, least of all the girl herself. By the time he hung up, Mabel Wilson thought she was getting a second Mrs Beeton in the making, and Margaret had a place on the training centre's current course.

Unfortunately Margaret had no protection against the malice of the other girls. With the highly developed herd instinct commonly found in tenement communities, they took one look at her and decided she did not belong. For a start, she had that funny northern accent; but worst of all, she was better dressed than any of them had so far dreamed of being, and they hated her for it.

Rose became aware of their hostility to the newcomer when she overheard three of her fellow trainees discussing Margaret just before supper on her first evening. 'Stuck-up little cow! Who does she think she is, turning up here dolled up to the nines? If she can afford clobber like that, she don't need no place here!' That was May Clancy, a girl Rose avoided whenever possible because she could be relied on to sneer about Rose's sucking up to the staff.

'Yeah, and why should she be let off all that scrubbing and sweeping we was all doing the first coupla weeks?' chimed in Ella Smith, the class whiner. 'It's all right for some, swanning along and picking up the lighter work when we've done the whole thing.'

Rose was surprised by the strength of her own reaction. She found it hard to subdue an impulse to join in and tell them to leave the newcomer in peace. But this time, at least, her natural inclination to remain aloof won. She merely sighed, gave them a cold look and moved off towards the dining room for supper. The new girl was isolated at the far end of an almost empty table. Nobody went to sit with her and two of the instructresses were regarding her with intense curiosity, obviously trying to work out where she had obtained her smart dress. Rose went to collect her plate of food and cup of tea with every intention of joining Margaret, but at the last moment her courage failed. The staff seemed almost as hostile to her as the other girls. Rose had no wish to make enemies with another five months of training ahead of her. She moved to another table and sat down, alone, like Margaret, hoping that seeing another solitary type might give the girl at least a little comfort.

Margaret would be issued her maid's uniform the next morning before formally commencing the course, so she remained conspicuous in her second-hand finery. She was beginning to regret her purchase. True, it had indirectly gained her back-door admission to this place, but she was wondering now whether she could endure the pressure of the other girls' hostility. It weighed so heavily on her that she entirely failed to notice Rose's sympathetic presence across the room.

Like Rose, she had never been close to people outside her own family, but no one had ever hated her, either. Until now, Margaret had passed unnoticed, a colourless schoolgirl with a few friends and acquaintances, a dutiful daughter who stuck close to her mother and never spoke to strangers. Now, to her consternation, she realised that some strangers might bear her malice for no better reason than that she was different. She quickly ate her supper then went off to bed, although it was still early.

She had been allocated one of two unoccupied beds in the dormitory next door to Rose's. A couple of hours later, Rose left her own shared room to go downstairs for a bath. Abruptly the door of Margaret's dormitory swung open and the girl rushed out as though she had been propelled, so careless in her haste that she cannoned into Rose and nearly knocked her down. Rose scarcely had time to react before she heard the chorus of cat-calls and jeers which followed Margaret. 'That's right, and stay out — we can do without your sort, thanks!' 'Miss Snotty-nose in her fancy togs. You're no better than us with your clothes off, luv!' There was much more in a similar vein.

The newcomer turned to Rose, skittish as a nervous animal. 'Please don't be cross,' she said. 'I don't think I could take it . . . not after all that.' She gestured towards the door, which had been slammed behind her, and as she did so she began to cry, murmuring, 'Sorry . . . so sorry . . . I didn't mean to show meself up like this.'

Rose found it impossible to remain aloof. She put an arm around Margaret's shoulder and said: 'You're not showing yourself up. They're a right bunch a cats, the whole lot a them. Come on, now, downstairs with me, before they know they've got at you.'

Two flights down, they had a whole floor to themselves. None of the other girls was over-keen on bathing, and Rose seldom had trouble in finding herself an unoccupied bathroom. Tonight was no exception. There were two, in adjoining rooms, one room tiled and the other painted to give the trainees experience of cleaning different types of wall surface.

'There's only a partition between the two,' she explained, 'so why don't you get yourself a bath in there and I'll have one here. We can talk over the partition top.'

Margaret's self possession was surging back, now. With another girl to turn to, life looked altogether brighter. Rose set the water running in her own bathroom. 'Go on, then,' she said, 'fill your bath up and get in and we can have a chat when the water's stopped.'

Up to her chin in steaming water, Margaret began, haltingly at first, to tell her story. In the telling it got easier, particularly as she was able to indulge in a little secret weeping when she came to the bit about seeing her mother across the street. No one could see her tears in here, not even her new friend Rose.

Finally the sad tale drew to a close. 'I suppose I mustn't complain too much really,' she ended. 'The lady at the dress agency couldn't have been kinder — nor the man up the Labour, come to that. But somehow I wish there was somewhere else for me.'

'I know the feeling, love. You needn't explain *that*.' Rose's tone was so charged with bitterness that Margaret glanced up, startled, towards the partition, half expecting to see the other girl's face peeping over it.

'Was it like that for you too, then?'

'No, not quite. But it came to the same thing in the end, didn't it? Listen, I gotta good idea. You and me are both all on our own. We're not going to make any friends among the rubbish in this place. What d'you say we stick together, you know, after we leave and get jobs? Dunno about you, but I'm sick to death of talking to meself all the time, and I think if I'd had a friend before, things wouldn't have seemed so bad.'

A glow of gratitude began spreading through Margaret. 'Do you really mean that? I'm not all that bright — never done anything exciting, like, or been anywhere you could boast about. The train trip down from Manchester's the furthest I've ever been.'

'Well then, you been hundreds of miles further than me! I never went out a London. Sometimes I don't think I ever will, neither,' Rose added darkly.

Margaret made a second timorous attempt to gain Rose's

confidence. 'D-do you want to tell me what happened to you, then? How you came here and all?'

'Not yet. Maybe some day, maybe not.' Rose's voice was different now, harsh, tightly controlled. 'It's too close . . . too nasty,' then, apologetically, she added, 'But if I ever *do* tell anybody, it'll be you, I promise. Nobody else knows at all, you see,' she ended lamely.

Margaret had already experienced enough suffering on her own account to recognise pain which went too deep to find expression. She simply said: 'That's all right. So long as you remember I'm your friend for good, now, and I always will be, whatever it is.'

'What on earth is going on in there? Do you girls realise what time it is? Rose Rush, I thought better of you — you usually have a sense of responsibility. Come out here at once!' It was Lottie Keenan, one of the instructresses whose sitting room was on the floor below. Rose hurriedly jumped out of the bath and swathed herself in a towel before opening the door.

'Sorry, Miss Keenan,' she murmured, eyes modestly downcast. 'I was, sort of, helping the new girl to settle in.'

'Settle in? At this time of night she should be asleep in her bed, not using up all the hot water and chattering away like a magpie. Now will you *please* tell me what's going on? Armstrong, come out at once!'

Suddenly Rose saw a way of minimising their present trouble and of getting Margaret out of the unpleasant conditions she faced upstairs. Without waiting for the other girl to emerge, she said: 'Please, Miss Keenan, I was trying to keep her out of the way of the others in the front dormitory. You know how rough they can be.'

Lottie Keenan had been embroiled in a heated argument with two of the cheekier girls only that afternoon, and now her cheeks flamed at the memory. She did not like to think they had bested her, but they had. 'Yes, you're right, Rush. They can be a handful. But that's no excuse for gallivanting down here at this time of night.'

'But, Miss, it was all I could think of, short of disturbing you and the other ladies,' said Rose, her tone wheedling. 'They were threatening poor Margaret with everything from slapping her around to ripping up her clothes. That's why she brought her bag and stuff with her − look.' As she spoke, Margaret had emerged from her own bathroom and her possessions were clearly visible behind her on the chair. In fact it had been pure instinct which had made her grab everything and run. At the time she had nursed some half-formed idea of leaving the centre that night. Only Rose's intervention had prevented her from trying to get out of the locked building.

Miss Keenan was softening by the minute. It was hard to resist Rose at her most deferential, and if those young hooligans in the front dorm were going to pick on the new girl, it would cause her and the other supervisors no end of trouble. 'Well, Rush, what d'you suggest I do about it? I'm no miracle worker and Armstrong has to go somewhere.'

'Yes, I know, that's what I was thinking. What's wrong with the room *I'm* in? Pauline Handyside was taken off to hospital yesterday, remember.'

'I know, I know − but she'll soon be back.' Miss Keenan's tone was lofty but Rose was as aware as the other trainees that poor Handyside had suffered some sort of brainstorm and was unlikely to be going anywhere in a hurry. Now she merely said: 'Well, when she comes back − *if* she comes back − she may prefer to be in the bigger room with all the others, you know, cheer herself up a bit?' Inwardly Rose shuddered at the thought of someone with delicate nerves being cheered up by the females in the big dormitory, but she pressed on. 'In the meantime Margaret could move into the little room with the two of us who are there now.'

'Linen,' said Miss Keenan. 'No linen. The bed hasn't been made up yet.'

'Well, if you could issue us with a set before we went back up, I'm sure we could see to that in two ticks without disturbing the others. Margaret hasn't touched her bed in the big room, so it won't be a matter of doubling up.'

'Is that true, Armstrong?'

Margaret nodded. 'Y-yes, Miss. They was so fierce to me I was afraid to undress and get in me bed.'

'All right, that settles it. And I'll see those young brats get a good talking to in the morning.' Margaret started to beg Miss Keenan not to make her position worse by mentioning the incident, but Rose silenced her with a pinch and a ferocious look.

As they trailed along behind Miss Keenan to the linen cupboard, she whispered: 'I know it'll make it a bit difficult, but better that than not moving at all. They'll have your guts if you go back in that big room tonight, and old Keenan's still not a hundred per cent sold on the idea. Leave her be if she's willing to go along with us now.'

The other girls certainly made life as uncomfortable as possible from that day on, but somehow that merely served to cement the friendship between Rose and Margaret. Their initial response to each other had been that of children — after all, both were only fourteen years old — and the vow of eternal friendship might have been as transitory as a spring shower. But the freezing reaction of the other trainees once the pair combined to defy the pack, turned childish whim into adult closeness. Within a week or two the girls found it inconceivable that either had ever managed without the support of the other.

The training course progressed at an incredibly slow pace. Margaret's education had been scanty and Rose's had virtually stopped after she learned to read, write and do elementary sums, but both were blessed with quick intelligence. Some of their fellow trainees had hardly been to school at all. Others had spent their time tucked away at the back of the class where the schools inspector would not see them and would remain unaware of their perennial illiteracy. With some it was not even mere lack of education, but the deadly, permanent torpor caused by an undernourished childhood. However hard some sympathetic teacher might try with these poor ruins, they would remain the slowest of the slow. Drunken parents and malnutrition had seen to that.

As a result, Rose and Margaret, both determined to get on, whisked through their work and were always available for extra jobs. After an initial period of wariness, the staff came to like it, because they had a manageable proportion of trainees who showed promise and initiative. They had no wish to train up a centre full of such prodigies — it would have been far too wearing constantly to find them something to do — but a couple of able pupils would help to ensure the continued existence of the centre, and of their jobs. The instructresses periodically felt threatened when they heard of yet another centre closing, either because of inefficient training practices, or because modern girls were unwilling to enter domestic service whatever the inducement.

But popularity with the staff merely acted as a counterbalance to the hostility of the girls. Both Rose and Margaret needed something else to stimulate their lively minds, and the public library proved the answer. It stood on the north side of Fulham Road, splendidly worthy and intimidating. The girls stared at it in awe for a long time before they eventually dared to go in, and then, to their amazement, discovered they could join free of charge as long as one of the instructresses signed a form for them.

Lottie Keenan completed the task with relish. 'Do you two good to read a few nice cheerful books,' she said. 'You want to try that Ethel M. Dell. Romantic? It's really lovely. Takes you right outa this place for days at a time. You ask for Ethel M. Dell.'

They had no reason to trust Miss Keenan's judgement of anything. She was one of the least competent and most ponderous of their instructors, often at a loss for the correct word and easily ridiculed by the sharper members of her training class. Once they had been issued with library tickets, Margaret and Rose headed straight for the shelves of titles on practical subjects. Their plans were simple enough. In a couple of weeks they would have to choose special skills which they would learn in addition to the more mundane domestic crafts. Both wanted to know what they could expect of the future and which jobs would take them where they wanted to go.

It was easy enough for Margaret. She had always loved young children and still missed her brothers very badly. Her idea of a perfect job was to be permitted to look after other people's babies. She started lapping up volumes on the latest theories of child care, on feeding, exercise, and even home sewing for babies. The more she learned, the happier she became about the prospect of working as a nursery-maid and eventually a nanny.

It was harder for Rose. She wanted no responsibility for other human beings, particularly infants. Briefly she considered cooking, only to dismiss it after a thorough study of Isabella Beeton's great work on cooker and household management. It might have been written for Victorian households, but some things had not changed and among them was the appallingly arduous route to supremacy in the kitchen. Starting off as a scullery-maid and spending years lighting coal-fired cooking ranges or learning to prepare vegetables all came too close to Rose's idea of drudgery.

She was becoming a little desperate when she began to consider the role of a parlour-maid. True, she would have her fair share of water-carrying and fire-lighting when she started, but if she worked hard — and she was used to that, now — she might progress quickly to looking after beautiful things: porcelain, cut glass, fine furniture, silver. She had never heard of objects harming you the way people could. If she did that well, she even had a good chance of ending up as housekeeper — a better job than cook any day, particularly if you were in one of those wonderful old country mansions.

There was no one to tell Rose that many of the books she read had been published before the Great War, and therefore talked of vast household staffs and opulent possessions which were far more thinly distributed in these days of austerity. Not that it would have mattered to her over-much. The fact remained that she would be dealing with objects rather than human beings, and in her present frame of mind that suited her admirably.

Throughout the last month of the training course, the staff organised a series of open days, in collaboration with the Labour Exchanges of West London. They served the dual purpose of giving the girls something to do after even the slowest trainees had learned all the centre had to teach them, and of introducing prospective employers to what they hoped would be their future domestic staff.

The days followed a uniform pattern. A list of housekeepers and women who engaged their own servants was drawn up, on the personal recommendation of the instructresses and from the lists of vacancies notified to the local Labour Exchanges. They were all invited to attend and inspect the work of the outgoing trainees, which extended from polishing and scrubbing, through laundry and bed-making to simple cookery. Those trainees who wished to take care of children also produced pieces of handiwork − crochet, darning or embroidery − which might be useful occupations in a nursery-maid's spare time.

Rose's contributions included a couple of special polish recipes she had copied from Mrs Beeton and adapted with modern additives; a piece of fine repair work on a linen tray cloth which had taken her hours of secret application before she managed a satisfactory job; and a couple of batches of plain cakes and buns to demonstrate her versatility just in case no one snapped her up as a parlour-maid. Margaret had knitted a layette, produced snowily laundered babies' napkins, and prepared what her child-care book described as a 'well-balanced nursery tea'. This was their first open day and they were very nervous. The centre staff had impressed upon all the girls that only the very best trainees were chosen on the first day, but that conversely, by the time the last one was held, it was possible that only one or two of the worst students would remain unemployed.

'We try to persuade our ladies to leave the girls until the end of the course,' Mabel Wilson explained, 'but when they need someone to start at once, we can hardly insist. Sometimes that's most unfortunate for the girls who are chosen last, because if we're down to just one or two, obviously we cancel the final open days.' She tried to sound sympathetic, but there was an undertone of satisfaction in her voice as she contemplated the lot of such unfortunates. 'After that it's get a job through the Labour Exchange and find yourself somewhere to live, because we can't keep people on once the course is finished, you know.'

Rose tried to tell herself that was what caused her panic as the moment approached when Mabel Wilson would open the door to the first visitors, but she knew she was deceiving herself. It had begun the previous night as she was drifting off to sleep, mentally exhausted by her repeated efforts to improve the mending job she had done on the tray cloth. The dream swirled out of nowhere. She was running, terrified, down a cobbled lane behind a line of tall, expensive town houses. Someone was pursuing her and although he remained invisible, she knew it was Alf Dobson. She flung herself down a flight of steps to the basement area outside the back door of one of the houses, and someone opened up for her as though they knew intuitively she had arrived. She blundered inside, sobbing for breath and with mixed terror and relief, as she began to explain she had been pursued. Then she looked up at the man who had opened the door for her, and who was now closing and bolting it. He was Alf Dobson.

Rose woke up with a start, convinced she had been crying out, but clearly she had remained silent throughout the nightmare, because the other three girls in the room were fast asleep. Sweating and trembling, she forced herself to examine the dream. It was still sufficiently clear for her to remember that she was a servant in the house to which she had been running. Presumably her sleeping mind had thrown together all sorts of jumbled impressions she had of girls hurrying back on the evening of their day off, and newspaper scare stories about mysterious men who attacked them in dark places. The whole thing was so patently absurd when she looked at it closely, that she wondered why on earth it had scared her so badly.

Then even that became clear and she uttered a grim chuckle. 'Alf Dobson, of course, you dunce!' she said aloud. She was much happier now. Drawing up the blankets tightly around her neck and shoulders, she burrowed down in the narrow bed and composed herself for sleep once more. It never occurred to her to question why her unconscious mind had planted the most monstrous figure from her past both outside and inside the fantasy version of whatever would turn out to be her new home. Indeed, at fourteen she was unaware she even possessed an unconscious mind.

There were no more dreams, but she passed a restless night and the next morning felt irritable and apprehensive. As they finished dressing in the unflattering maids' uniforms supplied by the centre, Margaret looked at her friend's hands and said: 'Why, Rose, what's the matter? You're trembling all over.'

Rose tried to smile and failed dismally. 'I know. Daft, innit? It's all I can do to stop my teeth chattering. I don't think I've ever been this nervous in me life.'

'But why? You know they're pleased with you. You'll be one of the first taken on, just mark my words.'

Rose blushed violently. 'I think maybe that's what I'm scared of.'

'You're making no sense at all. Surely you can't want to stay here any longer than you have to? If you do, you're the only one as does.'

'That's what I thought, too. Couldn't wait for someone to offer me a job in a house full of nice furniture and things. But ever since I got up this morning, I been thinking, this is really the only place I know any longer. I never had a proper home once Mother had died, so even if this is pretty horrible, it's better than I had before.'

Margaret was perplexed. 'All right, I understand that, I think. But what's wrong with going to something better still — a lot better, an' all, from what I hear?'

'It-it's not that, Mags. I wish I could understand myself.

Maybe I'd feel better then. But I'm dead scared of seeing all new people and having to start all over. What if they don't like me?'

That made Margaret hoot with laughter. 'You've managed with this lotta cats down here not liking you, and it hasn't seemed to give you a minute's trouble. Why should it start now?'

Even to Margaret, Rose found it impossible to articulate the real heart of the threat: there were bound to be men at whatever place she went to work. And for Rose, men amounted to deadly danger.

Unaware of any of this, Margaret went on smiling amiably at her friend. She patted Rose's arm and said: 'Come on, silly, or you won't need to worry where you might end up – they'll all have come and gone before they see us!'

Kate Higgins and Edna Warren were sitting together on the upper deck of a Number 14 bus as it made its way westward along Fulham Road. 'I don't know, Edna, really I don't. I've heard very mixed reports of these places. What guarantee do we have that we won't be sold a pair a pigs in a poke?'

'No more than we've got when we take on these young fools who arrive with character references from their vicar and a testimonial from the squire's cook. If the kid is so bright, why hasn't the squire taken her on himself? That's what I always wonder!'

'Suppose you've got a point there. And according to this circular they sent us from the Labour Exchange, we get a chance of looking at work the girls have done on their own. At least that should give us some idea of what they're capable of.'

'There you are, then. Look at the disaster we had last autumn around the time those two Welsh girls came. You must remember, the one went to Fenton.'

Mrs Higgins laughed mirthlessly. 'How could I ever forget? The other was Ellis.'

'God almighty, for a minute I'd forgotten that! Right little handful she is, too. But that isn't what I meant. Remember those two others?'

Mrs Higgins nodded and sighed. 'All right, Nanny, I admit it. We haven't done better anywhere else lately. We may as well try this.' The previous autumn, a day or two after Eleri Jones and Jane Ellis joined the Clifton establishment, two other girls, Londoners, had been about to start work at the London mansion. One had been destined for the nursery, the other for second housemaid's duties. Both were well recommended and neither had turned up. When housekeeper and nanny, furious at such slovenly timekeeping, contacted the girls' mothers, they drew a blank.

One was full of apologies but said her girl was adamant she would never go into service for anybody. She'd said it from the beginning, but they had hoped to make her come round. Now the parents had come round instead. They were letting her stay at school until a chance of a shop or factory job came up. The second girl had been taking no chances. While her mother finalised the nursery-maid's job in the Clifton household, she had been out ranging Oxford Street on her own account, and had found work. The senior servants had fulminated about the young no longer knowing when they were well off, but both vacancies had remained unfilled for the succeeding five months, and matters were now approaching crisis level, with a senior parlour-maid threatening to leave and Nanny Warren herself making ominous noises about early retirement.

Neither woman had viewed the Parsons Green Government Training Centre for Domestics as a likely source of good recruits, but they were given little say in the matter. Lady Clifton had paid a brief pre-season visit to the London house and had chanced to see the circular which advertised the series of open days. Exasperated at the lack of progress in filling domestic vacancies, she had called Mrs Higgins in and told her she and Nanny Warren were to attend the first open day. 'If you are there with the first group of visitors, you should have the pick of the crop,' she said. 'Why, it could be quite fun — like getting the best bargains at the January sales!'

'And what would she know about the January sales?' grumbled Nanny Warren when Mrs Higgins brought her the news. 'She always shops in Paris at the height of the season.'

After a short tour of the training centre, they were more impressed than they had expected to be. 'At least we shan't need to train them from scratch,' said Miss Warren. 'As long as we get bright types, we could pick up a pair with as good as a year's experience.'

Mabel Wilson was deeply deferential to the two senior servants. Their household was infinitely superior to those of the other visitors. In fact the open day leaflet had only been sent to the Cliftons and a few families like them as a formality. It was still generally assumed that they, at least, would have little difficulty in recruiting staff.

Determined to provide them with servants of sufficiently high quality to bring them back for more, Miss Wilson cast about for her best trainees. Of course — it had to be Rush and Armstrong. They were in a different class from most of the other girls here, just as these two women were above the normal run of potential employer. 'I think I have just the girls for you,' said Miss Wilson. 'If you'd care to come with me, you can see them at work.'

They found Rose cleaning silver forks in the draughty pantry behind the kitchen. She stood up politely and murmured a few words of acknowledgement when the housekeeper and nanny spoke to her, but her shyness was obvious to both of them. Secretly irritated at Rose's lacklustre response, Mabel Wilson made much of her competence and then hustled the women off to inspect Margaret's nursery tea.

This time there was no doubt in either woman's mind. When they emerged from the mocked-up nursery after a ten-minute talk with the girl and minute inspection of her work, Miss Warren said: 'I'm most impressed with that one — to tell the truth I never thought I'd find a girl of that calibre in this sort of place. But she'll do excellently for my nursery.

When Mrs Higgins is suited, we'll talk to Armstrong again in your office and arrange everything, shall we?'

Miss Wilson beamed her satisfaction. 'And — er — what about Rush, Mrs Higgins? If you're unhappy about her, I'm sure we can suit you with somebody else. Perhaps if you could tell me what you don't like about her? You saw her handiwork. It's quite good for an inexperienced girl . . . and that furniture stain remover she dreamed up is practically good enough to patent! We even use it around the centre.'

Mrs Higgins waved a hand dismissively. 'Not that,' she said. 'None of that bothers me. She's a neat, well turned-out young person and I can see she's a good worker. I've no doubts I could make an excellent parlour-maid of her as far as looking after the house is concerned. It's the — well, the social side that worries me. She'll have to do an awful lot of opening the front door to callers and announcing them, and she'll have to wait on table for some meals to help out the butler. Then there's the day to day business with the family . . . in our sort of establishment, the senior maids are in and out of the main rooms fetching and carrying all day long.'

'Surely you're not worried about the way she talks?' Mabel Wilson was dismayed. Rose was no worse than any other girl at the centre in that respect, and better than many.

Again the dismissive gesture. 'No, I'm not stupid. All girls pick up proper talk when it's going on around them all the time. It's the fact that she hardly seems to talk at *all* that worries me. She's like a frightened little mouse.'

'Oh, I know she's rather, well, reserved, but that's because she hasn't met any strangers for months while she's been here. Really, I'm sure you'll find that goes quite quickly.'

'Hmm, wish I thought you were right. I get the impression there's something in that girl makes her want to run away every time someone comes close to her.'

Edna Warren intervened, impatient that recruitment of one junior servant was turning into such a drawn-out process. 'Oh, come on, Kate! You're looking for a second housemaid, not a head parlour-maid! That child will be working in bedrooms and doing the stairs and fireplaces for at least a year, and nothing much more demanding for at least a year or two after that. She'll have forgotten what shyness is by then, I can tell you — in fact, you'll probably be wishing she'd stayed the way she is now by the time she starts getting followers round the kitchen door!'

Mrs Higgins sighed. 'Suppose you're right, really. She's certainly a pretty one, I'll give her that. Maybe the shyness isn't so bad after all, when I think a bit about it.' She was not contemplating possible future back-door suitors for Rose, but momentarily envisaging the possible masculine interest the girl might create within the house itself. 'I think I'd better look at a couple of your other girls before I decide, Miss Wilson.'

But the others proved a sorry procession. Most of the brighter trainees had chosen to specialise in nursery training or wanted to learn to cook, and those who aspired to be housemaids came from the duller end of an already unpromising group. After talking to three of them, and studying their sloppy responses and indifferent work, Mrs Higgins decided to take a chance. 'All right,' she told Mabel Wilson, 'Rush it must be. I'll just have to hope her temperament perks up a bit after she leaves here.'

Chapter Six
London, 1929

Once the bedroom door was safely closed, Jane Ellis skipped across to the wardrobe and opened it. First the coat, then the hat . . .

One of the few housemaid's jobs to which Jane had no objection was cleaning guests' bedrooms. Protected from their intrusion by their involvement in the post-breakfast activities which seemed to keep them down in the dining room until at least eleven o'clock, she could temporarily plunder their jewel cases and closets to make herself look like the rich girl she so desperately wanted to be. She'd had her eye on Ishbel Gilpin's room ever since she saw the woman swagger into the hall at Belgrave Square three days ago, sporting an ankle-length coat with a vast fox collar and a magnificent silk toque with an aigret bobbing saucily from the band. Now, for a few moments at least, the clothes were hers, and Jane intended to enjoy them to the full.

Before putting on the coat and hat, she repositioned the cheval glass and opened the wardrobe door wider, so that its interior mirror produced a double reflection with the other and enabled her to view herself back and front. The coat demanded to be thrown on – it was that sort of garment. Jane wrapped the oversized collar about herself and then gave a melodramatic shrug to make the fur ripple back over her shoulders. Who could ever want to wear anything else, if they had a coat like this? She remembered an oversight – that divine little hat, of course! She picked up the toque, discarded her white lace-trimmed cap and put it on. Then she stood back and uttered a sigh of sheer ecstasy at the overall effect.

'You look better in it than the Honourable Ishbel any day, kidda,' she told her mirror image. Then she began to stride around the room, making large gestures and silently mouthing the sort of bantering chatter she had heard on the lips of guests and family in the Clifton drawing room.

Somewhere along the way, she began to feel underdressed. What did she need to complete the picture? Gloves? No, that unlined, hand-sewn kid was so tight she'd never get them off and away if she heard someone approaching. Jewellery – that was it. Madam Gilpin had some very flashy rings. Jane flipped open the jewel case which nestled in the centre drawer of the dressing table. A huge squarecut amethyst twinkled wickedly at her out of the ring tray and she picked it up, somewhat gingerly because she was so impressed by its great size. It fitted her engagement finger, and as she pranced back and forth between the two mirrors, Jane languidly waved the bejewelled hand and pretended to herself that she had just become engaged to the Duke of Westminster.

She was startled almost into wetting herself by a sound from the doorway, a slow, ironical clapping of hands. 'And what d'you do as an encore, gradually take it all off?' drawled an equally mocking male voice.

Jane's first horrified reaction had been stimulated by the certainty that she had been caught by Ishbel Gilpin. She was still jumpy, but less frightened, to have been discovered by a man. 'Jesus Jones! You nearly gave me a heart attack!' she said.

The man laughed again, looking faintly surprised. 'Well, I'll give you one thing – you're a cool character. Do you always answer back when one of Lord Clifton's guests catches you dressing up in another guest's finery?'

Jane's smile was confident now. 'Only when it's a gentleman who catches me because he's creeping into a lady's room . . . a lady who isn't related to him in any way, unless I'm mistaken!'

There was respect in his expression now, along with

considerable wariness. 'Come — for all you know, I was collecting Ishbel for some innocent outing.'

Jane shook her head. 'That won't do. The guests always meet each other in the hall or drawing room. And why would you be bringing an envelope with you if you were on your way out with her? The guests always leave outgoing mail on the hall table for posting.'

Instinctively he glanced down at his own left hand. Jane could clearly see the words: 'To *la belle dame sans merci*' scrawled boldly across the snowy paper. She had no idea what it meant, but was willing to bet it was something suggestive.

The man shrugged. 'Touché!' He moved into the room, approaching her like a hunter stalking prey. 'I'll keep your secret if you'll keep mine. Now, if I were you, I'd take off those clothes and finish your work. I think Mrs Gilpin will be back up here in a few minutes.'

For the first time, Jane was really worried as she glanced at the carriage clock on the mantel shelf. It was almost eleven! Mrs Higgins would take her apart for wasting so much time. Fortunately for her prospects of continued employment, she always got through the main part of her work before indulging in a little dressing up. Now she had only to put the cheval glass back in position and replace the coat and hat in the wardrobe.

The intruding house guest was Harry Charteris, a friend of Lord Clifton's younger brother who was sufficiently well known and liked by the rest of the family to be invited to the Belgrave Square house occasionally when he came to London. He had a country house in Northamptonshire but did not bother to maintain his own London apartment because he spent relatively little time in the capital nowadays. Jane knew nothing about him except that he seemed to be a sort of court jester to his social group. Whenever she helped wait at table for luncheon or dinner parties which he attended, he kept everyone laughing. He was good looking, well dressed and unmarried, and had frequently figured as the central character in Jane's secret fantasies about escaping from her life of servitude. Now, as she bustled about putting the finishing touches to Ishbel Gilpin's room, she began speculating afresh. Perhaps he really *would* turn out to be her means of escape.

She fluffed up the eiderdown and gave the pillows a pat, then smiled at him with every ounce of appeal she could muster. 'Righto,' she said, 'I'll forget it with all the other little secrets I get told. But if I was you, I'd watch that Mrs Gilpin. She's a real man-eater.' And she flounced past him out on to the landing. As she passed the stairhead, Ishbel Gilpin was hurrying up the last flight. Jane breathed a silent sigh of relief. Too close for comfort, that one! She went round to the back of the guest-room landing and carried her equipment down the servants' staircase to the basement, where a scolding from Mrs Higgins awaited her.

With great care, Rose placed the large silver coffee pot and paper-thin cups on a small table in the morning room. That table was one of her favourite objects and she had no wish to see it damaged by a hot container or spilled liquid.

'Thank you, Rose. I'll ring when we're ready to go out.' Lady Clifton summoned up her most gracious smile for her favourite London servant. What on earth would they do without Rose?

In the basement, Mrs Higgins was thinking much the same thing. 'Where the devil have you been until this time?' she snapped at Jane. 'I know you do a good job on those bedrooms, but not so special you need twice as long as the other maids! If I thought you were going through the guests' things . . .' Her voice tailed off threateningly. Rose, coming through the door in time to catch the last words of the reproof, stifled a giggle. Nobody disliked Jane, because she was so bouncy and cheerful. And it was a treat to watch her flawless performance as outraged innocent accused of skulduggery. She launched into it now.

'Honestly, Mrs Higgins, if you could have seen those rooms! The men's were all right, but the ladies'! I'm sure I don't know where they were brought up. Stockings and underwear and spilled face powder all over the place. It was like cleaning up the chorus dressing room at the Coliseum!'

'And when were you ever in a chorus dressing room, I'd like to know?' retorted Mrs Higgins. Then, in spite of herself, she laughed. 'Oh, get away with you and catch up on your work. Rose has already had to take your turn at serving the coffee. But just remember, if I ever get so much as a whisper of any outa the way goings on, I'll have you on toast, my girl!'

'Don't worry, Mrs H – you'll never catch me!' Then, with an impish grin, she was gone, into the stillroom on some unrevealed errand of her own.

'She'll be the death a me, she really will,' Mrs Higgins told Rose. 'But somehow, it's impossible to stay angry with her. Have you noticed that, Rose?'

She nodded, still smiling. 'The way I look at it, anyone who can keep their sense of humour in this job deserves to get away with a lot.'

The housekeeper assumed a troubled expression. 'Still not settled after all these years and good promotion, then? It's such a shame, Rosie girl. You're that good at it. What is it you don't like so much?'

The parlour-maid sighed. 'Ah, nothing all that special – same as everyone else. Not being treated like a real person with feelings. Having to play deaf. Having to play stupid. Letting them upstairs have the last word about when I should come and go – you know, the things I bet *you* hate about it.'

Mrs Higgins tried to look severe. 'There's a lot worse things than that, my girl. Have you looked out on them streets lately? Plenty of poor devils roaming about with no seats to their trousers and no roof over their heads come night time. At least we're warm and comfortable and we know where the next meal is coming from.'

'Yeah, and we pay a bloody high price for it, too!'

'Rose Rush, I never heard you swear before!' Mrs Higgins's eyes were round with shock. Her sudden deflation cracked Rose's shell of anger and she giggled.

'Oh, Mrs Higgins, what's one little bloody among friends?

I don't know where you grew up, but down Shoreditch they thought that was the height of politeness.'

The housekeeper made another attempt to look grim. 'Now, Rose, this is no way to be carrying on. I'm in charge of you, remember. The way you're answering back today, I'm beginning to wonder if that Jane hasn't got at you.'

'Not deliberately,' said Rose, adding in an undertone, 'but, my God, I don't arf like her style!'

'Go along now, you must have plenty to do and Monsieur Auguste will go potty if that luncheon party is served late. But before you go, let me ask you something. Would it help if you were doing different work?'

Alarm flared in Rose's eyes. 'What sorta work? Better the devil you know than the one you don't. I can't think of another job in this house that's better for me than what I do already, 'cept yours of course, and you look fit enough for another twenty years if you don't mind me saying so.'

'What about lady's maid?'

'No – I couldn't! You know I'm no use with people.'

Mrs Higgins uttered a snort of contempt. 'Really, Rose, where's your backbone? This is a temporary job with Lady Clifton herself. You've known her nearly as long as you have me, and as a lady's maid you won't even have anything to do with the male servants.'

Rose glanced at her sharply. So Higgins had noticed that when she said 'people', she really meant men. Better take care, or they'd all begin to think she was funny in the head. 'Well, what's so special about being a lady's maid, then?' she asked truculently. 'Doesn't strike me as any great shakes.'

'That's where you're wrong. Now go upstairs and set the luncheon table and I'll have a longer talk with you after servants' dinner, all right? We should have twenty minutes to ourselves then.'

In the big rectangular dining room, Rose laid out the elaborate pattern of flatware and glasses required for a formal luncheon party and wondered what on earth she would say if they offered her a job as lady's maid. She knew she was a good servant: the conviction she had formed back at the training centre five years before had remained rock solid. If you were competent and courteous, you remained under the protection of whoever was employing you. Step out of line and you lost your security. 'And where would our Rosie be then, poor thing?' she murmured to herself.

She had never grown to like the work. True, the fine china and beautiful silver were delightful to handle and it was a pleasure to see a lovely old table or chest glow after it had been competently polished. But pride in such objects quickly palled when they belonged to someone else. And when that someone else could order you to do practically anything and expect unquestioning obedience, matters became even worse. There were, too, less pleasant aspects of looking after a house than cleaning attractive objects. Clearing grates and lighting fires for a start. Some winter mornings, she was tempted to believe she would never finish the task, but that she would complete the last ornate fire surround on the ground floor barely in time to re-start at the top of the house. The Cliftons scorned the new-fangled central heating which was being installed in many other houses around the square. The earl was fond of saying how much he enjoyed a good blaze. He would, wouldn't he, thought Rose savagely, when he doesn't have to spend hours on his hands and knees on a dust sheet, brushing, black-leading, lighting and then re-dusting the room after the inevitable fine ash dust had settled on the furniture and curtains. Sometimes, completing this task before dawn on a freezing winter morning, Rose wondered if there really had been no alternative to this slavish job. It made her ineffably sad to accept the obvious answer.

So why was she so resistant to being a lady's maid? People, of course. But as she grew older, Rose had come to realise that she regarded men rather than people in general as a threat to her safety. She knew why, and after suppressing the dreadful memories for months on end, had even built up the courage to disinter them and inspect what the rape by Alf Dobson had done to her. She needed no fancy modern explanations about psychology. It was clear that half the human race was strong enough and sufficiently aggressive physically to subject the other half to its appetites.

That was enough for Rose. She was determined never to be in such a position again. But how safe had her work as housemaid and then head parlour-maid really made her? She was aware of her own appeal for men. At nineteen she was tall, willowy and sufficiently graceful to get away with wearing a sack had she been forced to. In fact Lady Clifton chose reasonably flattering uniforms for her maids and on Rose they looked as if they were being modelled for a clothing catalogue, such was her outward poise and elegance. In 'real' clothes she looked a picture, as Jane and Mrs Higgins never tired of telling her. She liked her hair long, and in these days of the schoolboy-length shingle cut it was unusual to see a luxuriant mass of hair like hers. It was dark brown, almost black, and at the front formed a natural widow's peak which gave her face a heart-shaped look. She invariably wore it drawn back into a large soft chignon at the nape of the neck. Her complexion was silky-smooth and creamy, with a becoming flush beneath the cheekbones – 'Rose by name and Rose by looks,' Mrs Higgins said.

Rose was proud of her looks, but nervous too. She realised it would have been better for her own safety had she been afflicted with buck teeth and a squint. She smiled grimly at that. If she had been, Alf Dobson would never have fancied her and she wouldn't be in this state today. Still, it didn't alter the big advantage Mrs Higgins had pointed out to this lady's maid business. She would have virtually nothing to do with men and when she did it was likely to be something like taking a message to His Lordship from Her Ladyship. Hardly a scene of potential molestation. She began to consider the change more seriously as she worked.

Later that morning, after servants' dinner, Mrs Higgins was most persuasive. 'For a start, it'll not be permanent if you're not suited to it,' she said. 'Miss Rodwell handed in her notice yesterday to Lady Clifton. Her mother is dying, there's nobody else to look after her and Rodwell's too fond of the old girl to have her put away anywhere. Seems she's not the only one. Her Ladyship is too fond of Rodwell to put *her* away, if you get my meaning. She's offered to take on a temporary maid for up to a year, and if Rodwell's troubles are sorted out by then, she gets her job back. Whoever fills in will have trained properly as a lady's maid by then, and if there's nothing else going inside the family, there'd certainly be no trouble in getting a first-rate reference for a job somewhere else.'

Rose was still dubious. 'I've never really taken much notice of what ladies' maids actually do,' she said. 'I've got this silly idea of Rodwell helping Lady Clifton in and out of her stockings, of all things.'

'Don't laugh, my girl! When they're a new pair of the special fine silk ones for a big event, that's exactly what she does, but there's lots more to it than that.'

'Like what?'

'Well, for a start, you've got to be a good hairdresser. Now one look at your hair tells me you're good with it already. On top of that, you'll find Lady Clifton will send you along to the salon in Harrods for proper professional training. Then you look after all her beautiful clothes . . . you get to travel almost everywhere with her — I believe Rodwell had seen every foreign country Lady Clifton herself has visited this past ten years. You'll be better paid, and the perks are wonderful, you can see that for yourself — your pick of Her Ladyship's model dresses and suits, just a season after she gets them new. Rodwell always told me on the quiet she dressed in one half of what she chose and paid for her entertainment from what she got for selling the other half.'

'Is it really that good a perk?'

'In this house, yes. Lady Clifton may have her faults, but stinginess was never one a them. There's plenty of ladies give their maids just one or two outfits and then have the others sold to pay towards their next wardrobe, but not Lady Clifton. Rodwell must get between a dozen and fifteen outfits every year. How many a them d'you think she has time to wear herself?'

'Mmm, well, it sounds as if I'd make a lot more money than I do now, at any rate.'

'Yeah, and give you six months and you'll sound like a lady yourself. Us lot downstairs don't often manage that, but nannies and ladies' maids do because their jobs depend on it more than ours, and because they spend so much more time with the toffs. Mark my words, learn to talk proper and you'll add ten pounds a year to your salary.

'And you know you'll do better below stairs than you ever did as a parlour-maid, for service, and food and all the little things. You'll eat with us upper servants in the Room instead of out in the servants' hall. You'll get the same food as the family eats, and you'll get properly waited on at table, instead of having to fend for yourself. You'll even get wine with your supper a few nights a week!'

'Fancy that! I'll be taking over Fenton Parva next!'

Mrs Higgins scowled at her. 'Come on, Rose, stop being stubborn. You know you're beginning to like what you hear. What d'you say?'

Rose shrugged. 'Not much point me saying anything, yet, is there? Her Ladyship may not even think of offering me the job.'

'Oh, you daft little devil! Surely you don't think I'd be wasting my time chattering on a busy day like this if it wasn't on the cards? I may as well tell you now. She's had her eye on you all this week and she asked me to "sound you out", as she put it. Now I can hardly go back and tell her you chucked the job back in her face can I?'

Rose hardly heard the last words, so intense was her glow of inner satisfaction. So at least someone noticed she was doing her work well . . . she warmed to Lady Clifton. 'All right, Mrs H — tell Her Ladyship I shall be honoured to accept.' Inwardly she winced at the servility of her own tone, but Mrs Higgins found her response wholly suitable and positively twinkled at her as she got up to leave.

'That's my sensible girl,' she said. 'I'll see Lady Clifton

this afternoon and I'm sure she'll want to fix up all the details with you herself in the morning after she's done her letters. All right?'

'More than all right. Thank you for taking so much trouble.'

Mrs Higgins hesitated momentarily at the door, then turned and came back to the table. 'Rose,' she said, 'I don't want to embarrass you, but I've got to tell you this. When we came and saw you and Armstrong down in Parsons Green five years back, I really didn't want to take you on. Tell the truth, I thought you were a bit mental. You were so funny and — well, all wrapped up tight inside yourself, afraid to come out and face the world. But I listened to Nanny and did it, and it was the best thing that could have happened. It made you into a different girl in under a year, and I had one of the best maids I've ever been blessed with.'

A deep blush suffused Rose's face but Mrs Higgins merely squeezed her hand and went on: 'I think you've got on marvellously, really I do. It's just — that is, I felt I ought to tell you — I realise there was something very wrong then, and I don't think it's healed up to this day. If you ever need to talk to someone, you can come to me. I'll be only too happy to do what I can.'

Rose turned her head aside so that the housekeeper would not see the tears which filled her eyes, and managed to choke out: 'Th-thanks . . . I won't forget that I promise. But I can't do it yet, Mrs Higgins . . . not with anybody.'

The older woman broke their physical contact with a brisk but comforting pat and said: 'No, I realise some things go too deep. But don't just bottle it up forever for the want of someone to tell. I'm a good listener and I know how to keep a secret. All right?'

'All right.' Rose managed to smile through the tears. 'Now I better get back to my own work, hadn't I? Monsieur Auguste will be ready to serve upstairs luncheon by now.'

Chapter Seven

Venetia Clifton was studying Rose closely as she questioned the parlour-maid next day in her small private sitting room. Yes, it would certainly be possible to make something of her . . . four weeks under Rodwell's eagle eye should set her firmly on the road to satisfying Lady Clifton's smallest whim. The countess had never known what it was like to fend for herself and had no intention of learning about it now simply because her personal maid was about to disappear for an indefinite period. Lady Clifton had never washed her own hair, manicured her own nails or laundered a single item of her own clothing.

During twenty-one years of marriage, she had visited the kitchens of the Belgrave Square house twice, and those at Fenton Parva three times. Many years ago she had also taken a short, bored look at the servants' bedrooms in each establishment, but their bleakness had depressed her and she left all further inspections to her town and country housekeepers. Lady Clifton enjoyed good food and insisted on the highest standards in both her homes, but all she ever did to ensure those standards was to interview most of her own prospective staff before they were offered a job. Even this was something of an irrelevance, as the girls and men she saw had always been thoroughly vetted in advance by the senior servant under whom they would work. Whatever she thought she did, Lady Clifton's participation in domestic affairs amounted to nothing more than rubber-stamping the choices of butler, housekeeper and chef.

She was more attentive when an appointment affected her as directly as this one. The young woman who stood in front of her would spend more time with her than most of her closest friends. She would be responsible for the style of

Lady Clifton's hair and the perfection of her wardrobe. The countess always took an interest when her own comfort and convenience were involved.

She knew the importance of a good relationship with one's personal servants, and consequently treated Rose with great courtesy throughout the interview. In fact, although she was spoiled and self-centred, she treated all the servants well and most of them were conscious that domestics in some other houses around the square were regarded as barbarian halfwits by their aristocratic employers.

'I believe Mrs Higgins has given you a general idea of what your job would entail if you became my personal maid,' said the countess. 'You won't be expected to know how to do any of it at first, so don't let that worry you. Rodwell will give you a thorough grounding before she goes at the end of the month.' She smiled, as though offering a treat to a favourite child. 'And of course, I shall pay for you to take hairdressing lessons at the salon in Harrods. Now won't that be exciting?'

Be polite, smile, agree, you fool! Rose told herself as she fought to control an unaccustomed surge of rebellious anger. If she's a big enough idiot to think you get satisfaction from learning something for *her* benefit, that's her privilege. Still, said the unruly inner self, does she *have* to make it sound as if it's being done just for you?

Lady Clifton was bubbling happily on about the other benefits of the job. 'A room of your own, of course, no more sharing . . . and a maid to clean it for you. There! I don't suppose you ever expected to be in that position.' I shall have to refuse it, Rose was thinking. This woman will drive me mad in five minutes. Why haven't I ever noticed before what a patronising bitch she is?

'Then there are the clothes. You're a little taller than me, but otherwise we're close to the same size. I'm sure you'll love the things I shall be passing on to you.' In all her years as a co-opted member of the aristocracy, Lady Clifton had failed to learn that real ladies never prattled about such acts of generosity but merely passed on the occasional gift without comment. She was far too greedy for gratitude and appreciation ever to consider such an attitude. Now she beamed up at Rose, confident that the girl was overwhelmed by her own good fortune. 'That seems to be all, unless you have any questions.

'Yes, Milady. When would you be wanting me to start, and what would I have to wear while I was working?'

'Oh, we'll need to start you immediately. Poor Mrs Higgins is quite put out at losing her best parlour-maid, but I told her, the dusting can wait a day or two. I cannot be expected to entertain the earl's guests looking like an ill-kept field!' She gave a girlish laugh at the very idea of such a possibility, then added: 'Rodwell wants to get away to be with her mother as soon as possible, and if you really settle into the work quickly, I may be able to let her go in less than a month.'

Hmm, thought Rose. So much for asking me whether I wanted this damned job. She assumed I was going to take it before she ever talked to me. But when she considered her own precarious position in her old job should she refuse the transfer, and when she thought of poor Millie Rodwell fretting about her mother and unable to leave yet, she capitulated. She would take the job, whatever her feelings about Lady Clifton.

The countess was continuing ' – not anything like a standard maid's uniform. You'll have a smart black topcoat and dress for formal purposes, and most of the time you'll be kept well supplied with clothes of mine which I pass on to you. It never does for a lady to be seen with a dowdy maid trailing behind her. One of your great advantages is that you *look* so right for the job! Rodwell will take you to get the coat and frock during your training period. In the meantime, I've had her look out a couple of my things from last season and she'll bring them to your room later. That will give you the opportunity to make any alterations you need. Now, I have a busy day ahead of me, and I'm sure you have plenty to keep you occupied. Off you go, and we'll start the new routine tomorrow.'

Tomorrow! Dear God, what does she think I am, a sewing machine? thought Rose, as she hurried back down to the basement to continue her work. For all she knows, I mightn't even be able to hold a needle straight and she's giving me couture clothes to alter! And what will Mrs H say about me moving so quick? Jane's a good worker but she's not arf scatter-brained at times. With one maid short and Jane taking my job, she'll be doing her nut in a couple of days . . .

But Lady Clifton had arranged matters so that the change would cause scarcely a ripple. 'Milady's having one of the senior maids from Fenton sent up to replace you,' Mrs Higgins told Rose when the girl asked what would happen. She grinned and when she spoke again her tone dripped malice. 'That'll put Stanley's nose out of joint! She always did think Fenton's needs took first place over ours. Well, this'll show her!'

'That makes it awfully — well — permanent, doesn't it?' quavered Rose.

'Makes what awfully permanent? Getting another parlour-maid from Wiltshire?'

'Y-yes . . . means I've no way back. You know, if I don't like being a lady's maid.'

'Oh, Gawd, we're not still harping on that old tune, are we? What d'you want a way back to skivvying for once you've learned new tricks?'

Rose shrugged. 'I just thought, well, what if I don't *like* it?'

' "Like" isn't really a word anyone uses for our sorta work, love,' said the housekeeper. 'We earn our living the best way we can, and if we got the sense we were born with, we grab every chance that comes along to better ourselves.'

'I still can't really see how I'd be bettering myself, Mrs Higgins. Lady Clifton's putting up my wages by half-a-crown a week, but I know from what the others say that ladies' maids usually only get the same wages as parlour-maids, so where am I bettering myself there?'

'I've already told you — dozens of ways. A year from

now you'll be speaking like Lady Muck and wondering why you was ever content to be a skivvy, I guarantee it.'

'And what if I told you that the travelling and the lighter work and all that don't make up for having to fawn around Her Ladyship all the time?'

'I'd tell you that you were ready for putting away, that's what! Apart from anything else, d'you realise you're never going to have to get up at six in the morning again − or at least, not unless it's to catch the boat train for some fancy place abroad?'

Rose gaped at the housekeeper. 'You mean I get to lie in till a reasonable hour?'

'Course you do. I've yet to hear of a lady's maid cleaning out firegrates at the crack of dawn. You even get brought a cuppa tea when they bring me mine.'

Rose laughed, finally resigned to her lot. 'D'you know, that's probably the one thing that woulda swayed me, and nobody thought fit to mention it until now. In five years' work the one thing I never got used to was dragging meself out of bed in the dark and cold, knowing everyone else was warm and comfy in bed. And I'll never need to do it again! That's it, then. I better go up after staff dinner and see what these frocks are like that she's sending up for me.'

'I don't think they'll do anything to put you off, girl. If I'd ever had a chance to be a lady's maid, it woulda been the clothes that made the job worthwhile for me.'

The moment she saw the two outfits Millicent Rodwell had left for her, Rose decided she would have been crazy to refuse to change jobs.

Both were in subdued shades − even the most tolerant employer would not countenance being outshone by her maid − but the fabrics were rich and the cut impeccable. The first comprised a long cardigan and calf-length skirt in bias-cut double jersey wool the colour of a fresh caramel bon-bon, with a light-weight cashmere jumper to be worn under the jacket, combining the same shade of caramel with bitter chocolate and rich cream in horizontal chevron stripes that resembled florentine embroidery. Rose let out a gasp of pleasure when she saw it, and hurriedly bolted the door before trying it on. She shared a room with Jane and if the Welsh girl had seen any of the garments she would have contrived some way of wearing them herself when off duty.

The dress which Miss Rodwell had also left was of midnight-blue wool georgette. It had a loosely fitted bodice, cinched at the waist with a narrow belt of navy kid, and a skirt, bias-cut like the cardigan suit but considerably more full, so that it flared out elegantly when the wearer walked. The sleeves were its great design feature. Shaped like graceful, full-cut trumpets, they swirled down to elbow length and echoed the subtle motion of the skirt. 'And I'll be wearing clothes like this to *work*!' Rose said in an awed voice.

For ten minutes she pranced around the little bedroom, contriving somehow to catch glimpses of herself in the two small mirrors on the chest and bedside table. Finally, sighing with satisfaction, she took off the clothes and hung them in the back of the cupboard she shared with Jane, twitching her own sombre woollen coat forward to conceal the garments from her room-mate's endless curiosity. She had just finished when someone rapped on the locked door. Rose checked yet again that the new clothes were not visible, then went to open it. Millicent Rodwell stood outside. She smiled warmly at Rose, conscious that the girl's availability might enable her to save her job and meet her family obligations.

'Lady Clifton told me to come and speak to you about tomorrow,' said Rodwell. 'You're to report to me after kitchen breakfast, and after that we'll work together each day until I leave. You may wear either of the outfits I brought down earlier, and when Her Ladyship goes out to luncheon we must go through the other items she put aside to fit you with some more. The countess doesn't like to see her personal maid in the same clothes on two consecutive days, you understand.'

Rose nodded dumbly, deeply impressed by her sudden sartorial riches, and also thinking, My Gawd, will I ever get the hang of talking like that? She tried to console herself with the memory of Jane telling her Rodwell originally came from a small Shropshire town, and was the daughter of a baker and a laundress. Her talent for her mother's old trade had apparently set her on the trail of being a lady's maid by much the same route as Rose was now reaching it. In that case, she must have sounded every bit as rough as me at the beginning, thought Rose. I shall just have to learn, that's all.

Miss Rodwell was turning to leave when she remembered an oversight. 'Oh, yes, I forgot. As Milady is away all tomorrow afternoon, she's told me to take you along to Harrods to arrange those hairdressing lessons and measure you for your uniform frock and coat. You might feel you want to spend a little of your own money on shoes while we're out.' She looked down meaningfully at Rose's workaday lace-ups with their squat heels. 'You may think something a little lighter would do justice to your new clothes.'

Over the following months, Rose saw her own image transformed, almost as though she herself had nothing to do with it. She was expected to pay for her own shoes and underwear, but she had some savings and it would have been a sin, she told herself, to wear the beautiful clothes handed down by the countess with her clumpy maid's footwear. So she allowed Rodwell to steer her into the shoe department at Harrods, where she paid a breathtaking £3 – almost three weeks' wages – for a pair of black and a pair of beige leather shoes, both with high Louis heels and fancy-cut instep straps. Still aghast at her own extravagance, she crowned the exercise by spending thirteen shillings on two pairs of silk stockings with fancy clocks up the sides, and four shillings on a pair of suede gloves.

After that they went up to the beauty salon to arrange her hairdressing and hair waving lessons, and a course of instruction in manicure. That would cost even more than her shoes, stockings and gloves, but at least Lady Clifton was paying. Rose took a deep breath and agreed with Miss Rodwell that yes, she would love a cup of tea.

But Harrods was only the beginning. For a start, Lady Clifton knew that two outfits would hardly comprise a comprehensive wardrobe for her new maid. There were at least twenty day dresses and costumes hanging in Miss Rodwell's wardrobe, not to mention a couple of informal evening gowns and the obligatory plain black topcoat with matching, white-collared alpaca dress which was the nearest the countess's personal maids ever wore to a uniform. Now Rose found herself receiving a constant stream of such clothing. At first each fresh garment seemed more impressive than the one before it, but, as she grew more discriminating, she began developing preferences. After all, the clothes had originally been chosen for a well-rounded auburn-haired woman of average height. Rose was a tall, slender brunette. It would have been miraculous if everything that came her way had suited her.

One thing all the clothing had in common was its unsurpassable quality. There were no pieces of Parisian couture — even Lady Clifton tended to hang on to her Chanels and Vionnets as long as possible — but the best offerings of British designers were there in abundance, and it was now that Rose began to develop her lifelong love of impeccable tailoring and top quality materials.

The clothes held a magic of their own. When she wore them, she felt like a better person. She felt visible as an individual for the first time ever; and to a remarkable degree she felt free of the abuse inflicted on her years before by her father and his drunken crony. The solemn faced, elegant creature who gazed back at her from the full-length mirror in Lady Clifton's dressing room was almost beautiful. She was also a lady. Horrors like the incident with Alf Dobson did not happen to ladies. Rose was finally beginning to feel safe, protected by an impenetrable armour of silk and cashmere.

Chapter Eight

It was the first time Harry Charteris had ever taken an interest in a housemaid's afternoon off, but today he could think of few more riveting subjects. Jane Ellis had been on his mind a great deal since their confrontation in Ishbel Gilpin's room. He tried to be dismissive of his feelings. Ishbel had been an absolute pain lately – bossy, headstrong, uncontrollable – all the things Harry disliked in a woman. She still looked as good as ever, but dammit, personality had to count for something. He could not see their affair lasting much longer.

Now he was looking around for something different, and that little baggage Ellis might be just the ticket. He had seen her several times since their encounter in the bedroom, and since the first occasion, when she had looked apprehensive until it became clear he would keep her secret, she had invariably given him a huge and disrespectful wink when no one else was likely to see her.

The girl's familiar manner bothered him not at all. Harry was a snob, but he was so completely confident of his personal superiority to the rest of the human race that a little misplaced chaffing was of no concern to him. It merely spiced the encounter. Just how much spice Miss Ellis contained would perhaps become apparent today. He had encountered her in the hall at Belgrave Square when he was lunching with Bruno Clifton the previous Monday, and had murmured that it was a shame she seemed to have so little free time. 'Yes, I know. That's why I look forward to Wednesday afternoons so much,' the girl had said, laying undue emphasis on the last four words.

Charteris had taken a chance and responded: 'Then how

about taking full advantage of it and coming along somewhere interesting with me?'

Her eyes sparkled. 'Really? Would you really take me somewhere?'

'Why else would I ask? What would you like to do?'

Her expression was dreamy. 'Pity it isn't summer time. I know just what I'd like then – a boat on the Serpentine. I always fancied that.'

'I'd take you, even in this chilly weather, but they'll have the boats beached for the winter now. How about riding?'

Jane giggled. 'It would be the last time you'd be seen in public with me I can tell you! Seaside donkeys are the closest I ever got to that sorta thing.'

Harry had banked on her saying something of the sort. Bent as he was on seducing the girl, even a man with his sang-froid would have found it daunting to risk being seen riding in the Row with a maidservant. He felt reasonably safe from appearing with her in gallery or museum. She was hardly the type for that any more than for riding. 'I know,' she said, suddenly captivated by a new idea, 'how about a tea dance? I'd love that, and I've never been. I'm quite a good dancer, too.'

That was more like it! No fast young society women or debs' delights who might recognise him were likely to hang around a tea dance. Two years ago, maybe, but now they were just a little old hat. 'Done!' he said. 'Very well then, until Wednesday. Where shall we meet?'

'Ah, there you are, Harry! What're you doing bumbling around out here and stopping Ellis getting on with her work, eh? Come along, man, we're waiting for you!' The earl turned back into the drawing room and Charteris shrugged helplessly as he was led away. Nevertheless, he managed to corner Jane alone just before he left that afternoon, and dropped a slip of paper into her hand as she helped him into his overcoat. It merely said: 'Lyons Corner House, Piccadilly Circus, 2.30.'

As he strode off across the square, Jane made a pretence

of dusting the drawing room and gazed after him, starry-eyed. But she was not in the grip of a great passion for Harry Charteris. She was reflecting, with wild optimism, that he might be her ticket out of domestic service.

Harry had suffered several attacks of second thoughts by the time Wednesday afternoon came round. At first it had seemed such a jolly romp — a quick flirtation with a pretty housemaid. But he had not really thought how public the whole thing would be once he arranged a meeting, and although he had no fear of running into members of his own crowd either in a Lyons Corner House or in the Piccadilly Hotel's *thé dansant*, there was the road between the two places to be negotiated, and he could hardly let little Jane go back to her tube station or bus stop afterwards unescorted. It was all too easy to imagine someone like Margery Fabian or Iris Cavendish drifting out of Fortnum's after tea and running into them.

He wondered idly whether either woman ever noticed the looks of the servants who waited on them when they were guests at the Cliftons' Belgrave Square mansion, and decided that, yes, they probably did, at least when those servants were as personable as Jane. Unfortunately for him, the girl was pretty enough to excite their malice if they saw him with her, and then they wouldn't rest until they'd talked her out of a job and Harry out of the very useful friendship of the Earl and Countess of Clifton.

At that point he lost interest in any further speculation. Jane had arrived, and was threading her way between the tea tables towards him. He laughed at his own faint-heartedness. No one seeing this girl would ever associate her with a parlour-maid. Jane looked self-possessed, elegant and extremely attractive. A couple of male heads were turning to admire the girl herself, and several women were enviously eyeing her outfit. Strange, that, he thought as he rose to greet her. She must be as poor as a church mouse, but she looks positively prosperous.

She had also, it seemed, caught the drift of his thoughts, because she twinkled mischievously at him and said:

'Surprised you, did I? Surely you weren't expecting me to turn up in a cap and apron?'

'Of course not, you goose! It's just that you look so – well, so *expensive*, if you want the truth.'

Her giggle was delicious. 'I work on it, that's why. I spend every penny I get on clothes, but the most money goes on shoes and bags and gloves – hats, too, if they're special enough. I either make the frocks for myself, or make over stuff I buy from good second-hand shops.'

He stared at her, unsure whether he was more taken aback by her sophisticated understanding of how to look like ten pounds on five shillings, or by her candour in admitting to buying hand-me-downs. 'You are an amazing girl,' he said.

'Now how would you know that? All you've done is flirt with me a bit when His Lordship's back is turned, and said a few words to me this afternoon.'

Charteris shook his head. 'It's not necessary to know you well to see that you're exceptional. I can't imagine you being a housemaid for long.'

Her expression darkened. 'Been one too long already,' she said. 'D'you realise I been at that job five years, and I'm still a long way off my twentieth birthday?'

He shrugged. 'Surely that's the way it is if your parents can't afford to keep you? You're not alone in it – all the girls in service in London must have started out at about that age.'

'That doesn't make up for it!' she flashed back. 'I've done my share a that sort of skivvying and I'm not doing it for much longer. Trouble is, I can't see a way out yet.'

This conversation is getting too serious by half, Harry told himself. Aloud, he merely said, 'Come along, let's have a cup of tea and then go over to the dance. It *was* your choice for the afternoon, remember?'

She nodded, smiling, all moroseness dispersed by the thought of the treat ahead of her. 'Yes, you're right. Ooh, this tea is like that scenty sort that Lady Clifton drinks. Doesn't it taste nice?'

He winced at the servant-girl choice of words but smiled

encouragement. He had invited her. He had no right to expect more of her than she knew how to deliver.

Once they were inside the Piccadilly Hotel and on the dance floor, he lost all reservations about having invited her out. She really was a first-class ballroom dancer. As they settled themselves at one of the small round tables which surrounded the dance floor, the orchestra struck up a tango. Jane grinned at him. 'Start as we mean to go on, shall we? I s'pose you know how.'

'Who d'you think trained Valentino?'

She was as light as thistledown, exceptionally fit and possessed an excellent sense of rhythm. As the music pulsated suggestively, he swung her across the floor, executed one of the melodramatic turns beloved of tango dancers, and strode back to where they had started. She really was almost good enough to be an exhibition dancer, he thought. During the next hour they fox-trotted, waltzed and even executed a highly showy Charleston. Between sets, they sat at their little table with its rose-shaded lamp and ate cucumber sandwiches and drank China tea. Jane wanted it to go on forever, and in spite of the vulgarity of the whole interlude, Harry found himself enjoying every minute too.

Too soon, it was all over. Charteris, collecting their coats from the hat-check girl in the lobby, found himself viewing with regret the rapidly approaching separation from Jane. Funny, less than four hours ago he'd been on the point of disappearing quietly before she arrived at the Lyons Corner House. It had only been the embarrassment which would inevitably have ensued next time he visited the Cliftons that had made him keep the rendezvous. Now here he was, wishing he could live through it all again.

Outside, the short winter afternoon had already ended and raw, frosty darkness had set in, brightened here by the splashy electric signs of Piccadilly Circus. An idea nudged him gently. 'What time d'you have to be back at Belgrave Square?' he asked.

Jane was wide-eyed, not knowing what to expect next.

'Nine o'clock,' she said, 'though Mrs Higgins would probably put up with nine-thirty at a pinch.'

'In that case, how would you like an early supper in a little place I know just around the corner? Seems a shame to end such a promising day so abruptly.'

'Oh, I'd love it! That is, as long as you're sure I can get back before half-past nine.'

'I shall make it my personal responsibility, Miss Ellis.' And to her delight he made a deep, theatrical bow before her on the pavement.

They dined in an unpretentious Italian trattoria in Soho. It was an evening of new experiences for Jane: her first restaurant meal; her first wine; her first encounter with pasta; and finally, because they had dawdled, talking, for so long over liqueurs, her first ride in a taxi, summoned and pre-paid by Charteris to ensure that she got back before 9.30.

As they left the restaurant, Harry said: 'You must be available for longer stretches of time than this? I mean, how can a chap make any headway at all?'

'Only a full day once a month, I'm afraid. They don't seem to believe we live lives of our own. If you're interested, my next one is due on Saturday.'

Saturday usually saw Harry deep in the English countryside, either hosting or participating in a house party. But this looked like more interesting sport. 'If you felt like making a day of it, I could arrange a few things,' he said. 'We could start with a good tramp in the park, then get some lunch, and after that plan a rip-roaring afternoon and evening. Could you bring something suitable for a tour of the fleshpots, as well as your day clothes?'

Jane looked down dubiously at the frock she was wearing now. 'I haven't really got anything much better than this . . . oh, there is one thing for dancing . . . yes, I'll manage, don't worry.'

Within moments she was inside a taxi and her escort was kissing her lightly on the forehead through the open window. 'Until Saturday, then,' he said and the car drew away. Jane collapsed against the leather seat back, part thrilled, part exasperated, and muttered: 'If I'm to get anywhere at all, you'll have to move faster than that, Harry boy!'

Jane was a natural survivor. Having given vent to a few silent curses, she stopped blaming Charteris for the way Saturday turned out. After all, it was she who had said she did not want to spend the rest of her life as a parlour-maid.

At first it was what every girl from her background would have wanted. He met her mid-morning at Piccadilly Circus tube station and they strolled westward towards Hyde Park, Jane exclaiming at the opulence of the great houses which looked south from Mayfair across the green expanses that approached Buckingham Palace. She had taken great care to look sufficiently refined for him, and it said much for her natural good taste that she had carried it off.

They walked along the winding paths of Kensington Gardens and she was silently grateful to be young enough for the crystal-sharp sunlight to flatter her fair skin. As they turned back towards the West End she revelled in the knowledge that her red-gold hair looked as good when the wind played with it as when it was held firmly in place by hat or cap. By the time they were back in Shaftesbury Avenue, Jane was confident she had a slave in Harry Charteris.

'Soho again, I think, for lunch,' he said, his airy tone suggesting that it was the proximity of the neighbourhood rather than its discreet nature which drew him back to Greek Street. 'French this time, I think. I always think of Italian food as an *evening* sort of cuisine, don't you?'

Oh, you smooth bugger! thought Jane. You even remember to include me when you tell me what we're going to do, as if I had any say about an alternative. What if I suggested the Savoy Grill? Momentarily her innate sense of mischief played with the idea, but Jane was no fool. She sensed that if she wanted to escape him, such an idea was her chance of getting out. He would pursue her as long as she did not prove troublesome, but even a teasing reference to moving with him into his normal haunts would drive him away instantly. She had no romantic illusions about Harry and it would be suicidally silly to start behaving like a real flirt now. She was acting a part, and she must not forget it.

'That sounds lovely, Harry, just lovely. Of course, you'll have to choose the food and wine. But it would be *ever* so nice if you showed me how to do it.' Mentally she purred as she watched him soften up in face of her flattery. She could learn a lot from Harry, and all she had to do was flatter him.

All? Who's fooling who? said her inner self. She had been contemplating the other side of their nascent relationship since her afternoon off. The Charterises of this world were unlikely to be content with a few glimpses of fluttering petticoat lace and a puff of smoke from a Balkan cigarette. They could get that from their own kind, and not run the risk of ostracism by the smart set if they were found escorting off-duty servant-girls. No, she was here partly because he had a weakness for pretty redheads, and partly because he had been told from puberty that desirable parlour-maids were his for the seducing.

There was just one snag about that. Jane had only the sketchiest idea of what she had that he wanted. No one told housemaids in the best private houses about sex. It was assumed that they were 'good girls' who never indulged, and therefore there was no need for anything beyond an occasional warning to the fast ones. The system inevitably crumbled when confronted with girls who looked and behaved like Jane. They were natural flirts, looked wonderful — particularly in black-and-white uniforms — and appeared to carry all the knowledge of Lilith, Delilah and Salome inside their neatly capped heads.

The truth was more prosaic. Jane had been grabbed by an over-keen footman a couple of years ago, who bundled her into a recess along the corridor outside the kitchen and tried to get his hands up inside her voluminous uniform. She had shrieked for the housekeeper and after that she had never seen the footman again. Her reading of lightweight romantic fiction had given her to understand that after a certain amount of gazing into limpid eyes and stroking silky hair, respectably married men and women disappeared behind bedroom doors which closed firmly at the drop of a row of printed asterisks half way down the page.

She knew perfectly well that in the real world this was far from all it entailed. For a start, she had seen plenty of dashing young men like Charteris, single and married, pursuing pretty girls, and had known without needing to be told that marriage was the last thing they had in mind. She was also aware of the demands of her own body, although she was still hazy about their exact connection with whatever it was Harry had in mind. From her childhood in a house full of brothers and sisters, she knew, too, that men and women were shaped differently, and her chapel education had taught her God never did anything without a purpose in mind. Finally, and most important of all, she knew babies were mixed up in it somewhere.

There was far too much muttering, headshaking and lip-pursing among older women when unwanted births were in the offing for her to remain totally ignorant of the connection. But the only concrete information she had ever extracted from anyone had come from Mrs Higgins: 'Just you remember, Jane, when you're getting all worked up, men only want one thing and once they've got it they leave you to face the music.' Putting the hocus-pocus aside, Jane had decided that meant men did things to you because they fancied you and if you ended up expecting a baby they abandoned you. She had sufficient memories of heavily pregnant girls in the Valleys, shunned by all and the target of universal gossip, to have guessed long ago that the preliminary smooth romanticism had everything to do with the inevitable distortion of shape and production of unwanted progeny. Somewhere along the way, she had also heard whispers that such an outcome was not inevitable, and suspected that if she used the process sensibly, she could emerge free of kitchen and servant's attic for ever. All that was necessary was to find out how to protect herself.

No use asking one of the other maids or Mrs Higgins.

Mrs Higgins would have locked her in her room at the end of each day's work, and any one of the other maids might have betrayed her confidence on a whim, resulting in much the same thing. No, it had to be an outsider who told her all about it – better still, an outsider whose interests lay directly in her getting the proper information. At first, Harry Charteris had been earmarked largely as Jane's primary source of advice and her first experiment in breaking out, but already she was beginning to wonder whether he might be the only chance she would ever get. Perhaps she should stop rehearsing and regard Harry as her ultimate quarry.

In the event, she had little choice in the matter. Somehow, a merry lunch with endless supplies of Beaujolais drifted on into a trip to inspect Charteris's best friend's chambers in Jermyn Street, which Harry had borrowed for the week-end. Jane had no more idea that the chambers belonged to Bruno Charteris than Bruno had that Jane was Harry's chosen companion that afternoon. Once the door of the delightful bachelor apartment had closed behind them, chilled champagne appeared miraculously from the refrigerator and Jane found herself being edged towards the bedroom.

After that, it all got a little blurred. She had no more than the vaguest idea what Harry planned to do with her, and he, as it turned out, was equally perplexed when he realised she was a virgin. The afternoon passed in waves of bubbles, alcohol, seduction and anticlimax. It was not until shortly after six, when Jane found herself beginning to sober up in a deep bath full of fragrant hot water, that she truly grasped what had happened to her. She began to get out of the bath, then lassitude overtook her. She was hardly likely to get an opportunity like this again for a long time. Might as well enjoy it while she could.

She was still dozing in the water when Charteris tapped the door and came in, carrying two foaming glasses. 'Thought a little of the hair of the dog might not come amiss,' he told her, smiling lop-sidedly.

'I-I think I've already had a few too many hairs of the dog . . .' she said, '. . . I feel quite light-headed.'

'Come, now, it's not every day a girl loses her virtue, is it?' The tone was too forced for her to believe that he chatted in this manner every day of the week. Jane put on a brave face. 'I suppose it had to happen some time.'

She was about to lay on a little extra flattery about how irresistible he was, then mentally shrugged. To tell the truth she didn't feel at all like flattering anyone just now. She felt like lying back in the bath, sipping her champagne and then climbing back into that downy great bed all on her own and sleeping right through the night until nine or ten the next morning. She could no longer remember how it felt to wake up as late as ten in the morning.

Jane had brooded on her private thoughts a little too long for Harry's comfort. Now he leaned towards her, all concern, and gently touched her wet shoulder. 'I say . . . you know, I'm frightfully sorry about that . . . not usually my style at all . . . never realised for a moment. Hope it hasn't, er, upset you too much.'

'Does it make so much difference that no one has done that with me before?'

'Well, yes — I should say so. A chap likes to show a little decent respect. It was just that you didn't — I mean, I'd never have guessed — well, you know.'

'I do *now*, yes.'

He flushed and glanced away from her. 'If there's anything I can do to make up for it . . .'

Again she felt too overwhelmed by it all to try the obvious gold-digger's trick and say that of course he could. 'Such as what? It isn't as if anyone will be making enquiries or anything about my condition.' That word: condition. Abruptly, it concentrated Jane's mind. That was what the whisperers had invariably said back in the Valleys — *in an interesting condition . . . well, I'd like to know who got her in that condition in the first place . . .*

She felt the colour drain from her face as she sat up with exaggerated care and put down her half-empty glass on the rim of the bath. It was several seconds before she managed to summon up words for what she wanted to ask.

Finally she blurted out: 'Harry, tell me about babies — please!'

There was a note of rising panic in her voice as she finished the sentence and now he gaped at her, awestruck. 'Y-you mean you don't know? What precisely don't you know?'

'Any of it, really. I guessed what we've been up to can make it happen, but that's about all.'

'Merciful God, where have you been, child?' Charteris was gripped by an insane desire to rush out of the flat and never return. Let Bruno cope with the pretty redhead in the bath when he gets back on Monday, his brain gibbered at him. But he was essentially a decent enough man and after a couple of false starts managed to compose himself to explain to Jane matters which she would have benefited by learning a couple of years earlier.

When he had finished, it was her turn to gape at him. Then she said in a very small voice: 'So I might — that is I c-could be, after what we were doing in there . . .'

He nodded sombrely. 'Afraid so, old thing. But I don't think it's all that common the first time, not unless you're the original earth mother type. And you look more like a born flapper to me particularly with your uniform off!'

Abruptly, Jane burst into tears. 'Don't say that — don't remind me I've got to go back to it! Oh, Harry, I do so want to get out — I hate being a parlour-maid . . . hate it!'

He stood up and started pacing about the bathroom. Jane was crying in earnest now, at least as much from fury at her failure to handle the situation better as from the effects of an overwhelming day. Charteris was in a deeply embarrassing position. Dammit, he liked the girl. Engaging little thing. She showed signs of taking to the bed business like a good 'un, too, considering the circumstances (this was a handy excuse for his own somewhat feeble performance, which until now he had been mentally blaming on the Beaujolais). But what was a chap to do? He had no desire to set up a mistress in town — could not have afforded to do so even had he wished to. Anyway — and here was the rub — if he did, he'd want something a little more sophisticated than an ex-parlour-maid. On the other hand, he hated to see her so miserable, and 'Oh, God!' he said aloud. 'The time, look at the time!'

'As I don't own a watch and I'm sitting here stark naked, I'd have a bit of a job on, wouldn't I?' said Jane grumpily, brushing away the last of her tears. 'What time *is* it?'

'After nine. What about you getting back — what if you lose your job?' Charteris was visited by a horrific vision of this erstwhile virgin tagging along behind him all over London like the albatross around the Ancient Mariner's neck. He certainly couldn't ditch her after depriving her of her maidenhead and her job in one evening.

He was disconcerted when she laughed dismissively. 'Oh, is that all it is? Stop worrying — I've made arrangements.'

'Arrangements? What arrangements? You told me the only time you get a full week-end off is a couple of times a year to visit your family.'

'I know, but there's more ways than one of skinning a cat. Polly the scullery-maid sleeps in a little room behind the kitchen. Got a very handy little window out into the basement area, that room has. And Polly's never got enough money — she loves sweets and chocolates, you know, all she ever thinks about — so if any of us young ones wants to get in late, we give her a coupla bob or a bar a chocolate and she leaves her window a bit open for us. Works a treat.'

Suspicion flared in Harry's eyes where moments ago there had been only sympathy and concern. 'So why does an innocent little virgin like you need a window open late at night? Are you sure you've been entirely honest with me?'

He felt singed by the contemptuous look she flashed him. 'You mightn't have anything else on your mind than an endless supply of crumpet, but some of us have. How d'you think I got so good at dancing? I certainly never spent my time around the halls back home. I was years too young for a start. If you must know, Mr Smart-Alec, I stay out late once a week — twice when the family's away and I don't have to work so hard — and go dancing.'

He was still unable to dismiss his suspicion. 'Then why was that tea dance such a treat?'

Her hoot of mirth was as derisive as the look she had just given him. 'You're really slow about some things, aren't you, Harry? Course I never been to a tea dance, 'specially somewhere posh like the Piccadilly Hotel. On my money the best I can afford is one a the ballrooms — Hammersmith Palais or somewhere like that. They're common as muck but, by God, the blokes who go there know how to dance!'

'And you expect me to believe you've been going there regularly for — what? — a couple of years, fraternising with those types, and still stayed pure as the driven snow? I simply don't believe you!'

'Well, you better had, because I'm telling you I've had less familiarity from the lads I meet there in two years than ever I did from types like you catching me on my way from the morning room to the library! They go there to dance, that's all, and they're respectable chaps. They'd be shocked rigid at the idea of a girl like me sitting here like this talking to a man in the bathroom with no clothes on!' Her tears were close to the surface again, but this time she was determined to suppress them. As the conversation progressed, she was liking Harry Charteris less and less and she wanted to show him no signs of vulnerability now.

He had reddened again and Jane knew he had realised he was behaving badly. Now he made a visible effort to make amends. 'I dare say you won't want to be back at Belgrave Square until well after midnight,' he said. 'Mustn't risk being caught on the window sill by Venetia. I should think she can be terrible in wrath. I don't recommend prolonged occupation of that bath. It must be cooling pretty quickly by now. Why not let me dry you and we'll go and sit by the fire in the drawing room?'

Charteris turned away momentarily and picked up a blue Turkish towelling robe, to Jane's eyes as thick as a carpet. She was more accustomed to the scrappy towels issued to servants. As the girl stood up, he swaddled her in its luxurious depths and began rubbing her vigorously through the fabric. Within moments she was purring like a contented kitten. 'There,' he said eventually, 'feeling a little more relaxed now?'

Jane nodded and beamed at him. 'Much better, thanks. If we went and sat by that fire with another glass of bubbles, I'd feel better still.'

In the couple of hours that followed, Jane discovered Harry's better side. He was charming, polite, attentive, trying to make up for all his misdemeanours in the past few hours. Patiently he took her through a labyrinth of sexual instruction, explaining how she might avoid conception if she had been lucky this first time, and then moving on to other, wittier if less essential topics. Eventually, when Jane was quite relaxed and the miseries of the early evening seemed blurred, he gathered her into his arms and said: 'I think we have time for you really to find out what it's all about between men and women. I wasn't so wonderful myself earlier, you know.'

She gave a little start and he felt absurdly protective. 'Don't worry, darling. This time it's *my* responsibility to see you're all right . . . should have been from the start. I'm not always the most considerate of men, I fear.'

Jane turned her face up for his kiss, and this time it was fun. This time he was still no Don Juan, but she was not blundering about in a fog of champagne and ignorance. As she slipped forward against him on the thick, fleecy hearthrug, she wondered why everything in this place was so *comfortable*. When I'm rich, she thought, drowsy with desire, I'll bury myself in fluffy, furry stuff and drink nothing but champagne and have a centrally heated flat . . .

She enjoyed their lovemaking, but it never occurred to her that this was the core of the obsessive passion which had lost empires and caused murder, deceit and betrayal throughout history. If someone had told her so, she would have laughed dismissively. Somehow it just didn't seem important enough.

Not that she didn't like it. Harry's hands were strong and warm and they cupped her breasts pleasingly against his mouth as he bent to kiss them. He had a way of caressing the back of her neck, just below the hairline, with his fingertips, and sending a little shudder of pleasure the length of her spine to vanish tingling into her pelvis. He held her close against him and pressed her buttocks tightly together as he thrust her body up to his own from beneath. By the time he had been playing with her for half an hour or so, she was shaky and giggling, wondering tremulously where he would touch her next.

But somehow it didn't get any better than that. He parted her thighs and slipped inside her — an act that had frightened her earlier. Now it was unhurried and predictable and held no terrors. But it held little else, either. There was a pleasant feeling of pressure and she felt her body clasping and unclasping him. Charteris's own reactions were what distracted her now. What seemed to Jane a pleasurable diversion and little more appeared to have become the centre of Harry's world. He was thrusting himself forward into her body with a regular shuddering motion which increased its tempo as she moved under him. He was breathing harshly and his skin burned as if he was suffering a fever. He also began talking in a rapid monotone, an odd mixture of excited obscenities and half-articulated comments about her beautiful body. The entire performance was rapidly drawing Jane out of her own former high excitement. Not that it repelled her — she merely found it puzzling. Her own body was still moving, almost automatically, in rhythm with his own, and apparently he found this desperately exciting.

Suddenly, without warning, Charteris let out a long, shuddering cry and his deep, thrusting movements stopped. The red-hot dry fevered feel of his flesh changed with equal abruptness and he began sweating. Jane found this rather more pleasant than the fever and wriggled happily against him. The movement provoked a groan of pleasure and he reached up to brush back a stray tendril of moist hair from her forehead. Finally, smiling as though he had achieved something miraculous, he murmured: 'There — quite different, wasn't it?'

Jane was far from stupid and she knew her behaviour from now on might well decide what she was doing next week. 'Lovely,' she sighed with what she hoped was an ecstatic smile. 'I've never done anything like that before.' Well, it's true, she told her conscience with some indignation. But that doesn't mean the same as he thinks it does! her conscience retorted.

It was after two in the morning when Charteris helped Jane to negotiate Polly's basement window. 'Fine time to be in, I must say,' the girl grumbled drowsily. 'Didn't know you meant this late when you asked me.'

'Shh – stop complaining. I've brought you something special,' whispered Jane. 'Here, try one of these and you'll forget how late it is.' She handed over a two-pound box of Harrods' French handmade chocolates, which at £2.10s. had cost the equivalent of five weeks' wages for someone like Polly. Harry had raided a cupboard where Bruno kept a hoard of confectionery designed to bribe female relatives on their way to West End matinees. Now Jane left Polly gazing dumbfounded at the treasure trove and completely oblivious of the lateness of the hour.

Her own bauble was delivered the following week on her afternoon off, when Charteris met her as before at Piccadilly Lyons Corner House. 'Come on,' he said. 'This is a business meeting, not a lovers' tryst. I've set something up that might interest you.'

Once again, Jane spent an afternoon dancing, but this time to considerably more purpose. Today Charteris had taken her to The Silver Slipper, flagship of the infamous Ma Meyrick's nightclub empire. With its under-lit glass dance floor, The Slipper was the most renowned nightspot in Regent Street, and its dance hostesses some of the prettiest and most talented in London. After a half-hour audition, Jane was offered a job there. Once she had accepted it, Charteris took her through the side streets into the fringes of Soho, and led her up a steep staircase to a plainly furnished but clean and comfortable room. 'Think you could be happy living here?' he asked. 'If so, I'll treat you to a month's rent. Even if you stick to dancing and don't do anything else, you'll find you can easily afford it yourself after that.'

At the time, Jane did not even pause to consider what he meant about sticking to dancing and not doing anything else. She was far too starry-eyed about the room, the nightclub and the prospect of escape from black and white uniforms and one half-day off a week. In fact she appreciated his generosity and consideration so much that it required only the barest hint from Harry for her to remove her clothes and slide into bed for an hour's lovemaking with him.

Chapter Nine
Fenton Parva, Wiltshire

The jelly towered on the stillroom table, exquisite and insubstantial, the evening light striking glowing colour from its red-gold heart. Eleri adjusted the dish on which it sat, and the whole edifice quivered deliciously. 'For heaven's sake be careful — I don't know whether I expect it to collapse or fly away it's that light,' said Mrs Stanley. 'Honest, Eleri, I dunno how you manage it.'

The Welsh girl grinned at her. 'Nor me, but I'm ever so glad I can,' she said. 'Everybody should be good at something, or else what would be the point?'

'Point? Point of what, girl?'

Embarrassed, Eleri made a vague gesture with her hands. 'Well, you know, all this . . . hardly much in it for us if our lives were just down to fetching and carrying for them upstairs, is there?'

'But that's what we *are* doing, even if it's fancy jellies and pies we're carrying.'

'But surely, Cook, you must see that knowing you can do those things that they can't gives you just a little bitta something they haven't got?'

Maud Stanley sighed. 'S'pose you got a point, dear, but I wouldn't rely on it to hold off the arthritis when you're getting older. Your sense of achievement won't stand up to much a that, I can tell you.' Abruptly she turned away from her private reflections and said: 'Anyway, we got too much on to think about gloomy things like that now. How's the orange custard doing?'

'Oh, that's perfect,' said Eleri. 'I must say I like the whole idea. Bet they won't even notice, though.'

'Oh, I think they will — though you know better than to expect any of the guests to comment. Far too proper for that sort a thing,' Mrs Stanley replied. 'Just the same, I'll bet you anything Her Ladyship will find time to say something to us down here. Now, you make sure Hannah has washed those nectarines properly and I'll go and see to the meat.'

Eleri had been very lucky to train under Maud Stanley. The cook had liked the Welsh girl from the beginning, which had helped, but she also had a kindly temperament which ensured the new maid did not suffer many of the miseries commonly encountered by junior domestic staff in great houses. And when she discovered Eleri had a natural talent for food preparation, Mrs Stanley set aside any personal resentment of a would-be rival and taught the girl to the best of her ability. As a result, Eleri was out of the scullery in little over a year and working directly for Mrs Stanley on vegetable preparation and cooking the servants' meals. Not, perhaps, the pinnacle of achievement, but certainly a long step up from the scullery sinks.

Since then her progress had been steady and her training as sound as a country-house cook could make it. Eleri supplemented the knowledge she gained in the kitchens of Fenton Parva by voraciously reading Mrs Beeton at every opportunity. A year ago she had started experimenting with fancy puddings whenever she could persuade Mrs Stanley to give her permission. Now the cook was more than half convinced that her pupil had outstripped her. Characteristically, she was not jealous of Eleri, or apprehensive about losing her own supreme status below stairs. Apart from anything else, she understood intuitively that Eleri's talent pointed to a broader stage. Fenton Parva was a rich but conservative household, where much of the fare at even the grandest dinners reflected the saddle-of-mutton and fruit-tart tradition. Lady Clifton maintained a far more sophisticated table at Belgrave Square and Maud regarded it as inevitable that some day Eleri would be Cook in the London house. At present she was directing considerable effort to getting the girl's talents noticed by the countess, so that some thought might be given to wider opportunities for her assistant.

Tonight was a key occasion in Mrs Stanley's strategy. She herself had either cooked or supervised all the other courses for the formal dinner party the Cliftons were holding, to free Eleri to prepare a *pièce de résistance* which she had been conjuring in her imagination for weeks.

It was to comprise the feather-light tower of orange jelly, made from dozens of honey-sweet oranges, clarified to brilliant translucence and set with the lightest calf's foot jelly Eleri could manufacture. It rested on a cloud of orange confectioner's custard, its delicate flavour pointed up by the addition of a good measure of Grand Marnier. The blandness of the egg yolks and cream in the dish contrasted wonderfully with the tart orange jelly. Eleri's instinct, although she would have dismissed the idea as too grand for her, was to mix similar flavours with different textures and create what amounted to the gastronomic equivalent of musical counterpoint.

Eleri had two American guests to thank for her success that evening. The Cliftons still followed the unbreakable English upper-class principle that a gentleman never commented on the food offered by his host. Thus, however magnificent the meal, those who ate it were expected to taste each dish without comment. Under such a code, even the most innovative cook could expect little advancement unless her employer's attention was directly engaged by some stupendous effort. Then, and only then, would she be in line for preferment. In spite of Maud Stanley's hopes for her confection tonight, Eleri's expectations were not high. Lady Clifton was not fond of puddings and seldom paid much attention to them. She had once reduced Mrs Stanley to furious tears by dismissing a creation of pineapple ice cream and spun sugar which had taken two days to prepare as looking like a chorus girl's hat for a production of *The Merry Widow*.

Tonight's effort would undoubtedly have passed equally unappreciated, had it not been for the Americans.

Untrammelled by the conventions of British etiquette, Paula Church, a Mid-Westerner, threw up her hands in delight at the appearance of the orange pudding and cried: 'Why, that looks like a fairytale castle floating on a cloud! What a wonderful idea! It can't possibly taste as good as it looks.'

Her enthusiasm jerked the entire table from its conventional attitude and everyone was enthusiastic to try Eleri's creation. They even talked about it after they had tasted it. The butler's eye had been on the delicacy from the moment it appeared at table. To his fury, it disappeared on to the plates of the diners and there was not a single spoonful left for his luncheon the next day.

A couple of hours later, Eleri and Mrs Stanley were sitting beside the kitchen range, toasting their toes and enjoying a last cup of tea before bed. 'Well, love, even if Her Ladyship doesn't take any notice, you certainly got the thumbs up from her guests. I bet Americans will always be popular with you after this!'

Eleri smiled wearily. 'Yes, it was nice to hear some praise from above stairs for once. And I'm grateful to Timpson for bothering to come and tell us what they said.' Timpson was the first footman and had been in the dining room throughout the service of dinner. He had a soft spot for Eleri, and afterwards came hurrying downstairs to tell her of her triumph. 'Pity it doesn't seem to make any difference to Her Ladyship,' said Eleri with a sigh.

She had underestimated her employer. Next morning, when she had finished discussing the day's menus with Mrs Stanley, Venetia Clifton asked to see Eleri in the morning room.

'Our guests were most impressed by your efforts last night, Jones,' she said. 'So much so that they quite forgot their manners in order to shower you with compliments.'

Eleri blushed, unsure whether she was intended to feel flattered or chastened. Lady Clifton did not leave her in doubt for long. 'The opportunities for using a little culinary imagination are frightfully limited down here, and they're likely to remain so with the sort of guests the earl keeps inviting. I think it's time we tried you in Belgrave Square. See how you shape up when you're working for a French chef. Go along now — I shall let you know when I've made arrangements.' She turned back to her half-read morning post. Eleri had already ceased to exist for her.

'I really don't know whether to be pleased or sorry,' said Mrs Stanley. 'For a start, I'll miss you summat rotten. You've got just like a daughter to me this past coupla years. But on top a that, I wonder if I've been advising you to do the right thing. That Monsieur Auguste has got a terrible reputation.'

Eleri experienced her first misgivings about the new opportunity. 'I don't understand . . . I thought he was supposed to be marvellous.'

'Oh, he's that all right. That's half the trouble. He's jealous as hell of his reputation and won't give an inch when it comes to training up anybody else, just in case, you know . . .'

'Then what's the point of me being there? I'm no fully trained cook. You know I couldn't take over your job tomorrow if you got sick.'

'Bless you for saying that, my love, but I think you damn near could, once you got the confidence. I'd never have considered encouraging you towards promotion if I hadn't thought so. Come on, now, you know a lot a the things you can do are what you taught yourself — all them fancy sweets an' things. You'll just need to watch him like a hawk and pick up what you can.'

'But I'll never manage like that!'

'Then you're dafter than half the first-class cooks in England, that's all I can say! Listen, Eleri, you and me get on fine, and I've never been the jealous type anyway. But in most houses, the head kitchen-maid has practically got to spy on the cook if she wants to learn a single special recipe.

'They all keep their best things to themselves and go off to prepare the stuff away from prying eyes. I remember the cook I trained under had a thing about her raspberry sauce.

Every time she made it, she'd go off into a little pantry behind the kitchen and make it there by herself. And woe betide anybody who walked in on her while she was at it! That's what it's like in most places.'

'Oh, I never realised!' Always prone to blush, Eleri was red-faced yet again. 'I-I thought it was a credit to the cook if her girls were doing well.'

'Don't you believe it! True, I think like that, but precious few others do. Now don't fret about this Monsieur Auguste. He's a vain bugger, by all accounts, temperamental, too, and I'll bet he spends more time admiring his own cleverness than taking notice of anybody else. Keep your head down, don't miss a thing, and refuse to let him put you off. At the very worst, in a year or two you'll be good for a really decent job in another house; but my guess is you'll have Monsieur Auguste's billet. He's not at all popular with the staff in London, and I *did* hear Her Ladyship was getting a bit exasperated with him, an' all.'

Within a month of her move to London, Eleri was looking back on Fenton Parva with longing. She hated her life at the Belgrave Square house so violently that it destroyed any pleasure she might otherwise have derived from being in the capital. Auguste Lamarque was a martinet of the worst type, determined to extract every scrap of effort from his new head kitchen-maid in exchange for minimal credit when she did a good job.

There was no question of any interesting or responsible tasks devolving to her. Eleri sometimes wondered whether he would have made her peel vegetables, given the chance, but he had a scullery-maid and a junior kitchen-maid for such menial work and even Lamarque's malice was unequal to flouting the traditional kitchen hierarchy.

That did not stop him allocating the worst permissible cooking tasks to her. Breakfast, for instance. There was no kudos attached to poaching haddock to perfection, frying eggs and making toast so that both remained hot and fresh throughout a protracted breakfast hour. Complaints came thick and fast if anything fell short of the normal impeccable standard, and Eleri constantly found herself condemned to taking responsibility for it all.

When the main meals of the day were prepared, she was invariably ordered to knock up a batch of pastry or to clarify aspic; fussy, demanding tasks but nothing that tested her ability. When he assigned her to breadmaking for three successive days, she came close to shouting a refusal at him.

In the meantime, he continued to produce exquisite dishes for the luncheon and dinner parties beloved of Lady Clifton when she was in London to entertain her fashionable friends, and to create the irresistible light after-theatre suppers which were his speciality. He was a quick, intuitive type and was openly pleased to provoke Eleri so thoroughly. That in turn upset her further and within weeks she felt scarcely capable of an efficient day's work.

Preparation of food and the creation of imaginative menus had become Eleri's main intellectual outlet over the years of her apprenticeship. Now she found herself missing the mental stimulus she had gained from cooking as much as the physical satisfaction she derived from a perfect dish. Mrs Higgins, the housekeeper, eventually took pity on her. 'I really don't know how you stand that Lamarque,' she said. 'I said to the butler when they brought you up here, she won't last five minutes with that bully. I'm amazed you have — he broke the last girl in less than a month and now she's working in a house round in Eaton Square. She's the cook, there, too, and when she was here he used to say she wasn't fit to poach an egg!'

Eleri was grateful for the sympathy, but it did not get her far. 'If only I had something to keep my mind off it,' she said. 'You know, something that would help me improve my cooking without having to rely on him. But I can't really afford to buy cookery books for myself and if there are any in this house he keeps them well hidden.'

'Wait a minute.' Mrs Higgins beamed at her own brainwave. 'Her Ladyship hands on her old copies of *Vogue* to me — has done for years — and they're so lovely and expensive-looking I could never bear to throw any o' them away. Got them all tied up with string back to about 1925, '26, something like that. I take 'em out now and then and have a good gawp at all the expensive jewellery and things . . . there's a really posh chap writes about food in there, and sometimes he tells you how the stuff is cooked. Would you like to come in here from time to time and look at them, see if the articles are any use to you?'

'Oh, Mrs H, that's kind of you! Even if it's too highbrow for me, it'll be such a relief to get away from that old brute and just relax now and then!'

'Well, you're welcome. I'm off Wednesday afternoons and all day Saturdays. You got the run of the room then, and if there's ever a time you just want a cuppa tea and a talk, you know where to come.'

'Thank you, I do *now*. Anything's better than having to hang around him when he doesn't want me there.'

The magazines were a treasure hoard. Marcel Boulestin had started writing a food column in *Vogue* in the mid-1920s, sometimes about specific restaurants, more often about particular cuisines or individual foods and different ways of preparing them. He had a delicate, luxurious touch, considerable flair and an unerring eye for an impressive table. Eleri lapped up his articles, and when she discovered that Boulestin had his own restaurant in Leicester Square she put on her best clothes, took her courage and some of her savings in both hands, and spent part of a day off enjoying a sumptuous lunch at the restaurant. She emerged convinced that this was the kind of food she wanted to produce — if possible in the sort of surroundings featured in Boulestin's restaurant rather than in a private house. It was going to take more than a selfish poseur like Lamarque to stop her.

Her opportunity came sooner than she expected. Lamarque had been watching her covertly for some time, and had decided she was not so easily driven off as some of her predecessors. No use waiting until she has all the tricks of the trade at her disposal, he thought. Let's take drastic action now and get rid of her for good.

Lamarque suffered the classic weakness of the supreme egotist: he found it impossible to conceive that he was dispensable – and that was where he made his mistake. Lady Julia Clifton, the earl's eldest daughter, was part of a fashionable social set who enjoyed being seen at all the best places and in setting trends which lesser mortals would slavishly follow. This season it was the delicate little luncheon party.

There was no love lost between Lady Julia and Lamarque. He had decided long ago that she never accorded due reverence to his skills and merely saw him as a purveyor of food. Therefore he had no qualms about letting her down and chose to do so as a gesture which was sure to ruin Eleri.

Lady Julia's midweek luncheon for twelve was scheduled for Wednesday. Throughout dinner preparations on Tuesday evening, Lamarque mopped his brow, groaned piteously and announced repeatedly that he hardly knew how he remained standing, he felt so sick. He administered the *coup de grâce* by asking for an audience with the earl after dinner – the countess was abroad that week or he would have seen her – and informed his employer that thanks to a terrible attack of influenza or something like it, he would be unavailable to cook for the family the next day.

Clifton peered at him disbelievingly. 'But how are we to manage, man? Good God, for all I know, there are people lunching or dining. I'd better check with me wife's diary.' When he returned he seemed slightly mollified. 'Hmm, s'pose you could have chosen a worse time to fall ill, when all's said and done. Only got Caspar Partridge dining tomorrow and I've known old Caspar long enough to take him to the club. No one for lunch, so I'll have that out, too. Don't know about this luncheon of Julia's, though . . . hardly think she'll want to cancel and I'm certainly not footing the bill for her to take that crew to a restaurant!'

Lamarque's smile was catlike. 'No need, Milord, no need at all. I am sure Jones can handle such a small engagement. After all, she is always demanding to know why she may not take on more responsibility in the kitchen.'

'Is she, by Jove? Hmm, yes — come to think of it, I seem to remember some tomfool creation of hers down in Fenton causing no end of fuss with a pair of Americans. Seemed to think compliments were in order for just about everything. Well, if she's so good, we'll soon find out, shan't we?' He beamed at Lamarque, pleased that the man's illness would cause minimal disruption and otherwise totally indifferent to the enormity of asking an untried nineteen-year-old kitchen-maid to produce a luncheon for twelve people to master chef standards.

He would never have got away with it had Lady Clifton been at home, Lamarque reflected to himself as he headed for his bedroom. Her Ladyship would have been less interested in Eleri's tender feelings than in the tremendous blow her social reputation would suffer if a bunch of Bright Young People were about telling everyone of the disastrous meal they were served at the Cliftons'. Lady Clifton would have ensured that Monsieur Auguste cooked the luncheon if it had been necessary to nail him to the kitchen range.

Now Lamarque headed for bed, and once installed there rang for a manservant to give him the sad tidings of his indisposition. He also ordered himself a large hot toddy and a roast beef sandwich. Then he settled down with one of Escoffier's cookery primers and abandoned the household to get on with its own disaster.

'He've done WHAT?' Panic caused Eleri to drop both her carefully cultivated accent and her recently learned good grammar. Pure Valleys panic echoed in her speech patterns. 'Get 'im up! He can't just go off like that — I don't even know what they'm having for their lunch!'

'Neither did Monsieur Auguste,' explained the butler. 'You know how vague Lady Julia is about menus — none of your pre-planning like Her Ladyship. She just waved her hands and said he should get something amusing. He was waiting to see what the markets would come up with in the morning, I think.'

'But I can't do this on my own — I'll ruin it and then

they'll sack me!' wailed Eleri. 'Oh, Mr Watson, what am I going to do?'

The butler smiled at her kindly. Like the other servants, he was less than fond of Lamarque, but this was not really his problem and he did not propose to become entangled in it. 'Why not talk to Mrs Higgins? She always gives you good advice.'

'Yes . . . Mrs Higgins.' Eleri, gibbering now, concentrated on the housekeeper in an effort to exclude the prospect of tomorrow from her mind.

The housekeeper was brisker than she had expected. 'You'll do it, of course — that's what you'll do! I'm sure he did it to you deliberately — he'd never have risked it with Her Ladyship here — but how else would you ever get a chance to show what you could do, with him stopping you every time you tried? Pull yourself together, silly girl, and start planning. This one's worth staying up all night for if you have to.'

It almost amounted to that. At least they're modern-minded and they won't care for one of the whacking great meals the earl likes, thought Eleri in relief. Four courses should be ample, and the simpler the better.

After driving herself mad with all the possible combinations of food which would be in some way unsuitable, she turned in desperation to Mrs Higgins's store of old *Vogues* and started skipping through Boulestin again. She remembered something which would be just right, if only all the ingredients could be found. Yes, there it was, a piece headed 'The Finer Cooking,' featuring a luncheon party of *oeufs à la gelée*, seafood pilaff, stuffed partridge and pears in chocolate sauce. She could dispense with great piles of vegetables: the rice in the pilaff would be sufficient with that course, and straw potatoes and a green salad would be ample accompaniment to the partridges. Eleri began to feel a little better.

'Just to be on the safe side, I'll do the eggs tonight,' she muttered to herself. Ironically, Lamarque had detailed her to make aspic a couple of days ago and she had grumbled silently throughout the long-drawn-out process, which she had known inside out since her second year under Mrs Stanley. Now her labours were rewarded. She took a jar of the fine jelly from the stillroom refrigerator and stood it in a pan of hot water to liquefy. Then she went in search of fresh tarragon and a little sherry to flavour it. It was almost two in the morning by the time she dribbled the last of the half-set aspic into two fancy moulds which contained the remainder of the jelly, with perfect *oeufs mollets* hanging suspended in its recently firmed depths. The two containers went on to the slate slab at the back of the stillroom, where they would be cool enough to stay set without acquiring the flabby texture imparted by refrigeration.

Lamarque always allowed the butcher and fishmonger to deliver to him, visiting them at their shops only when the most important parties were in the offing and then having first made sure that the countess was aware he had attended to the selection personally. Eleri could have telephoned orders to the shops the following morning, but she was determined everything would go without a hitch and was now feeling so persecuted by Lamarque that she was half afraid the shopkeepers would send her inferior goods in order to pander to him.

At the fishmonger's she chose tiny, shining black Dieppe mussels, a large and very lively lobster and a quantity of Dublin Bay prawns. She also got some good fish trimmings to make a stock in which to cook her pilaff. Moving on to the butcher's, she stood over him while he minced a fresh batch of pork sausage meat with a good fatty texture to counter the dryness of the partridges. After that she selected prime chicken livers and wafer-thin slices of the best green bacon.

There were tinned truffles in the store cupboard, which was just as well because the fresh ones were out of season. Before departing on her own errand, she had despatched the second kitchen-maid to the greengrocer to buy watercress, slightly under-ripe pears and the salad greens. Everything else was in stock at the Belgrave Square house and she had peered into every cupboard at dawn that morning to check on the fact.

Back in her kitchen, Eleri set to work, at first still close to panic, then, gradually, realising she had hours in hand and that the beauty of all these sumptuous dishes lay in their simplicity of preparation for any professional. First she stuffed the partridges with a mixture of sausage meat, chicken livers, chopped truffles, egg yolk and cream, then wrapped the six birds in layers of bacon before putting them aside to await a brief roasting while the guests ate their first course.

Next she made a cream sauce, delicately flavoured with curry, and cooked the pilaff which it would accompany. The seafood was prepared and set beside the stove ready for frying in butter and paprika at the last minute as rice and sauce were re-heated.

The quartered unripe pears were poached in sugar and a little water, flavoured with a vanilla pod, until they softened. They were kept hot while she dissolved two bars of grated bitter chocolate in a little of the poaching liquid, and then brought the sauce up to a satiny gloss by whisking in a few pieces of butter.

By the time the four-course lunch had been transported upstairs, she collapsed in Mrs Higgins's fireside Windsor chair with an exhausted sigh, her expression triumphant. 'If that don't show the old sod what I can do, nothing ever will!' she exclaimed.

Chapter Ten

Three months as Lady Clifton's personal maid had altered Rose almost beyond recognition. She was probably more intensely aware of the superficial changes than anyone else. The more profound effects were visible to those who encountered her rather than Rose herself, and they gave those who did not know her a totally mistaken impression of her status and occupation.

The initial impact was made by the clothes the countess showered on her. Lady Clifton regarded her generosity as nothing more than insuring against her maid shaming her in public. Rose saw it as an opportunity of being reborn a lady.

In order to take advantage of such a fresh start, Rose needed to be away from the house and family where she played so subservient a role. Here, too, fate conspired to help her. Lady Clifton required Rose's undivided attention for much of the morning and for the vital hour or so before dinner. Generally she also demanded the girl's presence when she retired for the night – though as she frequently arrived home very late she had no objection to her maid snatching a couple of hours' sleep while she was out. As a result Rose found herself with far more freedom in the afternoons than she had ever enjoyed before; unfortunately it came at the expense of full days and afternoons off.

Not that she cared overmuch. There was nobody she could rush home to see; no loving family waiting for her news or a share of her wage packet. She had never been in touch with her father since the night she fled to Shepherdess Walk police station, and had no intention of ever doing so. Nor, thanks largely to what had happened to her then, was there any personable young man in her life. She avoided any but the most fleeting contact with men, and sometimes paused to wonder if she would ever forget her past sufficiently to make a romantic relationship.

At first, she enjoyed simply being free in the afternoons, strolling along the paths at the Knightsbridge end of Hyde Park or window-shopping in the expensive stores along Brompton Road. But inevitably it began to pall. She was a bright girl, and an endless progression of window displays, interleaved with strolls among the daffodils and tulips, were hardly sufficient to keep her occupied.

That was when she discovered the Victoria and Albert Museum. It opened up a world of beauty which made the furniture and ornaments of the Cliftons' Belgrave Square house look tawdry. Her first timid exploration of the vast building set her off on a quest for books to tell her more about the objects she saw. Overnight, she discovered a world of Chinese porcelain horses, medieval wooden house fronts and Gothic church paintings. She was no longer conscious of solitude. Suddenly her life was full of beauty on a level she had never suspected. For a short time it left room for little else.

Learning more about it proved harder than she had thought, but that in itself was an education. Starting with the scrappy second-hand bookstalls in a Pimlico street market, she painstakingly enquired where she would be likely to find bargains in books about furniture, architecture and painting. That led her to the warren of streets behind the British Museum where she found books aplenty within even her modest financial grasp. Unfortunately the more modern compact, manageable volumes were either brand-new or such recent hand-me-downs that they were still too expensive for her. She did not mind resorting to the heavier, less popular but infinitely more detailed works of the Victorian and Edwardian era, but each volume seemed to weigh a ton and sometimes she returned from one of her book-buying forays wishing she had a husky footman to carry her purchases. Normally she confined her reading to her own room in Belgrave Square, but one week when she was exploring the Chinese porcelain galleries, she took along her least bulky reference book in an attempt to learn more on the spot of the wonders she saw in the display cases.

'Hmm, that's rather heavy reading over tea, I'd have thought.' Rose glanced up, defensive, threatened. 'I-I couldn't find anything lightweight,' she muttered, half angry connoisseur, half apologetic servant. Tell him to mind his own damned business, said an anarchic inner voice. But five years of unquestioning obedience was too much for rebellion and she sat, biddable and receptive, waiting for his next remark.

'May I?' He gestured at the empty chair across the tea-room table. She nodded. 'Please forgive me for being so presumptuous. To see such a personable young woman weighed down by such an overwhelming tome was too much to pass unremarked.' He glanced around. There seemed to be a sudden shortage of staff. 'And to compensate for my rudeness, permit me to give you tea, should a waitress ever re-appear.'

She flushed and looked down at her hands, white-knuckled with the effort of supporting the heavy book. 'Th-that would be most kind. I haven't seen a waitress yet either, and I've been here *ages*!'

Her little speech made Rose want to blush even harder. After the first defensive response, she had decided impulsively that she was not going to retreat from this stranger, but she knew there was no possibility of her, little Rose Rush, holding a conversation with what she still secretly regarded as a toff. Then she thought, Why not do a Lady Mary? and she was away. Lady Mary was the second Clifton daughter, and left a trail of smitten men behind her thanks to an ingenuous manner and breathless upper-class-schoolgirl speech patterns. Almost instinctively, Rose took refuge in them, and it appeared they worked as well for her as for Lady Mary.

The man grinned at her and her heart lurched. He really was ravishingly good-looking. 'What a remarkable girl you are!' he said. 'You're reading one of the Empire's leading authorities on Chinese porcelain and you talk as if your governess had just released you for the day.' He glanced around the room. 'And furthermore, you're unchaperoned. What a mystery for an amateur detective to unravel!'

'Oh, no mystery, I can assure you. Just a rather sheltered life and an elderly father I can't get away from too often.' Improvising, Rose dropped her voice confidentially. 'Papa hasn't been out for so long he doesn't think about chaperons and such. I just tell him all that ended long ago and show him pictures of flappers. He's far too old to pursue it.'

As the man chuckled sympathetically, Rose gave herself a little shake. Where was this character coming from? She wasn't like this. She was Rose Rush, self-possessed lady's maid without an eye for man or woman unless it concerned her work. Where had this female ingenue with an ancient father emerged from? She even had a mental vision of the old codger. Mansion flat in Bloomsbury. Tea and muffins prepared by a cook-general. Solitary dinners with his daughter, the only comfort of his declining years, a beautiful afterthought born long after he had expected to have children . . .

Rosie girl, you've been reading too much Ethel M. Dell! she told herself guiltily . . . but this game was fun. The everyday Rose might find it impossible to chatter with eligible men in public places, but this alter ego of her imagination seemed to encounter no difficulties of that sort. Her attention snapped back to the man, who was now giving the waitress an order. 'And the scones with clotted cream, I think. Will that suit you, Miss – ah – ?' He paused meaningfully and she blushed again. Better not cheat on the name, too. 'Rush,' she said. 'Rose Rush.'

'Very well, Rose Rush, the works – cucumber sandwiches, toasted tea cakes, scones, cream and jam. Do you prefer Indian or China tea?'

'Oh – er – Indian.' She giggled kittenishly. 'I think the Chinese were better with the containers than the drink!'

It was the beginning of an odd little romance which Rose came to cherish as dearly as some women would a passionate love affair. The young man was called Edwin Taylor and he was preparing a monograph on the pottery demons which the Koreans traditionally used to decorate their house gables to ward off evil spirits. The Victoria and Albert had the finest collection in Europe, so he spent much of his time there.

'Of course, it's such a wonderful place that I spend about a quarter of the time I should with my demons and the rest just drifting around looking at miracles like that T'ang Dynasty camel and driver they have out in the main Chinese gallery,' he said. 'Hardly conducive to letting a fellow get on with his work!'

Naively, Rose said: 'But what work can you possibly do that makes it worth your while to come and look at Korean pottery figures day after day? I shouldn't have thought it would pay very well.'

He looked startled for a moment then burst out laughing. 'Pay? Not a sou, my dear! Good God, if I relied on that, I should be in the gutter. No, I have a bit of a university teaching post on the strength of it, but I have private means. It's like asking you whether your father earns enough to live from what he does.'

She was back in her role again. 'But he doesn't do anything!'

'Precisely. Neither do I. Well, not to live, anyway. I've often thought that would be a dreadful way to exist — forced to slave away in the City or something to keep body and soul together. No, thank heaven for provident ancestors, that's what I always say!' Then he began to look embarrassed. 'Really, Miss Rush, I must apologise. I'm chattering away about my financial affairs as if we'd known each other for years. Please forgive me for being so crass. My friends are always saying I show insufficient reticence about the decencies of life!'

'Think nothing of it!' Rose's gesture was almost regal. 'I've never attached any importance to that sort of thing.

Why must everyone be so — so *conventional* in their choice of conversational topics?'

He was looking at her now with open admiration. 'I'm so glad I was impertinent enough to speak to you, Miss Rush. You've quite transformed my afternoon. When we've finished tea, please permit me to show you my demons? We should have at least an hour before they begin to lock up.'

And so began what Rose always regarded as her phantom romances. Many years later, she admitted to herself that they probably turned her into a sane woman after the devastating damage wreaked on her by her girlhood. At the time they seemed no more than a playful way of passing the time.

There was a beguiling Cinderella element about such encounters, because Rose was never free after 6.30 in the evening, the hour when Lady Clifton would be leaving the drawing-room tea table to go upstairs and begin her preparations for dinner. Nevertheless, that gave her three to four hours each afternoon — five or more if Lady Clifton lunched away from Belgrave Square, which she frequently did. It gave Rose time for all sorts of adventures and freed her from any unpleasant consequences. At the hour when most men would be attempting to lure her to a dark corner in a nightclub, Rose was invariably drowsing in an armchair as she awaited her mistress's return from the latest party.

Rose surprised herself by discovering a seemingly endless capacity for role-playing and deception within herself. Edwin Taylor was something of an experiment, being the first man with whom she had even flirted. At first their contact had a studied casual air. There was no formal arrangement for a meeting, and yet as often as not they would happen upon one another in the porcelain galleries, the textile hall or the tea-room. They would talk about the excitements of their week — in Rose's case completely fictitious — have tea together, then part. After about a month of this social shadowboxing, Taylor invited her to a concert.

'Oh, I could never manage an evening engagement!' said Rose, amazed that she sounded so cool, feeling as flustered as she did. 'Papa can't bear to spend his evenings alone.'

Taylor merely smiled. 'No, I'd rather gathered that. So I got tickets for an afternoon concert. A little unfashionable, I know, but they're playing some of my favourite Mozart and I was sure you'd feel unable to come at night.'

Rose had never heard ensemble music played in public, except for the occasional military parade or silver band concert, and the afternoon came as a wonderful surprise. She sat through the formal, perfect music as though in a trance. When they emerged, Taylor said: 'I'm beginning to wonder where your faults lie, Rose. Modest, self-contained, a lover of ceramic art and a devotee of Mozart — I've been looking for a woman like you all my life.'

That brought her to earth with a bump. 'Oh, no, Edwin — don't say that. I'm no use to anyone . . . too many commitments . . . Papa, you know . . . just look on me as Cinderella.'

'I don't understand you.'

She sighed. 'Enjoy my company while the ball is on, but don't wait around for me out by the coach. The chances are that I shall have turned back into a kitchen-maid.'

Taylor laughed. 'You? The very idea! I've never seen a more refined young woman!' Then he became serious. 'But you really shouldn't let family commitments prey on your mind and your time so badly, you know. I'm sure we could arrange something one evening — someone to sit with your father — and then we could hear a full Mozart opera at Covent Garden and even go on to supper somewhere afterwards. Don't tell me you wouldn't like that.'

I'd like it more than almost anything else, she thought dreamily for a moment. And how would *you* like it when it dawned on you that I really *am* a kitchen-maid — or at least, not much better in your eyes? Better put a stop to it now, before it gets too painful, said the survivor in her.

All the same, she could not quite nerve herself to do it. Edwin had pinpointed a forthcoming production of *The Magic Flute* which was due to open in a month's time. He bought tickets and told Rose that he would not take no for an answer. If necessary he would go and confront her father to ask the old boy if he minded his only daughter absenting herself for just one evening.

Panic-stricken, Rose clutched at a straw. Lady Clifton was lunching with her oldest woman friend in three days' time. She always liked to leave Belgrave Square early and never came back until close to the dinner hour. Rose would have at least five hours free, much of it during lunchtime. She resolved she would placate Taylor with their first luncheon engagement — and break the news when she got there that it was to be their last meeting. She might even have weakened on this last resolution. In spite of her uncomfortable realisation that Edwin was in love with a Rose Rush who did not really exist, she had grown sufficiently besotted by him to wish their relationship might survive. Fortunately the decision was taken out of her hands. The day after the lunch engagement, Lady Clifton was going down to Fenton Parva and from there to France and Italy on an extended tour.

He took her to the River Room at the Savoy. Until that moment, Rose had told herself that Taylor was no more than a middle-class dilettante with a small private income. It was quite clear from the way the head waiter greeted him, his familiarity with menu and wine list, and his general ease in this, the most privileged of London's social milieux, that he was used to the best and could afford it.

Half way through their meal, Taylor put down his wine glass and said: 'You've agreed to see me today to tell me something I won't like, haven't you, Rose? Have you decided you won't come to see *The Magic Flute* after all?'

She shook her head, eyes downcast. 'I wish it were just that, Edwin. It-it's much more serious . . . we're going away, for some time.'

She would have given a lot to remove the stricken expression from his face. The rest of it might have been fun, but this wasn't. This was a real human being; one who was very fond of her and whom she held in considerable esteem. Still, there was no going back now. She pushed on.

'It's Papa. His doctor says he has to go away to the sun,

for a long time, perhaps indefinitely . . . We're going to France for a few weeks and then probably on to Italy. Oh, Edwin, I *am* sorry to be such a coward. We're off tomorrow and I haven't plucked up the courage to tell you until now!'

'Tomorrow?' His face was ashen. 'But that's no time at all . . . you can't . . . I don't know how . . .' His voice faded.

Rose reached out to touch his hand. 'It won't be forever,' she lied, her tone infinitely gentle. Then she added, wanting to cut out her tongue as she did so: 'And I'll write to you when we get there. We can keep in touch.'

'And what about when you get back?'

'I don't know how to answer that . . . you can guess what the doctor said about Papa's prospects.'

'I think so, yes. He'd hardly be sending away someone so old and frail if there were any chance of his lasting long here.'

'Exactly. I don't think it will be so very long, Edwin.'

'I shall wait, however long it is.'

'I don't think I should hold you to that.' Now she was fully immersed in her role. Inside her head, she really *was* a dutiful daughter about to take her dying father abroad.

'I want you to hold me to it. I've never met anyone like you, Rose.'

Reality flickered hysterically within her head. No, and you probably never will again, if only you knew it, she thought. Aloud, she replied: 'The time will pass much faster than either of us imagines now, Edwin. Let's try to concentrate on the future.'

He nodded, and she saw his eyes fill with tears. He reached inside his jacket pocket. 'We've never even told one another where we live,' he said. 'Most improper. Here, here's my card. Write to me as soon as you get to France. I shall be incapable of working until you do.' Silently, she put the piece of engraved pasteboard inside her bag and took another sip of wine. 'I shall go alone to see *The Magic Flute*,' he went on, 'and pretend you're with me. When you come back, we shall see it together, I promise.'

She gave him her best smile. 'I shall hold you to that. Now, I know we haven't really finished, but I think it would be best if we said goodbye. No — don't come with me. I'll leave you to recover a little over a brandy. Don't worry, Edwin, I'm used to getting about London on my own.'

He stood up and drew back her chair for her to leave the table, then kissed her lightly, first on one cheek, then on the other. 'Hurry back to me, my dearest,' he murmured. Then he let her go.

Watching the tall, elegant, dark-haired girl stride out of the restaurant, Lady Beatrice Duncan turned to her luncheon companion and said: 'If I didn't know better, I'd have sworn that was Venetia Clifton's maid. I must be mistaken, though. Who'd treat a servant-girl to sole and Chablis?'

Rose sat in front of her bedroom mirror and gazed at the calm, comely face reflected there. Why had she done it? Edwin was a kind, decent man and she found him very attractive. What had possessed her to make up a whole life which had no substance outside their afternoons together in gallery and tea-room? She had no ready answer. She only knew that after each meeting, she had returned to Belgrave Square feeling liberated. Each encounter had filled her with a sense of power, of her own attractions and, above all, her invulnerability. It had been the direct opposite of that dreadful night at Ladysmith Court, when she had nowhere else to go and no means of going there even had she found a possible sanctuary. Accidentally, she had discovered a world of power without responsibility, a world where she could be more or less whoever she wanted to be, where she was protected by the necessity of disappearing in the early evening, when the man she had ensnared was still hours away from becoming the sexual predator she had learned to fear so much.

At first Rose felt pangs of regret about her abandonment of Edwin Taylor. At the last moment, Lady Clifton postponed her trip abroad, but Rose felt almost as if they had really made the journey. Her fertile imagination conjured pictures of Edwin waiting every day for a letter from her in France, of his worry and subsequent despair when nothing materialised. Then the rigours of her own life closed in. What was such pain against physical possession and torment? He would forget her within a few weeks, and before that they had given each other a great deal of pleasure in an entirely harmless way. After all, her practical side reasoned, it wasn't as if he fell in love with Rose Rush the servant girl from Shoreditch . . . the girl he yearned to possess was a shy intellectual from Bloomsbury, with an ailing but entirely respectable father. Why, even if he thought he still wanted her, that illusion would wear off rapidly enough if she revealed her true origins! That made her feel much better. Why waste tears on a man who would only stay in love with a girl as long as he thought she came from a respectable background? To hell with the entire male sex! She had better things to do. The interlude with Taylor would be her first and last such adventure.

At least, that was what she told herself at first. The countess and her entourage departed for Wiltshire later that week. As usual, Rose travelled down with Lady Clifton in the Rolls-Royce, occupying the front passenger seat beside the chauffeur. In her boudoir, Venetia Clifton gossiped idly with Rose from time to time, but never while they were driving. Something about the chauffeur's presence seemed to constrain her. Probably thinks it would give him an opening to be too familiar, thought Rose with a touch of contempt. She did not actively dislike Lady Clifton, and felt positively grateful for her constant expensive gifts of clothes and scent, but felt no warmth for her employer. She was conscious that Venetia Clifton treated her well in the same manner as she cared for her favourite horse. If it were not well tended and at ease, it would not perform at its best for her. The same applied to her personal maid, so she was relatively considerate. There was no personal affection involved, and consequently she excited no answering warmth in Rose.

She had never grown wholly used to Fenton Parva. She

was urban to her fingertips and always felt a mild agoraphobic unease at the sheer area of open countryside which surrounded the Cliftons' country mansion. Paved streets and cobbled back alleys were more Rose's milieu. At first this visit was different. She was still too preoccupied with Edwin Taylor to do more than acknowledge the existence of the wide Wiltshire acres. After that her mind constantly returned to the man, his interest in her, the new paths he had opened in her mind, and the sheer thrill of the successful deception, which to her slight shame was growing all the time.

Rose intended to tell Margaret Armstrong about her adventure. Over the years, she and Margaret had developed a relationship far closer than any she enjoyed with the other Clifton servants. In practical terms they were often thrown together because both of them shuttled back and forth between London and Fenton Parva; but there was more to it than that. Both girls were quiet and reserved. Each had come into domestic service through an interlude of intense suffering and, on reaching the safe haven of live-in employment, had set about deliberately making herself inconspicuous. Each probably understood the other more than anyone else had ever done. Knowing this, they were both grateful for a little compassionate attention. Neither had known much affection in the past. If anyone were to be told about Edwin Taylor, it had to be Margaret.

But then Rose realised she was incapable of sharing her secret, even with Margaret – *particularly* with Margaret. Deep down, Rose knew what she had done was odd, maybe slightly deranged. Any girl might play up to a chap for a laugh – string him along for an afternoon and then disappear for ever after one meeting but there was something perverse about going back again and again, entrapping him until he was on the edge of proposing marriage, and then backing out in circumstances which would cause him the greatest possible anxiety and pain.

For the first time, Rose started feeling a touch of shame about her behaviour. As soon as she stopped thinking about confessing it all to Margaret, the guilt evaporated and the sense of delicious secrecy seeped back. It seemed ironical even to her that she had been able to confide anything to Margaret for years, but that the first time she had something that truly needed a confidante, she backed away. Now she hugged the secret to herself and the more she thought about it, the more she wanted to try it again.

After that it was only a matter of time before she went hunting a successor to Edwin Taylor. She had parted from him in mid-autumn. The Cliftons tended to spend what they called the Little Season shuttling between Wiltshire and Belgravia. Lady Clifton enjoyed the theatre and the occasional concert, but she was also fond of hunting, to which the earl was addicted. Hence the months from September to February tended to see them behaving like rich nomads, trailing their personal staff from town to country and back again. For a while Rose was too busy to have much time on her own in London, but in early November there was a lull. By now Rose was more than ready for another quasi-romantic encounter, and grasped the opportunity with enthusiasm.

This time the V&A was out as a hunting ground. There was no guarantee that her betrayal had driven Edwin Taylor away, particularly if he was still working on his monograph, and she did not trust herself to see him again with any equanimity. How about the British Museum? No, perhaps not; from what she had seen of it when she went on her second-hand book-buying trips, it was likely to contain dozens of dried-up old men who smelled of snuff and mouldy paper.

Did it have to be a museum? Hours of considering that problem brought no real answer. Pubs were out. There would be no shortage of suitors there, but they were unlikely to possess the forbearance of an Edwin Taylor and they would certainly not regard her as a respectable woman if they found her hanging around over a gin and tonic in the saloon bar of even the best public house. Rose had developed a real pleasure in museums during her repeated trips to the

Victoria and Albert, but after her first adventure she was loath to embark on an exact repetition of that encounter. At first the nature of the surroundings seemed bound to ensure that this would happen.

Perhaps she was approaching the dilemma from the wrong direction. What sort of girl did she want to be? It was useful to appear as a bit of a bluestocking, because that would certainly inhibit any over-physical yearnings in whoever she picked up. But last time all over again would be too much of a good thing. Rose wanted to be a little . . . well . . . racy. Then it came to her – of course, the Tate! Where better to be just that little bit bohemian? She had been there only once – on a Sunday afternoon – and had seen quite a number of young and middle-aged unattached females, drifting around the modern collections wearing anything from the latest fashion to weird assemblies of drapery which looked as if they had not been removed since 1913. 'I could even smoke in the tea-room!' she murmured to herself.' Just like that girl I saw!'

The girl who had stuck so firmly in her memory had been sitting elegantly behind a table in the Tate's ornate tea-room, sipping a glass of Russian tea and smoking something which looked to Rose like a long, very thin cigar, not much thicker than a cigarette. Together with the exotic tea glass, it made the young woman look like the mysterious heroine of a story about the Orient Express. Rose fancied herself in such a role, as long as she could remain secure from the romantic novel's inevitable embrace behind the closed door of an imaginary sleeping car.

Lady Clifton had given her a gorgeous afternoon dress of heavy dark-blue *peau de soie* – 'Hardly working clothes, I know, Rush, but I'm sure you'll get plenty of use from it during your time off,' she had said airily, as though unaware that Rose had taken no full days off since August. Well, she'd been right in a way, Rose reflected, planning her costume for next Saturday's drama. She had already treated herself to a glorious pair of fine silk stockings in a shade of midnight blue which complemented the dress and had the most daring scarlet hand-embroidered clocks running up from the ankle. Now she must find herself a suitable hat — a swathed silky turban, she thought, to imply a hint of the mystic East — and buy some of those wonderful cigarette things. Oh, she was going to enjoy this, even if no one took an interest in her!

Next day Rose visited a first-class tobacconist in Brompton Road. 'Perhaps you could advise me,' she told the salesman in her most meltingly refined voice, adapted from another of Lady Clifton's daughters. 'I wish to give my uncle a birthday present, but he smokes these things and I'm not entirely sure what they're called. They're long, about this long' — she indicated with her hands ' — and they're black. They smell a little like cigars but, er, *softer*, somehow. It would never occur to him that I know what they are and he'd be charmed if I got him some.'

The man smiled paternally at her, clearly as beguiled as her mythical uncle. 'Of course, Miss. They're cheroots. And as I'm sure he's a gentleman of discrimination, and you commented on the softness of the aroma, I'd hazard a guess they're the best Burmese.' He turned to the bank of small drawers behind him and produced a sample identical in every respect to the thing the girl had been smoking in the tea-room.

'Oh, how clever you are!' Rose clapped her hands like an excited child. 'That's exactly right. Do you think, let me see, fifty would be appropriate, just as a small gift?'

'Oh, yes, Miss. One doesn't smoke these at the speed of a cigarette. Fifty would be admirable.'

Bloody better be, at that price, thought Rose as she left the shop, clasping her booty. Talk about a vice of the rich!

Her next stop was Harrods' smokers' accessories department, where she invested ten shillings in a silver-plated matchbox, having learned with some relief from the cheroot salesman that it was sacrilege to pollute high-quality tobacco with the flame of a petrol lighter. She had noticed the daring young woman at the Tate kept her cheroots in a flat leather case, which relieved her of the necessity of parting with more of her precious savings for a silver-plated cigar case. This deception business was beginning to prove expensive. Perhaps the simple student approach she had adopted with Edwin had more going for it after all. But she was more optimistic once she had managed to buy the duplicate of her role-model's case for a couple of shillings in the small leather goods department, and returned to Belgrave Square to arrange Lady Clifton's hair for the evening's dinner party, feeling as if she had just bought half London for herself.

Rose spent most of her free time over the next couple of days mugging up anything she could find on paintings at the Tate — Lord Clifton was a surprisingly good source of information because he believed in self-improvement for servants and was delighted to lend Rose books from his library. If he knew *how* I'm planning to improve myself, he might change his mind a bit sharpish, she thought, suppressing a mischievous giggle with some difficulty. She was really beginning to enjoy her new hobby of deception now. It was not merely the thrill of a potential flirtation without any strings attached. It was the feeling of complete freedom she achieved by stepping out of the Clifton mansion and into another personality — one which had no idea of what it was to be a servant. One way and another, Rosie love, this wasn't a bad idea of yours, she told herself, lighting a cheroot in yet another attempt to accustom herself to the flavour and the acrid grip of the smoke on her throat and lungs.

She struck a bull's eye on her first visit to the Tate the following Saturday afternoon. It was a raw, cold day and she had put on her black alpaca coat over the luxurious silk dress. Amazing what a frock like this can do for a plain lady's maid's coat, she thought. She knew she looked both elegant and expensively turned out in her dark silk stockings and soft navy kid court shoes. The red clocks on her stockings added a daring touch but by now Rose's fashion judgement was sufficiently sure to know the rest of the outfit made it out of the question that she might be anything but respectable.

She became aware she was being followed about half-way around the eighteenth-century collections. She positioned herself before a large painting where she could see reflections in the glass and glanced up. He was tall, with very dark hair and high cheekbones, the olive skin suggesting that he had recently spent a long time abroad. His clothes seemed expensive but sightly eccentric. A Chelsea painter, perhaps, said her ever-active imagination. What a shame if he's not really following me . . .

But she was right – he was. She saw him close behind her at least three times more, in spite of having gone back for a second look at two canvases in order to let him move well ahead if he really was just an imaginary admirer. Time for a *café au lait* and a cheroot to intrigue him all the more, she thought. As she moved towards the tea-room, Rose was casting about for a reliable story to cover her decidedly scrappy knowledge of the works in the Tate.

Rose sat down, lit her cheroot and relaxed gracefully into what she hoped was an approximation of the position she had seen the girl adopt weeks before. She managed to inhale the sweet, aromatic smoke, expelling it dramatically through her nostrils. Then she took a nonchalant sip of her coffee and flipped open a soft-covered book on Turner which she had bought in the gallery shop. She heard him draw back a chair and sit down at the adjoining table, only six feet from her, and felt a thrill of anticipation. Who was it said a man chases a woman until she catches him?

Long moments passed, then he made contact in the most banal manner. 'Forgive me, but my lighter seems to be empty . . . may I trouble you for a light?' He had put down a gold cigarette case and matching lighter on the table top in front of him.

'Of course.' She hoped her tone was suitably relaxed. No girl of the type she was impersonating today would be thrown into confusion by the small familiarity of a man asking for a match. She managed a cool smile as he returned her little silver matchbox. 'You don't like lighters, I take it?'

'Hardly, with a cheroot.' She raised her eyebrows to an

appropriately pained level. 'It destroys the entire flavour of the tobacco. So much more subtle than cigarettes, you see.'

'Mmm, that's why you indulge in them, is it? You appreciate subtlety?'

'In tobacco, certainly. Not necessarily in everything.' Dear God, she thought, this could go on forever. Flirting is one thing. This back-chat is about as interesting as a discussion of the weather.

But it did not go on for long. He was merely trying to establish a little common ground, so that it was not too blatantly a pick-up when he sat down beside her. Finally he seemed to feel he had bumbled on meaninglessly for long enough and said: 'Look, I've interrupted your coffee. Please let me order two more and let's sit and chat awhile over them. I'm just back from Spain and no one I know seems to be in London at present, so you'll be doing a lonely chap a favour if you say yes.'

Rose gave him her most winning smile. 'Of course. Can't have intrepid travellers being left out in the cold, can we? I'd love another coffee.'

This one was called Mark Fletcher-Simms and he was a critic, not a painter. He had been in Spain for a couple of months indulging his twin passions for Velasquez and Goya, and was about to write a book about the great court painters of Europe. He could have been made for Rose and her deception game. She might be shaky on the Tate and therefore have no demonstrable reason for swanning around there looking blasé, but she could plead complete ignorance of Spain without raising any suspicion, then just sit back and let him enlighten her. That was precisely what she did.

Fletcher-Simms, starved of an audience of his usual acquaintances since his return from the Continent two days earlier, warmed in the sunlight of this pretty young woman's interest, and showed off unmercifully. After the first self-conscious quarter of an hour, Rose realised there was no need for her to play to the gallery. She really was fascinated by his stories — much more so than she had been by Edwin Taylor's more prosaic accounts of tracking down old porcelain and enamels. Almost before she was aware of it, the tea-room and the gallery itself were closing.

She glanced up at the clock and let out a gasp of unsimulated dismay: 'Oh, God, it's half-past five — I shall be late!' And losing her composure completely she snatched her cheroots and little matchbox and turned to flee.

To her consternation, Fletcher-Simms laughed heartily and took hold of her wrists. 'Oh, no you don't!' he said. 'I refuse to let anyone make an exit on me by doing a creditable impression of Alice's white rabbit. Why are you late, where are you going, and tell me, pretty maiden, who are you? You've let me bleat on at such length I've had no chance to find out.'

'Can't — no time!' Rose was breathless, partly in desperation at the thought of not getting back to Belgrave Square before Lady Clifton needed her, partly in panic at his firm grip on her arms. 'P-please let me go, Mr Fletcher-Simms!' She was too worried even to try and keep the rising fear out of her voice, and he realised she was genuinely upset.

'I say, look, don't take me seriously. Just tell me where I might get hold of you — telephone number will be fine — and I'll be in touch later. How about that?'

'N-no, I can't — no time to explain.' She realised that although he was still very friendly, he had no intention of losing touch with her, and grabbed at the first solution she could think of. 'Let me have your card, and I'll telephone you. Father's ill and we don't like incoming calls because they disturb him. Now, really must rush . . . should have relieved the nurse hours ago.'

He finally admitted defeat and produced a card. 'Don't you dare forget to ring me,' he said, shaking a finger, 'or I shall find you wherever you are. Just remember that — wherever you are.'

'Yes, all right . . . sorry about this.' She was backing away from him, dying to break into a run and not quite daring to do so on such a slight pretext. When she finally got outside it was already dark and there were plenty of taxis streaming past. To hell with the expense, she thought. If I'm not back there before six, it'll be my job, not just the cost of a taxi ride.

Rose arrived back at Belgrave Square just after ten minutes to six, giving her barely time to run to her room and remove the stockings which she knew would earn Lady Clifton's tantrum of disapproval. She liked her maid to be fashionable, but only within the dictates of her own taste. As Rose tapped on the countess's door in answer to the usual summons at 6.30 she heaved a sigh of relief at having returned unscathed and just about on time. She barely had an opportunity to calm herself completely before Venetia Clifton said: 'Surprising news, Rose. I don't know whether you will be glad or sorry. Rodwell telephoned today while you were out. Her mother is very close to the end now, and she expects to be ready to resume her old job as my personal maid by next spring. How do you feel about that?'

Chapter Eleven

The news burst over Rose like a bombshell. Return to carrying tea trays and dusting ornaments after this? She couldn't. She was still a servant, but experience had taught her it was a decidedly superior form of bondage. She had no intention of giving up the smart clothes and the secret afternoon outings just to let old Rodwell come back. Yes, the outings . . . with a start she realised how important they had become to her. Not just the two personable men she had managed to attract with apparently little effort, but the opportunity to go and look at the world in a way she had never been permitted to do before. She couldn't — wouldn't — give that up.

'Nothing to say at all, Rush? I'd have thought my news would provoke *some* sort of reaction.' Lady Clifton's spider-thin eyebrows were raised in mild curiosity.

'I-I'm rather shocked to tell the truth, Milady. It's been so long now, I feel quite settled in the job. I can't imagine doing anything else.'

'Well, you know what we discussed when I made the offer. It was all above board — Rodwell wanted to stay; I wanted to keep her; you wanted to acquire another string to your bow. We were all happy — but the original arrangement holds good, I'm afraid.'

Years of obedience were all that kept Rose from stamping her foot in outrage and yelling that this was not the way it had been put to her. She had been told it would be valuable training for her in the sense that should Rodwell return or not, Rose would never again need to contemplate working as an ordinary parlour-maid. Mrs Higgins had finally helped her make up her mind by pointing out that Rose would command a good job anywhere in Mayfair or Belgravia after training with Lady Clifton. But now there was no mention of any such thing. It appeared that Rose was to be relegated to the household ranks once again, without any acknowledgement of her greatly improved capability.

Only the old fear that to retaliate was to lose one's job and therefore one's home prevented Rose from pointing this out. Whatever she felt about the whole matter, she knew she would never dare apply for a job elsewhere and then approach the countess for a reference. She had seen Lady Clifton in action before when a member of staff took this line. There was a great deal of posturing and sulking and much unfavourable comment about the quality of the employee's work. Then some sort of reference was grudgingly produced, and Rose had formed the impression that it was invariably one which damned with faint praise. She had no desire to see her own years of hard work dismissed thus. She retreated into silence.

Lady Clifton regarded Rose in the mirror for a while, then shrugged dismissively. 'Well, there it is,' she finally said, 'make of it what you will. It won't happen overnight and I don't think you appreciate how fortunate you'll be until it does. I've had more than enough of this damp, gloomy winter. As I postponed it before, the earl is sending me off to France and Italy on an extended holiday until things brighten up back here. I shall need you with me, of course.'

Coming hard on the heels of such bad news, this announcement threw Rose into total confusion. France and Italy ... what a chance to see the world! To her disappointment, until now the foreign trips that Mrs Higgins and Rodwell had referred to had not materialised. The countess had been abroad three times since Rose became her personal maid, but on each occasion had travelled alone. With the earlier last-minute cancellation of the French and Italian trip, Rose's hopes had faded. Now France and Italy seemed to spread out at Rose's feet as a glorious compensation for the threat that her precious job would disappear.

In the housekeeper's room that evening, she told Mrs

Higgins what was likely to happen and that Rodwell planned to return in the spring. 'I'm thrilled about the trip abroad, Mrs H, don't think otherwise — but am I being so unreasonable in thinking she means to do me down over sending me back below stairs?'

Mrs Higgins was furious. 'No such thing! I was the one who advised you, remember? That one always was on the treacherous side! She swore to me she'd see you all right in a similar job if Rodwell ever put in another appearance. Now she wants it both ways.' Her expression cleared somewhat. 'One thing, though, don't worry about pushing her if you decide to go and find another job as a lady's maid. All that showing off when people give their notice is just so much swank. She likes to rub their nose in it — make it as difficult as possible for them to make the break. In fact, if they stick to their guns she always gives 'em a gilt-edged reference. Got to, you see, matter of personal pride. No one must accuse the Countess of Clifton of employing any but the best!'

'So she'd give me a decent reference even if she went over me the way I've seen her do with some of the other servants?'

'Yes, love, 'course she would. That's the last thing you need to worry about. It's still uncomfortable, though, having to go through nonsense like that just because she likes to show off. Anyway, I hope it doesn't come to that. You're a real asset to this house, Rose, and I'd hate it if we lost you. I dunno if you've any idea why she's turned so contrary, incidentally? I have. Proctor handed in her notice this morning and she's the best parlour-maid they ever had in this house apart from you. It'd just suit Her Ladyship nicely if you fitted back in that slot without a ripple and Rodwell took up where you'd left off as her maid. To hell with everyone else's convenience so long as she's satisfied!' Mrs Higgins finished her harangue with an indignant flourish of her powerful shoulders.

Rose stared at her. 'Surely she wouldn't do that? Break her word for such a small reason. Good parlour-maids are easy enough to come by.'

'Ah, but you still don't understand, do you, Rose? It's not *convenient* that way. And everything must be convenient.'

Reluctantly Rose acknowledged the housekeeper was right It made her feel wretched. She had no exaggerated sense of her own importance, but now and then she liked to think she had acquired some personal value with the family she served, not merely the worth attached to a household appliance or ornament.

Mrs Higgins was only partly right. Had Rose known the rest of Venetia Clifton's reasoning, perhaps she would have felt flattered rather than ill-used. In Rose, Lady Clifton had started out with an ugly duckling and found herself nurturing a swan. She had been watching Rush closely in recent weeks and had realised with a start that when the girl was dressed in good clothes, she was indistinguishable from a real lady. The parlour-maid who had painfully mimicked Lady Clifton's own refined speech patterns when she first started working as her maid, now spoke unaccented English with no apparent effort. Her vocabulary seemed considerably more extensive than that of Lady Clifton's second daughter, and – to be expected in a servant from years of observing her betters – her table manners were impeccable.

Rodwell had achieved all these goals; but Rodwell was ten years older than Lady Clifton and had never been pretty. Her hair was mouse-brown and her skin, although of good texture, was an unfortunate dingy shade. She made the most of herself in Lady Clifton's cast-off couture clothes, and succeeded in looking elegant enough; but Rush dressed so well that the countess had recently begun to get the uneasy feeling she herself was unable to carry off her own garments as effectively as her maid. When that started happening, someone had to go . . .

Thus reasoned Venetia Clifton. She would have laughed dismissively had anyone suggested she was building up a grudge against Rush. Nevertheless, once she heard about Rodwell's possible return to her old job, the countess set about fitting Rose back into the household in the humblest possible function for one so accomplished.

In the end it was the earl who saved Rose from such ignominy. At tea one afternoon, a woman friend of Lady Clifton was bemoaning the continued lack of good servants, and the countess said: 'I know — frightful, isn't it? I'm losing a first-rate parlour-maid, and it's pure good luck that I'm able to send my temporary maid back to her old job because Rodwell is finally coming back to me.'

The earl had been pouring himself a second cup of tea and now stopped, turning to stare at his wife as if he had not heard aright. 'D'you mean Rose, old girl? Is that who you're talking about'

'Yes, that's right. Rush.' For some reason Venetia found it irritating that George should refer to the maid by her first name. 'When I get back from abroad, Rodwell will return and Rush will take over as head parlour-maid again. What's so appalling about that? You look as if I've pulled down the roof about our ears.'

'But — but I say — you can't do that. The girl's worthy of so much better.'

'And how would you know that?'

'Well, it's obvious. Credit to any household. Quiet, capable, dignified — and damned pretty, even if that has nothing to do with it!' His tone held the slightly defiant hint that he suspected it had everything to do with it.

Venetia made a long-suffering face at Charlotte Creighton and said: 'I think the matter of ladies' maids and parlour-maids is best left to me, dear, don't you?'

George's stammer, evident only when he was sufficiently annoyed to defy his wife, surfaced rapidly, but he pressed on. 'N-no I d-d-don't — not this time, anyway. Th-that girl is worthy of s-something a l-lot better. You could place her tomorrow as a l-lady's m-maid if you really want Rodwell back here — she's worth her weight in g-gold!'

Venetia's tone had dropped dangerously low. 'And what, pray, makes you think that she's so worthy?'

He was sufficiently committed now not to recognise the

warning. 'Her self-improvement drive for a start. Ever since she became your maid, she's been reading whatever she can get her hands on — good stuff, mind, not those rubbishy modern romantic novels. I let her borrow art and ceramics stuff from my library. I only wish Julia or Mary were half as interested.'

Open suspicion now blazed in Lady Clifton's eyes. 'She's actually been conducting a self-improvement campaign in *my* time? How dare she? This will cost the girl her job!'

Spotting disaster too late, Lord Clifton rushed to mend fences. He knew Venetia too well to try the gentle approach. Instead he met her head-on with a counter-challenge. 'H-hardly that. Wh-when did you last give her a day off? And before you accuse me of an improper interest in the girl, I haven't a clue about her free time. But I do know that no personal maid of yours has ever received her full entitlement because you claim you can't manage your own hair and so on for a whole day at a time. Well?'

The countess looked away. 'Very well, George, perhaps I was a little hasty there. Better she should be reading books here at the house and listening for me than gallivanting about London where I can't find her . . . but what business does a maid have, reading books about art and porcelain?' She snorted contemptuously, 'It's not as if she's ever likely to be a collector, is it?'

Clifton found himself wanting to shake his wife for her heartless attitudes and lack of imagination, but he knew it was useless. Better be content with getting this one girl some fair treatment, and then keep out of Venetia's way for a while.

'All that's beside the point,' he said. 'Three months ago you were full of the fact that Julia has no maid of her own. I'd have thought Rush was ideal for the job. After all, she and Julia are practically the same age.' That stung Lady Clifton to further irritation. In her view, Rose had quite enough unfair advantages without also being only in her early twenties. But before she had a chance to respond, the earl continued: 'Hand her over to Julia when you get back from the Continent and see what they make of each other. If the whole plan falls through, I think the girl should still be entitled to a damned good reference when she goes for a job elsewhere – and as a lady's maid, too, not a parlour-maid!'

Venetia Clifton knew better than to push her husband when he was in this mood. She shook herself angrily and then murmured assent to his suggestion. To think they'd been trapped into a squabble like this over such a trivial matter, and in the company of one of the biggest gossips in Mayfair! No doubt by this time next week, they'd all be saying George had a thing going on with Lady Clifton's maid.

When Rose received the news that she was to continue as a lady's maid after her return from abroad, her first sweeping sense of relief was followed by apprehension. She knew little of Julia Clifton, but was not at all enthusiastic about the girl. She seemed a typical product of the tail-end of the flapper era – spoiled, opinionated and glamorous, assured of her own ability to outdo anyone else and in truth lacking either the native intelligence or education to be anything but a social butterfly.

'Cheer up, love,' said Mrs Higgins. 'At least you'll be staying where the perks are, and it may be more fun to look after a really young, fashionable woman for a change. If you don't mind my saying it, you're not quite old enough yet for all that middle-aged elegance you've picked up off Lady Clifton!'

The countess had a weakness for the traditional French reveillon celebrations. Although not a Catholic, she gloried in the ornate ceremonies of the Medieval French New Year, Midnight Mass, followed by a widely indulgent supper party where not a single child appeared on the guest list. She had decided to depart from England on Boxing Day in order to reach the Riviera in time to enjoy the new year festivities to the full. That gave Rose about six weeks – at least ten days of the time to be spent in Fenton Parva and she was soon wondering what to do about Mark Fletcher-Simms.

Caution told her to drop the whole thing, and to stay away from the Tate. The trip abroad would make a satisfactorily permanent break and when she returned to England it would be to a markedly different life. Rose was tempted, nevertheless. Fletcher-Simms was quite different from Edwin Taylor: that was part of his attraction. He was an adventurer through and through (she was sure of this, although she had no experience whatsoever of adventurers or any other male types). In her role of secret *femme fatale* it would be fun to dally with him before disappearing as conclusively as she had from Taylor's life. But when Fletcher-Simms had said he would find her wherever she was, Rose experienced the chilling thought that he might manage to do just that. After brooding on the matter at some length, she found his card and telephoned him.

His voice had a tigerish, purring quality which almost frightened her into hanging up without speaking. Instead, she took a deep breath and said: 'Hello, Mr Fletcher-Simms. I felt I must ring to apologise for my appalling behaviour the other afternoon, but I get so worried about dear Father that it preys on my mind . . .' She trailed off into silence and his laugh boomed down the telephone.

'Well, well, if it's not the beautiful cheroot-smoking white rabbit! If you'd remained in your burrow much longer, my girl, I'd have been forced to come and hunt you out!'

'Well, here I am now. I really am most frightfully sorry.'

'How do you plan to make up for it?'

'W-well, I thought, perhaps you'd have time to show me some of the Spanish Masters in the National Gallery. I still have this difficulty with leaving Father alone after five-thirty, you see,' she added hurriedly. A vision of Joe Rush sprawling drunkenly over a piece of ruined furniture in the old days at Ladysmith Court rose unbidden in her memory, and she suppressed a giggle of pure hysteria.

'Of course, of course! I think that's an admirable idea. How about a spot of lunch first?'

Damn! It really *would* be fun to have lunch with Fletcher-

Simms . . . Rose's mind went to Lady Clifton's diary. Were there any lunch-and-through-the-afternoon engagements coming up in the near future? Yes, of course! She was seeing Frances Munster on Wednesday. Frances had just come back from Florence, so she would be bursting with tips for Lady Clifton on her forthcoming holiday. They were meeting at 12.30 and the countess would never be back before five. 'Wednesday,' she said breathlessly, 'how about that? Otherwise things are a bit tight this week.'

'In that case I shall make sure it's all right. You seem to lead a somewhat busy life — much busier than mine, I'll be bound.'

You can say that again! thought Rose. But you'll never know what I work *at*!

The meeting with Fletcher-Simms went well — so well that Rose had constantly to remind herself she was not the daughter of an elderly academic who had moved to London on his retirement from Oxford. Somehow the role seemed to fit her perfectly: the hint of rebellion offered by her fast stockings and rakish cheroots; the apparent determination to plough her own furrow, supervising the care of a difficult, sick relative while still contriving to live the life she wanted. Mark was not the only one to be enchanted by the Rose Rush who met him at a smart little restaurant in King Street — Rose herself was half in love with the character too.

For one thing, she started on absolutely firm ground. The art gallery might pose problems, but no restaurant menu would ever do so. Rose had been assisting at Monsieur Auguste's luncheons and dinners for long enough to know every classic dish which was likely to appear on a menu, as well as the appropriate flatware with which to eat it. She knew what not to order if one wished to avoid glutinous sauces dripping down one's blouse; what to avoid if it were felt that the sound of crunching small birds' internal bones would upset one's companion. She even knew what sort of wine she liked.

Fletcher-Simms handed her a menu and said : 'I hate the

type of fellow who expects his female guest to accept what he orders for her. Tell me what you'd like from that lot.' He himself fell to studying the wine list.

Rose contemplated the menu with such happy greed that at first she did not realise he had set aside the wine list and was watching her in some amusement. 'To think I had reservations about bringing you here in case the Vales of Academe had steeped you in overdone mutton and rice pudding throughout a puritanical childhood!' he said when she looked up enquiringly.

Rose smiled. 'Ah, no, we were never like that. Father is too ill to enjoy his meals nowadays, of course, but he always kept a very civilised table. He was particularly fond of Florentine cuisine — Tuscan food in general, come to that — and I share his enthusiasm. As it happens, I was just wondering about their *frito misto* . . .'

'Ah, that's really a man's dish in this restaurant!' He was fighting not to patronise her but Rose noticed with amusement that he was losing the battle. Didn't men like women who knew as much as they did about food? It seemed an odd idea. Politics, yes. Motor mechanics, perhaps . . . far more men's topics than women's. But *food*? With the exception of establishments like Monsieur Auguste's, women did most of the cooking, after all! She bounced back: 'What's so frightening about their *frito misto*, for heaven's sake?'

He was grinning broadly now. 'Not for them the dreary northern version with a dab of calf's liver and a veal cutlet,' he said. 'They put in kidneys, brains, sweetbreads — you name it!'

'I should hope so! I'd send it back if they didn't,' she announced. 'In any case, I don't think they'd have a good strong Barbaresco sufficiently *chambré* to accompany it. Perhaps we could save it for another day and you could warn them in advance about the wine?'

He laughed. 'I think you won that round without even extending yourself. As we're now such *intimate* adversaries, don't you think we should change from Miss Rush and Mr Fletcher-Simms to Rose and Mark.'

'I should like that very much. And I warn you, if we come back for the *frito misto*, you have to eat it too!'

'Nothing would give me greater pleasure – I thrive on offal – but I've yet to see a female of your looks and spirit who could put up with it in any quantity.'

'If you don't stop throwing down challenges all over the place, I'll have brain fritters to start my meal – and they're on the menu, so don't think I'm pretending!'

Fletcher-Simms raised his hands in mock surrender. 'Very well, fair maid: I shall assume your revered parent was a French peasant farmer before finding an academic vocation, and that you acquired your strange appetites on his lonely smallholding. How about that?'

She smiled at him. 'That's better. Now, perhaps you'll let me choose my real lunch before that poor waiter dozes off? I *must* start with a dozen Colchester Natives – they beat the French oysters hollow, don't you think?' And before Fletcher-Simms had a chance to express further surprise at the sophistication of her gastronomic tastes, she had completed a tour of the menu, moving from oysters to chilled lobster soufflé and thence to saddle of venison with rowanberry sauce. 'Then if I have any room left at the end, I shall have a pineapple ice,' she concluded. 'This looks like the sort of place that would make wonderful pineapple ices!'

Mark was now openly amused at her loudly announced pleasure in good food. Even in his bohemian circle, there were still too many people in London who approached dinner as if it were one of the Seven Deadly Sins and forbore to say anything about their enjoyment or otherwise of what was put before them. Rose was well aware of the convention, but in taking on her role as arty girl-about-town had decided it was far too boring to follow the convention and deliberately overdid things in the other direction.

Fletcher-Simms handed over the wine list. 'I know what I was going to suggest,' he said, 'but you say you were interested. What shall we have?'

'Hmm, well, with the oysters and the lobster, Chablis is the only thing, really, isn't it? I'd happily stick to Burgundy for my venison and have the Beaune — but that Chateauneuf-du-Pape looks interesting, too.'

'Well done, Rose! How did you know I was so fond of it? It looks as if I shall have to order the same lunch as you to keep in step with the wine. So be it!' He snapped the leather-covered wine list shut and in due course their luncheon order was taken.

'How on earth do you expect me to walk round the National Gallery this afternoon after consuming this lot?' he asked in mock despair. 'I was having visions of a delicate little truffled omelette followed by a sorbet, with maybe hock-and-seltzer to drink.'

'Do I look like the sort of girl who'd be seen dead drinking hock-and-seltzer?'

He considered her gravely for a long moment. 'No — vintage champagne, perhaps . . . no — got it! Black velvet! That's a drink that might have been invented for you!'

She vaguely remembered Lord Clifton and some of his brother's more raffish friends sending the butler off to make black velvet, years ago, when she had been bringing in a pot of coffee for one of the guests who had temporarily given up alcohol. 'Isn't that champagne and stout mixed?' she said. 'I've never tried it . . . now *that* really doesn't strike me as a woman's drink, if there's ever been such a thing!'

'No, perhaps not — although more adventurous females have been known to quaff it by the quart. Still, there's something about the mixture of smoothness and dark sparkle that's just you, Rose. Perhaps we shall try some the day we come back for our *frito misto*.'

'Now that sounds like a really killing combination!'

Chapter Twelve

So much for dancing my way to the good life, thought Jane as she walked gloomily down Dean Street at the beginning of her evening's work. It had hardly lasted long enough for her to get some decent clothes together, let alone anything else.

At first she had been surprised at the ease with which she slid into the routine at The Silver Slipper. The girls there were not so very different from her. They came from a wide variety of backgrounds but there were certainly no runaway heiresses or dukes' wayward daughters among them. To a girl, they were ill-equipped to earn the sort of living they wanted at the jobs which would have been available to them. Dance hostessing offered a good wage for a moderately strenuous job, but possessed the added attraction of enabling them to work in pretty clothes and giving them a chance to meet the most attractive men in London. Many of them embarked on highly profitable love affairs with those men, and some — though very few — were even lucky enough to marry them.

It had suited Jane admirably. All she cared about was the pretty clothes, the good money and the freedom. True she had to work late at night, but that did not worry her. Far more important was the fact that once away from the nightclub, she was in charge of her own fate and there was no one to tell her what to do. She could sleep as late as she wished in the morning, and spend the afternoons shopping, exploring London and meeting her new workmates — in fact whatever came into her head. There was no housekeeper to order her back to her post, and no godlike family constantly impressing her with their superiority to her.

Then Harry started giving her a little trouble.

Charteris was the sort of man who liked people to remember he had done them a favour, and to be suitably co-operative when he decided it was time to call in the debt. Jane's time came soon enough. During her first few weeks, she spent a certain amount of time fending off unwelcome suggestions from her dance partners, but ten minutes' talk with the other girls convinced her that was no more than a normal hazard of the job. Harry's request was different, because although he said it politely, it came across as an order.

'I thought of dropping in with a couple of – ah – associates of mine tomorrow, sweetie,' he said with a studiedly casual air one evening. Jane had already learned to distrust that tone. It meant he was going to ask her to do something she wouldn't like. But Jane knew she still needed every friend she could get and responded politely enough. 'I expect they'll enjoy it,' she said. 'That new Blues quartet from Harlem is starting tomorrow. Don't forget to reserve a table.'

'Of course I won't, silly. But I don't think Eddie will be that interested in the band. Actually, he's – er – expressed a strong desire to meet *you*.'

'Oh, that's nice.' Jane's voice sounded small and flat, even to her own ears.

'My, such enthusiasm! What's the matter?'

'Well, why should he be so keen to meet me? I know I look all right, and I'm a good dancer – otherwise not even you could have got me this job. But I don't fool myself that I'm such a cracker men flock from miles around for a glimpse of my stocking tops.'

'No need to be vulgar, Jane. It doesn't become you, you know that. I told him about you, of course. That's why he's interested.'

'But why should you want to make him interested in me? I'm your girl, aren't I.'

'Hmm, well, yes; in a manner of speaking. But, look here, Janie, I owe this chap a number of favours. He could be extremely useful to me in the future if I make him really happy with his night out tomorrow.'

'So you want me to keep him sweet and see his champagne glass is topped up, is that it?' She knew instinctively that this was far from being it, but wanted to postpone the inevitable revelation as long as possible.

Harry was sufficiently embarrassed now to start blustering. 'Dammit, Jane, do I have to spell it out? I want you to do that, yes . . . but after I've got you properly introduced to each other, Charlie and I will probably slip away somewhere and leave you two together. I want you to really butter him up . . . you know, take him home with you . . . let him stay.'

There, he'd said it. Jane bit her lip and looked away from Harry. Bloody, bloody men! She didn't love him. Why did it hurt so much, then, that he wanted her to do this? Because he's treating you like a bottle of wine or a plate of food, that's why, she thought. Nothing to do with whether the bastard loves you . . . everything to do with him being prepared to sell you without a second thought. And where does he think your freedom to decide comes in?

'Well? Why are you playing the wronged woman all of a sudden? Surely you're not green enough to think the girls who work here only come for the dancing?'

Jane turned her gaze back to Charteris and contemplated him silently for a long time before she answered. 'Of course I know what a lot of them do. I also happen to know they choose to do it, Harry. They're not given their orders.'

His laugh was raw and contemptuous. 'If you believe that, you'll believe anything! Sure, some of them choose the way they live. But plenty of them have a big strong man back at home who tells them how many fellows they need to sleep with this week to make the books balance. D'you call that freedom to choose?'

He had shocked her — it had never occurred to her that so many of the girls were part-time tarts helping to support some idle male. But still she felt he was deliberately misrepresenting their lives. 'They've still had a choice somewhere along the line, Harry. What choice did I have? You helped me to get away from service, and I was very grateful for it, but you've had plenty of fun out of that, too, it wasn't only me. I didn't know there was a price tag and I think you should have told me there would be.'

Again the brutal laugh. 'Why the hell should I do that? A housemaid who gets whipped out of the servants' hall and set up in her own room with pretty frocks can hardly think she's being helped by a charitable patron!'

Jane was forgetting her hurt now as her anger grew. 'Do me a favour! That little adventure with me didn't cost more than pocket money by your standards! A month's rent for a pokey room in Soho, and three sequined ready-made dance dresses? An afternoon's racing at Ascot would cost you three times that and you wouldn't even notice!'

'Things are never quite what they seem, my dear. Why d'you think I spend most of my time in London staying with friends?'

'Because you can't be bothered to set yourself up in a permanent place, of course, 'specially while you've got that great pile down in Northamptonshire for weekends. What's that got to do with anything?'

He sighed. 'You still have a lot to learn, Jane, although you look so sophisticated. I could easily stay at one of my clubs rather than sponging off friends. The truth of it is, I'm just about at the end of my rope.'

'Rope? I don't understand.'

'Jane, you're so determinedly naive I'm beginning to get cross with you. I – have run – out – of – money. Is that clear enough for you?'

'B-but you can't have! Everybody who came to the Cliftons' used to go on about you being as rich as Croesus.'

'Yes, my dear. I'm no mean actor when it's a question of survival. If one needs to sponge on one's own set, it's advisable not to let them know one is in need. Amazing how generous they are when they think it's unnecessary – and how damned tight-fisted they can be when they scent penury coming on!'

'It doesn't make sense. You've got far too much ready cash to be broke.'

He made a small, irritated gesture with his hands which simultaneously excluded her from his confidence and made it clear he regarded her as incapable of understanding a gentleman's problems. 'Pocket-money! I'm talking about the sort of sums necessary to pay my tailor and bootmaker — not to mention the butcher, the baker and the candlestick maker!'

'Well, if it's that serious, what on earth is the use of bundling me into bed with some chap on the off-chance he'll help you? He's hardly likely to lend you enough to pay all that off, is he? And if he did, you'd need more money to keep it all going.' I may be bloody green, she thought, but once I get the drift of things I pick it up fast enough.

He glanced at her speculatively. 'It's not as simple as that. Actually, he might have a job for me . . . a sort of unofficial job, but one that will pay oodles.'

Now it was Jane's turn to laugh. 'I thought *I* was the one who was supposed to be green! You told me yourself you're not qualified to do anything — you were quite proud of it, remember? Who'd pay you enough to go on living the high life for what you can do?'

'A couple of months ago, I might have been tempted to take the same point of view,' said Charteris, smiling at the memory. 'Then I met Eddie Anderton and we changed one another's outlooks.'

'And Eddie Anderton is this bloke you're pairing me up with, no doubt.'

He nodded. 'You're not going to get sticky now you know how important it is, are you, old thing?' He was using his most persuasive tone, which would normally have given Jane considerable satisfaction. Tonight it left her unmoved.

She shrugged. 'I dare say I could get used to the idea — but I don't like it, Harry, and I'm sure it won't work. Oh, and another thing — don't ask me to do anything like this again. This time is because I owe you, but after this we're quits, all right?'

'All right. First and last, I promise. But you really have missed the point. You're a gorgeous girl, darling, but don't imagine I'm thinking that merely lining you up for him will swing it. I'm working hard at showing him I can fix whatever he wants, and provide the best. You're one part of it; my stately acres are another. I'm taking him to my club tomorrow and I shall make damned sure we happen to run into some very influential people there. By the time we've gone through the whole Grand Tour, he'll be putty in my hands.'

Jane shook her head. 'I'm sorry, I just don't understand. Why should any of that get you this job with him?'

'Because it shows him I can lay on what he wants, of course. He's an industrialist and he's always got great crowds of potential clients coming over from foreign countries. His products are good, but there are plenty of others in the same field. So he's hit on this idea of having a tame aristo – yours truly, I hope – who will wine and dine them and fix them up with the prettiest girls in London, take them shooting and to the races using his country mansion as a base, and generally treat them as if they were English lords re-living the high Edwardian summer. I think the man's a genius to think of it, and I'd give my eye teeth to be in on the ground floor. Apart from anything else, I have a feeling I shall be very good at it – very good indeed.'

Jane stared at him, her contempt growing as she thought through his project. 'Yeah, p'raps you would,' she said. 'It's only fair, really, if you're turning me into a tart, that you become one yourself.'

For a moment she thought he would hit her. 'How dare you?' he finally grated out through clenched teeth. 'I've never taken talk like that from anyone, let alone a . . . a . . .'

'Go on, Harry, say it – a jumped-up housemaid. Maybe it takes a tart to know a tart. At least I'm not afraid to tell you what I think of you. You're afraid to do the same with me, aren't you, because I'm the tastiest bit of crumpet you can lay hands on at such short notice who'll go along with your nasty little game. You can't be too rude to me until after I've done what you want, can you?'

'That's nonsense!' But his manner shouted that she had interpreted his motives with complete accuracy.

They parted early that evening. Once Charteris had finished outlining his strategy for a secure future, a chilly silence descended on them. Jane was surprised at her own reaction. Until now, though not in love with Harry, she had enjoyed his company and taken pleasure in their lovemaking. Alone in her big double bed after Charteris left, she conducted an interminable argument with herself about why she felt so wretched.

What had she expected when she left Belgrave Square? She was alone, defenceless, with nothing except her own wits to protect her. She knew there were wolves out in the streets, no less ferocious because they wore clean white shirts and business suits and went on two legs instead of four. She knew Charteris was a temporary stop along her road. Above all she knew – or should have known – that once she was sexually compromised and working on the fringes of café society, she could expect to have to defend herself. So why was she so demoralised merely because Charteris had run to type and betrayed her? One betrayal was much the same as another, and although the nature of this treachery was unexpected, it was no worse or better than any other. With that thought fixed firmly in her head, Jane thumped her pillow back into shape and composed herself for sleep.

Eddie Anderton gave her no trouble. The self-made millionaire son of a provincial carpenter, he had been apprenticed early to a Birmingham engineer and learned his trade with admirable speed. At twenty-one he was a self-employed workshop proprietor, at twenty-five he bought his first factory and at thirty made his first million as a small arms manufacturer. After that he had never looked back. His fortune expanded as explosively as his products performed, but his tastes remained firmly embedded in his humble lower middle-class origins. He was a business genius and he had swiftly recognised that Charteris was exactly what he had in mind to run the odd, unofficial department he wanted to institute in his company. He liked to think of it as his customer relations department, but was far too reticent to use the term in public. He had decided to employ Charteris more than a week earlier, but saw no reason why he should not keep the man in suspense for long enough to sample the delights which would in future be offered to his clients.

When he saw Jane Ellis, he could hardly believe his luck. Anderton was in his early forties, physically fit and vigorous, with a sexual appetite sharpened by fifteen years of marriage to a worthy, shapeless female whose attractions had included a well-capitalised father and a large marriage settlement. She had – reluctantly – transferred her allegiance from the Methodist to the Anglican Church, but apart from that she remained determinedly a member of the solid, respectable classes who found physical pleasure closely akin to wickedness.

Jane was a mass of glossy hair, smooth skin and curvy flesh, a great deal of which was visible above and below the brief dance frock she wore. Apart from a slight lilt in her speech, she sounded reasonably cultivated, but Anderton knew instinctively that she came from similar roots to his own. That drew him even more strongly. She flirted with him, constantly topped up his champagne glass, taught him the Charleston – he had been far too busy earning millions to take lessons when the dance swept the country in the 1920s – and nuzzled close to him like an affectionate kitten when they got into a taxi for the brief drive back to her lodgings.

He bounded into the big bed with her, passion undimmed by the considerable quantity of alcohol he had consumed, and treated Jane to a boisterous, laughter-filled night. When the early sunlight spilled over the adjoining rooftops, she got up and made a pot of strong tea, which she served in thick mugs, heavily sweetened. He took a deep draught from the cup and then turned back to give Jane a big, smacking kiss. 'You're a lovely kid,' he said, 'I don't want just to disappear and leave you like this – you're too much fun. Look . . . I've never done this sort of thing before – too busy, I s'pose,' he added, sheepishly, 'but I think we'd get on great. If I found us a little place where I could come and see you, would you be — y'know — interested? I'd take care of all the expenses, o' course. Wouldn't want you to have to go on working in that old job.'

Jane was studying him carefully over the top of her tea mug. 'Are you sure this isn't just 'cos you got a really nice jump off after a long time, and we had fun?'

Anderton shook his head. 'You can get that anywhere, love, if you're in the mood. No — you make me laugh; and you make me feel twenty. Funny, that. When I *was* twenty, I always felt about forty-five!'

Jane put down her cup, leaned across and kissed him, almost chastely, on the forehead. 'I don't think so, Andy. Maybe I should have met you in a different way, I dunno . . . whatever it is, I like you too much for this.' She gestured around her at the obvious tart's bedroom they occupied. 'You'd never be able to forget this, would you? And the daft thing is, I've only been here about a month. I was ever so respectable before that. And I'll tell you something — we'd never have met at all if I'd stayed respectable.'

Anderton was bewildered. 'I don't care about any of that. I like you. I want to spend a lot of time with you and I don't want to share you with anyone else. Now, what d'you say? Are you on?'

Jane thought of Charteris; thought of the job she knew he already had. Her own native intelligence had led her to that conclusion within minutes of her first conversation with Anderton. Harry couldn't see the man was pushing him around a bit and keeping him in suspense; she could. And she knew she would never fit into a world which included Charteris in the role Anderton had in mind for him, and herself in the role he had assigned to her.

'No, Andy. I think you're smashing, but it really is the wrong time and place. I had a lovely night with you — never a dull moment — but I want to keep it like that. Too many loose ends, love. It'd never work, believe me.'

He shook his head. 'I think you're wrong, but I'm not

going to push you. I think people have been pushing you since before you were old enough to walk about on your own.' He fell silent for a while as he digested the logic of what he had said to her, then he added, 'Get away from this lot, though. That Harry isn't gonna leave you alone, you know that. You're one of his best assets. Get out from under before he gets used to you, there's a good girl.'

Her laugh was forced. 'Oh, yeah, just like that! To what? At least I'm earning enough to keep this place going and Harry isn't too hard to handle.'

'He will be, believe me. Give him a few months to get used to the job I got in mind for him, and you'll be on tap twenty-four hours a day. Come to me, or get away from him some other way, but don't stay, whatever you've got to do.'

She stared at him. 'You do know what you're saying, don't you?'

He nodded mutely.

'Why d'you think I'd be better off making my own way? It's a cruel world.'

'I know, Jane. I been out in it since I was twelve, remember? I don't think girls are that different.'

'Oh, yes, we are. We've only got one thing to sell.'

'So bloody go and sell it! The one thing you learn when you start out on your own, is that if you got any sense, next year you won't still be doing what you're doing now. And the cleverer you are, the more likely it is you'll be doing something else. Just remember, all any of us can work with is what we got. If all you got is what you're sitting on, girl, that's what you use. But only use it till you get a chance at something better. Some of the great business tragedies have been because people haven't known when to move on. 'Course, you could still change your mind and come with me.'

Jane was close to tears, but she swallowed them and said: 'No chance, you tough old bastard. You're right, and you know it. Now come over here and gimme a cuddle before you go off and become a respectable business tycoon again.'

* * *

The next evening Jane arrived for her evening's work at The Silver Slipper and handed in her notice to the nightclub manager. He gave her a surprised look. 'Why d'you want to go? You're a very popular hostess. We'll miss you. Has one of the regulars been annoying you?'

She shook her head. 'No, Mr Laszlo. It's something personal, really. Everyone's treated me well here. I just need to move on.'

'All right, dear. But if you fancy coming back, pop in and see me, okay? You're good, and you don't make a fuss. I'll always find a place for you.'

Touched, she leaned forward and kissed his cheek. He grinned. 'Well, if it's bribery you got in mind, maybe we should re-negotiate your pay!'

Jane winked at him as she departed. 'Come on, Joe! I happen to know there are seven little Laszlos back in Camden, all waiting for Daddy to bring back the porridge!'

A week later she put on the most garish make-up she had ever applied, and started parading up and down Shaftesbury Avenue where she accosted men and took them to her room to copulate with them in exchange for a reasonably high hourly rate of pay.

Chapter Thirteen

On balance, Jane decided, she had preferred life as a dance hostess. But her new occupation was still a lot better than domestic service and she made five times as much money as she ever had at The Silver Slipper.

As long as she stuck to Piccadilly and Shaftesbury Avenue, she was safe from assault by other girls who resented an invasion of their patch. The streets of Soho seemed to belong to a specialist crowd — girls who looked dangerous, who claimed French or Italian names and hinted they were ready for all sorts of odd behaviour if the customer was prepared to pay. Jane soon learned from the regulars that Piccadilly was one of London's safer patches. Around here and down the Haymarket, you got a steady stream of respectable, prosperous men from the provinces, whose only real sexual problem was that they were not able to get it when they wanted it. The girls who swarmed the pavements and so annoyed the more innocent sort of tourist were young and personable and were seldom required to do more than what the men would have asked of their wives, had they dared.

'Looking at this lot, you'd never believe a whore got old,' Jane told her new acquaintance Minna Lennard one evening a they strolled towards the Eros statue.

Minna hooted with mirth. 'Course not, you daft thing — go an' take a look around the main railway stations or go up Islington or Camden . . . place is swarming with old slags, but you never see 'em down here. When they start going to the dogs a bit, they seem to sense it. Probably stop getting as many tricks as they used to. One thing you learn fast in this game — there's always someone who'll pay you for it, as long as the price is right. When you start falling apart, you just move where the lights ain't so bright and the competition's not up to much.'

Jane shuddered. 'God forbid that should ever happen to me! Doesn't it scare the daylights out of you just thinking about it?'

'Of course it does! Trick is to get out while the going's good. You'll hear half the brasses along the 'dilly saying that to you, mind, but I mean it. I started off as a shopgirl up Oxford Street. I still live on the same money they paid me there and I put all the rest in savings.' She giggled at a memory. 'I even got one a my Joes to advise me, once. He was a head clerk in a bank. Told me about the right savings accounts and so on.' She seized Jane's arm and squeezed it with the fierce enthusiasm of an excited child. 'The minute I got enough I'm gonna buy meself a pub – in the country, mind, none a your London rubbish – and retire to a life of respectability.'

'Gawd, you certainly believe in planning ahead, don't you?' Jane was deeply impressed. She was putting aside some of her money, but at present it resided in a biscuit tin in her chest of drawers, not in a savings bank. Perhaps she should make a plan for her own future.

Minna said: 'Listen, kid, you're new at all this and there's an awful lot can go wrong at the beginning. Once it does, everything will go to hell. Take a couple a tips from me: save every bit of spare cash – in the bank, not at home, mind – and steer clear of the pimps. Once a girl gets lumbered with a pimp she can forget any future beyond the Essex Road or Camden High Street.'

At first it seemed easy enough to follow Minna's advice. Jane was immune to the charms of the loudly dressed, thuggish young men who strutted the Soho streets displaying a spurious masculinity which existed only because it was underpinned by the earnings of prostitutes. Such males held no physical appeal for her. She was always drawn to upper-class playboy types rather than imitation Apaches. She opened a savings account and was surprised at the amount of cash in her biscuit tin when she counted it out before making her first deposit.

Then she met a man who set aside her preconceptions about pimps looking like second-hand Rudolph Valentinos. He was dressed in classic gentlemanly style — conservative jacket in a good tweed, impeccably cut; old-fashioned hand-made shoes; nondescript tie. He was enjoying a late afternoon drink at one of Ma Meyrick's West End clubs where she sometimes called for a pick-me-up before starting her evening's work.

When she ordered her usual large gin and tonic, he said, barely looking up from his own glass, 'Put the lady's drink on my tab, Gerry.'

Jane knew Gerry the barman quite well by now and trusted his judgement, but for some reason she never understood, she chose to ignore the barely visible shake of the head he gave as he looked across at her. Why should Gerry be all-knowing all of a sudden? This chap was just what she liked: clean hair; clear complexion; strong profile; expensive clothes. She turned and smiled brightly at him. 'Isn't it a little early in the day for a chap to be buying a girl's drinks for her?'

He looked at her directly for the first time and her stomach tilted slightly. 'Not if he thinks it may be the only chance he ever gets. Did anyone ever tell you that you have an extremely winning smile, Miss — er . . .?'

'Just call me Jane. Everyone else does. There are lots of winning smiles around. What's so special about mine?'

He leaned back on his bar stool and made much of studying her. 'Don't know . . . something special, that's all. I don't think I want you to move on anywhere else, Jane, even if you were planning to.'

'Well, I have to move some time. Can't prop up Ma's bar forever, you know, however pleasant the thought may be.'

'Not even if I asked you as an extra-special favour?'

Time to let him know how you pay the rent, she told herself, however much you'd like to pretend it wasn't.

'A girl has to earn a living.'

'Ah, yes. Thought so.' Dammit, thought Jane, was it *that* obvious?

'I'm James Teal,' he went on. 'Don't worry about the rest of the evening. I'm sure we can sort out something between us.' He stared into her face and she was transfixed by the crystalline blueness of his eyes. 'After all, you can't work every minute of every day, can you now?'

Even as they moved over to one of the luxurious banquettes along the back wall of the cocktail bar, Jane knew there was something not quite right about him. But he was simply too good-looking for her to pay attention to the danger signals. Wrong-wrong-wrong! her sixth sense shrieked at her. Gerry was still sending her warning signals too, but she chose to ignore them. There was something about this man . . . something she had to have. Jane took a long swallow of her gin and tonic and ignored the pricking of her thumbs.

They stayed at Ma's for an hour or so, then her new friend said: 'How about a bite of supper or something? Don't want to stay here . . . it never warms up until after eleven, anyway.'

They ended up in the inevitable small Soho French restaurant. Jane had almost lost count of the shy punters who had suggested a visit to one of these places before the inevitable confrontation back in her room. For some reason, the dispensation of mounds of foreign food seemed to calm their nerves. This one seemed to need no calming influences, though. He was full of himself — and full of appeal for Jane.

She never could remember the details of the silly badinage they exchanged over their *soupe à l'oignon* and sole *dieppoise*. She was too bewitched by the icy-blue intensity of his eyes and the tanned strength of his wrist as he poured the wine. When they had finished their coffee, she was almost desperate to get him back to her room.

They walked arm in arm along Frith Street and she said: 'What takes someone like you to Ma Meyrick's at that hour of the day? I'd have thought you'd have far more important fish to fry.'

'Oh, a business meeting that didn't take off, that's all,' he answered airily. Surreptitiously, Jane looked again at his clothes. He hadn't been planning any business meeting in that outfit . . . that was rich boy's come-out-to-play uniform. Why was she being so trusting? If ever she'd seen trouble, this was it.

But it made no difference. The planes of his face reflected in the raw light of the street lamps; the expensive, straight-across crop of his hair; the clean smell of expensive soap, and above all those unique eyes, had taken her prisoner. She knew there was something wrong about him, but he was irresistible.

She barely had time to close the door of her room before he was on her, perfectly sculpted mouth pressing along her throat and shoulder as if he had rehearsed the act countless times. He pushed her gently back against the wall and ran his hands down her body. 'Mmm, everything in its place and just enough of it,' he murmured.

Just like a salesman checking out his goods, was Jane's last thought before she surrendered herself deliciously to his embrace.

He was the lover she might have expected Harry Charteris to be; the lover who would have saved her had he been Eddie Anderton. But he was James Teal, and James Teal was a singular creature.

He eased the skimpy silk frock down her shoulders and kissed her again, as before, on the soft flesh of her body rather than her lips. There was something about that, something so sensual she found it almost unbearable. She turned her face up to his and then his lips clamped over hers, his tongue probing inside her mouth while his fingers went on easing the dress from her body.

In moments she was standing before him in nothing but a brief pair of silk panties and her stockings, rolled just above her knees to avoid the need for garters or suspenders. He knelt in front of her and peeled each stocking from her leg, peppering her calves with butterfly-light kisses as he did so. Then he stood up and pressed the panties down over her hips, until they were sufficiently low for her to kick free of them. He was still fully clothed, but now pressed her to him, his hands exploring her freely as he kissed her cheeks and eyelids.

Jane was almost incoherent by now. 'Undress,' she moaned, 'please, darling, take your clothes off. I want to touch you all over.'

'You do it for me. Give yourself a treat.'

She started with his tie, slowly undoing the knot and casting it away somewhere behind her. Then she unbuttoned the shirt before turning her attention to his jacket. Once it was off, she buried her face against his chest and murmured, 'Please, James, take the rest off − I want you so much.'

'No − you. It's more fun.'

With increasingly frantic fingers, she finished undoing the shirt and moved to unbutton his fly. His hand stopped her. 'No, no!' There was a teasing note in his voice. 'Men look so silly stark naked when they still have shoes and socks on, don't you think? First things first!' He sat down on the edge of the bed and she knelt before him, slavishly, to unlace his shoes and remove his socks.

He laughed again. 'There! Now virtue gets its reward!' And he pulled her up level with him, guiding her hands back to his trouser fastenings.

His body had the most beautiful golden tan she had ever seen. Jane caught herself wondering momentarily how he had managed to achieve such a colour, then his sheer beauty swamped her and she leaned forward to engulf his mouth in her own.

Teal pulled her across him and drew her down so that she lay along the length of his body. 'Mmm, you're as soft as a piece of velvet,' he said. 'What little tricks are you going to show me now?' Again the danger signal. Tricks? She was so excited she would have done anything to have him possess her and he was discussing little tricks she might try . . . but before she could fully realise the extent of his detachment, he had shifted her body so that his big, stiff penis was trapped between her thighs. 'There,' he murmured, 'what would you like to do with that?' And before she could respond, he had lifted her in some way she could not understand, and impaled her on himself. She writhed with pleasure at the unexpectedly abrupt invasion of her body, moaning and reaching out in an attempt to press herself down on him again. But Teal preferred to have her sitting astride him and pinned her upright above him, thrusting himself up into her with a prodigious strength which seemed inexhaustible.

Jane had never experienced anything to compare with this insistent, repetitive push of maleness. Just as she felt she would collapse under the assault, he turned her body and she found herself under him. Instead of spending himself in her, he slid away and began running his hands over her with a smooth rhythmic motion compulsively reminiscent of the brief, dynamic penetration, which made her long for him to enter her again.

Moments later, she was electrified by the pressure of his lips as they moved over the flesh of her breasts, belly and thighs, with a delicate biting motion, ending only as he pressed his face deep between her legs and slid his tongue up into the warm, moist flesh of her vulva. He was out of her again before she went through the huge orgasm which was boiling up within her, and finally pressed his full weight on her small body, burying his penis in her again and bringing the whole act to an explosively pleasurable climax.

Jane fell back against the mounded pillows, sobbing in sheer exhilaration. She was too far gone fully to realise that Teal seemed less disoriented than she. Eventually, reaching up and trailing a limp hand down his back, she murmured: 'I never did anything like that before.'

His laugh was mundane, out of step with her exalted mood. 'What, when you make a living at this sort of thing?'

To her mortification, Jane felt herself blushing. 'I-I didn't mean that . . . I meant it had never been like that for me before.'

Abruptly, he appeared to collect himself, eased away from her and began stroking her hair. 'Forgive me, my pet, I can be a brute at times. It was pretty marvellous for me, too, you know. Tell me where everything is and I'll make us some tea or coffee..'

'Then you're not leaving?' She cursed herself for the leaping relief in her tone which must have been as audible to him as it was to her. What a fool to let him know how cock-a-hoop she was about him.

'Never love a lady and leave her, it's impolite,' he said, laughing, then added: 'And, anyway, you're such a gorgeous little baggage I don't think I'd have the strength of will to go yet.'

Jane's idyll lasted a week before she realised she had fallen victim to one of the oldest tricks in the book – she had acquired a pimp.

In spite of having known from the beginning there had been something not quite right about Teal, she was sufficiently besotted by him to ignore the first warning signs. They had started even before she got to know the man, she remembered later. Gerry the barman had spent half an hour trying to capture her attention and tell her to stay away from James, but she had stayed away from Gerry instead. After that, it was impossible to ignore the fact that Teal appeared to have fewer social or professional obligations than any man of his type Jane had met so far. She had known plenty of his sort who had no need to work for a living; half Lord Clifton's friends fell into that category. But their days were as full as if they occupied posts in the City or the Law Courts. They went racing, looked in at their clubs, spent plenty of time in the country hunting or shooting, and seemed set on an unending round of social calls, plays, concerts and dinner parties.

James Teal was the genuine article, she would have laid bets on it. She had not spent years below stairs seeing the boot-boy clean the hand-made shoes of the Clifton men every evening without learning to recognise the shape and cut of the most expensive footwear. She was accustomed to putting away woollens and linen of the quality worn by Teal and could spot the difference between best and third rate at fifty paces in bad light. She would have sworn he got his hair cut at Trumpers in Curzon Street — no other barber could achieve quite that air of expensive Englishness — and his talk, though peppered with all the current slang, rested on an authentic old Etonian accent.

All of which was strange, because had it not been for these totems, she would have been sure he was an extremely attractive guttersnipe.

After their first night together, he stayed for three days. Naturally, Jane spent her time with him and that meant no Piccadilly strolling, no customers and no earnings. Mentally she shrugged. So what? Since her chat with Minna Lennard she had been saving like mad. She had enough put away to take a little holiday. Nevertheless, when the third night had passed and still James showed no sign of any plan to depart, she became edgy. So far he had left her only to go to his own place — which he vaguely designated as 'nearer the River than this' — and pick up more clothes. They went out together to eat at restaurants, and he paid the bills.

Theoretically she had no cause for concern, passionately involved with him as she was. That, little girl, is beside the point, she told herself as she sat at her mirror, applying what she thought of as her professional make-up for her first working night that week. He's said nothing about any permanent arrangement, and I can't assume he intends paying my way in future — not unless he asks me straight out, and he hasn't yet. It's not as if he doesn't know what I do for a living.

That in itself gave her further cause for concern. Harry Charteris had placed any job Jane might do on the same level — housemaid, dance hostess, tart they were all the same to him, and all contemptible. He would never have considered moving in with Jane; that would have been letting the side down in some obscure way. She did not understand the reasoning behind it but she understood the outcome easily enough. The conventions said he could set her up in a flat and spend a lot of time there with her. That was slightly naughty, man-about-town activity, nothing worse. But it would be highly irregular for him to live in the flat with her instead of merely visiting when he felt like it. That was definitely not acceptable behaviour among the best people. Actually moving into a tart's room with her must rank as the lowest depth to which a man could sink – and that was what James Teal seemed perfectly content to do.

Jane was able to put aside the problem for a while, because when James came in and saw her preparing for work, he grinned broadly and said: 'Don't worry, darling. I get the message. I shall make myself scarce. Don't worry about my turning up here tonight and wrecking things.' He seemed quite cheerful about the whole thing. They might have been talking about her conducting a home sewing circle. Momentarily, Jane wished he would make a fuss; tell her he didn't want her going with other men; say to hell with it, he'd find her a cosy little place to live and subsidise her if she went back to being a dance hostess at The Silver Slipper. Then her innate realism re-asserted itself. If there had been any likelihood of that, he'd have suggested it long before this. Time to go back to work, and sort out the conundrum of who or what James Teal was later on.

He did not return for six days. For the first two, Jane felt nothing beyond a vague sense of displacement at not having him near when he had been in her pocket for almost four days. Then she began to miss him in earnest, and to worry about him. She went to the two restaurants which seemed to be his favourite Soho haunts, but there was no sign of him and she was too proud to ask the waiters if he had been in. Then, reluctantly, she went back to Ma Meyrick's Forty-Two Club. Gerry obviously knew a lot more about James Teal than she did. He might even know where her lover was now. She had held back this long only because she did not really want to know more about James's background.

It was as if Gerry had read her mind. Her gin and tonic was poured and waiting for her as she drew up one of the high bar stools. 'Disappeared?' he said laconically.

Jane nodded. 'You don't sound surprised. Does he make a habit of it?'

'From time to time, dear, I believe he does. Always comes back, though, and he's seldom gone longer than a week.' He paused, waiting for her to ask more questions. Jane only gave him a weary grin. 'No, Gerry, I don't really want to know more about him — not yet, anyway. I know it's daft, but I dare say we all make fools of ourselves now and again.'

His answering smile was sympathetic. 'Of course we do,' he said, 'but just remember, when you *do* decide it's time you knew, I can fill you in on him. Oh, and Jane, there's something else . . .'

'Do I need to know this?' she asked, her stomach lurching at the prospect of bad news.

'I'm afraid you do. Be careful with him. He really *is* an English gentleman, but remember, some English gentlemen have very funny habits. Believe me, I wouldn't be warning you like this if I didn't think it was important.'

'But he can't do anything to me . . . this is London in the twentieth century. I'm free to do as I please, aren't I?'

'Are you? That's more than most of us can say, I'll bet. Take my word: *be careful*. Just don't get off alone with him anywhere out of earshot of plenty of people, that's all.'

'All? What are you saying?'

He glanced around the bar, which was still almost empty because it was so early, and leaned towards her. 'Really, Jane, why don't you let me tell you? I can't just go on saying "heed the gypsy's warning" all night, can I?'

'No, you're right. I'll think about it, Gerry.' She gazed morosely into her gin glass as he turned away to serve two new arrivals. The men wanted complicated cocktails, and Gerry spent some time assembling and mixing the ingredients. Jane sat brooding for a few minutes, then muttered to herself, 'It's no good — I don't want to know,' drained her glass, stood up, called, 'Cheerio, Gerry, be seeing you!' then turned away and hurried out before he could move to intercept her.

Chapter Fourteen

It had been a long, hard night, one that Jane preferred to put out of her mind even more speedily than usual. At two in the morning, she walked tiredly back into Soho from her final trick at the Regent Palace Hotel — never an arrangement she liked because it involved such demeaning dodging of the hotel staff to get to the client's room. As she came out of the last side street and turned the corner towards her building, she glanced up instinctively at her bedroom window. The light was on.

She tried to control the violent trembling which seized her as she hurried up the steep staircase to the top floor. It was all too likely that she had forgotten to switch off the light . . . she sometimes did forget. Yes, and you know you gave James a key, too, mocked an inner voice. You're acting like a baby because you hope he's there. Pull yourself together, you little fool, don't let him see what a hold he's got on you.

Her instinct proved accurate. He was back. He seemed not to hear her high heels clattering up the staircase, or the sound of the front door lock clicking as she let herself in. What on earth was he doing?

Teal stood near the window, bending over Jane's open chest of drawers. Underwear and blouses were scattered on the bed behind him, but he appeared to have stopped rummaging now. 'What are you doing?' she asked, still more bewildered than angry at the intrusion.

He straightened and turned towards her, his face set in a strange, tight expression which chilled her to the bone. 'Perhaps you'd care to explain this?' he said, raising his hand and brandishing the biscuit tin she used as a moneybox.

'Explain? Why?' She was utterly confused now.

He stormed towards her. 'I'll tell you why — because

there's just ten pounds in there, that's why! What have you been doing this week — lying in bed on your own all day eating chocolates? And where's the rest?'

The reason for his inquisition was beginning to penetrate at last. Even now, though, Jane was reluctant to believe it, and she hedged. 'There's ten pounds in the tin because I went to pay the rest into my account yesterday, and that's last night's money. As for the rest, I don't know what you're on about.'

'Don't you dare lie to me, you whore! You've been on the game now — what? — three months? With a face and body like yours, you must be coining it. Where have you put it? You girls always tuck away their takings somewhere like this, so tell me where the money is before I take everything in this room apart.'

What he said was made worse by the deceptive softness with which the words were uttered. Anyone just out of earshot would have thought he was expressing affection or having a peaceful conversation. At point blank range it gave the words an added edge of horror. Jane was terrified, but determined to stand her ground. 'It's not your concern, but since you're so keen to know, it's all in the bank, earning me a bit of interest. I've got no intention of staying on the game until I rot, I promise you.'

He was very close to her now and it was all she could do not to flinch, for she was convinced he would hit her. Instead, he smiled lopsidedly and said: 'Who's a clever girl? As long as it's safe.' He turned away from her and replaced the biscuit tin in the drawer, without removing the ten pounds. Then he picked up the jumble of clothes on the bed and folded them with surprising care, replacing them in proper order as if he remembered exactly where everything had been. After that he came back to Jane and said: 'It's so good to see you again, darling — I have had the devil of a week, nothing but work, work and more work!'

'At what? You never got round to telling me what you actually do, James.'

'Oh, dealing of course. A word here, a word there, a top-level meeting in some other place, and then the cash starts flowing . . . dull stuff, I assure you, but it pays the bills.'

'Hmm, is that why you were so concerned about *my* bit of money?'

His laugh was dismissive. 'Oh, that was rather silly of me! One of my cronies told me about some silly little female who kept all her money around the house and got robbed blind the other day. I was suddenly scared you might have done the same and it became something of an obsession — hence the mess.'

They both knew she did not believe him, but beneath her outrage, Jane still felt the irresistible pull of his sexual allure and, at least for the moment, she let the matter rest. As she stood indecisively before him, he moved towards her like a big, sleek panther, and in seconds his hands were sliding over her shoulders and neck, easing away her doubt and fear in a surge of renewed sexual attraction. That night he made love to her with even more passionate expertise than before, and when he shook her awake soon after dawn, she thought it was a prelude to further pleasure.

Abruptly, she realised he had twisted her arms behind her back. 'Up — out!' he hissed at her. 'Time for naughty little girls to learn a lesson!'

Jane could not remember ever having been so frightened. He was not hurting her — yet — but his grip on her crossed arms was so sure that she was incapable of breaking it. Her imagination was already far ahead of her. What did he plan to do to her, and why? Her mind was still foggy about last night and if she had not forgotten his strange, intrusive behaviour, it was certainly still muffled by drowsiness.

Not for long, though. Within seconds James had twisted her out of bed on to the floor, and then virtually tumbled her across to the little stick-backed chair in front of the dressing table. Only then did he loosen his grip on her arms. Momentarily freeing her, he grabbed her again by the wrists and pressed her hands, palms down, on the dressing table. 'Jimmy, what are you doing? What the bloody hell are you playing at?' she cried in mounting panic.

He was panting, with excitement rather than exertion. 'Keep still,' he said, so ominously that her hands froze where he had placed them. Dear God, the man was mad! That was what Gerry had been trying to tell her, and what she had been so determined to ignore.

Belatedly, her sense of self-preservation came into play and she moved to withdraw her exposed hands from the position where he had spread them.

'I said no, you bitch!' he almost screamed, and then she realised he was holding a flexible tapering bamboo cane. As its significance dawned on Jane, he brought down the cane with all his strength across her knuckles. The pain and the surprise were so intense that they froze her hands in position. After that there seemed to be nothing in the room — in the world — except the whirling cane slashing down again and again on her hands, and the terrible pain which sliced through her whole body with every blow. His assault was so abrupt, so unexpected and so agonising that she actually began to lose consciousness and slip down out of the chair without making a further attempt to move her hands.

He wrenched her upright again, turning her by her hair as he did so, into a position where she was facing him directly. The additional pain in her scalp dragged her back to full consciousness and she found herself looking directly into his face. That was when she lost hope of getting away from him. The face was set in an almost idiot expression of glee, and his eyes were flat, glazed, and fixed on some imperceptible horizon. Whatever he was seeing, it was not Jane Ellis, his new lover. It was some helpless victim born to suffer at his hands throughout eternity, and there seemed no end to his plans for making that suffering fill the infinite time available to him.

Jane wriggled against his grip on her hair. There was a whistling sound and the cane cut downward again, this time not on her hands, but across her legs immediately below the knee. He continued to thrash her between knees and ankles for at least five minutes, the longest five minutes in Jane's life, then she passed out.

When she opened her eyes, Jane found it difficult to believe it possible that she could be suffering so much pain in so many different places. The events of the early morning came back to her before she opened her eyes, and she lay completely still for a long time without daring to move, in case he began thrashing her again. Eventually she peeped through squinched-up eyelids, trying desperately to see without being seen. She was lying on her left side, on the left-hand side of the bed, facing the window. Bright sunlight poured through the uncurtained glass, illuminating a scene of apparent normality. Where was he? Had he really gone? It seemed too good to be true.

It was. As she dared to stretch to her full length and open her eyes, a hand pressed against her shoulder. 'Hallo, darling,' murmured the now terrifying voice. 'You slept so long I thought you might manage the whole twenty-four hours.' And then, while she was still lying beside him seized with terror at what he might do next, he turned her over to face him and began making love to her as if nothing had happened between them to cause any discord. Jane was far too frightened to resist him, but the tricks and talents which had pleased her so much until twelve hours ago now left her unmoved or actively repelled her. Each time she opened her eyes, the angle of his head or body would jolt her into remembrance of what he had done to her since their last love-making, and she wanted to kill him.

Teal seemed unaware of her revulsion. When he had performed his great lover routine, he slid away from her, sighing luxuriously, and murmured, 'You are the most adorable girl, Janey. I'm *so* glad we met.'

She held her breath, desperately seeking a neutral answer which would not infuriate him again, but would not make her feel she had colluded with his sadism. She could find nothing to say. Fortunately, it did not matter. Presumably the combination of the beating and the love-making had satisfied him sufficiently to blunt his sensibilities. Now he dozed off to sleep as abruptly as she had fallen into unconsciousness earlier.

Jane lay absolutely still for an interminable period. He had turned slightly once or twice to take pressure off an arm or leg muscle, but clearly he was enjoying a deep, untroubled slumber. She eased out of bed, intending to grab an armful of clothes and creep into her tiny kitchen to dress. To her dismay she found herself sliding towards the floor. Her legs refused to support her. Biting back tears, she forced herself upright and propelled herself across to the little chair where he had inflicted so much pain on her. From there, clinging to the edge of her dressing table, she managed to circumnavigate the room until she reached the kitchen door, and staggered through it. On her way she had managed to salvage a pair of stockings and panties, a dress and a pair of shoes. She was never sure afterwards how she had carried the bundle of clothing, because her fingers hurt more than her legs.

She looked longingly at the kettle. A cup of tea would go down so well . . . but no. If she stopped for that, he might wake up. More likely, she would start hurting too much to finish dressing before her strength ran out. Ignoring the tea things, Jane gritted her teeth and started to pull on her stockings.

'Dear God, Jane, why didn't you listen to me?' Gerry remembered to whisper the words but his tone suggested he wanted to shout at the top of his voice.

'All right, Gerry, I know I was pigheaded but I'm here now aren't I? What time d'you get off?'

'Not until the end of the evening. You can't possibly hang around that late in the state you're in. Look, tell you what' – he looked at his watch – 'I've got a half-hour break in about forty minutes' time. I'll mix you a great big drink and bring it to you in that far booth over the other side. Nobody'll bother you there this early. When I get my break, you come out the back and share my supper, then I'll tell you what you've been playing with. After that, we'll make some plans for looking after you tonight, okay?'

Jane nodded dumbly. She had used up all her strength

in dressing and getting round to the Forty-Two, and now she had no idea what she would do next.

At seven thirty, Gerry took his break, collecting her from the booth where she had been nodding and half-drowsing over the biggest brandy she had ever seen. He ushered her out to the staff room at the back of the club and went to collect a plate of food from the kitchen. He returned with a smaller plate for her, tricked out with tiny tastes of the rarer delicacies on the club menu.

'I knew you wouldn't be up to anything like boeuf bourgignon in your state, dear, so I just got you some snacks. Now eat up, for God's sake, or I can see you passing out on me.'

His slightly bullying kindness was just what she needed, and she picked away with a certain amount of enthusiasm at the canapés on her plate. After a while, she fixed him with a direct gaze and said: 'All right, Gerry, I'm as ready as I'll ever be. Spill the beans.'

He shrugged. 'Just remember, we all make fools of ourselves sometimes. You're no better or worse than the rest of us, love. Let's just hope you've had a chance to learn your lesson early.'

By the time he finished telling her what he knew of James Teal's life story, Jane was torn between nausea and overwhelming gratitude that she was still alive. Not that Teal was on record as actually having killed anyone yet, but it had been a near-run thing on various occasions.

She was right about Teal's exalted origins, Gerry told her. James was a peer's son, educated at the best schools and then at Cambridge, finished off with a couple of terms at the Sorbonne. That was where the first breath of scandal had touched him. Gerry had heard on the clubland grapevine that Teal had been extricated only with great difficulty by his father's wealth and excellent French diplomatic contacts. It was something to do with knocking a French tart about, but no further detail was forthcoming, then or later.

'Of course, at the time we all thought he just had a taste for the rough stuff,' Gerry explained, 'and you've been around long enough to know there are plenty of tough little girls up Greek Street and Dean Street to satisfy that sort of thing if the price is right. Everybody assumed the girl had tried to blackmail him after agreeing to let him knock her about. When I got to know more about the Honourable James Teal, I started thinking that mightn't be the whole story.'

It seemed Teal had returned prematurely to England after the suppressed scandal, and family connections had fixed a job in the City for him. 'That didn't last long, either,' said Gerry. 'He's far from stupid — got a brain like a razor when he's interested in something — but banking wasn't his idea of an exciting life. He started being late, messing up his work, you can imagine the rest. His dear Dad's pull kept him there long after you or I would have got the old heave-ho, but eventually even that wasn't enough. The bank fired him and his father told him if he flunked the next job, it was his last chance. No more parental help.'

'And I suppose he did flunk it,' said Jane.

'Never got there for long enough to find out. Apparently he told the old man to stick his job where the monkey stuck his nuts, said he could make his own way in the world and that he didn't care whether his father cut him off. Funny with that sort of family. If you call their bluff, they don't necessarily carry out their threats. Jimmy Teal's father was that sort. Chucked his son out, all right, and stopped his allowance, but didn't disinherit him. It's stood the bastard in good stead now and again, I can tell you. When the going gets rough, he can pick up credit on the strength of the inheritance in less time than it'd take either of us to down a gin and tonic.'

Gerry fell silent at this point and concentrated on polishing off his supper. Jane was gazing at him morosely, brooding over what she had just heard. Finally, though, she could no longer stand the suspense. 'Come on, Gerry, you were the one who said there was a tale to tell. Let's have the rest. None of what you've said so far really explains what he did to me this morning.'

The barman sighed. 'Oh, Christ, I wish I'd never started this. I hate being a Job's comforter. But I was so worried you'd get hurt.'

'Well, you were right, so enjoy the feeling and tell me the rest. You've explained how he gets his hands on credit, but how does he stay alive day-to-day? Not even an Honourable can keep going indefinitely on tick.'

'Jane, my love, I wish there was some way of making you stay as young as you obviously still are. Hasn't it dawned on you yet?'

She shook her head, more bewildered than ever. 'He's a bloody pimp, you little goose! He's got brasses staked out all over London, from juicy little pieces of prime flesh like you to old hags scraping by on a couple of cheap tricks a day in back rooms down Stockwell way. Don't tell me — let me guess. Your little set-to with him was caused either by you spending more time with a trick than he thought was sensible, or because he couldn't get his hands on your earnings.'

'Something like that,' she said, barely above a whisper, looking down at her bruised hands and blinking rapidly to disperse the tears which filled her eyes.

Gerry leaned across and touched her shoulder, very gently, in case she had been beaten about the body, too. 'I know this may sound harsh now, love, but it isn't, really. So long as you don't start getting all dewy-eyed about the bugger again — don't you flounce at me, I've seen that happen more times than you've had hot dinners! Anyway, so long as you don't, you've got off lightly.'

'Gerry — look at my hands! My legs are at least as bad, except these dark stockings cover the worst of it. How can you say that?'

'You could ask Lily Challoner, 'cept the last I heard, Lily was locked up in a home for incurable drunks. Or there was a kid called Dorothea . . . Dorothea Price, was it? No matter; she bumped herself off. There's at least three more I could tell you about who found their careers on the game went straight from the Haymarket to Kennington almost overnight after the way your dear lover boy permanently re-arranged their looks. Believe me, darling, you're one of the lucky ones — if you stay away from him now, that is.'

She nodded, brooding on the horrible tale. 'But what did he *do* to them, and why? And how come you know such a lot about it?'

'I know a lot about it because Mrs Meyrick's known about it for years, and she doesn't want Teal battening on any of her girls. She doesn't like banning people outright, and she's had so much trouble with police raids she's a bit hesitant about a bastard like Teal in case he takes revenge by tattling to the law about illegal gambling here. But she trusts me, and I've turned into a sort of Teal-watchdog over the years. Believe me, if you'd been working for Ma Meyrick, you'd have had no option about being told the sod's life history, then barred from seeing him again on pain of losing your job. It was your freelance status that got you into trouble.

'As for knowing so much — Ma supplied some of the gossip, but I know for certain he's been in prison once. That was for what he did to Lily. Little Dorothea had just agreed to give evidence against him in another case, but he got to her again and the next day she went over the parapet of Waterloo Bridge in front of a few hundred witnesses. She just didn't want to live any more with the sort of punishment he dished out, and I suppose the poor kid couldn't live without him, either.'

That thought seemed to jolt his full attention back to Jane. 'I hope you haven't still got any notions about him being the love of your life!'

She smiled bleakly at him and shook her head. 'If the bastard came anywhere near me now, I'd kill him,' she said.

'In that case, I'll tell you the bare facts and then we'll drop it. His habits aren't for the ears of decent people. In a way, you could say you were lucky only to get the cane.'

'Lucky? Right now I'm practically a cripple and I don't kid myself it won't get worse until after the bruises come out. And my, aren't I going to look pretty while that's happening? Looks as if I'm out of work for a week at least.'

'Better than for ever, love, take my word for it. The cane is one of his favourite toys. The others are a hammer and a brick wrapped in a fine linen cloth.'

'A hammer! Jesus, what does he do with it?'

'Roughly what he did to you with the cane, but the effects are a bit more permanent. The brick is a more recent refinement. He's been known to take that to their faces. That's what did for Lily Challoner's looks — and a couple of the others he ruined along the way.'

Jane was crying quietly. The tidiness of her grief somehow made it worse. 'How could I ever have let him touch me? Why don't people see monsters for what they are?'

'If the world was like that, Janey, I dare say we'd all get bored after a while. One of the sad things about human nature, I suppose. And a lot of us have little harmless secrets that have to be hidden from the world. Doesn't make us wicked, but it's better for us if the world doesn't know what we are.'

Her tears were already drying on her cheeks and she was looking sharply at Gerry. 'Nothing'd make me believe *you* ever went around hurting people!'

'There are other sorts of secret. There are even some people who'd say what I hide is worse than your friend Teal. I don't happen to agree with them, but that's just my opinion.'

'Gerry, what's so terrible — so terrible you think that?'

He reddened and looked away past her shoulder. 'I-I don't like women the way most men do . . . I prefer men.' Whatever else he had been about to say was choked off by the anguish of his confession. Eventually he added: 'Perhaps that will make you not want anything more to do with me.'

He was thoroughly disconcerted when she laughed for the first time since limping into the club to tell her tragic little story. 'Me, not want anything more to do with you? A tuppenny tart who lets some posh thug beat the daylights out of her? Do me a favour, Gerry, I'm bloody lucky you're still bothering with me!'

He leaned across and kissed her lightly on the lips. Now

it was his turn to laugh. 'Probably the only kiss you'll get from a man for a long time that won't give you the heeby-jeebies!'

After that they sat in companionable silence for a few minutes, leisurely finishing their supper. Eventually Gerry glanced up at the clock and said: 'My God — better get back behind the bar or Peter will be crying blue murder I'm not pulling my weight. Look, don't rush off straight away.'

Jane glanced down ironically at her swollen legs. 'That's hardly likely, is it, with my pins the way they are?'

'Shut up and listen. Stay out here and have a couple a drinks. I got an idea that may solve more problems than just yours.' He stopped and made a small impatient sound. 'Oh, hell, call me Mister Tact! I just realised. You've not really got anywhere you can go home to, have you? Don't hang around. Take this.'

He dug into his pocket and produced a key. 'My spare. Spend a few days round at my place. Come through to the bar when you've finished your drink and I'll have the address written down for you. I'll tell you my idea when I get home tonight. Try to have a sleep while you're waiting.'

Chapter Fifteen

Gerry introduced Jane to Gavin Lange after she had been staying at his flat for three days. Lange was one of the most good-looking men Jane had ever seen, and she was understandably wary of him as a result.

After an awkward five minutes, Gerry followed her to his little kitchen, where she was making tea, and set her mind at rest. 'No need to concern yourself about Gavin giving you the Teal treatment,' he said with a grin. 'He's tarred with the same brush as me. That's partly why I wanted you to meet him. Now come on back in the sitting room and listen to my idea.'

Feeling much more relaxed, Jane sat down opposite Lange and studied him more closely. He really was fabulously handsome.

'Mmm, and it's quite a problem,' said Gerry, apparently reading her mind. 'That's why I thought you two might be able to do each other a favour.'

His strategy had all the simplicity of genius. Gavin played the piano at a nightclub off Bond Street. He was a popular artiste but his looks and his single state brought him constant trouble. The way Gerry told it, half the young women who used the club were in the habit of coming to drool at Lange across the lacquered top of his white Steinway. When he rejected their advances, they either turned tearful or vindictive — either reaction spelled trouble for him. Occasionally someone or other who came to the club would guess the truth about him, and so far that had resulted in everything from unwanted attention from fellow homosexuals to blackmail attempts by those who had no erotic interest in him. One way and another, the very attributes which had won him a nightclub career were now adding unnecessary complications to his life.

He had an attractive flat near the club and the man with whom he shared it had recently moved out. If he had a female sharer, particularly one as attractive as Jane, reasoned Gerry, it would deal with all the unwelcome attention. All Jane would need to do was to put in the occasional appearance at the club and make it clear for the benefit of clients and staff that they were on intimate terms.

'It would be pretty useful for you, too,' he added. 'I know the streets aren't exactly full of perverts like Teal, but you hardly need me to tell you it's just a matter of time before the pimps move in on you as a purely commercial proposition. You're far too nice a bit of goods for them to let you go on your own sweet way much longer. In fact it was probably only Jimmy Teal's reputation that kept the sharks off for so long.

'Gavin can put you on to a fair bit of work, I should think, too. It's like with me — pianists and barmen are always being asked to fix something or other naughty for the customers. Gavin's no pimp, but you'd be safe with him and I'm sure you'd get on well with each other.'

It seemed too good to be true to Jane. She turned slowly from one man to the other, studying their faces minutely for some trace of dissemblance. After a while, Gerry said: 'What's the matter, pet? You look as if I'm trying to trick you. Honestly, I'm not. I'm just doing my best for two people I like.'

Jane shook her head. 'It's not that, Gerry. It's — well, it's just a little bit too much, that's all. Of course I can see what's in it for me; I'd be stupid not to. But for Gavin? All right, so he gets pestered. So what? I know people give you boys a bad time. I still feel embarrassed about looking shocked when you told me about yourself. But it can't be worth so much to you, can it, Gavin? I just don't see that you get as much from the deal as I do.'

Lange shook his elegant head and smiled resignedly at Gerry. 'I told you she sounded too sharp to be taken in,' he said. 'Tell her the rest. I trust her.'

'No, you tell me. If we're to share a place it's daft for Gerry to go on acting the match-making go-between, isn't it?' Jane intervened.

Lange shrugged. 'Very well. It hardly matters which of us tells you. You must have noticed Lange's a foreign-sounding name. It is – German. I'm as British by background as you or Gerry, but not according to the law. My mother came to this country by a very round-about route, and there are a few little hitches in my papers . . . nothing very terrible; nothing the police would notice in the normal way. But if one of those awkward customers makes a fuss in the wrong place because they take a dislike to me, I'm out. And something tells me Germany will not be a comfortable place for some time to come for an adoptive Englishman with funny sexual tastes.'

Jane let out a long sigh of relief. 'Well, if that's all there is . . . when d'you want me to move in?'

Both men laughed heartily. 'I'll give you one thing, Janey: once you make up your mind about anything, you don't hang around. You're satisfied now, then?'

''Course I am. But use your loaf! You can't con someone by leaving out the most important part of the story. If you'd told me right at the start, I wouldn't even have taken this long.'

The merriment left Lange's face. 'That was my fault,' he said. 'I've been dwelling on the whole thing so much lately that it blew up out of all proportion. I was afraid to tell anybody. Only Gerry knows about it, you see. I have this – well, I suppose you could almost call it a superstition – that if anyone knows, one night a couple of foreign-looking types in soft hats and long leather coats will come calling.'

'Well, love, your secret's safe with me. It must be like being in prison, and I'd never help keep someone locked in like that. Now, I want one of you big strong lads to go round to my room and get my things. If Jimmy is still hanging around there, I may end up hurting a lot more than I did the last time he got his hands on me.'

'You're right there. I'll go,' said Gerry. 'Teal is just the sort of bastard who'd try and make trouble for Gavin if they met. He knows you and I are pals, so no harm done if he's about when I go there. Until now he's always been a damned sight less brave with big strong fellows to contend with than when he's got a little girl cornered.'

'Let's just hope he stays that way. I need all the friends I can get and I don't want him beating you up.'

Gerry's laugh was dismissive. 'Look, I may not look any tougher than Teal, but with five years in the Merchant Marine behind me and another seven as a barman, I could eat him for breakfast without even belching.'

It was inevitable that eventually Teal would find out roughly what had happened to Jane. Their world was cosmopolitan but tiny, more or less bounded by the West End of London and a scattering of roadhouses outside the capital. Apart from the passing stream of out-of-towners, the same faces appeared night after night in the West End clubs. Teal did not witness Gerry Hamilton removing Jane's belongings from her room, but a couple of weeks later he stalked into the Forty-Two, white-faced, demanding to know what the barman had done with what he referred to as his piece.

'I take it you mean Jane Ellis,' said Gerry with an exaggerated air of weariness. 'Look, Teal, the lady walked out on you — isn't that enough? If she'd wanted anything more to do with you, she'd hardly have done that.'

'Don't take that tone with me, you guttersnipe!' snarled Teal. 'In case you've forgotten, you're the bar tender in this place. I'm not only a paying customer — I'm a paying customer with better connections than you'll ever dream about. Now I'll ask you again: what have you done with her?'

Gerry leaned across the bar and dropped his voice so that Teal could barely hear him. He said: 'If you go anywhere near her, I've got her signed deposition, and mine, and one from a doctor, about the state you got her in the last time you saw her. If you so much as *breathe* on her again, it'll all be put in the hands of the police. From what I hear they've been looking for just that sort of dirt on you for a very long time. Now, do me a favour and piss off — and take your time about coming back in here, too.'

Then he drew back, smiled courteously and finished, in his normal voice, 'So if that's all, Sir? . . .'

The tale about the depositions contained not a word of truth. Gerry had grasped it out of the air in the hope it would make Teal leave them all alone. There was every sign that the other man believed him.

'You'll suffer for that, you bastard!' Teal spat back at him. 'If you see that little bitch, tell her I'll get her in the end.' And he turned and stormed out of the club.

Gerry knew it was only a matter of time before the same grapevine that had led him to the Forty-Two would redirect Teal to Gavin Lange. He shrugged. An eventful life had taught him long ago that fretting never changed anything and that it was better to ride trouble when it met you, not go out looking for it. He went back to polishing glasses.

A week later, Gavin was warming up for his evening's work at the Keynote Club by running through a string of light music hits. He broke off as a shadow fell across the keyboard, and glanced up to encounter the flat, inward-looking stare of a madman. God in heaven, he thought, this must be the man who knocked Jane about . . . there can't be two who look that crazy. Inconsequentially he wondered how she could have failed to notice the fellow's strangeness, then dismissed the thought. He himself had been ready to ignore enough oddities when he fancied someone.

'You have something that belongs to me,' said the man, in a low voice which matched the terrible eyes.

'Really? I can't think what it might be,' Gavin retorted and returned his attention to his playing.

'You know damned well what I'm talking about,' said the man. 'Ellis — Jane Ellis. What have you done with her?'

Lange shrugged. 'I don't "do anything with" human beings, sir. No one has that right. Perhaps the answer to your question lies in the fact that you have no such reservations?'

'Don't get clever with me, sonny. I know how to deal with customers like you!'

'Do you? Do you really?' Gavin's beautifully modulated voice with its faint hint of foreign influences had not altered, but as he spoke he stood up. He was six feet three inches tall, and his lean, muscular frame made him look considerably taller. Teal was not a small man, but Lange dwarfed him. Imperceptibly Lange moved closer, so that he stood gazing glacially down and Teal was forced to crane his neck in order to maintain eye contact. 'Perhaps you would care to give me a demonstration,' said Gavin.

Teal stepped back a couple of paces, flustered. 'Hardly the appropriate place for it, is it?' he mumbled sullenly.

Gavin's chuckle was smooth and easy, as though he were doing no more than enjoying a good joke with an old friend. 'Something tells me nowhere on this earth is appropriate for what you have in mind,' he said. 'Now, please, I have a job to do. There is nothing for us to discuss. The person you referred to has no wish to see you again – ever – and I am invariably within reach to see that her wishes are observed. I suggest you find a couple of different clubs and confine your activities to your other – er – ladies.'

A couple of early evening revellers over by the bar had noticed Teal's agitation and were beginning to take an interest in what was going on. Lange made a barely noticeable gesture in their direction. 'No one cares when scandal touches nightclub pianists, Mr Teal. They are exotic creatures whom everyone assumes to be mixed up in excitement day and night. But I rather think you prefer to avoid public demonstrations of intemperance. People do so love to gossip, and we both inhabit a surprisingly small world.'

Teal was so angry now that he had difficulty in refraining from stamping his foot. He was hamstrung – partly because he knew instinctively that the big man would cut him to pieces in a fight, partly because the speculation about a public row had hit the mark. Finally he let out his pent-up breath in a great rush and choked: 'Don't think I'll ever forget this, Lange. I shan't. And I shall get even, don't ever doubt it.' With that he turned and hurried away.

Gavin raised his voice only slightly to say: 'I wouldn't dream of doubting you, but as I have nothing to lose, I do not feel threatened.' If only that were true, he told himself. That man could turn into the worst enemy I ever had. Perhaps this partnership with Jane Ellis wasn't such a good notion after all . . . He resumed his seat at the piano and began playing a slow, haunting blues number. Stupid thought! Already she was his close friend. Already he looked forward to seeing her impish little face when he came in at night, and to sitting down with her over a last drink while they verbally assassinated her less attractive customers. She had become part of his life in a very short time. She was worth a little trouble and worry.

He glanced up at the swing door which had just closed behind Teal. But in the end that one might prove to be more than a little trouble and worry, he thought.

Chapter Sixteen

Provence absorbed Rose like a lover. She had never seen anything as alluring as the rich ochre and rusted yellows of the south country in winter, and thrilled to the sight of the tall thin cypress trees lashed by the evil-tempered Mistral.

Venetia Clifton found cause for complaint as usual. She was delighted to see her French and expatriate English acquaintances again after a long separation, and enjoyed the New Year parties every bit as much as she had hoped. But she carped about the demoralising effects of the Mistral and complained that the Provençal wines which tasted so fresh in summer were thin and comfortless at this time of year.

At first Rose was apprehensive about the countess's reaction, in case she should decide to abandon this magical place early, but she was quickly reassured when she entered a room one evening in time to overhear two of Lady Clifton's visitors agreeing that Venetia would have managed to find something to complain about in Paradise. After that, Rose realised her mistress was merely behaving as she always did at home, and began to relax. It looked as if 1931 would be a very good year for her.

Knowing his wife's exacting standards and capacity for complaining on the slightest pretext, the earl had rented fully staffed houses in both Provence and Tuscany instead of making hotel reservations. Only Rose travelled with Lady Clifton from London, and this heightened her feeling of disconnection from her normal menial position in a large household. The Provençal house was an ancient *mas*, modernised to provide every convenience, including a swimming pool. Rose had been assigned a delightful room with its own wide first-floor veranda, its clay-tiled roof supported by massive old pillars swathed in creeper. The glazed doors from bedroom to veranda also offered a view of the long, deep valley that slashed its way towards the sea. Whenever Rose looked through it, she glimpsed a new combination of colour and texture in the winter vegetation. Beneath a screen of recently thinned trees, the river gleamed like polished slate, blooming into a pewter-silver glow when the sun shone. Rose found it difficult to imagine a better place to spend the winter.

Lady Clifton, accustomed to the arctic temperatures of English country houses, was impervious to the occasional chill in the air and went swimming in the pool each day. When she discovered that Rose was slightly wary of deep water, she teased the maid until she felt she must try the pool for herself. To Rose's own amazement, she enjoyed the water, and after a couple of days she persuaded Philomene, the cook, to ask her gardener husband to provide swimming instruction. Within a month of their arrival, Rose was swimming with growing confidence, and was learning French with equal enthusiasm from both Philomene and Georges the gardener.

Angelique Sharpe, the French widow of an English brewing associate of Lady Clifton's father, was among the dinner guests who stayed on after a larger group had departed from the *mas* one evening. She sat opposite Venetia beside the massive stone fireplace where half a tree trunk sent sparks and flames up the broad chimney, and eyed her friend speculatively.

'This maid of yours is quite a change from Rodwell, isn't she?' she eventually asked. Lady Clifton said nothing, merely raising her eyebrows in regal enquiry. 'Don't play the innocent, Venetia. You know precisely what I mean . . . all this swimming and chattering away in French, and getting Philomene's daughter to take her down to the local museum on her day off. Good heavens — Rodwell could never be winkled out of her room except to follow in your footsteps like a duenna! I always thought Abroad frightened her more than the Devil himself.'

Lady Clifton expelled an exasperated sigh. 'I keep telling myself the girl is doing nothing I didn't suggest to her when I told her I was bringing her with me — so why on earth do I resent it? She'd never have gone near that damned swimming pool if I hadn't provoked her into learning to swim! I really don't know what drives me, Angelique!'

The Frenchwoman laughed. 'Then I am a long way ahead of you. I know exactly what it is. The girl is too young, too glamorous and far too independent! My dear, it's good old-fashioned jealousy! What gives me pause is the fact that you chose her yourself.'

Lady Clifton shook her head. 'I can assure you she was quite different when I engaged her — and remained so right up until we came to France, as far as I can tell. She's always been fairly personable, but when I promoted her from parlour-maid, she was such a mouse! How was I to know she'd blossom like this the moment she got some smart clothes on her back? And there's been such a change in her attitude! You've met Rodwell often enough. You know that's the sort of personal maid I prefer — quiet, obedient, always ready to do what is required of her. No more, no less. When I took Rush, I thought I was getting more of the same thing.

'Darling, I've never known your judgement to let you down so badly!'

'Quite. Oh, Angelique, she irritates me unspeakably! I shall be so damned glad when we go back to England in May and I can get rid of her.'

'Is she moving to another household, then?'

'Oh, no. When Rodwell comes back, I shall pass Rush over to Julia. I think we can rely on her to keep Rush in her place.'

Angelique's look was sceptical. 'I am glad you think so, my dear. I think perhaps Julia will have a more difficult task than you anticipate.'

'Nonsense! She's far more stubborn than I — and far more spoiled. She won't stand any nonsense from Rose.'

'But from what you say, the maid has done nothing wrong. Quite the reverse, in fact.'

Lady Clifton was beginning to tire of the conversation. She waved a hand irritably. 'Oh, I know what I *said*, but confronting the girl is quite another matter. No, the sooner she goes to Julia, the better.'

'Well, if you permit me an opinion, I think you would do better to get rid of her altogether. A refusal to provide another lady's maid post within your family and the promise of a good reference will solve the problem for good. Why wish her on to Julia?'

'Really, Angelique, you're taking all this far too seriously. She's only a *maid*, for pity's sake!'

'And I think that before you finally end your association with Mademoiselle Rose Rush, she will be a great deal more — perhaps at the expense of your family. I believe she is a rare type in England, but I have seen a number of girls like her here in France, apparently doomed by a slum background, but clever, persistent and ambitious. They invariably get what they want. Be careful she doesn't want the same things as you and yours!'

'I forbid you to continue with this stupid conversation. Anyone would think we were discussing the descent of Attila on the Roman Empire!'

'Perhaps we are, my dear — perhaps we are.'

Tuscany offered Rose a different set of new experiences which she grasped with as much enthusiasm as she had shown in France. When they left Provence after seven weeks, she was close to tears, and spent sleepless hours the night before their departure, trying to work out some way of remaining there permanently. If winter here was so good, what would it be like in spring and summer? Philomene had already told her of the cascading crops of early flowers, of Mardi Gras and then of how the burning sun of midsummer toasted the marvellous landscape into some magical form the northern mind could only begin to guess at. Rose wanted it — all of it — and it was not until she had despaired of finding a way to stay that she realised her fear of being alone and unprotected was gradually dissolving.

In the event she need not have worried. Italy swamped her with a whole set of fresh sensations which, without displacing Provence, gave her so much that was new to digest and explore that her earlier paradise was relegated to memory for the time being.

Whatever her feelings about the maid, Venetia Clifton lacked any real power to restrict Rose because she needed the girl's co-operation in fulfilling her own whims, and secretly knew she already took unfair advantage of her servant. Rose's English working life continued essentially undisturbed in Florence, with long afternoons to herself but no question of much freedom at night or of any full days off. Lord Clifton had rented a graceful small villa at Fiesole, serviced by an Italian couple who lived in. Now Rose found herself able to fill every moment when Venetia Clifton did not require her in visiting the great galleries or simply walking the streets of Florence, experiencing the beauties of the finest churches and best sculpture with the help of an old Baedeker. She even got an opportunity to visit Siena and Arezzo, when Lady Clifton went to both places to stay for a couple of days and did not contemplate travelling without her maid.

As in Provence, Rose found it surprisingly easy to befriend the local people, and revelled in her previously undiscovered facility for foreign languages. By the time they had been in Italy for a month, her spoken Italian was as good as the French she had picked up, her only problem a tendency to mix the two languages because she had learned them so quickly at such a short interval.

By the time they were homeward bound, she was as changed as she had been by the initial period of training as the countess's personal maid. The Rose Rush who boarded the Orient Express early in May fifteen minutes ahead of her mistress, to check that the first-class sleeper was in order, was a different woman from the nervous girl who had hidden among the porcelain and fine furniture of the Cliftons' London house just two years earlier.

Lady Clifton was even more conscious of the change than Rose herself, and for the last three days of their trip had been barely able to tolerate her maid's presence. Now she was itching to get back to London and to accept Rodwell's undemanding ministrations again. Let Julia handle this changeling — I've had more than enough of her! thought Venetia as the train gathered speed outward bound from Milan station.

It appeared that Rose's travelling days had barely begun. By the time they got back to London, the summer social season was under way and Julia had acquired a male admirer who seemed more permanent than any of the other men in her life.

Alexander Moncreiff was a twenty-six-year-old American, heir to a comfortable fortune and based in Virginia. Moncreiff had partly formed ambitions to pursue a political career. He had met Lady Julia at a New Year party in London, where he was paying an extended visit to his best friend, the American Ambassador's son. Julia was pretty, fashionable and enjoyed an impeccable social background; and Moncreiff was looking for a wife. Julia boasted almost all the characteristics on his mental shopping list, with the exception of a sparkling sense of humour — but even that lack was concealed by her sharp wit.

Within a couple of weeks, Moncreiff was seriously courting the girl. If he was going to achieve the sort of political dreams he had begun to entertain, he would need the right wife, and the marriage must last. A wise man chose his bride early, got the background and children established, then set out to realise his life's ambition. This young English thoroughbred, with her perfect manners and distinguished looks, was the most appropriate prospect yet.

Venetia Clifton entered her eldest daughter's room immediately before the cocktail hour two days after returning from Italy. Julia was discontentedly blowing away drifts of face powder which had showered from her overloaded powder puff on to the glass surface of her dressing table, and now threatened to engulf everything from scent bottles to jewel case.

'Really, Mama, how much longer am I expected to manage without my own maid? All the girls in my set whose fathers aren't actually bankrupt have them, and this place is a pigsty without someone to take special care of it!'

Venetia's smile was sphinx-like. 'Precisely why I was coming to see you, darling. You know Rodwell is coming back permanently next week?'

'Rodwell? Oh, no, Mummy! Rodwell's fine for someone older, but for a girl of my age? I want a maid who knows exactly what the young people are doing, and knows how to get the look.' Seeing her mother's gaze begin to harden, Julia became more diplomatic. 'It's different for you — you already have the dress sense and the make-up tricks to tell her what you want. But I need advice on the latest things.'

Somewhat mollified, Lady Clifton said: 'I did *not* have Rodwell in mind for you, as it happens. I value her personal services far too much myself. I was about to suggest you took over Rose Rush from me.'

'Rose? Good gracious, I'd never thought of that! But she's so — so *accomplished*!'

'Quite. I should think you'll find her more than capable of interpreting the most up-to-date ideas to your satisfaction. If you feel the same way, I suggest she comes to you from Monday, when Rodwell returns.'

'Mama — wait. I . . . it's a very personal decision. After all, she'll practically be living with me! I want to think it over before I say yes or no.'

Venetia was at a loss to understand what was driving her. Was it a small, malicious desire that her daughter should experience a little of the unease she herself had gone through at Rose's innocent hands? Whatever the reason, now she replied: 'No, Julia, that's simply not convenient. If you don't want Rush, I feel I owe it to the girl to tell her and discuss her future. Mary certainly can't have her own maid yet, so it would mean Rush getting a job outside this family.

I'd have to let her know immediately. You decide, and I shall tell her one way or the other tonight when she is preparing me for bed.'

Lady Julia made a gesture which fell somewhere between a flounce and a shrug. She was determined to acquire her own lady's maid, and to tell the truth only Rush's extreme good looks had made her hesitate so long. Like her mother, Julia Clifton wanted no competition. But what competition? The girl was a servant, that was all – and from the way the Old Girl's general appearance had snapped up to date in the past year or so, she was a damn' good one.

'Very well, Mama, I'll have her,' she said. 'Perhaps you'd send her for a chat with me in the morning after you've finished with her?'

'Of course, darling.' Having achieved her objective, Lady Clifton was all sweetness and light. 'It will be quite a change to be able to visit you in your room without leaving covered in tons of face powder!'

It had not occurred to either Lady Clifton or her daughter to ask Rose herself what she wanted to do though, had they done so, she would have been at a loss for an answer. For all her recently acquired sophistication, she had always done what she was told at work. Since the chilly dawn when Sergeant Hampson had consigned her to the care of the matron of St Luke's Workhouse, she had been told what to do and had done it to the best of her ability. She had no reason now to question the system which assigned her such a role; she merely got on with her job and waited to see what came up next. At present she was far more interested in catching up with gossip in Mrs Higgins's sitting room than in what was going on upstairs.

Mrs Higgins was tearfully patting the present Rose had brought her from Florence – a beautiful varicoloured alabaster bowl of such translucency that it looked more like opaque glass than stone. 'It's lovely, Rose, one a the prettiest things I ever got,' she said. 'And that dear little lid! The way it fits on, like bits of a jigsaw puzzle . . . how *do* they do it.'

Rose launched into a breathless description of the workshop, beside a fifteenth-century black-and-white monastic church overlooking a quiet square in a Florentine backwater. 'There's no place like it, Mrs H, there really isn't. If I ever had the money, I think I'd go back there to live . . . when we were in Provence, I thought that about settling there, but once I saw Tuscany! Everywhere you look there's beauty, and colour, and sunlight.' She gave a little shiver of pure pleasure. 'Not a sign of a slum or a rough-house anywhere – not that they don't exist, I'm sure. It's just that you don't get your nose rubbed in the poverty as you do here.'

'Whatever it was, you're blooming on it, love,' said Mrs Higgins. 'I've never seen you look so lovely – or so smart. No wonder Her Nibs's nose is out of joint.'

'I don't understand.'

Mrs Higgins laughed delightedly. 'You must be half blind then. Her Ladyship is livid that you're turning into a beauty. All this nonsense about Rodwell coming back and you going to work for Lady Julia – if you were ugly, she'd hang on to you like a leech and shove old Rodwell off on to the girl. Truth to tell, she's a bit jealous a Julia an' all. I really think she's got some bee in her bonnet about sticking you both together and letting you stew in your own juice!'

Rose was truly confused now. 'But why on earth would she want to do that? I'm just her maid. I can't do anything to her.'

'Not the point! Not the point at all. You're living proof that we're all sisters under the skin. She looks at you in her last year's frock and knows you carry it off better than she does. While you were bobbing about in a cap and apron, dusting the knick-knacks, nobody noticed you. But dress you up and you'd pass for one a them, any day. That's what really kills her pig!'

Rose shook her head, at a loss to deal with any of it. She had been without any sort of family for too long to have any notion of mother and daughter jealousy, so Lady Clifton's willingness to hand her over to her own daughter seemed the most incomprehensible act of all, if the countess truly harboured malice towards Rose. Not that any of it mattered, in any case. Tonight, or tomorrow, Lady Clifton would tell her what she planned to do, and in due course Rose would do it. That was the way matters had always been and always would be.

She stood up, bent over the housekeeper and lightly kissed her forehead. 'It's lovely to see you again, Mrs H. You and Margaret Armstrong are the only family I've got. Glad you like your present. I'll say goodnight, now.'

'Goodnight, my dear — and thank you ever so much.'

By the time Rose went to see Lady Julia the next morning, her prospective new employer had thought long and hard over the prospect of having her as personal maid. On balance, she had decided she liked the idea. Julia was far more confident about her own attractions than her mother had ever been, and after a few minutes' consideration of the drawbacks of having such a glamorous maid, she had decided her own charms were infinitely superior. Now she was on her best behaviour, in an effort to give Rose the impression they would be suited to one another.

'I expect you'll find it strange at first, working for a younger woman than my mother,' she said, 'but I'm sure we shall get on splendidly. I'm not at all clear yet about time off and that sort of thing, but I'm sure we can sort all that out as we go along. Perhaps we can get started now by doing something with my hair? It really is in the most frightful state!'

In many respects, Lady Julia proved far less demanding than her mother. Lady Clifton had defied certain fashionable edicts and one of them had been the length of her hair. She had beautiful hair, long, silky and richly honey-coloured, and had no intention of wasting her best asset by suffering an Eton Crop or even a bob. Consequently Rose had been forced to wash the hip-length mass three times a week, and to dress it in elaborate chignon styles three or four times a day. Her last task before bed was always to administer two hundred thorough strokes with a close-bristled hair brush, a job which seldom took less than twenty minutes. Lady Julia had sported the shortest of shingle cuts for two years or so, and even now that styles were softening had only grown her hair to jaw length at the sides, leaving it shorter at the back. 'Otherwise it looks absolutely wretched with all my hats,' she said.

Lady Clifton had always demanded that Rose should apply her make-up: 'If I do it myself, I shall end up with one of those disgusting lines around my jaw where the face cream ends and the uncovered flesh begins,' she said. Lady Julia wanted none of that. She took a pride in her ability to paint her own face with the latest cosmetic look and had no desire to credit a maid with the skill. Instead she picked Rose's brain for tips about the latest face creams and eye-shadow colours, devouring each snippet of news and frequently tossing Rose her unread copy of *Vogue* with the instruction: 'You see what they have to say, Rush, then tell me while you're dressing me for dinner. I shall be far too busy to look today.'

Soon Rose was working far less than she had for Lady Clifton, and now she was getting the benefit of more up-to-date clothes, too. She was not altogether sure that suited her. On balance, the more mature designs favoured by the countess had been an excellent foil for Rose's stately good looks, whereas in garments from the tail-end of the flapper era she looked more like a faintly bewildered wild creature wrapped in gaudy trimmings which had never been intended for it.

That soon changed, though. As the spring of 1931 turned to high summer, she began to receive hand-me-downs from Lady Julia's previous season, and the gauzy, bias-cut styles were far more suited to her than the skin-tight cropped skirts and vertiginously cut bodices of the 1920s. Rose was silently thankful for the transformation, because the flapper dresses had begun to have an effect on her private fantasy life outside the Belgravia house.

Lady Clifton's long trip to the Continent had extricated Rose neatly from a potentially explosive situation with Mark Fletcher-Simms. After their long lunch and an afternoon in the National Gallery, he had been most reluctant to part company with her. She had put him off firmly by saying that her father's doctor had ordered a winter in the southern sun for her ailing parent, and that unless he showed strong signs of improvement by the spring, they might even stay abroad permanently. Eventually Fletcher-Simms had given in, on condition that Rose wrote to him while she was away. She had given the promise readily enough, and that was the last Fletcher-Simms had heard of her. Now she was back in London, Rose's main problem was to find a new hunting ground for her excursions in search of personable men.

At first, Lady Julia's cast-off clothing seemed to offer a solution. The skimpy frocks were hardly suitable for sorties to museums. Rose's attention turned to dance halls, and she tried a number of *thés dansants* before admitting ruefully to herself that they were not for her. Part of it was that the young men who came to dance at the Lyceum and the Piccadilly Hotel were usually on the lookout for attractive girlfriends. That was the last thing Rose wanted. She had endless reasons not to have a persistent follower escorting her back to Belgrave Square, let alone running the risk of him groping for her stocking tops or trying to kiss her. Suitors like these were unlikely to accept tales of an invalid father or mother back in Bloomsbury.

The other drawback lay in her own attitude. To her dismay, she realised that in her way she was as much of a snob as her aristocratic employers. She did not like what she mentally termed the 'pardon me' school of etiquette to which they universally subscribed. She did not like the carefully maintained but cheap, often shiny, suits they wore. Above all she loathed the tones of mock gentility they used so painfully each time they addressed her.

From the beginning she was much in demand as a dancing partner. She was, after all, a very striking young woman. But once she had been whirled around the floor a few times with an increasingly uncomfortable young man struggling gamely to raise suitable conversational gambits, both she and they were eager to be gone. Too much of Rose's assumed background had rubbed off on her. She had acquired all the trimmings of a lady without the air of arrogant relaxation used effortlessly by truly upper-class types to make themselves at ease with their social inferiors. She could not unbend sufficiently to be merely an ordinary young woman; and if she resumed the persona of her childhood, which she could have done easily enough with a little thought, she would have fallen as far below the young men in their own estimation as she now felt they were beneath her. There was no answer save retirement from that particular fantasy. Unless it was fun, it served no purpose anyway.

There followed an interlude when she no longer pursued such equivocal pleasures. But Lady Julia, though less demanding than her mother in the tasks she required of her maid, was infinitely more tiresome on an emotional level. She was a moody girl, and used Rose as the butt for much of her ill humour. Although Rose enjoyed more free time now than when she worked for Lady Clifton, a full day off was still a rarity, and when three months had passed since her last secret outing, she was feeling the strain.

That was when the softer, more up-to-date clothes began to be handed down to her, and Rose decided to risk the world of museums and art galleries again. London offered an infinite variety of both, after all, and as long as she was reasonably vigilant it was unlikely she would see either Edwin or Mark again. Knowing Mark, he would have drifted off back to Europe by now. He had freely admitted that he needed regular injections of continental sculpture and painting rather than an unbroken regime of English material. That autumn, Rose took her first tentative steps inside the National Gallery for almost a year, and felt she was coming home.

The season she had spent away from her old haunts had been full of incident, for her employer if not for her.

Alexander Moncreiff had assiduously pursued Lady Julia throughout the summer, escorting her to all the big social events and triumphantly accomplishing an invitation to stay with the family on the Isle of Wight for Cowes Week. After that, he accompanied them back to Fenton Parva and made himself a favourite with the women of the family before going off for a week's shooting with the earl in Scotland. He planned to return to his family estate in Virginia after that, but promised he would be back in the autumn.

The evening before his departure, he cornered the earl in his library and asked his permission to propose marriage to Lady Julia. He was somewhat taken aback when the peer responded: 'Certainly, my boy. Thought you'd never ask!' Clifton brooded for a few seconds then added: 'Better not tell young Julia I said that, y'know. Might take it amiss, and I am fond of the child. It's just that she's been unfit to live with recently. Think she's rather taken to you and she's getting worried you may never pop the question.'

'Possibly, My Lord. I thought she'd have realised by now what my intentions were, but perhaps I was wrong. I'll put matters right this evening.'

Lady Julia had, indeed, become nervous about the young American. She would be twenty-four that winter, and all her friends were engaged or married by that age. At least half-a-dozen of them had married before they were twenty and Julia, with two attractive younger sisters hard on her heels, was beginning to feel she had been left on a very high shelf. Now it was all different. She was making a perfect match with the handsome son of a highly regarded, rich American family, and from what Alexander had said to her about his plans for the future, there was every prospect of him rising to the top.

He proposed, on the loggia at Fenton Parva, under a fat harvest moon which clothed the immaculate grounds in an appropriately romantic glimmer. By the time he had bought her a huge solitaire diamond engagement ring and their betrothal had been sealed by a *Times* announcement and a cripplingly expensive party at the Belgrave Square house that autumn, Lady Julia was a changed woman, contented to the edge of smugness and easier to live with than any of her family could remember.

It was understood from the beginning that they would live in America, and the earl bowed to Moncreiff's request that the marriage should take place on the Virginia estate, as his mother was a semi-invalid and unable to travel to London for the ceremony. 'Quite relieved, really,' he said privately to Venetia. 'After that engagement bash, paying for the wedding as well would probably have bankrupted me!'

'Oh, don't exaggerate, George! We'll never go short. There's always my money.'

'Not always, my dear. This is a different world from the one in which we were married. Have you any idea what a case of single malt costs these days?'

'No, but it would hardly amount to financial ruin, would it?'

'Hmm, maybe not. All I'm saying is that I welcome an excuse for someone else to foot the bills for Julia's nuptials. Pity the others aren't likely to manage it when their turn comes.'

'If you say another word about money, I shall leave the room. It's all some imaginary worry you've conjured up out of nowhere, I'm sure!'

That winter and the following spring, Rose brightened her life with a series of afternoon assignations with two men she met at the Wallace Collection and in the British Museum. She produced the same mythical parents as before, and re-created for herself the role with which she identified most closely: cheroot-smoking bohemian with a taste for avant-garde painting and – since her first exploration of the British Museum – for Egyptian antiquities.

Almost imperceptibly, her true reasons for visiting the cultural institutions were changing. The prospect of romance remained her central aim, but she found herself increasingly absorbed by what she was looking at in the display cases, rather than by trying to see whether a potential admirer was studying her rapt face. Often, she found herself skipping an opportunity to rush off to the Tate or the National Portrait Gallery and instead staying in her room to work on the simple French and Italian self-tutor books she had bought following her return from the trip abroad with Lady Clifton.

Occasionally she paused to consider what would happen to her in the longer term. She knew she could not go on living this odd half life for ever, but was at a loss to find something else to fill her life. Her panic-stricken reaction to masculine interest had almost ceased now, but she was intelligent enough to know this was because she held control of her own emotional life and that it existed at all only as a fantasy.

She found the answer where her father had found a solution to his problems — in a bottle. She now thoroughly enjoyed the elegant cheroots she had started smoking merely as an exotic pose, and one day decided they would combine ideally with some sort of alcoholic drink. Almost without a second thought, Rose bought herself a large bottle of gin and experimented with mixers from lemonade to Indian tonic water before deciding the tonic provided her favourite combination. She took care never to overdo her new habit — one large drink in her afternoon free period and another after Lady Julia had finished with her at night was her daily limit. But she came to enjoy her drinks almost as much as she relished accomplishing a difficult new chapter in her Italian primer, or attracting the attention of yet another admirer at one of the museums.

She was still preoccupied with thoughts of how her life might develop along more normal lines when any need to act for herself was abruptly removed. Lady Julia set her wedding date for early June and invited her maid to accompany her permanently to America. Rose had not come to like Lady Julia any better on closer acquaintance, but the prospect of this vast change of scene wiped out such considerations. America! She had naively absorbed all the mythology of the USA as the land of universal opportunity. Perhaps that was exactly what she needed to set her on a different course. And what did she have to keep her in England? An on-and-off romance with a scatterbrained young man who had encountered her in the National Gallery when he went there to look at a painting once owned by his ancestors; a few memories of similar unfinished liaisons; and a passing connection with the Cliftons' London housekeeper and their country house nanny as substitutes for a family life.

That night Rose indulged in two gins before she went to bed. As she sipped the second, she gazed at herself in her bedroom mirror. 'Here's to you, Rosie,' she said. 'P'raps this is where you start growing up!' The spirit slipped down her throat, smoothing the creases of the day, and she composed herself for sleep with a sense of rising optimism.

Chapter Seventeen

Eleri knew it would turn out badly when Lady Julia sent down a special request that she and not Monsieur Auguste should prepare the food for an informal post-engagement dinner Her Ladyship was planning for mid-October.

'I tried to tell her Monsieur Auguste would be expecting to pull out all the stops for this one, but she was having none of it.' Mrs Higgins's tone was apologetic. Of the younger servants, she liked Eleri almost as much as Rose, and as her quasi-parental relationship with Rose was too special to admit of any rivalries, that was no small honour. Now she was not only protective of the young assistant cook against the chef, but had the added drive of a dread of any upsets below stairs which would make her central role as housekeeper harder than usual. Lady Julia had really set the cat among the pigeons this time . . .

'Why won't she have him? You know he do thrive on parties like that one.'

'Well for a start she doesn't like him much more than you do — haven't you noticed? If there's one thing in this house unites above and below stairs straight off, it's hating Monsieur Auguste.'

'Well, why do they keep him on, then?'

'Because Milady doesn't hate him, that's why. He always sucks up to her and he also makes damned sure she has some of the best dinner parties in London.' Mrs Higgins uttered a long-suffering sigh. 'I get really tired of telling you younger ones the same thing all the time: all Lady Clifton cares about is her own convenience, and Monsieur Auguste makes sure he contributes to that.'

'What am I going to do, Mrs Higgins? He'll crucify me when you tell him.'

'Tell him – me? I'm not telling the bugger! I'm nearly as scared of him as you are!'

'Well, I'm not going to! You were the one Lady Julia gave the orders to. It's your place.' Eleri's truculent tone softened. 'Please, please, Mrs H! You're at least on his pecking level, maybe even a bit higher. He can tie me in knots but he can only grumble at you.'

'Oh, all right then,' said the good-natured housekeeper. 'I'm ever so sorry about this little lot, Eleri. I know how that man rides you, and I got a good idea what he'll have to say on the subject when he hears this bitta news. I just can't see any way round it, that's all.'

Disconsolately, Eleri shook her head, then said: 'Oh, bugger Lady Julia! Why can't she leave well enough alone?'

'Come on, now, love. You know you wouldn't be any happier doing little skivvying jobs for that pig. At least you got another chance to shine – and I'll tell you one thing for free: you won't find our Monsieur Auguste throwing a bout of the collywobbles and taking to his bed this time. He'll be too damned worried you might upstage him again.'

Mrs Higgins was right about the unlikelihood of another attack of feigned sickness, but this time the chef attempted to sabotage Eleri by complaining directly to the earl. Barely pausing to tap on the door, he stormed into his employer's library and began demanding stridently that Eleri, to whom he referred throughout as 'that Welsh kitchen-maid', should be forbidden to prepare Lady Julia's dinner.

Lord Clifton looked at him in some consternation. He was indifferent to whoever cooked Julia's dinner, but was all too aware that such a slight was likely to make Monsieur Auguste abandon his post at a moment's notice. Venetia would hold the earl himself personally responsible, then there would be hell to pay. She was quite capable of sacking this Jones girl simply to keep the Frenchman sweet, and something in that smacked to the earl of injustice.

At the same time, he had a wild mental glimpse of the misery the chef's departure would cause him, and fumbled for a solution which would keep everyone happy. Why, of course! Why hadn't he thought about it before? That was the evening they were going with that odd fellow Schlegel to the first night of some fancy new German play. The answer came to him in a split second and he favoured Lamarque with his most charming smile.

'Hold your horses, old chap,' he said. 'If Lady Julia had begged for your services on bended knee for that evening, she couldn't have had them. The countess has just arranged a theatre party for the eighteenth and she'll be bringing a group of friends back here for one of your special suppers afterwards. Couldn't possibly ask you to do two big parties on one evening, now could we?'

'But – I . . . I could have supervised them both!' But Lamarque knew how lame that sounded. Why jeopardise the success of two big functions when he had a thoroughly competent assistant who could tackle the less important event without trouble? He muttered appropriate thanks for the flowery compliments Lord Clifton now poured on him to mollify him further, and departed for the kitchens. He remained furious, however, and without formulating a precise revenge against Eleri he stoked the fire of his resentment, determined that she would not succeed again in eclipsing his own talent.

Karl Schlegel was something of an oddity in the Cliftons' circle. The earl enjoyed certain branches of fine art, collected in a modest way, and nursed a passion for Chelsea porcelain. His wife was equally keen on the theatre. But their claims to enjoy intellectual pursuits extended no further. Schlegel was almost a caricature of the eccentric German professor. He was quite capable of arriving in the stalls of a West End theatre clad in a Norfolk jacket, walking boots, knee-length socks and shooting breeches. He sang snatches of light opera in the street, spent an inordinate amount of time in the British Museum reading room, and left London at a moment's notice for weeks on end if he took a sudden fancy to go hill walking.

A constantly changing pageant of fellow eccentrics and

intellectuals from five continents drifted through his untidy Gower Street house, the only thing they had in common being that they were always active participants in their chosen fields rather than dried-out academics. Schlegel's own speciality, if such a polymath could be said to have one, was plant and animal biology. He had spent his twenties and early thirties in the islands and coral reefs of the Pacific Rim in pursuit of the exotic fauna and flora which were his main passion.

Somewhere along the way he had also developed an enthusiasm for psychology and psychiatry, and thence had taken a leap into political philosophy. He came of a family of exceedingly rich Austrian-Jewish merchant bankers, but his hugely diverse interests and early enthusiasm for foreign travel had completely destroyed any class consciousness he might have possessed. Schlegel treated servants and friends alike with identical courtesy, and it had lost him so many servants he had stopped keeping a tally.

He had first crossed the Cliftons' path when the earl's brother, an enthusiastic amateur botanist, invited him to lunch during a weekend house party at Fenton Parva. To their mutual amazement, both the earl and the countess had been charmed by him. Even Julia had succumbed to his remarkable traveller's tales about the South Seas, Japan and the Great Barrier Reef of Australia. Behind her mother's back, she had often said Venetia cultivated Schlegel much as aristocratic ladies had once gone accompanied by dwarves or even monkeys in order to enhance their own beauty, but Julia knew as well as anyone else that the German was of the rare breed that attracted everyone because of some special interior magic.

Nowadays he frequently visited the family, both in London and the country. When he joined a theatre party clad in his country walking gear, Lady Clifton merely dismissed the matter with a laugh by saying he offered a welcome contrast to all the white ties and tails which threatened to swamp them.

On the day of the two parties at the Belgrave Square

house, Schlegel had arranged to spend the afternoon with Lord Clifton. There was an auction of Chelsea figurines at Sotheby's and George Clifton knew he was likely to be swept away by enthusiasm for what was on offer. He wanted a friendly, restraining hand, but not restraining enough to stop him from buying anything at all. Schlegel would be the perfect companion. They planned to lunch at Clifton's London club, go on to the sale room and return from there to Belgravia. Schlegel would share a light dinner with the Cliftons before the theatre, coming back to the house afterwards for the supper party. The complicated routine was to change Eleri Jones's life beyond recognition.

Eleri had designed a menu which looked as pretty as it tasted delicious, for she knew Lady Julia put at least as much value on appearance as flavour. The cold hors d'oeuvres were followed by a small, fiendishly rich dish of her own devising: a little cube of bread about four inches along each edge, hollowed in the centre, brushed with butter and baked until it was crisp and golden. It was lined with a puddle of pink hollandaise sauce mixed with prawns and strips of smoked salmon. This mixture was topped by a poached egg, masked on top with more hollandaise and a few more shreds of smoked salmon; the whole dish was served warm. It was followed by grilled devilled sole, then a pheasant sautée with a salade Rachel – truffles, celery, artichoke bottoms and lightly cooked sliced potatoes with thin mayonnaise. The meal ended with glazed fruit tartlets for those with delicate appetites and a feather-light but lethally rich chocolate mousse for more robust constitutions.

She had taken on the complex assembly of dishes secure in the belief that Lamarque had been distracted from his enmity for her by the need to provide a perfect supper later that evening. Nothing could have been further from the truth.

Eleri was at the height of her preparations. It was seven o'clock and dinner was to be served at eight-thirty. Only the puddings and the hors d'oeuvres, which were intended to be eaten cold, were complete and safely tucked away on the stillroom slab and in the refrigerator. Otherwise everything was half done. The pheasants were jointed and waiting to be plunged into foaming butter in the deep sautée pan called a *poelen*. The eggs were poached and floating, like ethereal clouds, in a large bowl of cold water where they would stay soft and retain their clear white-and-yellow colour. The hollandaise was made up and sitting on a double saucepan of barely warm water to maintain it at just the right semi-liquid state until it was required. The bread cases had been hollowed, buttered and baked and awaited their filling. But the sole could be cooked only at the last minute and the whole fish, skinned, were now lying on a large oval platter in the refrigerator. The salad ingredients were prepared and the mayonnaise made, but Eleri would assemble that, too, at the last minute because otherwise the colour of the truffles would disfigure the other ingredients.

Everything was going according to her timetable, and as she heated the butter for the pheasant sautée, Eleri began to relax. That was the moment Auguste Lamarque chose to erupt into the room, shouting: 'What is the meaning of this shambles? Clear it at once – I need to start work on Her Ladyship's theatre supper!' Whereupon he pinned his own menu to the kitchen noticeboard with a horribly final slap of satisfaction, and turned to confront his arch-rival across the huge deal table.

Pat, the young kitchen-maid, was gaping at him in a mixture of awe and horror, clearly convinced that all their collective work on Lady Julia's dinner party was about to be swept away. Eleri had no such fears. She wanted to kill Lamarque for disrupting her concentration at such a crucial time, but felt quite capable of dealing with it. She drew herself up to her not very great height and fixed Lamarque with the most intimidating glare she could muster.

'Monsieur Auguste,' she said, 'I shall need at least another hour in this kitchen, and as Lady Julia isn't planning to start dinner until eight-thirty, you can add another hour on to that. I'm prepared to share the kitchen with you once I've had that first hour, if it's absolutely necessary, but that's the most I can do. Now, if you'll excuse me, the sooner you leave me to get on, the sooner you'll have the place to yourself.'

He exploded. 'This is *my* kitchen and I am about to prepare *my* supper party. If you were so moronic that you could not consult me you must expect to ruin your meal. I need the space – all of it – this minute, not part of it in an hour. Now get this pigswill away from me and don't come back!'

Without saying any more, he began picking up bowls of partially prepared food and thrusting them on to the old-fashioned buffet sideboard which normally held china waiting to be washed up in the scullery.

'Get your bloody meddlesome hands off my cooking!' yelled Eleri. 'You come in yere when I'm ready, and not a minute before, understand?' Whereupon she lunged across the chef's extended arms and began snatching back her precious preparations. Seconds later their hands were locked together on the handle of the *poelen*, which Lamarque had removed from the stove as the first two pheasant portions began sizzling in the butter, and the pair of them seemed locked together for the evening.

Pat had run to find Mrs Higgins, in the hope that she would know what to do. The housekeeper came bustling into the kitchen, saying, 'Now what *is* going on here? Surely two grown people . . . Jesus Christ almighty, what a carry-on!' as she saw for herself just how far the dispute had advanced. 'Eleri, you damned fool, let go a that pan! You been cooking long enough to know you don't mess about with bubbling hot butter. Chef – what the hell d'you think you're up to?'

Eleri was so schooled to obedience that the sound of a friendly, if scandalised, voice ordering her to do something quite reasonable, produced an immediate response. She abruptly let go of the *poelen* and it swung wildly as Lamarque's grip on it tightened, spattering a little hot butter on his bare forearm and producing a furious Gallic oath.

'Come on, we don't discuss matters like this in front of junior staff. My room will do.' Mrs Higgins turned majestically to lead the way to her domain, giving herself time to rack her brain for a peace formula as they moved.

But Lamarque had no intention of behaving reasonably. 'I will not tolerate this!' he bawled. 'I take no orders from female servants!' Still carrying the hot pan, he shouldered his way past both Eleri and Mrs Higgins and headed for the staircase.

'Monsieur! Monsieur Auguste! You can't go up there with a *cooking pot*!' Now it was the housekeeper's turn to shout. 'Come back, for God's sake, and cool down a minute!' But already he had swung round the newel post and disappeared up the staircase towards the green baize door which opened into the main hall of the Cliftons' town house.

'Eleri – come back here, girl! Where d'you think you're going? It'll mean your job . . .'

Mrs Higgins's voice faded as Eleri raced up the stairs behind Lamarque. Bugger the bloody job, she was thinking. He's not wrecking my whole week's work and my reputation with it. Abruptly, she was out of the servants' area and in the main part of the house. Brilliant light from the electrolier in the hall flooded down on her. Lamarque, immaculate in his chef's whites but looking on the edge of madness, was forging his way across the chequered marble floor, still clutching the *poelen* which contained three portions of pheasant and a large puddle of rapidly congealing butter.

'Monsieur Auguste! You give that back this minute!' she yelled after him. 'It's not yours to go off with, and what the devil d'you plan doing with it anyway?'

He glanced over his shoulder. 'You will soon see – just follow me!' he spat out.

Then things grew confused. The front door opened and the earl came in, shepherding Karl Schlegel ahead of him. 'Good God! What on earth is going on?' he said.

Lamarque rounded on him. 'This – this Welsh trollop – is proposing to serve this rubbish to your daughter's guests tonight!' he cried. 'I looked in to the kitchen and when I saw what she intended – *ma foi*! I was overwhelmed and thought Her Ladyship must see what disgrace her household faced before it was too late.'

Schlegel, with an air of almost professional interest, peered into the *poelen*. 'Hmm — it does not appear to be rubbish to me. That is pheasant, no? And fine unsalted butter . . . of course it looks a little strange now, because it has been off the stove for some time, but —' he bent his head over the pan and drew in a deep breath' — it still smells divine. It would make a very good dinner. Smell it, George.'

But the earl was already recoiling, embarrassed beyond speech by this unseemly scene in his own hall. At that point, Eleri lost control.

''Course it'll make a very good dinner — 'specially with what I got cooking for before and after. But he've ruined the rest and run off with that. What am I supposed to do?' Her appeal was directed straight at George Clifton. She had encountered Schlegel before, but only as an odd figure sitting at the dinner table.

'I — er — um, that is . . .' The earl was beetroot-red and desperately casting about for an escape route. At that point, Venetia Clifton, just finishing her toilette for the evening, came out of her second-floor bedroom to find out what the fuss was all about.

She peered myopically down the twisting stairwell of the great house. 'George — what on earth is going on down there? It sounds like Mardi Gras at Nice!'

Clifton turned to her like a drowning man reaching for a lifebelt. 'Ah, Venetia — I think you'd better come down. Bit of an embarrassment, I fear.'

As his wife began the long descent of the staircase, Eleri made a last desperate attempt to recover her pheasant from Lamarque. By the time Venetia Clifton was in the hall, the two were grappling with one another again, much as they had been when Mrs Higgins intervened below stairs.

'Stop that this instant.' Lady Clifton had not raised her voice but it cut through the confusion like a splinter of ice. The two combatants froze and half turned so that they could look at her. 'I will *not* tolerate such behaviour from anyone in my own front hall. Has it occurred to either of you that you are servants in this house?'

'A servant — me?' Lamarque's outrage was as great as Venetia Clifton's. 'I am an artist, Madame, not a servant.' He released one hand from the *poelen* in order to point dramatically at Eleri. 'Look at that. *That*, Milady, is a servant.'

Still angrier with Monsieur Auguste than she was in awe of Lady Clifton, Eleri pressed home the advantage of his partial surrender of her pan. She wrested it out of his hand and wheeled back across the hall towards the green baize door. 'Jones, where do you think you are going?' demanded Lady Clifton.

'Back to the kitchen, Milady. I've still got to try and save your daughter's dinner party after what that madman have done.'

'Enough! I will not have my assistant cook calling her superior a madman. Whatever the rights and wrongs of this incident, a servant's duty is to defer to her superiors. You will go back to work, Jones, finish preparing the dinner, and then keep out of Monsieur Auguste's way. I shall consider overnight whether I wish you to continue in my employment but if I do, I assure you it will only be after you have made a full apology to Monsieur Auguste.'

She had finally succeeded in pushing the girl beyond caution, something Lamarque had not managed in weeks of constant provocation. Eleri, in the act of pushing open the door, had her back to Lady Clifton when the countess spoke to her. Now she stood absolutely still for about ten seconds, the quality of her stillness somehow restraining any of the others from further action. Then she turned, almost in slow motion, and moved gracefully back across the hall, carrying her cooking pot as if it were some holy chalice.

She faced Lady Clifton from barely two feet away, and said in a high, clear voice: 'No need to think about dismissing me, Your Ladyship. I — hereby — resign!' Then, with ceremonial deliberation, she dropped the pot. As cast iron struck marble, the *poelen* split in two and one of the square white floor slabs cracked. The noise was startlingly loud. Seconds later, it was compounded by enraged feminine shrieks as Lady Clifton looked down and realised that congealing butter had splashed all over her silk stockings and handmade court shoes.

Eleri reacted as if she were alone in the hall, marching across it and starting to ascend the stairs. 'Wh-where are you going, Jones?' The scene in the hall had brought back Lord Clifton's stammer at full strength.

She turned on the fourth stair and smiled down at the earl. 'I'm going to pack, sir. And just for once, I'm going up the front stairs instead of the back, right?' He reddened and looked down. Eleri studied the top of his head for a few seconds, then continued her progress up the staircase.

Chapter Eighteen

Not much here to show for nearly seven years of my life, Eleri reflected as she emptied her two drawers from the chest she shared with the head parlour-maid. Just a few cheap blouses and petticoats, a couple of decent day dresses, a woollen winter coat and two pairs of shoes. Over the years she had sent home as much money as she could, knowing the family needed it, so even her savings did not amount to much.

She wondered whether she stood a chance of getting a reference from Lady Clifton. Without one, she was finished for first-class service. Even in these days of permanent domestic staff shortage, the better off would not dream of taking an employee with no reference. Much as Eleri hated the system, she could even understand their point of view. It wasn't so much the work; a week's trial would always sort that out. It was the need for utter trustworthiness. The owner of any house crammed with precious paintings, furniture and silver must know beyond reasonable doubt that he was not letting a criminal into his household. Otherwise, some day he might arrive back from a week in the country to find his home stripped of its most valuable contents and the culprit gone without trace.

She gave herself an angry little shake. What am I doing, brooding here about such nonsense? she asked herself. I've no job, no friends. Can't even get at Mrs Higgins without tangling myself up with that bastard Lamarque again. She knew all too well that Monsieur Auguste would by now have taken charge in the kitchen to supervise the completion of her dinner-party food before moving on to the supper preparations. Then he would doubtless take all the credit for saving the family in a small crisis and be right back in the countess's good books. Not for the first time, Eleri reflected how unfair life could be. As she packed her meagre belongings, she came to a decision about the reference. She would write a farewell note to Mrs Higgins – she wanted to say goodbye, anyway – and ask the housekeeper to arrange for her to collect the fibreboard trunk containing her larger possessions, which was kept locked in the attic. At the same time she could enquire about the possibility of a reference. If anyone could succeed in coaxing such a thing out of Lady Clifton, it was Mrs Higgins. And if that didn't work, the housekeeper was quite capable of approaching Lady Julia and flattering her into producing one. It didn't really matter who provided it, as long as it came on headed paper from a good address and, preferably, from someone with a title. Lady Julia fitted those rules as well as her mother, and as she disliked Auguste Lamarque so much she was quite likely to be a willing conspirator.

Eleri took out the pad and envelopes she kept to write to her mother in South Wales, and composed a graceful little note to Mrs Higgins. Then she put the writing materials into her bag with her other belongings, and departed.

She used the front staircase again, this time less from bravado than because she did not want to go anywhere near the kitchen. To use the servants' stairs and entrance, she would have had to. The hall was empty when she descended to it. Someone had hastily removed the broken pan and mopped up the grease, but the spider-web crack remained on the marble floor tile as a mute reminder of what had happened. There were no signs of occupation, but Eleri could hear the faint sound of voices rising and falling somewhere off the inner hall – probably the library. Perhaps they'd all gone in there for a couple of drinks to calm themselves down after the disruption of the previous half-hour. She chuckled grimly. Maybe she should follow their example, find a pub and get plastered. At least then she could put off thinking about what she was going to do with the rest of her life.

'Come on, you silly cow!' she muttered. 'No good feeling

sorry for yourself. You been wanting to get out from under for long enough, so go on and do it.' Yes, her cautious side responded, but not on a few quid in the Post Office and no reference for another job. 'P'raps that makes it better,' she told herself. 'Start as you mean to go on, innit? Always easier when there ent no other way.' She propped the sealed envelope for Mrs Higgins on the hall table, unconsciously squared her shoulders, opened the massive front door and descended the four front steps into the soft autumn evening.

She had gone less than fifty yards when she heard hurrying footsteps behind her. Then a male voice called out: 'Miss Jones! Miss Jones, would you mind if I walk with you a little way?'

Her first thought was, No one calls me Miss Jones. Her second was, I don't know anyone in London. After that sheer curiosity made her turn to confront her pursuer. It was Karl Schlegel, for once dressed quite conventionally for the city, if not for an evening at the theatre. She was on the point of telling him she wanted nothing to do with friends of the Cliftons and turning away, when she recalled afresh that she was going nowhere. 'All right,' she said, 'please yourself. Makes no odds to me.'

'Good.' He nodded happily and fell into step beside her, apparently unoffended by her cold manner. Eleri remained silent, largely because she could think of nothing to say to this comparative stranger. They walked along Grosvenor Street and past the entrance to St George's Hospital. Schlegel peered into her face as it was illumined by the entrance hall lights and said: 'Good girl. No sign of tears.'

'You think I'd waste tears on that lot?' Eleri tossed her head scornfully. 'I save my misery for things that are worth crying for.'

'I should think that chef has driven many young women to tears, and will again.'

'P'raps so. Far as I'm concerned he do just make me feel violent.' She gave a shamefaced little giggle. 'Oh, dear, hark at me! I've been sounding like a right *sionni oi* all evening thanks to that devil. He do make me that angry, all my posh speaking do fly outa the window!'

'I could listen to it all day, Miss Jones. The words may not be refined, but it runs like music. Quite enchanting.'

Eleri had never been in the habit of dwelling on herself for long. Now, she abruptly recalled that Schlegel had been planning to go to the theatre with the Cliftons and various other friends. 'I just thought,' she said, 'what happened to your party? You shouldn't be out here with me. You'll be late.'

He shrugged dismissively. 'Somehow I lost the taste for it. Real life is so much more interesting. And tonight I did not much like the Cliftons. I thought the aristocracy was supposed to act on the principle of *noblesse oblige*. There was nothing noble or obliging about the way they behaved tonight. Now, unless you have something else in mind, perhaps you would care to join me in a restaurant for dinner?' After studying her facial expression he chuckled. 'It's all right, my intentions are entirely honourable. I think you have been through quite enough today without having to fend off a middle-aged foreigner.'

'You *are* kind,' said Eleri, 'but I couldn't go into a decent restaurant like this. My God, the one time I took myself off to a really swish place, I wore the best clothes I had and I still felt out of place. And that was only lunchtime, too.'

'My dear, you would grace the Savoy Grill and I should be happy to take you there if you wished. But if you feel more comfortable in informal surroundings, Soho is only a few minutes away.'

'Yes, maybe that would suit me better. I've been far too conspicuous today. I want just to melt into the background now.'

'Very well, so you shall. Incidentally, where was this "swish place" to which you treated yourself?'

She laughed at the memory. 'Boulestin's. I'd been reading his articles in *Vogue* and they made my mouth water. When I found out he had his own place, I was determined to go if it cost me every penny of my savings. It almost did, an' all.'

He was regarding her with something like wonder. 'But did you think the experience worth the outlay?'

'Worth every penny, and more. If you come from my sort of family, there's no way of finding out about things like that unless you get a magic wand waved over you. I do always think of reading those articles and having a little bitta money put away as my magic wand. It taught me more than any number of books.'

'Such as what?'

'More than anything, the *feel* of good food. Funny, that. However long you work in a big house, your place as a servant stops you feeling the food. You eat it regular enough – once you're fairly senior, you get a lot of the same meals as the people above stairs, even if it's usually left from the day before. But so many servants just see food as fuel. They pile it on their plates, then sup up heavy beer with delicate sauces. They don't have no respect for it. When you get out and go to a good restaurant as a paying customer, you see food being treated with respect and you respect it yourself.'

'I see I have fallen into the clutches of a youthful connoisseur. Have you ever eaten the food of Eastern Europe or Russia?'

She shook her head. 'I've seen it mentioned on some menus, but that's all. I wouldn't even know how to start cooking it.'

'You aren't going to need to. Tonight you will be waited on and explore a whole new cuisine. I hope you are hungry.'

Eleri considered that in silence for a while, then said: 'You know, I'm ravenous. If anyone had ever asked me how I'd feel about food after the sort of rows I've just gone through, I'd have said I never wanted to eat again. But at this minute I could put away anything that's set in front of me.'

'Then we must set something in front of you, and quickly!' Schlegel took her suitcase from her, then hailed a taxi and gave the driver a Greek Street address.

The Blue Danube restaurant offered itself to the world with an air of shabby baroque beauty reminiscent of an ageing but still bewitching woman. Its atmosphere intoxicated the customers before they ever tasted the food. Many of them thought the place had been there since Victorian days but in fact it had been created by a Hungarian emigré named Imri Mikes barely eleven years previously when he fled to London from his German establishment which was ruined by the Great War. He had hunted down distressed fabrics and worn plasterwork cherubs with the tenacity of an expert and within a few months of the opening he had a success on his hands.

By the early 1930s he was offering an eclectic collection of dishes from the Austro-Hungarian Empire, Russia, Czechoslovakia, Poland and the Balkans. It said much for Mikes's talent that exiles from all the source countries happily ate at the Blue Danube, and left assuring Imri that he must have spent years in their particular region in order to know the cuisine so well. In fact he had grown up in Budapest and trained in Vienna. The other exotica were all the product of a fertile imagination and an instinctive understanding of good food.

Tonight Eleri was introduced to East European cuisine with the finest Russian caviar served on buckwheat blinis and sour cream. 'We will drink wine with the other dishes,' said Schlegel, 'but the caviar calls for vodka.' He chose a particularly potent Polish brand and taught her the correct way of eating some blini and caviar, then throwing down a tot of the iced spirit as a digestive. Next came a feather-light pike mousse with beetroot sauce and wafer-thin slices of cucumber dressed in sugar and vinegar. Schlegel even managed to find a suitable wine which stood up to the highly seasoned food – a spicy Gewurtztraminer that Eleri could have gone on sipping forever.

'Something a little more bland, now, to prepare us for our main dish,' he explained. Ordering the course, he had used its Hungarian name and Eleri had no idea what it could be. *Toltott Kalarabé* turned out to be kohlrabi, hollowed out and stuffed with minced pork and veal, then cloaked in a light parsley sauce. It was delicious, and by the time she finished it Eleri was laughing helplessly at the idea of eating anything else. 'I think a sorbet and a long sleep are about all I can cope with,' she told Schlegel.

He looked quite crushed. 'My dear child, how can you say such a thing? In a moment you will experience the *pièce de résistance* of Russian fish cookery.'

'Well, maybe just a taste.' He reminded her of that remark later when she was finishing her second helping.

Coulibiac was as much a mystery to Eleri as some of the exotically named dishes she had tried earlier, but after her visit to the Blue Danube it became a lifelong favourite. It was a vast, oval pillow of unsweetened brioche, filled with layers of hot buckwheat, mushrooms, finely chopped herbs, hard-boiled eggs, salmon and pike-perch in a sauce of white wine and melted butter. The outside had been buttered and coated with breadcrumbs before baking, and now offered a wonderful toasted invitation to the diner to cut through them and eat the pie.

Eleri was speechless in her delight at the first plateful. By the second, she had found her tongue again and plagued Schlegel for instructions on its preparation. He told her as best he could, then added: 'I am merely an amateur, Miss Jones. I shall bring you here again soon, and get Imri to tell you. I am sure he will be powerless to resist such a charming enthusiast!' Abruptly, he became serious. 'Throughout our meal, I have been trying to raise the courage to ask you something, but I fail each time.' He broke off to pat her arm earnestly. 'Do not mistake my intentions. They are still entirely honourable. It — it is just a rather delicate matter . . .'

'Well, I think I'm fit to cope with the most delicate subjects on earth after eating that. Better get on with it.'

'I wondered . . . have you had time yet to make plans for your future?'

She shook her head. 'It's not easy to find a new place as a cook with no reference at seven o'clock at night,' she said, trying to keep her tone light and almost succeeding.

'I thought not. I am not good at holding on to my housekeepers. I think they suspect me of lese-majesty because I treat servants as friends. My latest lady left two weeks ago. Would you be interested in taking over her job?'

Eleri set down her fork with exaggerated care and gaped at him. 'You'd give me a job, after seeing the way I carried on tonight?'

'Especially after seeing the way you carried on tonight. It took considerable courage for one so young and so heavily outnumbered to do as you did. I was proud to witness it. Oh dear, I have made you cry. I thought you did not waste tears.'

'That's because nobody's ever been this kind to me. Never knew myself it would make me behave like a baby.' She passed her hand across her eyes, remained in apparent thought for a moment, then looked up at him again, dry-eyed. 'I'll come and work for you on two conditions. First, don't call me Miss Jones. My name is Eleri. Second, if you ever want to entertain the Cliftons at your place, count me out. I'd probably poison their bloody soup.'

'Don't worry. After seeing them as I did tonight, I should probably help you! But really, that is all? You have no questions about hours, or wages, or what you would have to do?'

'None. You may have been studying me this evening, but I was doing the same with you. And I can only speak as I find. Anybody who'll run out and rescue someone the way you did me, then take them out like this and treat them like – like a civilised human being, has got to be worth working for. You can tell me all about it now, if you like, but consider the position filled.'

His smile was a trifle shamefaced now. 'I am appallingly untidy and the house is dreadful at present. In two weeks without domestic help I could probably reduce the Palace of Versailles to chaos. It is far worse in a house of modest size. Perhaps you had better spend tonight in a ladies' hotel – I will pay for it – because it pains me to confess that the linen on your bed is still what Mrs Chivers slept in for the last three days of her tenure.'

Eleri merely laughed. 'If you think I'd let you waste

money on an hotel when it's just a case of grubby sheets, you've got me wrong. You have *got* some clean ones, I take it?' He nodded. 'Right, then. When we go back I'll make it up with fresh linen – bet your bed needs changing an' all – and then I'll start doing the place through first thing tomorrow. How about that?'

'But you cannot start bedmaking after an evening of such rich food and wine!'

'God bless us all, I'd rather do it like that than on an empty stomach! In my days with the Cliftons, I'd often be up after midnight just making sure everyone had enough fresh coffee and petits fours, and that would be at the end of a sixteen-hour working day with my last meal five hours earlier. Don't you worry about that for a minute.'

'In that case – Eleri – I think we will celebrate with cream-cheese pancakes and a bottle of sweet champagne. How does that sound to you?'

'Bloody disgraceful, and yes.'

Karl Schlegel's house *was* a shambles. He was good at making coffee and tea, but otherwise domestically incompetent. Every cup and saucer in the place was dirty and there seemed to be one sitting in a little drift of dust on every flat surface. The filter coffee pot was clean enough, otherwise he would have run out of the means of making his drinks. All four of his teapots had stale wet dregs in them. There was a good delicatessen close to the house, and everywhere there was evidence of his reliance on its made-up food when he was not eating at restaurants or with friends. Slicks of dried-up Russian salad, fragments of pie pastry and other unlovely scraps littered every plate and most of the kitchen work surfaces.

Schlegel stood diffidently behind Eleri under the pitiless glare of the electric lights and said: 'I told you that you should stay in an hotel tonight, Miss Jones. It is far worse than I realised and I would have made it at least a little better by tomorrow. Have I put you off completely?'

She laughed. 'I told you to call me by my first name,

remember? Don't worry about any of this. I'll just change the beds and then I'll start on the rest tomorrow. At least it shows you really need me!'

She made up two clean beds, cleared some space around the kitchen sink so that she could get the worst of the cutlery and crockery out of the way quickly next day, then bade Schlegel an affectionate goodnight and went off to her room, completely untroubled at being alone with an eccentric male stranger.

For minutes after her departure, Schlegel stood in the hall, touching his cheek where she had patted it as she said goodnight. 'You are a remarkable girl, Eleri Jones,' he said at last, 'truly remarkable.'

When he awoke next morning what he saw reinforced his initial judgement. The morning room was already sparkling clean, the circular mahogany breakfast table glowing with fresh polish, a crisp white linen place mat and napkin set out on its glossy surface. It seemed she had already discovered the delicatessen on the corner, as there was a basket of still warm rolls and brioches awaiting him. The coffee pot was clean outside as well as inside, and fragrant steam curled invitingly from the spout. Eleri had turfed out a smaller, lidded milk pot to match it and it was beside the coffee, full of hot, frothy milk. Normandy butter and an assortment of honeys and jams completed the offering.

'How did you manage? You have no money for these things, and no door key,' said Schlegel, breathless with wonder.

She laughed. 'Dr Schlegel, I'm sure you're ever such a subtle chap at brainy things, but I know your sort. You never trust yourselves with just the keys in your pocket, so there's always a doormat or a flowerpot with spares tucked in. No wonder so many well-off people get robbed! I looked at your front porch and after a couple a minutes it stood out a mile that the little metal grid half-way up the wall could be pulled open. It was child's play after that. Where else would you put the keys?'

He shook his head. 'Very well, I consider myself

reprimanded about the keys. What about buying all this food?'

'There was a whole bunch of paper bags from that fancy grocer's in your kitchen rubbish. Stood to reason you wouldn't be wanting to bother with cash in there all the time, so I went in, ordered everything we'd need this morning, then said in a really brazen voice: "Put it on Dr Schlegel's account, please. I'm the new housekeeper." After that I picked up my stuff and swept out! Child's play.'

'But what if I had not held an account there? What would you have done?'

'Opened one, o' course! Good God, Sir, you don't arf make some things difficult!'

He veered to another matter. 'No "Sir" and no "Dr Schlegel", if you please, Eleri. If you are Eleri, I am Karl. Understood?'

Now it was her turn to look dazed. 'But I can't do that! It — it wouldn't be proper!'

'That is the first reactionary thing I have heard you say. I am no better than you and you are no better than me. We are just different, and the important difference is that I have more money. I choose to use some of it to pay you, a skilled woman, to look after me. That is all. I do not consider this means you should call me "Sir". It is unnatural.'

She snorted. 'I bet the other housekeepers gave you a talking to when you said that sorta thing to them.'

His grin was sheepish. 'They invariably departed long before that stage. I don't recall this ever arising before, because they called me "Dr Schlegel" and I went on calling them "Mrs Chivers" or whichever one it was at the time. No, they began getting restless if I ever suggested they should sit down and share an evening meal with me at the dinner table, or come into the drawing room and join in a cup of coffee with some of my friends.'

'Good God, you *are* bloody odd!' The words spilled out before Eleri could stop herself and she covered her mouth with her hand, horrified at her own discourtesy.

He was unruffled. 'Perhaps so. All I know is that

mankind does not thrive on division. The better we understand each other, the more likely we are to live together in peace as a happy society. I see precious little happiness in this society.'

'Come on, your coffee's getting cold. Sit down and enjoy it and stop nattering,' said Eleri, trying to hide how deeply his simple goodness had touched her. 'I got to get the rest of this place straight if you're not going to catch plague or something from all the rotting food and tea leaves!'

She spent a thoroughly satisfying day cleaning the lower floors of the house. It was an attractive place under the dust and disruption, with tall, stately rooms often crammed floor to ceiling with books, a superbly equipped kitchen and two up-to-date bathrooms, both of which Schlegel appeared to have been using in a vain attempt to minimise the muddle in either. Naturally the effect was exactly opposite to that he had intended.

Eleri had bought a selection of cold hors d'oeuvres at the delicatessen, and served them to Schlegel for his lunch, followed by a feather-light mushroom omelette and a green salad with a walnut oil dressing. 'After our efforts last night, I thought a pudding wouldn't be a good idea,' she told him, suddenly schoolmarmish, then relented and added: 'But I'll do you something special tonight, all right?'

'I think you have more than enough on your hands getting this house straight. We will eat together at a restaurant again.'

'Indeed we won't. The very idea! Last night was a special treat, not for every day. How long is it since you were able to enjoy a good dinner in the comfort of your own home?'

'Hmm, it does sound tempting. If you're sure you won't be worn out by so much work . . .?'

'Me? I been working harder than I am today since I was fourteen. Any girl who've done a year or two as a scullery-maid never thinks she has to work hard again once she's out of it. It won't be the most elaborate dinner you ever had, but it'll be a good one.'

'Very well. And you will join me in the dining room.'

She opened her mouth to protest, and he cut through her objection before she had time to voice it. 'I will hear no excuses. You know my views about this matter. We get on well together, so it cannot be that you will feel bored. Forget convention. Your life will be much more entertaining.'

'All right, then. And thank you for being the best employer in the world.'

'No labels, please. Such a reputation would be too hard to live up to.'

They ate a late dinner – old-fashioned homely dishes including pork chops, fried onions and mashed potatoes, and ending with a Welsh apple tart, the top crust sugar-coated crisp shortcrust pastry, the undercrust meltingly softened by the juice of the Bramley apple filling.

By now Eleri had cleaned all the reception rooms, the kitchen and bathrooms, and only the bedrooms remained. 'What d'you normally do about the cleaning?' she asked. 'I can't imagine the average cook-housekeeper being prepared to do all that and get your meals and so on.'

'Oh, gracious, I would never expect it!' His tone was agitated. 'The trouble was that Mrs Chivers had engaged the woman who did all the cleaning work, and when she left Mrs Perkins never came again, either. That's why the place got so filthy. And then it was so bad I hardly liked to approach a domestic staff agency for someone. When it is all straight, either you find someone or I shall call in an agency. Whichever you prefer.'

'I'm sure I could get a reliable woman who lives around here, once I know the area,' said Eleri. 'In general you get better work out of a local, because she wants to keep her end up with the neighbours. Just leave it to me. If I fall down on it, I'll come back to you for help.'

'Now, young woman, let us get back to you. You would not come out tonight, in spite of such a hard day, and I suspect you will insist on working all day tomorrow. On Sunday I insist on giving you a treat.'

She was wary. 'Not the Danube again. I want to keep that special.'

'No, no. I thought you might enjoy a little food safari. I was planning to take you down to the East End for a taste of authentic Jewish nourishment.'

Her eyes sparkled. 'Ooh, I'd love that! Tell me all about it.'

'No, I shall save that for Sunday. It's enough for you to know we must be up very early. The street market down there starts at dawn.'

The area around Brick Lane and Club Row was the nearest London came to possessing a ghetto. Since the dying years of the nineteenth century, it had been the first point of settlement for East European and Russian Jews, driven continually westward by the pogroms they faced in their old countries. Now a second and third generation had established themselves. Many of the early arrivals had made their fortunes and moved out to the salubrious suburbs of North London. But a constant trickle of newcomers replaced them, and there were plenty of the first immigrants who had either failed to make good or simply preferred the ability of their close-knit East End community to maintain an older tradition.

Sunday was a normal working day for many of the local people, who had celebrated their sabbath on Saturday. Now as the first light of an autumnal Sunday morning dawned, the stalls were already set up and bustling: second-hand furniture and clothing, bric-a-brac, tattered books, cheap linen and mass-produced china all jostled for the visitor's attention. And at every intersection was a corner grocer's, a bakery or a tiny café, the vast majority of them kosher, all selling delicious food.

Eleri spent a blissful hour flitting from stall to stall, picking up a cheap book here, a trinket there. She found an earthenware butter dish with a brightly painted cow reclining on the lid, and a cream jug in white ironstone, which was actually shaped like a cow. She bought both, deciding that now she had some independence she would start collecting such objects for her room. Schlegel was as greedy as Eleri and as interested in exotic food. They had a field day, accumulating unusual vegetables, bags of buckwheat and various other delicacies seldom seen in provision shops further west.

When they had finished, Schlegel took her first to a tiny Jewish general store where he bought pickled herrings by the pound from a capacious barrel, a large container of sour cream and some dark red onions. From a kosher bakery nearby he acquired a mound of fresh bagels. 'I know you will never have eaten these,' he said, twinkling with pleasure at introducing her to yet another new taste. 'They are hardly the breakfast food of people like the Cliftons, and I doubt whether there is a Jewish family living within miles of Fenton Parva!'

They staggered back into the Gower Street house soon after nine in the morning, giggling like naughty schoolchildren at their own self-indulgence. 'Oh, Karl, you're a genius at thinking up treats!' said Eleri. 'First the Blue Danube, then this . . . what are you going to think of next?'

'You would be most surprised if I told you, and I have no intention of doing so yet. It would spoil the surprises. But, yes, I have a few things in mind. You will learn about them in the end.'

Chapter Nineteen

Had the trip to America been made in the company of anyone but Julia Clifton, it would have been the journey of a lifetime. Even with such a spoiled young snob, it had its moments.

They started from Paris, where Lady Julia was having final fittings for her trousseau and awaiting its delivery while doing some more minor shopping. After that they took the boat train to Cherbourg and set sail aboard the *Ile de France* for New York.

Rose had known about the trip for almost two months, but she still had to pinch herself occasionally to believe she was making it. At first it had looked as if she was to travel cabin class, hurrying up to Lady Julia's boat deck stateroom each time her employer wanted something. Then Alexander Moncreiff had come to her rescue, although he had insisted it was for the sake of Julia's convenience.

'You can't go through nearly a week of shipboard entertainment with a maid a couple of decks below you,' he told her. 'That's utterly ridiculous. My father travelled with a valet in his suite, and he didn't need anything like the cossetting a woman always wants! I'll book a suite, Julia, and the maid can have a single stateroom opening on the far side of your sitting room. That way she'll always be on hand when you want her.'

'Oh, Alex, you really *do* spoil me!' Julia's smile had been pure honey, but privately she had felt considerable resentment against Rose. Why should a mere maid get the five-star treatment just so that she could be close to her mistress? Someone really should write to the likes of Cunard and French Line and tell them servants' rooms would be useful adjoining the upper deck staterooms.

But if any shipping company had such intentions, they were far in the future. The two young women found themselves sharing a three-roomed suite with a large central drawing room separating two bedrooms, one a roomy double, the second a perfectly adequate single. After all, it was first class. Like the drawing room, both bedrooms had doors on to the companionway outside. The shipping company was sufficiently flexible to have designed bedrooms that could be closed off and used separately if no one was booking them as part of a full suite.

Lady Julia was oddly reticent about the fact that her maid shared her quarters. There were at least four other female passengers travelling, as they were, in a mistress-and-servant relationship. Two of the servants were paid companions. The other pairs, like Julia and Rose, were rich women with their maids. The essential difference was that the others were Frenchwomen. They had the hard-headed, almost commercial, assurance too often lacking in the English. They paid their maids and trusted in external appearances to draw distinction between mistress and servant.

With Julia Clifton it was different. All her life she had been wrapped up in the cotton-wool of privilege. Her physical position at the top of her society was enough to keep her superior to servants and the lower classes. She had never really rubbed shoulders with the lower orders as she now had to with Rose, and was at a loss about how to behave. Her reaction was to try and pretend the maid did not exist. She kept conversation to the minimum, did as much as possible for herself, and gave Rose more free time than ever before. She did not identify the girl as a servant to the fellow passengers she met at dinner on the first night, and spent a great deal of time privately wondering why she had brought her own maid from England.

At first, Rose was unhappy and perplexed about the position in which Lady Julia had left her. She did not know where to take her meals, where to go for walks, where to enjoy her leisure. She was almost as free as the other first-class passengers, so much had Lady Julia's professional demands diminished. Sometimes Rose wished Lady Julia would use her as much as she had ashore. Anything would have been better than the limbo in which she now found herself.

Three years earlier, she would have kept her misgivings to herself, but she had developed a shell of self-confidence since then and now she confronted Lady Julia for an answer.

Julia Clifton shrugged. 'How should I know what you are to do?' she said sulkily. 'I only know this arrangement doesn't suit me at all.'

'I realise that, Milady, but I came to you in the hope that you'd tell me where I shouldn't go, and when. If you can give me some idea . . .'

Almost imperceptibly, Julia brightened. Of course! Why hadn't she thought of that? 'What had you in mind?' she asked, wary of sounding too enthusiastic.

'Well, Milady, meals are an obvious thing. I could have most of mine in the suite, and when it got too isolated I could go to one of the coffee shops or whatever when I knew you would be in the main restaurant.' Gradually Rose built up a convenient plan for getting them across the Atlantic without causing too much embarrassment to either of them.

The whole strategy appealed enormously to Lady Julia, but at the last moment she began fussing about her maid's getting enough exercise and some pleasure from the trip. Rose was thrown by her sudden concern. It was the first time she could recall Julia Clifton showing any anxiety for the well-being of anyone else, let alone a servant. Then she understood. Lady Julia was afraid her fiancé would quiz the maid about the joys of her first cruise, and would turn on Julia in anger if he learned that Rose had been a voluntary prisoner rather than embarrass her mistress.

But the arrangement proved simple enough to work out. The *Ile de France* was a big liner and it was easy to avoid someone if one worked at it. Once they had fixed their timetable, both women were relieved. Nevertheless it left Julia Clifton with yet another small, half-identi*̇* resentment against Rose. The girl was altogether too *̇*

too diplomatic, too efficient, too bloody self-effacing. Julia wondered how long she would put up with Rush once they got to America.

They had been at sea for two days. Early on the third evening, Rose was crossing the drawing room after tidying Lady Julia's stateroom. Her employer had already left for cocktails in the glittering full-size Parisian pavement café which was a star feature of the *Ile de France*. She had told Rose she would not want her again that evening, and Rose suspected that she was involved in some sort of brief shipboard romance. Where, she wondered, did Alexander Moncreiff fit in with that?

As she crossed the Persian rug in front of the drawing room's imitation fireplace, there was a discreet rap on the door. Surprised, she went to open it. It was at least an hour before her normal dinner time, and she had not yet submitted an order for cabin service.

Outside the door stood a steward, bearing a silver-plated tray with a bottle of champagne, a bottle of Guinness, an ice bucket, a chilled pitcher and cocktail stirrer, and two half-pint tankards. For a moment, Rose wondered if she were having an hallucination. Then she made a small irritated sound at her own stupidity. 'This is Suite A4,' she told the steward. 'You have the wrong place. No one here ordered that.'

The steward smiled. 'No, Miss. There's a note on the tray. Comes with the compliments of one of your fellow-passengers — for Miss Rose Rush.'

The note, unsigned, merely said: '*I promised we would try this together some time. Well, tonight's the night!*' It came as such a shock that she almost dropped it like an overheated dish. The steward regarded her with faint surprise. 'Shall I bring it in, Miss?'

Rose forced herself to smile and said: 'Oh — oh, forgive me, I was miles away! Just put it inside on the table, please. The bottles can go into the ice bucket. I have no idea when my guest will arrive.'

She sounded calm enough, even to her own ears, but

inside she was seething. What did it mean? Who could have . . .? 'Oh, Christ!' she exclaimed aloud, suddenly realising the source of the drinks. In her day-to-day life, she was so cut off from her fantasy afternoons that it had quite slipped her mind. Mark Fletcher-Simms must be aboard the *Ile de France*!

At first the very idea filled her with panic. This was Rose Rush, the lady's maid, not the bohemian beauty with glamorous dark blue stockings and a fondness for cheroots. How could she be anything but terrified? Here she was, alone and unprotected in the suite, and a man − a strong, hot-blooded man − was on his way to see her . . . Then she began considering her surroundings in a different light. The ship was as unreal as her fantastic voyages around artistic London. The woman called Rose Rush who inhabited the de luxe 'A' Deck suite was not really anything like the lady's maid who spent her time looking after a spoiled young society woman. The Rose Rush who was making this voyage was as fictitious as those long-legged art-loving females she had played with such panache in London. Any flirtation that went on now between herself and Fletcher-Simms would be as transient and as harmless as her silly girlish adventures in London. Why not welcome him, make up a story to suit present circumstances, and enjoy it? Rose turned and went into her bathroom to check her appearance in the full-length mirror behind the door. Hmm, not bad, she decided, if a little too restrained. Some scent and that organza dinner gown should do the trick . . .

Twenty minutes later Mark Fletcher-Simms arrived at the suite. He looked ridiculously handsome in his dinner jacket, his skin still deep olive, his black hair cut *en brosse* and springing back from a perfectly boned face. As she opened the drawing-room door, he shook a finger at her and tutted exaggeratedly. 'I should be coming along to spank you, not present you with the makings of a jug of Black Velvet, you bad girl!'

Rose gave him a shame-faced smile and stood aside to let him in. 'How did you find me?' she asked.

'I could never have forgotten that fallen angel's face,' he said. 'I'm still rather surprised you didn't notice *me*.'

'Where was I?'

'Sitting in the pavement café, with a large *café au lait* in a glass, smoking a cheroot and looking every bit the beauty I lost last year. I was strolling along the deck outside. I didn't come tearing in after you because I was determined that this time I wouldn't let you escape so easily. So I tiptoed away and eventually got hold of a co-operative steward who parted with your suite number for a price not far short of a round-trip ticket to New York.'

'Oh, dear! I am sorry.'

'Don't be. It was worth every penny. Now, while I mix us some Black Velvet, I think you have a little explaining to do. Fire away.'

As he stood over the bottles and ice bucket, Rose recounted her hastily composed story. 'I really meant to get in touch with you from Italy, Mark, honestly. But it — it was all just too much for poor Father. We'd only been there a week and he had a couple of bad attacks. After that, he went downhill at a gallop, and I was beyond thinking of anyone but him. He died there, you see. I don't know whether you have any idea how complicated it is to arrange preservation of a body and have it shipped back to England from abroad, but take my word, it seems to go on forever. By the time I got home and we'd held the burial service, I went into a sort of black depression. I must have been in quite a bad way, although I don't remember much of it now.

'Such family as we have is distant and rather grand — from my mother's side — and they all disapproved of Papa, so there wasn't much contact. They were very kind over this business, though. Came to the funeral and insisted on one or the other coming to see me at regular intervals. For a while they were the only people I *did* see, except for tradesmen.' (Well, she told her conscience wryly, there *have* been long spells when the Cliftons were the only people I saw much of!) 'There was some money left after I sold up the flat and some of the furniture and paintings — and my father had a little invested, enough for us to live in modest comfort.

'I was going to get right away from London — open a tea-shop in the Cotswolds or something like that — when one of the Clifton cousins came along and asked me if I'd care to take a trip to America before I moved. She's going over to get married. The family are paying for my round-trip ticket or I could never have considered it. Naturally I jumped at the chance. I shouldn't think I shall ever get the same opportunity again.'

'Poor butterfly!' he said, turning back towards her with two foaming mugs of Black Velvet. 'You've obviously been having a beastly time of it and I haven't helped by bursting in so bossily. How will this kinswoman of yours take to finding a man with you?'

Panic momentarily gripped Rose again. 'Oh — she mustn't! It's out of the question . . . that is . . . she wouldn't approve at all of my striking up a shipboard acquaintance, and she'd never believe we knew each other before. Anyway, she's likely to be out very late and to go straight into her room from the companionway when she gets back. We'd still better be gone when she does come, though.'

His smile was conspiratorial. 'Bit of a dragon, eh? Well, we'd better not make her breathe fire. How would you like to go along for a light supper at the pavement café?'

Rose glanced up at the clock. It was past 8.30. Lady Julia would certainly have moved on to the restaurant by now, and the dinners there were so sumptuous that she and Mark were bound to have finished their own meal if she decided to return to the café for after-dinner drinks. 'I'd love to,' she said. It was a very pleasant prospect, and it removed her from an altogether too risky situation here in the suite.

But he proved much harder to manipulate than she had expected. He gave her a delightful evening at the café, and she could not remember ever having relaxed so completely in anyone's company, male or female. Almost before she was aware of it, he was escorting her back to the suite, and she was protesting that if they stayed in the drawing room, her 'cousin' might catch them and be angry. 'Which door is yours?' he asked, almost casually. She indicated the one on the left of the drawing room. He strolled back across to her and extended his hands down to her, pulling her to her feet from the small bergère chair she was sitting in.

It was impossible to misunderstand his intention to kiss her, and Rose wondered for ever afterwards why she did not dodge away from him. How could she have changed so suddenly from fear of men to desire to be held and touched by one? The only explanation she could offer herself was that Fletcher-Simms was precisely the right man in precisely the right circumstance.

His kiss was delicious, gentle, exploratory and carrying the faint echo of the Napoleon brandy he had drunk after supper. When he eventually released her, Rose was quite breathless. 'You taste delicious,' he told her. 'I've been chasing you in my dreams ever since you disappeared from my life. I'm not letting you go again.' He bent to kiss her once more, and again, to her delight, she responded with pleasure instead of fear.

He glanced around the drawing room. 'Look, there's no trace of unauthorised revels in here,' he said. 'The steward must have cleared the stuff from the Black Velvet while we were at supper. If we simply drifted into your room, then shut the door, your dear cousin would never know you'd been out, let alone with a man!'

'It's quite a small room,' said Rose, a trifle dubious now.

His smile, like his intentions, was perfectly open. 'I'm sure it's sufficiently spacious for what we have in mind.' He opened her stateroom door and, leading her by the hand, went in. To her own unending astonishment, Rose followed him without protest.

That night re-made Rose's life. Years later, she read psychology textbooks in an effort to understand her own responses, but she never found a precise explanation, only glimpses of why her world had suddenly come right. When Mark Fletcher-Simms closed the stateroom door behind them and turned to embrace her, she melted into his arms and responded to his love-making as if no one had ever done anything to frighten or harm her.

'Wait a moment, my darling, I want to see that hair when it's down,' he murmured. Switching on the smallest, dimmest light in the cabin, he turned back to her and loosened the pins which fastened the dark luxuriance in place.

She laughed somewhat nervously as he did it. 'It's not really the way they say in the cheap romances, you know. It sticks, and stands out, and . . . oh!' As she rambled he had let down her hair, and it was exactly as it was in the cheap romances. Rose's hair was so heavy that, instead of bushing unattractively around her face, it cascaded down beyond waist level, a glossy dark stream which seemed to hold the essence of night in its shining coils.

'Exquisite,' Fletcher-Simms murmured. 'You could be some nymph, or a mermaid perhaps – not a flesh-and-blood woman at all.' He ran his hands lightly down her body and added: 'Then I *feel* the flesh and blood and know I was wrong. Oh, Rose, it's been such a long time . . . I've never wanted a woman so much, never!' He buried his face against her throat, kissing the hollows in her white flesh and the silky gloss of her hair in a series of intoxicating caresses.

Rose felt passion rising within herself, with a speed and intensity she would not have thought possible only a few hours ago. Why now, why him? The questions passed fleetingly through her mind and were gone as quickly as they occurred. She did not care. His hands were tracing a path of exquisite torment down her body, over the sinuous silky fabric of her dinner gown. Within seconds he had encircled her body and was unfastening the tiny buttons which held the garment in place. He slipped the fine organza off her shoulders and the gown slithered gracefully to the floor, surrounding her like a giant rosebud.

Mark stood back with a gasp which combined lust and admiration in equal degrees. 'What a beauty you are,' he said. 'Rose, you're unique! I've never encountered a woman remotely like you.'

She stepped out of the discarded gown and stood inches from him, clad only in panties and stockings. 'And never will, I hope,' she said, barely above a whisper.

He pressed her back on to the bed, and when she was lying down, carefully unrolled the dark silk stockings, then slipped off the satin panties. 'You're just like Goya's *Naked Maja*,' he told her. 'It's like making love to a boyhood dream.'

Rose smiled lazily at him. 'Don't you think you'd better take off some clothes, too? I'm beginning to feel under-dressed!'

He laughed, bent to kiss her forehead, then stood up and began undressing. She watched avidly, savouring the compactness of his muscular male beauty, longing for him to touch her again. Some instinct warned her not to make speeches about being new to such encounters. This was a man who liked exotic, experienced women, not shy little girls. It was a role Rose took to as a duck to water.

Rose had been sexually ruined by a man who stank, who looked ugly and behaved violently, and had been ravished with the connivance of and in the presence of her own father. Nothing could have been more different from that terrible night than what happened between her and Mark, and perhaps it was the simple fact of her freedom to choose, as well as her temporary escape from her prosaic identity as lady's maid, which enabled her to relish it so much.

Mark was the polar opposite of Alf Dobson. He was scrupulously clean, as fit as an Olympic athlete, and almost impossibly handsome. There was a smell about him of good brandy and cigars overlaying expensive soaps and toiletries. His teeth were even and perfect; his breath sweet. The body which slid between the sheets beside her was hard as whipcord and ready to give them both pleasure. As his fingers trailed over her skin, Rose was almost delirious with her desire for him. She knew what he was going to do to her, and it seemed the only desirable conclusion to their encounter. As she reached for him, her long, slender legs twined around his and her arms drew him against her soft body. Mark pressed his head between her breasts, and began nuzzling them with his lips. He sucked her small pink nipples until they stiffened and bloomed under his caress, then drew back momentarily to look at her body. 'You really are the most beautiful woman I've ever seen, Rose,' he murmured. 'Oh, for the talent to paint you!'

'No need for painting talent with what you've got. Oh, Mark love me, please love me!'

He slipped his fingers down between her legs, parting the soft lips of flesh beneath the little bush of crisp hair, and seeking out the seat of her excitement. Rose uttered a sharp gasp as he began to press his hands rhythmically against her. 'What are you doing? Stop it, I can't bear . . . no, I can't bear you to stop, either! Oh, please, Mark, fill me up!'

'I don't think I can wait much longer, either,' he murmured, shifting his weight slightly. And then it was the moment Rose had always dreaded most: the moment when a man pressed his full weight down on her and penetrated – possessed – her body. But instead of fear, this time she felt only a great rolling wave of excitement. She lay back against the mound of pillows, arching her body up to meet his, and he mounted her like some prize stallion, beautiful, fluid, entirely desirable. He thrust deep inside her and his erect penis slid into her as smoothly as silk. Her own body picked up the rhythm of his movements, and to all intents and purposes they were one being. As his passion and the speed of his movements into her increased, so her own excitement mounted, and as Mark spent himself in her and slumped down on to her soft, pliant flesh, Rose felt her own consciousness cut itself adrift and throw her into a delicious limbo where nothing counted except the completeness of her union with this beautiful male.

Mark stayed with her until past four in the morning, making love to her three times after the first, perfect, coupling. Nothing could duplicate the intensity of that pleasure for Rose. Now she never completely lost control or awareness of her individuality. She still enjoyed every moment. She was vaguely aware of Lady Julia returning to her own stateroom in the small hours, and wondered once again what Alexander Moncreiff would have to say if he knew of her behaviour. Vaguely, she wondered if the American had booked her into a suite with his fiancée as much as a chaperon as a maid. But she set aside the idea. It was no concern of hers. She took her orders from Julia Clifton and she seemed to want as little as possible to do with Rose on this voyage. That suited her perfectly. With a companion like Mark Fletcher-Simms on hand, who needed an employer breathing down her neck day and night?

Her idyll with Mark continued for the remainder of the crossing. He spent the major part of the next three nights in Rose's bed, revelling in their shared pleasure as they grew more accustomed to each other — indeed, in Rose's case as she became more accustomed to any physical contact with a man. He made a perfect companion for her, because he was sufficiently unconventional to refrain from interrogating her about her sex life before they met. It was obvious that he assumed she had had one, and going on the image of a glamorous bohemian which she had worked at projecting to him, she was unsurprised. She paid little attention to the past, because as the days at sea slid by, she was increasingly concerned about the future.

Alone after preparing Lady Julia for a grand entrance at some shipboard party or other, Rose had time to do plenty of thinking about Mark Fletcher-Simms. After a couple of days, their affair was showing signs of becoming something else. Perhaps that suited him. It most certainly did not suit Rose. Although she had shaken off much of the mental maiming she had received as a child, a great deal remained of which Rose herself remained largely unaware.

Her parents had been legally married and ostensibly respectable, and yet her father had failed to provide for the family, had neglected his younger daughter to the extent that she died, and had beaten his wife to death. After that, he had not only failed to provide for the surviving child, but had sold her to a drunken crony. Rose was capable of summarising her childhood in those terms. She did not fully understand that it made her irrationally wary of the married state, or of anything which smacked of a woman volunteering to put herself under the control of a man. Mark Fletcher-Simms attracted and excited her, but what guarantee did she have that he was any different from the lowest costermonger?

Nor had she seen much evidence that matters differed greatly in other classes than her own. In Belgrave Square, the Earl of Clifton made much of going in fear of his wife's unpredictable rages, but there was no question of who ruled. He did as he pleased, neglecting her for long stretches of the year while he went off heaven knew where with vague excuses about shooting or looking at paintings, and dismissing her resultant bad behaviour with a casual wave of the hand as evidence of the fickleness of womanhood. Rose wanted none of that any more than she wanted to be tied to a parasitic wife-beater.

There were other, more immediate, complications, too. Fletcher-Simms had swallowed Rose's explanation of her earlier disappearance without questioning it. Having caught a glimpse of Lady Julia in a particularly sulky mood the day after his and Rose's first love-making, he also fully understood why Rose wished to keep their relationship a secret. Beyond being somewhat surprised at Lady Julia's youth, he had found nothing odd in the story. But now he was talking about some serious permanent attachment to Rose, and if that happened, her true origins were bound to come out. Rose was convinced she knew how he would react. No man in his position would attach himself permanently to a former servant-girl. Either he would abandon her, or she would be turned into some sordid little kept woman, tucked away in a flat in St John's Wood or Chelsea. Rose was not enthusiastic about remaining a lady's maid, but on balance she preferred that prospect to the alternative of being pigeon-holed as a paid mistress.

All of which left her with a considerable problem: how to ditch Fletcher-Simms when they reached New York without him knowing where she was bound. The dilemma recurred with increasing frequency throughout the remainder of the voyage, but Rose was at a loss to solve it.

In the end it solved itself. Mark was deeply in love with her by now, and he was a wealthy, profoundly self-indulgent young man, still at the age when the whole world seemed attainable to him. Indeed one of Rose's misgivings about his feelings arose from a suspicion that he wanted her so much now because she had disappeared before he could define the terms of their earlier relationship. He regarded the Atlantic crossing as one of the great romantic events of his life and became increasingly misty-eyed as they drew closer to America and the end of the voyage. By the last evening he was weltering in a pool of freshly generated nostalgia for the past few days. Rose inadvertently compounded his starry-eyed attitude by announcing that she would be prepared to eat publicly with him that evening in the liner's main first class restaurant. Lady Julia had given her express permission to do so after accepting an invitation to a cocktail party and private dinner in the *Ile de France*'s most luxurious suite. Rose had few doubts that the dinner would be *à deux*, and that Lady Julia would be saying a few intimate private farewells to whoever she had been seeing for the past few days.

Nevertheless it gave Rose a chance to appear in public and to shine brightly, enslaving Mark even more deeply when he saw her behave impeccably and look wonderful in such a grand setting. Here was a woman he could take anywhere and be complimented on his choice of partner! He never ceased to be amazed that a mere university professor's daughter could turn out to be as sophisticated, fashionable and self-possessed as Rose.

As a result of his immense satisfaction, he drank far too much. He escorted Rose unsteadily back to the suite, but when they arrived even he could see that if he came in, he might well still be there the next morning. Rather than risk such an embarrassment, he made much of kissing her hand and giving her a flourishing goodnight bow out on the companionway. Then he departed for his own stateroom, saying over his shoulder: 'I shall be up to see you first thing, and we'll make arrangements to meet up in New York. After that, dear girl, I have plans for you!' Then he was gone, taking the corner to the lifts with a slight stagger.

Rose hurried inside and went straight through to Lady Julia's stateroom to check the state of her packing. Yes, everything was in order apart from what Lady Julia had worn tonight, and her cosmetics and scent. It would be the work of a moment to finish that off in the morning. Her own preparations were equally close to completion. She took a bath, then retired alone to bed for the first time in four nights, to lie awake trying to work out some way of dodging Mark the next day.

She need not have worried. As the great liner approached New York the following morning and the passengers lined the rails for a first glimpse of the famous skyline, there was no sign of him. Lady Julia was sulky and preoccupied, extremely reluctant to look anywhere over to her left, where Rose assumed that her temporary romantic interest must be standing. As soon as the great ship nudged into its pier, she was chafing to be off. Rose followed her with a huge silent sigh of relief, wondering what on earth had happened to Mark but immensely glad that something had.

In fact, as the ship docked, he was still fast asleep in his stateroom. Too much burgundy, too much brandy, and a succession of delightfully sleepless nights had combined to give Rose the most prosaic escape route in the world: a man who overslept his appointment with destiny. By eleven o'clock, Lady Julia and her maid were sweeping through midtown Manhattan in a taxi, en route to the hotel where they would stay for a couple of days before Alexander Moncreiff met them to escort them to Virginia. Rose Rush, glamorous bohemian daughter of a dead professor of classics, had once more changed her identity to Rose Rush, lady's maid, and Mark Fletcher-Simms had lost his madonna yet again.

Chapter Twenty

Safely ashore, Lady Julia instantly readopted the mistress-servant relationship. That entirely suited Rose, who had felt faintly disorientated throughout the ocean crossing by her untypical behaviour. By the time they had settled in at their New York hotel, she had almost succeeded in convincing herself that Lady Julia's changed manner had been responsible for her own surrender to Mark. If only she'd had a clear idea of her own position . . . if only there had been some strong focus in her world, instead of the quicksilver, elusive Lady Julia.

But there Rose was forced to stop herself. The truth of it was, she admitted to herself, that she still had no explanation for her total surrender to Fletcher-Simms, and no rational grounds for having run from him when they docked. True, the explanation of her servile status might have caused embarrassment, but neither she nor anyone else could be certain of his reaction. At their last rendezvous, Mark had shown every sign of being permanently besotted. As she played the real lady so convincingly, it was at least possible that he would not have cared two hoots that it was all an act — might even have laughed with her about it.

Too late now to brood about any of it. She had no desire to go on waiting hand and foot on Lady Julia, but there was no avoiding the fact that she had no wish, either, to escape the life by any act as drastic as marriage. Rose felt vaguely ashamed of her own coldness at the thought of Mark waking to find he had lost her again. Somehow, just as the Rose he knew ceased to exist in this world, she managed to change him from a flesh-and-blood man into a fairytale figure when her reality reasserted itself.

As she busied herself hanging the clothes Lady Julia

wanted unpacked for the brief stay in New York, she was left with just one cause for deep unease. She remembered an earlier parting from Fletcher-Simms, when she was about to go to Italy with the countess. He had said then, only half teasingly, 'Don't you dare forget, or I shall find you wherever you are. Just remember that — wherever you are.'

How silly! she reprimanded herself. What possible chance did he have of finding her? He had not done so when she went off to France and Italy — for all she knew had not even tried — and it was even less likely now that he could locate her in this vast continent. Rose went to find Lady Julia's favourite shampoo and setting lotion. Doubtless she would want her hair washed and styled before Mr Moncreiff arrived this afternoon.

If Lady Julia's private dalliance aboard the *Ile de France* had left her with a guilty conscience, she hid it well. Alexander Moncreiff arrived in time for a late lunch, and spirited his fiancée off to some fashionable restaurant he had mentioned in a letter. Lady Julia went off cooing like a tame pigeon, responding flirtatiously to his compliments and occasionally flashing Rose the odd glance as if to make sure the maid would not betray any confidences. Though God knows why, thought Rose. I've no idea what she was up to. I was far too careful about keeping out of her way.

That afternoon she went out for a long walk, to gaze at opulent shops and buildings taller than any she had ever seen. What a place! There was something instantly intoxicating about it, and Rose wished they were staying more than two days. She could feel the city calling her to come out and *use* it, goddammit, and there was no question of her wishing to project herself into a series of fantasies here. The city was enough. It was its own fantasy, a place she felt she could explore with delight until the end of her life.

It was different with Washington. She could find little charm there when she first saw it, or later when she got to know it better. They did not visit the capital at first, apart from arriving at the Union Station. A chauffeur-driven limousine met them there and whisked them off to Manley

Heights, the Moncreiff family estate in Virginia, overlooking the Potomac. That was certainly impressive, drawing a gasp of admiration even from the blasé Lady Julia, who had lived in and visited grand houses all her life.

Perhaps Manley Heights impressed Julia Clifton because it was a modern house. She knew all about the draughts, the rising damp, endless corridors and remote kitchens of England's finer stately homes and they did not impress her. But Manley Heights combined the grace of neo-colonial architecture with the convenience of a modern Bauhaus-designed villa. The original plantation house had burned to its foundations in 1910, and Alexander's grandfather had set about finding an architect who could design a new mansion that reflected the family's dignity without being either avant garde or conservative-monstrous.

'He certainly succeeded. What a glorious place!' said Lady Julia as Alexander explained. 'When was it finished?'

'Not until 1916, and that was just the main house. The staff quarters and the pool were added in the early 1920s — not that they weren't in the original plans; it's just that Grandfather was getting frail by then and the family decided to postpone the final work awhile. The old boy never lived to see the whole thing completed.'

The house was long, low and white, with big sash windows, each with double shutters. Creating staff accommodation in a neat row of apartments that looked like cottages had made it unnecessary to tack on a third floor to house them, and the result was a seemingly endless low-slung run of elegant windows in minimal walls. The architect had paid homage to the traditional southern plantation house his design replaced by creating an enclosed front porch complete with columns and pediment, echoing the original long, open gallery that had run along the façade of the ante-bellum mansion.

At the northern end of the building, overlooking the Potomac River, was a feather-light parody of a Victorian conservatory, all graceful cast-iron arches, painted white and sugar-candy pastel shades. Instead of the usual old-fashioned winter garden palms and tropical ferns, it was stocked with a spectacular range of exotic flowering plants. 'Grandfather was a fanatical orchid grower,' said Alexander. 'Mother doesn't like orchids, so when she and Father took over after Grandfather died, she converted it. The far wall had to be almost entirely glass, because it gives fabulous views down to the river.'

Tucked discreetly out of sight behind the house was the biggest privately owned swimming pool Lady Julia had ever seen, complete with a range of changing cabins. Mature trees alongside the winding front drive led the eye to the house – 'We were lucky, the trees weren't damaged in the fire,' explained Moncreiff – and to complete the ravishing picture a number of very expensive-looking horses grazed in the sloping meadows between the house and the public highway.

'I could live here for ever,' said Julia, starry-eyed.

Moncreiff hardly seemed to notice her enthusiasm, as his own was elsewhere. 'Only vacations and weekends, I'm afraid, darling,' he told her. 'Remember my plans. Washington will be home for us. I plan to run for Congress in two years. By then I want to know every wrinkle of Washington from an insider's point of view, and that means living there. It also means you exercising every ounce of your upper crust English charm to see they all have us pegged as Washington's most glamorous newlyweds.'

'I'm beginning to wonder if that isn't why you proposed to me: "Gosh, here's a good looking young Englishwoman of the right class. She could be just what I need . . ." '

He had been contemplating the front of the house. Now he turned and looked at her sharply. 'What is it, Julia? This is quite unlike you. Did something go wrong aboard ship?'

'N-no . . . I just . . . oh, never mind! I expect I'm just jumpy over the huge change in my life and everything, and all of a sudden it seemed you were more interested in *what* I was than *who* I was. Let's just forget about it, shall we?' But in the back of her mind there lingered the picture of the tall, blond, slender and penniless young German who had turned her head aboard the *Ile de France*. He had been convinced they should run away together and live in hope her father would give Julia a handsome allowance which would keep them both. With all her heart, Julia had wanted to accept, but her head was more mercenary than her emotions. Finally, with infinite reluctance, she had said goodbye to him.

Now, as the Virginia spring turned to full, luxurious early summer, she enjoyed Manley Heights while she could and prepared for what sounded like the wedding of the year. She had known since their engagement was announced precisely the wedding gown she wanted, and that she would have to exert every ounce of available charm, tantrum and blackmail she could lay hands on to persuade her father to pay for it. In the event Alexander unwittingly provided her with the perfect weapon by asking to stage the wedding in Virginia. Relieved of the bill for a vast society marriage in England, George Clifton could hardly cavil at paying for a rather indulgent bridal gown.

It had been the talk of Coco Chanel's show in Paris in August 1931, because Chanel had always scorned the couture tradition of ending the show with a wedding gown until this year. All the gossip columnists picked up the fact that this year she had made an exception as a farewell gesture to her lover, the Duke of Westminster, from whom she had just parted. Not only was the story meat and drink to the popular press, the design to which it drew attention was one of the most beautiful Lady Julia had ever seen.

She was a tall, excessively slender woman, with dark reddish-brown hair and the long legs and ribcage which showed off Chanel clothes to perfection. The wedding gown was made of ivory slipper satin, with a waistline cut high beneath the breasts and accentuated by two bands of bias-cut fabric. Where they met the vee-neckline of the gown, a stiffened collar curved up and back to frame the wearer's neck and face. Observers had always said La Grande Mademoiselle had a long, graceful neck. This was the design which demanded a similar endowment in the client who wore it. The collar curved up like the backing for a Tudor princess's ruff, ending so high that it was almost a support for the bride's head. Chanel, always a showman at heart, had taken account that most people saw more of the bride's rear view than anything else. A vertical row of tiny satin-covered spherical buttons ran from the base of the collar back, bisected the waistbands and ended just where the cleft of the buttocks would have shown had the bride been naked. The sleeves of the gown were long and skintight. At the back, the skirt extended into a train almost four yards long which required strong corn-fed American girls and hearty English huntresses to bear it behind the bride.

A veil of finest silk tulle overlaid the gown, held in place by a tiny Juliet cap of ivory satin, trimmed with colourful miniature flowers. The drawing which had captivated Lady Julia showed the bride carrying a great sheaf of Arum lilies, and she ordered them as soon as she arrived at Manley Heights.

No society wedding of the time was complete without its regiment of bridesmaids. Julia's two grown-up younger sisters were to be her attendants, supported by Moncreiff's sister Eleanor and his cousin Jenny. Lord Clifton had rebelled at the idea of outfitting them, too, in Chanel, claiming that he could have invited half London to a home-produced wedding reception at a fraction of the price. As a result their gowns were designed and made by a London dressmaker, but so skilfully that they matched the line and mood of the bride's Chanel creation.

Rose envied her mistress the half-dozen couture outfits which were Alexander Moncreiff's main gift to his bride, but not the wedding gown. It was the last type of garment that interested her. Instead, she coveted the wonderfully simple jersey knit Chanel cardigan suit, the swirling Vionnet afternoon frock, and above all a classically draped evening gown in sky blue by Madame Alix at the house of Grès. Hanging them in their monogrammed dress bags in Lady Julia's closet, Rose stroked the Alix gown almost reverently and whispered: 'One day, somehow, *I'm* going to have clothes like this!' She never took the fantasy further, because there seemed no way of making it a reality. And this was one daydream she desperately wanted to come true.

* * *

Julia Clifton had gone to America six weeks before the wedding. Her family guests arrived a few days before the ceremony, her sisters Mary and Ruth itching with impatience both to meet eligible American men and to wear their peach silk bridesmaids' gowns. They drove Julia to distraction, because by now she was working up her own private head of nerves about whether the wedding would go off smoothly; whether marrying here in Virginia would seem quite as smart in the eyes of her ex-deb friends as it had in a wintry London townscape; whether she would be able to cope with the dreaded move into Washington, and above all whether her indispensable lady's maid was heading for a mental breakdown at the very time when her services were most needed.

Rose was wondering herself if the sky was about to fall on her. It was looking terribly as if the one problem had arisen now which had never entered her head during her short affair with Fletcher-Simms: she was pregnant. As she lay, sleepless, in her pleasant room in the staff terrace, she would curl herself into a tight ball and mutter unceasingly: 'Don't let it be true . . . it can't be . . . it's not fair . . . I was just . . .' And all the time her saner self seemed to be standing aside, a faintly exasperated onlooker, telling her that if she had thought the possibility of pregnancy was all part of a fictional world of her own creation, she was about to be proved wrong.

Already she felt sick in the mornings; she who could normally get up at any hour and eat whatever was available as breakfast, now found the mere thought of food and drink nauseating for at least an hour after she awoke. Her periods, for years as regular as a military band, had stopped. She had been due ten days after her arrival in New York. That had been five weeks ago, and still nothing had happened. In moments of panic, Rose even suspected her waist was beginning to thicken, but at that stage her native common sense generally saved her. Nevertheless she went about her work distractedly, gave monosyllabic answers to Lady Julia's questions, and was generally a shadow of her former self. Not that she became incompetent. Rose could never have been that; she was too conscientious and too well-trained. But for a couple of weeks she functioned as no more than a run-of-the-mill lady's maid, and the change was shockingly obvious to Lady Julia.

In a way, Rose was lucky Julia Clifton was now her employer instead of the countess. Venetia Clifton was a far shrewder observer of human frailties than her daughter would ever be. She had also borne six children of her own, and knew the signs in some women before they were aware of their own condition. At least Rose had only to contend with Lady Julia. In Julia's mind, there was only one possible explanation for Rose's distraction: she was insanely jealous.

Julia never succeeded in seeing a world which did not revolve around herself, and in this case she thought it obvious that a girl in Rose's subservient position, witnessing all this glamour and wealth, and getting to know Alexander Moncreiff, who clearly knew how to charm every female in the neighbourhood, would be sick with envy. That made Julia more indulgent. She liked to be the object of such feelings – it meant she had all sorts of good things someone else lacked, and even if that someone else were just a servant, it was something. She bore with Rose's lacklustre performance and enjoyed the feeling of added superiority it gave her.

After a while, Rose's panic faded, although her intense worry did not diminish. Helpless to remedy her condition, she was forced to get on with her life, and after a week of intense misery she settled to the round of doing her job with her old competence.

The wedding ceremony was to be held in the long drawing room at Manley Heights. A huge marquee on the Moncreiffs' lawn was to house the reception, giving guests a choice of staying under the shade of the pink and white canvas or of strolling on the grass and enjoying the view. Little groups of white wrought-iron tables and chairs had been arranged on lawns and terrace, and by early afternoon on Lady Julia's wedding day, the whole scene resembled a feature in a smart magazine. Which was precisely what it had been designed for.

One of the glossies had been invited to send a reporter and photographer to the wedding – the Moncreiffs regarded mass coverage as too vulgar for words, but Alexander was determined to obtain the desirable type of coverage to help lay the foundations of his political future. The newly-weds were photographed talking to all the correct people; the bride's parents were given particularly reverent attention as English aristocrats, and the reporter mopped up information about 'your divine family home', as she insisted on calling it.

When Moncreiff carefully let slip that they were renovating a two-hundred-year-old house in the down-at-heel Washington suburb of Georgetown as their permanent base in the capital, the reporter picked it up without breaking her stride and pestered Lady Julia to be permitted to come and interview her about the project as soon as she returned from her honeymoon. Venetia Clifton would have refused the request out of hand. In twenty-five years of marriage she had put a great deal of work into outclassing the aristocracy. Had she been able to buy public amnesia about her origins in the brewery trade, she would have. Failing that, she merely became one of the most regal women in society. Permitting magazines to run features on one's houses qualified as the depth of vulgarity for Lady Clifton. For Julia it was a blissful opportunity to show off, and she jumped at it.

Alexander and Julia were honeymooning at Westport, Connecticut, where a college friend of Alex's had lent them his ocean-front house with its own private beach. In the interests of newly wed privacy, they had decided not to take any servants with them. There was a resident cook-housekeeper who shared a cottage in the grounds with her husband, the head gardener and estate caretaker. She was to be their sole protection from fending for themselves for the two weeks which were all Moncreiff said he could spare away from Washington.

As their enormous car bowled off down the drive in mid-afternoon, followed by the cries of well-wishers, Rose relaxed with a sigh of relief. Two weeks to be her own person! It seemed almost too good to be true. Admittedly she had promised Lady Julia she would keep an eye on what the decorators were doing with the Georgetown house, but that was more to ensure they finished on time, than to supervise the work. The Moncreiffs had agreed firm designs for all the rooms and the decorators were sufficiently careful of their high reputation not to jeopardise it by deviating from the plans.

Lady Julia's attitude to living in Washington had lightened when she saw Georgetown. True, it was shabby and run-down; but anyone looking closely could see it was about to zoom back into fashion. And there at its heart would be that clever young Moncreiff couple. She could already hear admirers murmuring: 'Of course, they had the sense to see its potential and move in before prices went through the roof.'

It was Alex who had drawn her attention to the inevitability of Georgetown's resurrection. 'Look around you,' he said. 'Georgetown was an established, busy settlement when Washington was still a fever-laden marsh. The houses are all at least one hundred and fifty years old, most of them much older. That one and the one down at the end there are still lived in by the descendants of the people who built them. Three across from where we're standing are all being renovated after some clever risk-taker snapped them up. It's time we did the same.

'The sort of people coming into Washington now won't want to live in nasty modern suburbs. They'll want this sort of elegance. And just think, you'd be living in a place as good-looking as an English mansion without any of the inconvenient plumbing and faraway kitchens. British tradition meets American know-how. It can't fail. Just like us, when you think of it!'

In a rare sunny mood, Lady Julia squeezed his arm, smiled radiantly and repeated: '*Just* like us, darling!'

It was a sultry afternoon in mid-July. The doorbell made a subdued jangle somewhere deep inside the bandbox-smart house. Within moments an immaculate butler opened the door and in due course told the caller that if he cared to wait in the hall, he would enquire whether madam was at home. Eventually the young man was shown into a small sitting room furnished perfectly to fit in with the exterior design of the house. The woman who came towards him was as smooth and sophisticated as a marron glacé.

'Good afternoon, Mr Fletcher-Simms,' said Lady Julia Moncreiff. 'How can I help you?'

It was Rose's afternoon off, and she had used the time to explore some of Washington's public buildings and monuments. Normally such an expedition would have filled her with enthusiasm, but today her feet felt leaden and she shuffled about attempting without success to be interested in what she saw.

She was now almost three months pregnant, and still no solution presented itself. She had not sought confirmation from a doctor, but for the past two weeks she had needed to do no more than look at her own naked body to know it was true. There was now a small but distinct bulge in her abdomen, and her breasts were fuller and more tender than they had been in the past. Physically, she was once more in the bloom of good health. The nausea had gone, except for an occasional twinge of queasiness in the afternoon. Her skin glowed, her hair was even silkier than ever, and people were apt to turn in the street to admire her good looks. When she momentarily forgot her condition, she felt marvellous, but inevitably a cloud of gloom would descend once more when she remembered the circumstances.

At last she decided to return to Georgetown. She would be much too early to start helping Lady Julia to prepare for dinner, but wandering about like this was no way to spend her time. Rose decided she would prefer to curl up in her room with a book until she was required.

As she let herself in through the servants' entrance, Willa James, the cook, said: 'Lady Julia said you was to go see her as soon as you came in.'

Rose was taken aback. 'But I'm not at the end of my time off, yet. Surely she remembered it's my free afternoon?'

'Don' know nuffin about that. She jus' said to tell yer, an' I'm tellin' yer.' The cook's expression was surly. When will I ever get used to these unwilling domestics? Rose wondered. One met plenty of servants in England who hated their lot, but none who took such scant pains to hide the fact. Rose shrugged and left the kitchen, wondering what bee Lady Julia had in her bonnet this time.

She did not remain ignorant for long. Julia Moncreiff heard her mounting the steep staircase from the basement kitchen, and as Rose reached the top she practically bounded out of her sitting room into the inner hall. 'So there you are, Rush! I want a word with you!'

'Of course, my lady. I hope it wasn't inconvenient for me to take my afternoon off . . . it *is* my usual day.'

'As a matter of fact it *was* inconvenient – damned inconvenient, not to mention deeply embarrassing. Come into my sitting room at once.'

She can't know I'm pregnant; no one knows, not even a doctor, thought Rose. What on earth can be making her so angry?

'Close that door,' snapped Lady Julia. 'This is strictly between you and me. I don't want the other servants getting to know about it.' Rose had hardly turned from the door when she went on: 'Are you going to deny that the name Mark Fletcher-Simms means anything to you?'

Oh God, oh God, oh God, thought Rose. She reached out blindly and clutched the back of a stiff chair to keep herself upright. 'How did you find out?' she said faintly.

'Find out? I didn't need to find out. He came and told me!'

'He what?'

'He came here – here to my house – to tell me he was looking for my cousin and ask if I knew where she was. My cousin! I feel like killing you for that, Rush. You're my maid. My *maid*, d'you hear me? How dare you claim me as your kinswoman?'

'I-I couldn't think of any other explanation at the time, Milady, and he was someone I'd known before who had no idea I was a servant.'

'I should think not! He's clearly a man of some refinement and taste. He'd hardly spend his time running about in public with a maidservant, would he?'

'No, Milady.' Rose's voice was barely above a whisper.

'Then why lie to him in the first place?'

'I-it seemed so harmless. After all, when I knew him in London, there was nothing serious about it. It was just lunches and visits to galleries.'

'You went to art galleries with this man?'

For the first time since the confrontation began, Rose met her employer's eyes defiantly. 'It's not against the law for even a maidservant to look at pictures on public display, as far as I know, Milady.'

It was Julia Moncreiff's turn to glance away, her face flushing slightly. 'Maybe not — but I'm sure that contributed a great deal to these ridiculous ideas you seem to have of your own social importance. I'm far more concerned about the way you lied to me, and to Mr Fletcher-Simms, aboard the *Ile de France*.'

'I can't quite see why it was so harmful to you, Milady. You said yourself that the less we saw of each other on the crossing the better, and I merely arranged matters to fit around what you wanted to do. No one could have been more surprised than I was when Mark Fletcher-Simms showed up aboard, and I only saw him at times when you didn't want me. Surely you don't believe servants should be stopped from having any sort of social life or friends of their own?'

Julia Moncreiff thought precisely that — it was too advanced by far for her liking. Some modern customs appealed to her far less than others. One could hardly imagine a servant like Rush answering back in her mother's youth. But she was aware that few people would publicly support her approval of friendless, celibate domestic staff, so she returned to another tack.

'What about all these disgraceful lies?' she demanded. 'What have you to say about that?'

'I can only apologise again, Milady. But even that did no harm. Only Mark heard them.'

'That's not the point — not the point at all!' Lady Julia pressed on with juggernaut force. 'I'm going to give the matter serious thought, but I think you may find yourself out of a job by tomorrow, Rush!'

Rose, who had been experiencing waves of nausea for the last couple of minutes, let out a little gasp of protest and leaned more heavily against the chairback. Then, before Lady Julia's horrified gaze, she was violently sick on the Aubusson carpet before collapsing in a dead faint.

When Rose regained consciousness she was in bed in her own room. The seventeen-year-old parlour-maid, Lizzie, a far friendlier girl than the cook, was bobbing about the room, apparently intent on flicking away non-existent dust from the furniture. Rose assumed she had been ordered to remain there until she herself came round. She ran her tongue over her dry lips. The inside of her mouth tasted terrible.

'Lizzie,' she murmured, her voice sounding cracked and strained to her own ears, 'how long have I been like this?'

The maid, whose back had been turned to Rose, gave a violent start and turned. 'Oh, Rose, you gave me a fright! You've been out for nearly two hours — had us all worried.'

Two hours! My God, it didn't seem possible . . . her mind began to reconnect, hazily at first then with too much clarity. She gasped and pressed a hand to her mouth. 'Milady's carpet! Was I really sick all over it?'

'Threw up from one end to the other,' said Lizzie with a certain grim satisfaction. 'Cook said she woulda thought you was too skimpy ta hold that much!'

Rose shuddered. 'Don't! It's bad enough that it happened. What did Lady Julia do about it?'

'Yelled her head off for Lambert and me and told us to get you up here and for me to undress you an' clean you up. Then she called the doctor on the telephone.'

'Oh, no. When is he coming?'

'Been and gone already, so there's no call for you to fret, Rose.'

Panic flared inside her. 'But he can't have! I would have come to.'

'He said you'd passed into a something-or-other sleep, natural, after the faint wore off, and you'd be better left undisturbed as you never moved a muscle when he took a look at you. Didn't seem to think there was too much wrong.'

'Did he say anything apart from that?'

Lizzie giggled. 'Not to me, dope! I'm just part a the help in this house. I think he was with Lady Julia for a while downstairs, though.'

Rose closed her eyes wearily as despair replaced the panic. Oh, well, if there had been anything to salvage before, it was quite gone now. Lizzie came over to the bed and gave her arm a little shake. 'Don't go back to sleep, now. Lady Julia said I was to fetch her the minute you woke up.'

'All right, then. Go down and get it over with.' Rose lay back against the pillow and awaited the catastrophe she knew was at hand.

Julia Moncreiff was prey to a handful of warring emotions at that moment. She was angrier than ever at Rose for having vomited all over her precious carpet. Certainly, it could be cleaned to look like new, but Julia would be unable to look at it again without remembering the disgusting incident. Hard on the heels of her anger came guilt. She was still incensed that Rose had pretended they were related, but was also aware she had been completely excessive in her reaction. She was able to put two and two together from what the doctor had said and come up with the unpalatable fact that stress and harassment had directly caused Rose's collapse.

Fortunately, the doctor did not know of the scene immediately before Rose passed out, and when he had examined the maid thoroughly he came up with the probable cause of the strain. She was about three months pregnant and clearly had no one to whom she could turn in a foreign country. The prospect of inevitable dismissal from her job and the lack of any means of returning home to England had undoubtedly done the rest.

The news of Rose's pregnancy had filled Julia first with surprise and then relief. While she awaited the doctor's arrival, she had been casting about for a reasonable explanation she could offer Alexander for Rose's abrupt dismissal. She could hardly tell the truth, for if he learned of the existence of Fletcher-Simms and his visit to the house, the whole story of her own behaviour during the Atlantic crossing would come out. She knew that would drop her into more trouble than Rose over the whole matter. Now she could simply tell Alexander, truthfully, that Rose was pregnant and was therefore being dismissed. No decent man would tolerate, let alone expect his wife to retain a servant in such circumstances.

And Rose? said the already-fading voice of her conscience. 'Damn you to hell, Rush!' she spat out. Lady Julia still had not the faintest idea why she had reacted so violently to Fletcher-Simms's tale of shipboard romance, beyond resentment that the younger woman seemed to have got away with having a better time than she herself. Fletcher-Simms had been completely frank with her, having arrived at the house still convinced she was Rose's cousin who could direct him to her.

When she disabused him, at first he was stunned, then, responding to suitably malicious observations from Julia, increasingly angry with Rose. By the time Julia had finished making a few unflattering adjustments to the truth about her maid, Fletcher-Simms was vowing he never wanted anything more to do with the girl and cursing himself for a fool at having been involved in the first place. Wherever else Rush might care to look for salvation, she thought savagely, Fletcher-Simms was not it.

Lizzie tapped timidly on the door of the small sitting room. 'Please, Milady, you said to let you know when Rose woke up. She came round about five minutes ago.'

Lady Julia stood up and moved to the door. 'Thank you, Carter. I shall ring if I require anything. You can go back down to the kitchen and get on with those jobs you were doing for Cook.' She wanted no eavesdropping by other servants on this confrontation.

Chapter Twenty-one

Lady Julia had learned the art of manipulation early in her girlhood when she subjugated her younger sisters with a mixture of bribes, threats and tittle-tattle. She had used similar tactics on her friends, and because of her family's social standing, her good looks and capacity for enjoying a good time, they endured her tricks instead of deserting her.

She had been less successful with young men, much to her fury. They tended to start off finding her irresistible, then to cool off gradually as they tired of her brittle manner and dedicated self-centredness. That was why she had swooned so gracefully into Alex Moncreiff's arms. She chose to ignore his frank statement of his plans for the future, secretly convinced she would change his mind when the time came. And her vanity forbade her even to consider the thought that his proposal of marriage was prompted not by overwhelming passion but by the careful calculation that she would be an invaluable political accessory.

Now that the initial gloss had worn off the surface of the bride's life, she was beginning to question whether she had achieved what she wanted from life, and rapidly concluding she had not. All of which boosted her considerable existing ill-will for the world in general, and ensured that she would give Rose Rush an extremely hard time.

In the maid's bedroom, she said: 'Well, Rose, what have you to say for yourself? The doctor told me about your — ah — unfortunate condition. I hope you were not entertaining any thoughts of concealing it and staying on here.'

Rose, her face red with shame, stared down at the counterpane and murmured: 'I had no idea of what I should do. I certainly never meant to deceive you — I just had nowhere to go.'

'You should have thought of that when you got yourself into trouble in the first place. Too late now to play the injured innocent. I think there is little point in further discussion of the rights and wrongs of the matter. You've chosen to take a certain course and it's up to you to make your way.

'The doctor tells me your general health is extremely good and there are unlikely to be complications in your pregnancy. Given that it still has some months to run, I think it would be best for you to start making your arrangements as quickly as possible. You can stay here for another week, but after that I shall require the bedroom for your replacement. I'm sure you will have firm plans by then.'

She hesitated for a while, avid for an overwhelmed reaction from Rose. But the maid did not give her the satisfaction of tears or pleas for charity. She did not even look at Lady Julia, continuing to stare at the bed cover. At last she said, very quietly, 'I shall make sure I'm gone by next Friday.' Lady Julia had to be satisfied with that, for Rose neither said nor did anything further.

It was different after she heard her mistress's footsteps retreating along the landing and starting down the stairs. She buried her face in the pillow and sobbed until there seemed to be no tears left. Then she got up and went along the landing to the servants' bathroom, where she ran herself a deep bath of tepid water and relaxed in it for an hour to refresh herself in the afternoon heat. By the time she emerged, her emotions were back under control. You're Rosie, remember? Skinny little Rose Rush from up Ladysmith Court. She can live on chucked-out bits of fried fish and sleep on pavements if she has to, and she still survives. She doesn't need anybody, *not anybody* to get her by . . . A vivid picture of the police sergeant who had helped her so long ago, and whose name she had never known, flashed through her mind. Yes, perhaps there had been someone, once, after all. Never mind. All that was a long time ago and a continent away. She would manage here, and she had no intention of crawling to Julia Moncreiff in a misguided attempt to save her skin.

When Rose had stiffened her courage sufficiently to confront her mistress again, she went down to see her. Lady Julia glared across at her from the elegant little writing table where she had been writing invitations to some party or other. 'I was under the impression that we had nothing left to say to each other,' she said in a fair imitation of her mother's iciest tones.

Rose remained calm and looked directly at her. 'Forgive me for bothering you, Milady, but I thought I should ask whether you will want me to act as your maid for the next week.'

The thought had yet to cross Julia's mind. Her lady's maid played such a major, though normally unremarked, role in her life that she had not stopped to think what would happen until she found a new girl. Perhaps she should — no, the idea was appalling, after the trouncing she had handed out today. However great the inconvenience, she couldn't possibly have a silent, resentful Rose going about her normal tasks until the day of her departure.

'Out of the question!' she snapped, as if Rose had been asking a favour rather than seeking instructions. 'I couldn't possibly permit you to continue now. I shall just have to arrange something to tide me over.'

She would have taken pleasure in dismissing the maid in a sufficiently churlish manner to make her feel worse than ever, but Rose was armoured against hurt now, and denied her the opportunity. 'Very well, Lady Julia. I shall go back to my room and start sorting my own things. I'll be there if I'm wanted.' Then she left, closing the door silently behind her.

The following week was one of the most difficult of Rose's life. She felt like a ghost, haunting a building where once, however briefly, she had been at home. Lady Julia quickly acquired a temporary maid through one of her husband's family contacts, and after that, life in the Georgetown house appeared to continue without a ripple. Rose kept to her room as much as possible, or made quick sorties to eat at small, inexpensive restaurants. She had no intention of giving Lady Julia the satisfaction of saying she had fed her maid during an inactive period of notice.

The one bright spot occurred the day before Rose was due to leave. As far as she knew, she was to be paid for her last month — the week of confinement completed the term — and would receive nothing else. She had some money saved, but was not at all sure how far it would take her at American prices. Everything seemed so different here than in England. Then, on her penultimate day, she saw Lady Julia leave the house and get into the family limousine. Moments later, someone tapped on the door and when she told them to come in, it turned out to be Lizzie.

'Mr Moncreiff wants to see you, Rose. He's down in the library, and could you come down as soon as possible, please?' she said.

In the library, Moncreiff gave her a friendly smile and waved her to a chair. 'I understand you've had a few problems lately, Rose,' he said. 'I'm sorry you have to leave us, but there seems to be no way of arranging things so that you can stay with my wife.'

'I wouldn't have expected it, sir. It's entirely my responsibility.'

His smile was approving, but he did not pursue her response. 'The reason I'm talking to you now is that I think circumstances have conspired to make things very uncomfortable for you. I think the least we can do is to give you a good start.'

'In what way, Sir? I don't see what you're getting at.'

'Well, for one thing, I thought you might be happier back in England, among your own people, at a time like this. I was proposing to buy you a boat ticket and give you something to put you on your feet at the other side.'

Rose's laugh was derisive. 'What on earth would I go back to? Mr Moncreiff, can you begin to imagine what would drive a young girl or boy into domestic service?'

For the first time, it seemed, he looked at her as a human being instead of some part of the household fixtures and fittings. 'No, I can't say I have. Go on.'

'I won't bore you with what might be called my family life. Let's say that a twelve-hour day as an under-housemaid was a better bet. England never gave me anything. I hacked out everything I needed, and nobody helped. Why should I want to go back? There's nobody to look after me.'

Moncreiff found it difficult to control the lump in his throat. The girl who sat at the other side of his desk was beautiful, calm and apparently resourceful. She had described hell in a tiny masterpiece of understatement. And he had been sitting there playing the grand gentleman, offering a boat ticket back to torment.

'What were you planning to do?' he asked.

She shrugged, then smiled, and her face was transformed. 'I've spent this week asking myself the same thing. I haven't come to any useful conclusions yet, but I'm damned if I'll let it beat me. When we docked in New York and stayed there a couple of days, I started to fall in love with it. I think I could start again there, with everything new.' He tried to break in but she stopped him with an impulsive gesture. 'No need to remind me that New York is Harlem and Rivington Street and the Bowery just as much as Central Park and Fifth Avenue. Even the slums are new by London standards. I grew up among people who were sinners before the Dutch had bought Manhattan from the Indians!'

He managed a rueful laugh. 'That was exactly what I intended to say. How do you propose to conquer it? New York is quite a citadel.'

'And I'm quite a fighter. I shall manage. You can help me, though, with advice if nothing else.'

'Name it.'

'Well, for a start, your wife hasn't mentioned a reference. I have no intention of begging, Mr Moncreiff, and you may feel as reluctant as she does about it. If you do, so be it. But please let me point out that no one has criticised my ability as a maid. Lady Julia's mother recommended me to her daughter because I was so competent. I've worked to the best of my ability, and I've always given her the highest level of service. Would you be prepared to give me a really good reference? It would make all the difference in the world.'

'Of course I will. My wife is still a little upset about the entire business, so we won't discuss it with her. I'll give you a reference on headed writing paper, and if anyone wants to follow through, tell them to contact me direct. What else?'

She gave a little shamefaced giggle. 'I know this might sound childish to someone who knows his way around as you do, but I've never applied for a job, not even back in England. I know there are domestic employment agencies, but I don't know how to start choosing one, and I don't know anything about their registration procedure or fees or anything. If you could tell me, it would help a lot.'

'Of course. My secretary can get that information in half an hour. I'll get her on to it this afternoon. What next?'

She looked at him blankly. 'Well . . . nothing. That would be most helpful. What else could I reasonably ask?'

'Much more than that, I think. Hasn't it occurred to you that this sort of conversation isn't too common between an employer's husband and a soon-to-be ex-lady's maid?'

'I wouldn't know. It's the first time I've ever been a soon-to-be ex-lady's maid!'

He grinned back at her. 'Okay. We won't go into that too deeply. Let's leave it at saying that when you followed Lady Julia over here, you weren't to know it would be such a short-term engagement. Whatever the rights and wrongs of the situation, I think we have a moral obligation to see you aren't destitute over here. At the very least we have to pay to transport you back home. If you prefer to remain here, we should look at spending the same on giving you a reasonable start over here. If you really think you can handle New York, I think that adds up to a train ticket from here to there, and some ready cash to set you up.'

He opened a small cash box at his elbow and counted out a sheaf of bills. 'I was thinking in terms of three hundred dollars. That should see you don't starve, at least. No arguments, please! I have a feeling I've heard something less than the full story of this little incident. Let's regard the three hundred as compensation. Whatever it may be, it isn't charity. I'll also give you my business card. I think you may need a little extra support sometime, and if you do, don't hesitate to contact me.'

Rose was fighting back tears. 'Why are you doing this for me?'

He shrugged. 'I've asked myself that. One reason is just what I told you: I don't think I've heard the full story. But even if I have, I get the feeling you're an exceptional young woman. I'd hate to think of you being washed up for lack of three hundred dollars. And let's face it, it will hardly bankrupt me!'

Rose looked down at the business card and wad of banknotes in her hand, then raised her eyes to Moncreiff once more. 'You're a very understanding man,' she said. 'I hope Lady Julia realises how fortunate she is.'

She got up and moved to the door. As she opened it, Moncreiff said: 'I'll put the reference and agency information in a sealed envelope and have Lizzie slip it under your door, or get you to come down and collect it here tomorrow. Try not to worry too much. With your spirit, you'll ride this trouble and come out on top. I'll be in there pitching for you.'

'Thank you, Sir. I think I shall need all the good wishes I can get.'

Three days after her arrival in New York, Rose was becoming desperate. She had registered in a cheap boarding house for women, and had set out bright and early on her first day to try the domestic employment agencies on the list supplied by Alex Moncreiff's secretary. They were all strung out along Sixth Avenue, and her first sight of them did nothing to reassure Rose.

The Williams Employment Agency occupied the upper floor of a shabby building next door to a doughnut stand. Dilapidated signs on the outer wall made it clear that the agency derived its income from the workers it placed, not the employers.

announced the biggest sign. Beneath it was a list of the type of worker they offered, ranging from restaurant waiters and waitresses through hotel staff to housemaids and cooks for private households. A short line of aspiring employees queued outside the street door, all of them smartly if cheaply turned out. Taking their numbers as an indication that this must be a good place, Rose joined the queue.

Half an hour later, she was interviewed by a grim-faced harpy in a black jacket and skirt. The woman glanced at Rose's carefully prepared training and employment record (Rose had decided the Parsons Green Training Centre might seem impressive to people who had never been in suburban West London), then turned to the reference from Moncreiff. She sniffed suspiciously. 'I don't recall ever seeing a female domestic's reference provided by a man,' she said. 'You sure this is above board?'

Rose raised her eyebrows and looked as superior as possible. 'Of course it's above board! Would I have produced it if it were not?' The woman's expression indicated that was all too likely, so Rose improvised hastily. 'Mr Moncreiff's wife, Lady Julia, broke her wrist a couple of weeks ago and she still can't write. She's going to be out of the social swim for a long time and doesn't really have use for a lady's maid until she's recovered. She asked me whether I'd prefer to work as parlour-maid until then, or find another job more appropriate to my experience. Check on it if you wish – the telephone number is on the letterhead.'

She made the last suggestion with her fingers crossed behind her back. It was a reasonable explanation, and this did not look like the sort of establishment to waste money on a long distance call if the evidence seemed sound. If she lost the gamble, there were four other domestic agencies and two office appointment bureaux on Alexander Moncreiff's list, so all was not lost. The woman appeared to give the matter extended consideration and then, reluctantly, nodded. 'Okay. Suppose it sounds reasonable enough. You realise New York isn't the best place for private service these days? The Crash made an awful lot of people learn they could get by cheaper with less human help and more kitchen gadgets.'

'I know times are not good, but I have worked at the best houses, I've learned hairdressing at one of the best salons in existence, and I'm a first-class needlewoman. Surely that makes me easy enough to place?'

The woman pursed her lips. 'Don't be too sure of that, Miss Rush. There's a lotta my ladies would curl up and die of embarrassment if they had a maid like that. They're just not used to it. They feel more comfortable with a girl who's just up to getting them by.'

Rose bit back a sarcastic comment and there was a short silence while the woman skimmed through the register of vacancies in front of her. After a while she looked up and said: 'Hmm, if you want my opinion, you'd do better going to an hotel. I could fix you up in one of the big ones with no trouble.'

Rose was aghast. 'Doing what? I'm a lady's maid, not a bed maker!'

'Well, the luxury places all offer a personal maid service. Clients who want one just ring down and get assigned one from the pool.'

'And between assignments? I take it I'd be cleaning bedrooms and dusting furniture. I've never heard of an hotel keeping idle staff around on the chance of a booking.'

'Yeah, more or less. But what's so bad about that? One sorta help's much the same as another.'

Rose stood up and held out her hand. 'Not for me, I'm afraid. May I have my papers back? My apologies if I wasted your time. It seems we can't be of use to each other after all.'

The woman shrugged and handed over Rose's documents. 'Suit yourself, Miss Rush, but I wouldn't go getting too many big ideas if I were you. You'll get the same story from every agency along Sixth Avenue.'

She was right. Each one seemed more fly-blown than the

last. Each interviewer seemed more bored or contemptuous with the job applicants. By the third day, Rose was frantic. She had noted a couple of other domestic bureaux and tried them. All were terribly similar to those on Moncreiff's list.

In the end he had personally handed over the list, cash and a train ticket to New York. 'It seemed churlish just to let Lizzie push it under your door,' he had said.

Looking at the agencies, Rose had said: 'There are two office employment bureaux down here. It's very kind of you, but I have no experience of that sort.'

'No, but I have a hunch that what you find at those other places will be anything but what you're expecting. A good-looking, smart girl like you could hold down a job as a receptionist without any trouble. It's just an extra suggestion, that's all.'

Now she was going to see whether he had been right. She could not stand the thought of yet another of those pathetic fly-blown agencies which universally described her and her kind as 'help'.

The Adams Office Staff agency could not have been more different from the other places she had visited. A fashionably dressed woman seated Rose at a table and gave her a form to fill in, covering her background, training, experience and desired type of work. After that she waited in a spacious outer room while her application and reference went to whoever would be interviewing her. Unfortunately the pleasant surroundings produced no more optimistic results than the squalid domestic bureaux had.

Her interviewer, a courteous young man, was apologetic. 'Five years ago, I could have placed you in any of a hundred offices at a really good wage,' he told her. 'You have the looks any businessman would pay to have fronting up his organisation as a receptionist. But since the Slump started, times have changed. They have fifty to choose from now where there were six of them clamouring for one member of staff before. I can see that the sort of domestic work you were doing would fit you for a receptionist job just as much as it did for dealing with demanding employers, but they wouldn't even bother to find that out in times like this. Quite frankly, Miss Rush, I have a couple of ex-Vassar girls on my books who'd be happy to get the sort of job you're talking about.'

Rose sighed and gave him a glum nod. 'It was worth a try, anyway,' she said. 'I simply couldn't stand another of those terrible domestic agencies.'

He was sympathetic. 'All I can offer is advice, Miss Rush.' He gave her a winning smile. 'I may not be able to get you a job, but I'd love to buy you a drink after work today and pass on a few tips. How about it?'

She opened her mouth to refuse and then thought, Stop it, Rose. You've stopped living in a dream world, remember? This man is reality. She forced a smile. 'You're on. Where shall we meet?'

They arranged to see each other in an hotel coffee shop round the corner from the bureau, then Rose got up to leave. 'It's not that I'm reluctant to work as a maid,' she explained. 'It's just that they all seem to think I'm only good for scrubbing floors or making beds in hotels, and I'm not prepared to do either.'

She was half-way out through the open door of his office as she uttered the last words, and as she turned to leave, a woman who had been coming from the room next door said: 'Not so fast — please don't just disappear — you're English!'

Rose turned back. 'Yes. What about it?'

'Oh — well, it was just a bit of a surprise. Sorry to stop you like that, but I am, too, and it was so lovely to hear a voice from home . . .' Embarrassed, she stammered to silence, and Rose responded with a friendly smile.

'I should apologise for being so rude. I'm a little on edge from having been trodden on so often lately, I expect.'

The other smiled tremulously back. 'You too, eh? Grim, isn't it? Are you off to another place now?'

'No. I think I've had all I can take for one day. What about you?'

'Same here. D'you eat lunch, or are you on a fresh-air diet?'

Rose laughed. 'I still manage the lunch queue. How about you?'

Another tremulous smile. 'I get either lunch or dinner, so if I make it lunch today . . .'

Suddenly Rose wanted to make a kind gesture and to share a little of her pent-up frustration with someone who understood her predicament. 'I can stake us to lunch, then you'll still manage dinner tonight. I didn't get a bad pay-off at my last place. No arguments, come on. We'll find a good deli and eat there.'

The other Englishwoman was called Lilian Shaw. She was an experienced secretary and had been doing well enough in England until the slump around the 1926 General Strike. 'I must be the original Jonah,' she said, 'because no sooner did I come over here to work for a big American company than they had their Crash. I held on to my job for a couple of years — even if it sounds boastful, I'm ever so good at my work — but six months ago the company collapsed under us. There were only a handful of us left by then, and we all went under together.

'I looked at my savings account and worked out I could go eight months if I lived on ten dollars a week. I shared an apartment then with two American girls, but my share of the rent and bills was twelve dollars a week, so I had to pull out. I found a furnished room for five dollars. I allow myself four dollars for food and anything else that comes up, and put aside a dollar for the week's car fares to go looking for work. You can see how far that's got me!'

'But as you're so competent, what's the problem?'

'I'm too expensive, dear, that's what. I was earning a damned good wage with Omega Finance and in a very trustworthy position. I'm still not quite badly off enough to take a dive into some typing pool or lawyer's back office for the privilege of earning ten dollars a week. I can live on that anyway until my savings run out.'

'How long have you got to go before that happens?'

Lilian's smile slipped. 'Two months. Timed it badly, didn't I, to run out of money in the Fall? Much easier if you do it in April. At least you've got the summer in front of you then.'

Both women turned instinctively from the unlovely thought and concentrated on their vast sandwiches of pastrami on dark rye bread. After a while, comforted by the warmth of the rich, fatty cured beef, Lilian said: 'So how grim are things with you? I get the impression you haven't been job-hunting as long as me.'

To her own astonishment, Rose found herself telling Lilian almost everything. The only part she left out was the fantasy encounters with people like Mark, merely keeping him as 'someone I knew in London who turned up again on the ocean crossing'. Afterwards she considered again and again the fact that she had never even been capable of confiding in her friend Margaret Armstrong, yet here she was, unburdening her life's miseries to a complete stranger.

When she had finished, Lilian gave her a gentle smile. 'I wondered if pregnancy had anything to do with it,' she said.

'Oh, God, does it show? I was hoping . . .'

'No, it's all right. I went through almost the same thing seven years ago back in England, so I know the signs inside out.' Her eyes held a faraway look. 'No question of marriage; no question of supporting the poor little mite when he was born, either. So I had to part with him. He was adopted by a very nice couple, they told me after.' Abruptly she pulled herself together. 'This is daft. You make your own life once you're grown up, and you have to live with what you do. Let's think about you.'

'I don't see how thinking about me will help,' said Rose with a sigh. 'I should hate to work in an hotel, but I suppose I might at least stand a chance of getting good tips if it was one of the fancy places. That would be something towards when the baby comes.'

'You're going to need an awful lot more than good hotel tips to survive with a kid in New York,' said Lilian. 'Look what's happening to *my* savings. Money just melts in this city.'

'Yes. I'm afraid it took what you said to bring it home to me. When I got that three hundred dollars I thought as long as I could get a job to fill in, that would pay for the baby and everything. I'm just beginning to realise it won't.'

Lilian played about with her coffee spoon for a while, then said: 'How much are you paying in this boarding house?'

'Eight dollars a week and they give you coffee and rolls for breakfast in the price.'

'Christ, I'd expect ham and eggs for that! Makes it easier to say what's on my mind. There's a two-roomed place going in the little apartment house where I live, and it's eight dollars a week. I'd like it, because it's quite recently refurnished and of course it's far roomier than my little place. What would you say to sharing? If you got sick or anything, at least you'd be with someone who knew about your condition.'

'Would you be willing to do that, just on the strength of a couple of hours' acquaintance?'

'Good grief, love, when you were in service before you got to be a lady's maid, I bet they just put you in to share with anyone who was handy. And from my point of view, this meeting is long compared with some of the snap introductions you get to possible room-mates if you answer adverts in this city. What d'you say?'

'I think I'd be happier than I've been for some time,' said Rose. A wistful tone crept into her voice. 'It would be so nice to have someone I could trust to talk to.'

Lilian laughed. 'Well don't get too hooked on it, kid. I may be out on my ear by the end of September if something doesn't come up pretty damn quick!'

Rose had quite forgotten her drinks date with Eddie Hansen from the employment agency. Now she recalled it abruptly and said: 'Hey, I'm seeing the employment interviewer for drinks when he finishes work this evening. Maybe he'll have some ideas.'

Lilian almost choked on her coffee. 'Telling me he'll have some ideas, with a girl who looks like you! Just you watch your step. You've got enough troubles as it is.'

'Go on — a couple of drinks never hurt anyone and I've got a head like solid teak for spirits. I'll be all right. Might even get a free dinner out of it,' Rose added, grinning.

'That's as may be. Just remember, city boys are sharp in New York. He doesn't sound like an imported hayseed to me. They're the only ones who generally get taken for dinner and drinks in New York without getting anything back.'

They chattered on amiably to each other for a long time. When they parted, Lilian went off to arrange a transfer to the two-room flat at the end of the week, Rose to give notice at her boarding house that she was leaving. Both women felt better than they could remember.

At six o'clock, Rose was bathed and changed and back downtown for her rendezvous with Eddie Hansen. He slid into the coffee shop booth opposite her and smiled broadly. 'My, but you're a sight for sore eyes after a hard day!' he said.

'Compliments will get you everywhere.'

'If only I believed that, I'd be the happiest man in New York. No, I promise, I'll rack my brains for helpful suggestions and I shall be as gentlemanly as your gorgeous looks permit.'

'You *are* nice. Let's go and have that drink.'

When they had settled themselves into a cocktail lounge and Rose began working steadily through a series of large gin-and-tonics without apparent effect, Hansen began to look more and more impressed. 'Hey, you never ran one of those old-time gin palaces back in London, did you?'

'My family invented them. Don't worry, my speciality is failing to slide under the table! Forget the gin. I want to pick your brains.'

'Be my guest. I only wish it could be more useful to you than it will be. What d'you want to know?'

'I want someone in the business to explain why there's such a vast difference over here between your sort of agency and those that place people in domestic service. In England they certainly look different from one another, but they operate the same way and there's no question of the domestic places looking shabbier or treating clients any worse than the office bureaux..'

'That's simple — it's a different world over here. I've never managed to work out whether Americans resent waiting on people because we're a nation of natural free spirits, or because so many of us had our roots in countries where we weren't much better than slaves and we arrived here determined we'd never be treated like that again. Either way, the whole domestic service scene has a crummy air about it, whereas our side is fixing up smart, or clever, or well-qualified young people with the sort of jobs they identify as leading them somewhere. For "somewhere", read up the ladder of success. They all regard domestic work as something you do as a last resort.'

'But don't the agency proprietors see that they degrade the business themselves by making it so sordid?'

He was fatalistic. 'What can you expect? The employers are unenthusiastic about paying to hire help, so the agencies load their fees on to the staff they engage. That means low fees — basic salaries aren't anything to boast about — and it often takes a while for the new employee to scrape up the cash to pay. That means they operate the tightest ship you ever saw — certainly too tight for smart offices with waiting rooms and so on.'

'I was beginning to wonder if it was something like that . . . and that's making me wonder if it can be changed.'

Hansen touched the brim of an imaginary hat in mock wonder. 'Jee-zuz, lady, there's a word for what you're being now.'

'What's that?'

'Chutzpah. A Jewish friend of mine explained it as what you see when a guy is on trial for murdering his parents and pleads the mercy of the court because he's an orphan. You're an unemployed lady's maid. How can you even *think* of taking on a sector of New York business and winning?'

'But, Eddie, the more I think of it, the more convinced I am that it would work like a dream if it was done properly. I'd advertise it in the posh newspapers, make a thing of the fact that I was the agency who expected the employer to pay, because you only get the best if you pay for it. I'd start with a small office, but it would be at a decent address and it would look like a million dollars. And I – wouldn't – use American staff! The real secret would be that they'd all be English-trained domestics, with the best manners imaginable. What d'you think?'

He was gaping at her again, even more astonished than when she had started drinking steadily. Finally, he said: 'You're a great girl, Rosie, but I think you're crazy. I think you're crazy and I think you'll probably end up in jail. But, goddammit, there's a little bit of me that thinks it might just work. Whatever happens, I wish you success from the bottom of my heart. What is it your countrymen say? The best of British luck to you.'

Her eyes were shining. 'That's it! That's what I'll call it – Best of British. Come and see me in five years, Eddie. I'll be a millionaire.'

'Don't you mean millionairess?'

'Silly – who wants to be a millionairess when they can be a millionaire?'

Chapter Twenty-two

Eddie Hansen took Rose out to dinner and spent most of his time with her trying to dissuade her from what he considered a crazy scheme. 'Have you the faintest idea of how much money it takes to set up any sort of new business here?' he asked. 'D'you imagine those people who run the domestic employment agencies *want* them to look shabby and run-down? If there was profit in it, they'd have done it long ago!'

But Rose was determined. 'Rubbish!' she told him. 'You know as well as I do, they keep their premises like that because they don't give a damn what the customers think about the surroundings. And why not? Because the people who pay them aren't the rich employers, they're the poor workers. If the employers were paying the commission, you'd be trampled in the rush as they roared off to the interior decorators!'

Her enthusiasm outran all his objections and lasted until she was back in the boarding house. Then she began to have doubts of her own. By midnight she was convinced she was merely inventing a new set of daydreams. Eventually she drifted off to sleep, depressed and confused.

It was different in the morning. When she began to pick over the poor corpse of her great idea, she realised it might not be dead after all. 'Planning – that's what it needs!' she muttered. 'I'll sit down and work it out on paper.'

Rose had never undertaken an exercise like this before. Her domestic work had never involved her in the sort of budgeting and provisioning carried out daily by cooks and housekeepers. Nevertheless, she had managed her own meagre wages efficiently, in order to afford silk stockings and good shoes to match her expensive hand-me-down clothes, not to mention the cheroots and the occasional bottle of gin.

It couldn't be that much harder to work out what it would cost to run a little business. In any case, there was no time like the present for finding out.

After breakfast she went back to her room and dug out the exercise book she used for her Italian practice. Turning to the back of it, she wrote out laboriously: 'Best Of British – estimated costs'. She spent half the morning writing down everything she could think of, then went downstairs and called Lilian's apartment house from the payphone in the hall. Rose half expected her new friend to be out job-hunting, but Lilian said she had decided to give it a miss today because she had lost heart in the whole business. 'I was starting to get my things together for our move,' she said. A tone of anxiety crept into her voice. 'You're not trying to find a nice way of saying you changed your mind?'

'No, silly – I'm as keen as you. I just have this big idea and I think two heads are better than one. My date last night seemed to think it was a complete non-starter, but I want another opinion. If I went out and grabbed us a bag of sandwiches, would you fancy coming over here for the afternoon to talk it over?'

'You're kidding! Food *and* decent company? It's the best offer I've had in weeks. Expect me in an hour or so.'

Rose went out to buy a huge bag of deli sandwiches. On the way back she begged a bowl of ice cubes from the landlady, a friendly enough soul so long as her young women paid their rent regularly and refrained from smuggling men into their rooms. When Rose informed her she had a girl friend coming to share cold lunch in her room, the landlady positively glowed at her. Something told Rose this might be a good day to consume the last of her precious gin, and it was only half as delicious without ice.

Lilian duly arrived with two enormous containers of hot coffee, which they drank with the sandwiches. 'So what's this big idea you've had, then?' asked Lilian, her voice muffled by a mouthful of ham and cheese.

'I'm losing my nerve about telling you, now. I started out convinced I could do it, but first Eddie Hansen said I was off my head and I have a feeling you'll think the same. Tell you what — let's leave it until after we've eaten. I've got some gin and it mightn't sound so daft with a bit of mother's ruin to smooth the way.'

'Gin? Dear God, I haven't had a gin since the week I lost my job! I'll say yes to anything if you give me a few sips of that!'

Rose grinned at her. 'Thought you might. There, why should we worry? When we run out of cash we can always take up residence in Skid Row.'

'Have you ever *seen* Skid Row? Thought not. Believe me, it's enough to put you off booze forever!'

Rose poured two generous gin-and-tonics and they sat sipping them for a while before Lilian's curiosity got the better of her. 'All right, you've softened me up. Let's hear the big idea.'

Faltering at first, but speeding up as she gathered confidence, Rose outlined the idea behind Best of British. When she had finished, Lilian smiled doubtfully. 'I think I need another gin if you can spare it.'

Rose poured them another drink. 'Does that mean you're going to tell me it's out of the question?'

'It's hard to say, love. I think it's a wonderful idea, and I certainly think the combination of snob appeal and a chance of top quality servants will attract rich people like flies. But you'll never be able to afford it, that's what bothers me.'

Rose nodded glumly. 'Yes, I know that's the weakest point of the whole thing. But suppose I could scrape together some cash. What d'you think?'

'If you could keep afloat for six months, you'd be made. But Rose, you'll never even raise the deposit for office accommodation, let alone anything else.'

'I still have two hundred and fifty dollars left of the money Mr Moncreiff gave me — and twenty dollars savings I brought from England.'

'Oh, little Miss Bigshot! I can just imagine how far that would go. Probably cover an office with no cash left to stay alive on, let alone anything else.'

'I was afraid you might say that. Of course, there is another way — maybe.'

'Which is?'

'Mr Moncreiff said if I needed any help or advice, to call. I have his business card, so I wouldn't need to contact him at home.'

'And what would you say when you got hold of him?'

'I'd offer him a share in my surefire business success, in return for an investment of — shall we say — fifteen hundred dollars?'

'We can *say* twenty thousand, ducky. Getting it is another matter entirely. What does this benefactor get for his money?'

'A choice of his money back with bank interest on top, after the first or second year, or a cut of the business — perhaps twenty per cent.'

'You're crazy, but I like your style!'

'Well, let's pretend I have the money. Look at what I've written down in this notebook. Can you see anything I've missed out?'

Lilian took the notes and began to read, smiling indulgently at the name of the proposed business. Then the smile gradually faded. 'Hey, Rosie, where did you learn to think like this? It's so — so precise! You haven't missed a thing that I can see.'

Rose's basic proposal was to rent small but good offices as a base, then advertise, either in the domestic service columns of the newspaper classified sections, or to organise a mail shot to all the best addresses in Manhattan. The whole selling strategy would be aimed at telling people they only got the best if they paid for it; that for centuries the British had been training and employing domestic staff and that they were still world leaders at it; that Best of British had an unequalled network of contacts in London who could supply the sort of servants wealthy New Yorkers sought in vain among their own countrymen and -women.

'Just one thing, Rose, as well as the little matter of finance: where are all these British contacts of yours?'

Rose waved a hand airily. 'I'd simply get in touch with three or four of the middle-range domestic employment agencies in London and offer to share commission on any placements we made here of people registered on their books. I can also try the housekeeper at my ex-employer's place. I got on really well with her, and she'd be bound to come up with some promising ones.'

'Rose, you just said "we". Don't tell me you're roping this chap Hansen in with you!'

Rose was momentarily incredulous, then burst out laughing. 'I meant *you* and me, idiot!'

'Oh, no! No chance. On second thoughts, Skid Row doesn't seem such a terrible choice after all . . .'

Alexander Moncreiff was reading Rose's business plan for the fifth time and shaking his head in wonder. It didn't seem possible that a girl without any but the most primitive formal education, who had gone into domestic service at an age when more privileged children were just outgrowing their dolls, could have acquired the intellectual skills necessary to work out something so dynamic. But she had, and she had been bright enough to write it all down legibly and send it to him after their telephone conversation on the subject. He felt faintly guilty about his own patronising attitude when she had first contacted him. After all, he *had* told her to get in touch if there was anything he could do . . . it was just that 'anything' had not been to stake her in business. It would never have occurred to him that she had it in her, for a start.

Well, now she had more than half convinced him, and he was in New York to discuss the whole thing in detail. Julia knew nothing about it. She thought he was going to the city for a couple of meetings with important Democratic politicians. In fact he was seeing a couple of them. No point in confining the trip to just one interest. Time wasn't necessarily money, but it was a vital commodity to anyone as hungry for power as he.

He met Rose and Lilian at the apartment they shared. It was small and modest, but immaculate. Rose introduced

Lilian as 'my right hand if we ever get this agency going'. Moncreiff talked to them for more than an hour, with Rose saying most but Lilian contributing sufficiently to convince him she had a shrewd head on her shoulders. Finally, Rose had covered everything she could think of, except to add: 'Of course, if it really got off the ground, I'd cut the weak link — the London agency connection — and open a branch over there to assess and recommend people. That way we could guarantee the standard we offered.'

'That clinches it,' said Moncreiff. 'Rose, I'm afraid I won't lend you fifteen hundred dollars.'

Lilian uttered a despairing sigh. 'Told you not to raise your hopes too far, didn't I?' she said.

Moncreiff merely grinned at her. 'I didn't say I wouldn't help, Miss Shaw. I happen to think that with just fifteen hundred dollars and change in your safe, you'd sink without trace and I'd lose every penny of my investment. Now, if we made it five thousand dollars, you'd have a far better chance.'

'I might faint,' said Lilian.

Rose was radiant but there was a hollow feeling of fright beneath it. 'I told you, the choice would be repayment in a year or two years, or a share of the business, Mr Moncreiff. I'd have to withdraw the choice. The agency would never make enough early on to repay you. You'd have to take a share of the firm without the option.'

'I wouldn't consider investing on any other basis. For goodness sake, I'm doing this for fun as much as anything. Since when was it fun just to lend somebody money?'

'I wouldn't know, Mr Moncreiff. I've never had enough for anyone to come to me for a loan.'

Lilian was gaping at him, for once shocked out of her chirpy self-containment. Eventually she said: 'If you go under a taxicab on your way out, I bet your soul will go straight to heaven!'

Laughing, Moncreiff said: 'Come on, I'm taking you girls out to lunch. After that, we'll get you some money and open a bank account on your behalf, Rose. I have a good attorney who'll draw up the necessary papers. Oh, and another thing

– you're going to need more references than you'd believe possible. I'll prepare a handful of the things, and when they run out, you can have more.'

'For what? I'm not applying for jobs.'

'You wait until you see how the average New York property developer reacts to having a woman try to rent an office suite . . . or an office equipment company dealing with a request for lease of furniture and machines. They'd laugh in your face unless you had the sort of solid male backing that convinced them you were just a front organisation.'

'I think that's disgusting.'

'Maybe, but unless you accept that it exists and go along with it, you'll still be looking for premises long after the money runs out.'

It took them a month to organise an office suite, furnish it and prepare a good mail shot. The classified advertisements were used as back-up. Rose had written to Mrs Higgins and to four good middle-range domestic agencies in London and Birmingham, proposing a straight commission share with the agencies and a fee per engagement with Mrs Higgins. Two London agencies and one in Birmingham had replied favourably. Mrs Higgins had written an effusive letter, accompanied by two recommendations. 'We're in business, Lil, start unrolling the red carpet!' Rose shouted after reading the housekeeper's letter.

The two months that followed were the most hectic in Rose's working life. Mail shot and classified advertisement had both started with the line: 'You wouldn't expect to get the same quality in goods you receive free as from those you pay for, so why expect the same from domestic servants? Best of British gives you the best help with the best training – and that extra something implied by an English accent – but it costs a lot. If you value quality more than economy, why not call us? We'll have something interesting to tell you.'

Lilian had been terrified that they would get a response and have no potential employees lined up; but by the time the mail shot had circulated and the advertisements had appeared, the agencies had supplied comprehensive lists of applicants who were eager to work abroad, almost all of whom had impeccable references and good training. By then, Mrs Higgins had come up with three more and was promising a much bigger influx when she got her little intelligence network posted.

By Christmas, they were making a modest profit and their first English butlers and parlour-maids had started work in Park Avenue mansions. Rose had bought herself a corset and was lacing it tighter each week to conceal the advanced state of her pregnancy, and Lilian was wondering how she would ever manage alone for the month which was all Rose would allow herself to give birth, recover and get back to work. Best of British was on its way to the top.

The two Englishwomen spent Christmas together in their little apartment, indulging in all the small luxuries they normally did not consider buying. Then, after they had eaten roast turkey with three different stuffings, English bacon rolls and tiny sausages, Lilian said: 'I'm sorry to raise the ugly topic of work, dear, but in case you hadn't noticed, we have a waiting list of twenty prospective employers and three candidates on our books. Any suggestions?'

'Yes. A very large gin and I'll think about it tomorrow.'

'There you go!'

Inevitably, tomorrow came, and with it, a happy surprise. Rose had written to her old friend Margaret, now the senior nanny at Fenton Parva, back in June, and had received a miserable, incoherent note in reply. Since then, all had been silent. Now a belated Christmas card arrived, announcing that Margaret had left the Cliftons and was in an unhappy position with a prosperous London family. Mrs Higgins had trawled the Fenton Parva staff for likely Best of British recruits and the housekeeper there had, in turn, been in touch with Margaret. Would Rose be interested in finding her a job through her Best of British agency?

Reading the sad little note, Rose let out a whoop of joy. 'Lilian – come and see this! I think we've just opened a London office!' she yelled.

Chapter Twenty-three
London, 1932

Margaret Armstrong had finally left the Cliftons' employment when her position became unbearable. Since then she had lacked all sense of purpose and spent much of her time wondering what she had to live for.

Since 1924, the Cliftons had been the only family she knew, even if they regarded her as nothing more than an employee. To the younger children, she was far more than that. They returned her adoration with a fierce affection of their own.

The Earl and Countess of Clifton had a large family which split naturally into senior and junior branches. George Clifton had married Venetia Haskins in 1906, when she was eighteen and he was twenty-six. She was pretty, self-assured and very rich. George was poor but came of impeccable lineage and was heir to two great houses. Their families were mutually delighted at the match and raised no objections that Venetia was too young. She was married within a couple of months of her presentation at Court. Her first child, Julia, was born in 1908, followed by Mary in 1911 and Ruth in 1913. Venetia found childbirth easy and enjoyed a large family, since she was cushioned from its demands by an even larger domestic staff. She also wanted to ensure her continued ascendancy with George by producing a son to inherit the title.

The Great War threw a huge obstacle in her way. George volunteered to return to his old regiment, the Life Guards, within days of the start of hostilities. He served throughout the war, largely on the Western Front, and only suffered two slight wounds from which he swiftly recovered. His mental state was a different matter. Peace found him a morose, withdrawn man, uninterested in anything except solitary rambles around the Wiltshire estate. He had apparently lost all interest in sex, and when an exasperated Venetia reminded him sharply after a couple of years' virtually separate existence that they would never beget a son at this rate, he merely shrugged and replied that it was no world into which to bring a male child, anyway.

Matters remained thus until summer 1923, when Venetia, now almost thirty-five and ripening into a mature beauty, embarked on an intense flirtation with a young man five years her junior during Cowes Week. She never knew whether George had simply required a sting to his male pride, or whether he had been on the edge of putting the post-war gloom behind him, but whatever the reason, he finally turned to her with rekindled passion and carried her off for an extended late summer holiday on Lake Balaton and in Budapest.

While they were away, she conceived her only son, Henry, who was born during the Easter weekend of 1924. Two more daughters — Imogen and Claire — were to follow in 1926 and 1927. Venetia always told her closest woman friend she was convinced that voluntary work against the 1926 strikers had worked George up to the final fling of procreative passion which resulted in Claire. After that he lapsed into middle age, reserving his physical energies for long walks and field sports.

Margaret had been engaged to train under the ageing Fenton Parva nanny after the birth of Lord Henry. Nanny had been with the family since George, his brother and sisters were babies, and had always intended retiring in 1926. Venetia Clifton wanted to make sure she had a competently instructed, young and healthy replacement ready to look after her 'second' family.

Margaret had taken to her role with enthusiasm, and the reading habit both she and Rose had developed out of loneliness and boredom at the Parsons Green Training Centre became permanent, keeping her up to date in all the latest advances in baby care and feeding. By the time Claire was a toddler, Lady Clifton's children enjoyed a reputation as some of the most comely and well-behaved in Wiltshire, and Margaret was in charge of the nursery.

All should have been running smoothly. She went abroad a couple of times when the Cliftons travelled en famille to Le Touquet and Biarritz; the children adored her; she loved her work and lived in one of the most beautiful parts of rural England, with occasional London visits thrown in as a bonus. But there was a serpent in her paradise and eventually he destroyed it for her.

The earl's brother, Bruno, was the youngest child of his generation of Cliftons. There were two sisters between George Clifton and him, and all were born at long intervals. Bruno was sixteen years younger than George. He, too, had served in the Life Guards during the War, had suffered a serious leg wound in 1915 which prevented him from returning to active service. Once sufficiently recovered, he served out the rest of the hostilities at a desk job in the War Office, but as he had been decorated for bravery in the action which shattered his leg, this was regarded as no disgrace. When peace returned, the family agreed quietly that poor old George might never again be in a fit state to run the estate, so Bruno was installed as land agent, working alongside the professional who was already employed to do this work and in reality acting as the earl's proxy. He had his own quarters in the west wing at Fenton Parva, but took his meals with the family and to all intents and purposes lived with them as he had when he was a boy.

Bruno was handsome in the way aristocratic Englishmen were portrayed in popular romances: tall, lithe, with fair hair and brilliant blue eyes. By the mid-1920s his leg wound had healed sufficiently to leave him with only slight stiffness, a trait which if anything added to his appeal. He spent much of his time out of doors, so his naturally fair skin was always lightly tanned, and the classic straightness of his features was given a certain boyish charm by the scattering of freckles across the bridge of his nose.

The fifteen-year-old Margaret Armstrong took one look at this young god and developed a schoolgirl obsession for him. It hardly mattered that Bruno was almost twice her age: he was so utterly unattainable on countless other grounds that it was merely one more fact about him. In her lowly position, no one ever noticed her or consulted her wishes. Bruno came often to the nursery, because he was especially fond of Henry, his godson, and Margaret was given plenty of opportunity to study him covertly and daydream about her very own hero.

But everything changes, and inevitably, Margaret grew up. In the meantime, Bruno showed no inclination to marry and make his own life outside Fenton Parva. Frequently the subject of gossip among the servants, Bruno seemed to charm every woman he knew and to leave a trail of conquests behind him, all hoping that one day he would return. When his attention fell on Margaret after she had been with the Cliftons for four years, her childish passion for him was undimmed.

Lady Clifton had decided that the children might have a special treat in 1928 when she went up to London to do her Christmas shopping, and go with her so that Nanny could take them to visit Santa Claus's Grotto in Harrods. It was Margaret's first winter in charge of the nursery, and she felt enormously proud of her new position of responsibility.

They had been to the great store, the children had sat on Santa's knee and had duly received gaily wrapped parcels which they now hugged possessively. That year fashionable infants' outdoor clothes tended to follow the style of stage elves and pixies. The three youngest Cliftons were clad in forest-green leggings, tabard-like woollen jackets and knitted caps in brilliant colours, with long pointed hoods finishing in tassels. The combination of such pretty children with such smart clothing and bright Christmas parcels made them look like a charming greetings card, and everywhere people were watching them approvingly.

Margaret was holding Lady Imogen's hand and Lord

Henry was lurching along in front, connected to her by leather reins which fastened around his chest and arms. She was wearing her smart nanny's uniform and was followed by Catherine, the nursery-maid who had taken over her old job when she was promoted, with Lady Claire in a push-chair.

As they reached the pavement, a heart-stoppingly familiar voice said: 'Well, I must say, no fond uncle could have wished for a prettier family portrait!' Bruno Clifton had been walking along the pavement when he saw the little party and had stood watching with pleasure the minor stir they caused among the other shoppers.

'Oh! Good afternoon, Sir . . . they do look nice, don't they?'

'Nice? Nanny, that's the understatement of the month! They look delicious. In fact, I can't resist the temptation to take them out to tea.'

'I-I'm afraid that's quite impossible, Mr Clifton . . . nursery tea . . . Lady Clifton is most particular . . .'

'Come now, the countess would be the first to want her nestlings shown off! All youngsters deserve to get hold of a really sticky chocolate cake now and then. Makes them appreciate bread-and-butter more, y'know!'

This was getting out of hand. Much as Margaret would have loved to fulfil his every whim, she knew the likely consequences of consigning the children to someone else's care, even that of the countess's brother-in-law. 'I really am sorry, Sir, but it's out of the question. I'd lose my job if I left the children for a moment, even in your care. And they are a bit of a handful when they're excited,' she added doubtfully.

He laughed heartily. 'Good God, Nanny, I wouldn't take them on myself! Permit me to know my own limitations. I was proposing to give you and young Jenkins here tea as well. All got up in those uniforms, no one could think I was trying to lead either of you astray, could they?'

It would be too rude to refuse, Margaret told herself

hastily, knowing the real reason for accepting was her adoration of their prospective host. She also knew, without needing to be told, that Lady Clifton would be only slightly less angry if she knew her nursery staff were being entertained in a teashop by her brother-in-law than if Margaret had left them alone with him. After all, in Knightsbridge it was quite possibly an establishment she herself patronised and the very idea of two of her servants going there would put her off for good.

Three-quarters of an hour later, flushed and giggling from Clifton's unending stream of flattery and witticism, they re-emerged from one of the most luxurious tea-rooms in Brompton Road. Bruno patted Margaret's shoulder and she felt as if she had been scorched.

'I don't want either of you worrying about Lady Clifton and what she'll say about this little treat. I shall tell her as soon as I get back that I insisted on giving the children tea and you rightly refused to abandon them to my tender mercies. Don't worry about a thing. I'll see I let you know what she says. And now I'll let you get back – goodbye!' With that he turned into the twilit afternoon and left them to walk back to Belgrave Square.

Venetia Clifton was no more immune than any other female to her brother-in-law's charm. When he embarked on his account of the afternoon over a cup of tea in her boudoir, the countess was ready to explode. By the time he had finished praising the joint and several charms of her three younger children, with frequent references to their having their mother's good looks, she was willing to accept almost anything.

'You really are a bit of a vulgarian, Bruno! Imagine taking Nanny and the nursery-maid out to tea just to entertain your nephew and nieces.'

He chuckled. 'You can hardly expect me to cope with that trio single-handed. They're a delightful little tribe, but given half a chance they turn into Chicago gangsters. It required Armstrong to handle them and I could hardly have taken her without that other one – what's her name? – Jenkins.

Now I could have understood your anger if I'd done *that* . . .'

'You bad boy. Somehow you always manage to get your own way. I don't know why I tolerate you.'

'Because I may be a cad, but I'm a devilish good-looking one!' he told her, doing his celebrated melodrama villain impersonation.

Closing the door behind him, he leaned against it momentarily and uttered a huge sigh of relief. On his way back to the house he had begun to see the small, unimportant incident through Venetia's scandalised eyes, and by the time he reached the square he was half convinced he might have lost that poor little Armstrong her job.

'That poor little Armstrong' promptly faded into insignificance in his memory as he went through the pre-Christmas London social round. Bruno took an infantile delight in all sorts of parties, and he was sufficiently well-connected, handsome and attractive to be asked to anything worth attending. He often told Venetia so when she twitted him about never having settled down to marriage. 'Why on earth should a fellow want to do that when he's a sort of eternal male belle of the ball?' he had once retorted.

Watching him flit effortlessly from engagement to engagement, Lady Clifton was forced to admit he was right. It was so unfair that good-looking men seemed to improve with age rather than getting worn out like women!

Bruno was spending Christmas with the family at Fenton Parva, and Lady Clifton had decided this year to revive the Victorian tradition of a servants' ball. When she read about these events in detail, she modified the idea slightly. She had no intention of waiting on her own cook, housekeeper or butler as the Victorians had. What might have seemed like a quaint inversion in their secure imperial high noon had an altogether too ambiguous side in these uncertain days. Instead of going the whole hog, the family would join in the servants' entertainment, the men dancing with the female domestics, Lady Clifton and her daughters partnering the butler, chauffeur and footmen. Outside caterers would provide a suitably lavish supper and everyone would return to their allotted tasks the following day revelling in what a generous family they worked for.

Letter from Margaret Armstrong in Fenton Parva, Wiltshire, to Rose Rush in London, 2 December 1928:

Dear Rose

I feel like the happiest girl in the country today. You know how long I have liked our Honourable Bruno? Well, at the Servants' Ball last night, he danced with me THREE TIMES, and during the last waltz he swung us both out into the hall, under a great big bunch of mistletoe, and kissed me. Twice. Right on the lips. And then he said, 'By the Lord Harry, little Armstrong, I never noticed how pretty you've been getting lately.' Goodness knows what would have happened next, but Jilkes came dancing out with Catherine, so Mr Bruno whisked me back into the ballroom and we just danced ordinary until the tune ended. Then he bowed to me, just as if I'd been a proper lady, and said, 'That was a greater pleasure than you could possibly imagine, but now I must do my duty,' and went off to talk to the earl. Oh, Rosie, I know it's hopeless, but I do so love him! Maybe something magic will happen to bring us together again . . . and even if it doesn't, at least I can look at him a lot. Now he's home for Christmas, he seems to be up in the nursery suite an awful lot. Keep your fingers crossed I might get a New Year's miracle, all right?

Your loving friend,
Margaret

Margaret had looked more like a guest of the Cliftons than one of the servants at the Christmas ball. She had remained taller than average as she began living a healthier life at Fenton Parva. Now she was almost five feet nine inches. Her silvery pale hair had deepened to a rich corn colour, and like Rose she had chosen not to cut it in line with the dictates of fashion. It was parted in the middle and pulled back severely into a big coil at the back of her head, an arrangement which only enhanced its beauty, suggesting that it might uncoil at any minute in a golden cascade.

She had found a dress in London when they visited before the holidays. It was midnight blue, a soft, very slippery satin, with wide shoulder straps which fanned into a complicated bias-cut bodice. The bodice, in turn, spread into two layered skirts cut on an even more extreme bias, which made them flare naturally at knee and calf level as Margaret walked. Only a girl of her slenderness and height could have carried it off, and when dressed she bore no resemblance to the shy, biddable nanny in a severe grey uniform.

When the family assembled in the ballroom to receive the servants, twenty-year-old Lady Julia hissed indignantly at her mother: 'We've got a gate-crasher! I'll soon sort . . . Good heavens, it's *Armstrong*!' She watched the nanny half the evening, furious with envy that a girl who earned less than two pounds a week and her keep could find, buy and carry off such an elegant frock. She knew enough about quality to recognise the gown was not in any class she would have considered, but the fact that this jumped-up creature could do so much for it infuriated her further. Lady Clifton smiled secretly. She was already experiencing slight pangs of rivalry with her eldest daughter. It would do Julia no harm at all to realise she was not the only young woman who looked good in the right clothes.

After the servants' treat had ended and everyone had drifted away to bed, Bruno Clifton stood alone on the terrace, smoking a cigar and looking up at the frosty stars. Well, well . . . it looked as if not all the servants were ugly ducklings after all. At least one of them had blossomed into an extremely desirable swan. As he ground out the cigar and turned to go to the west wing, he resolved to spend more time in the nursery over the next couple of weeks.

The seduction of Margaret Armstrong was surprisingly easy to accomplish. For months afterwards, Bruno caught himself wondering why he continued to find her so ravishing. Usually any female who was so readily available bored him in next to no time. But there was something about Margaret's vulnerability, coupled with the adoration for him which she never attempted to conceal, which made him return constantly to her. Perhaps it was her very difference from any of the female types he normally found attractive which drew him back.

Bruno's women tended to fall into two groups: the 'respectable' types, which had nothing to do with morality but everything to do with background and breeding; and the fun girls, who could be minor show business performers, servants or even tarts. He made no distinction about his pleasure in their company — generally speaking he enjoyed them all equally — but he drew a very firm line over where he was seen with girls from one group as opposed to the other.

The Respectables as he mentally called them accompanied him to the first nights of West End shows, to Henley and to Hurlingham for the polo. If he took them to nightclubs, it was always somewhere glossy, smart and expensive, like the Ambassadors. He gave them lunch at the Savoy Grill or the Ritz, tea at Brown's and morning rides on the best hired hacks in Rotten Row. They frequently made appearances as his house party guests in Fenton Parva, and occasionally had been members of parties of himself and friends who went abroad to ski or sunbathe.

The Fun Girls were another matter. He went nightclubbing with them all right — but it was invariably to an outpost of Ma Meyrick's raffish empire, or even to one of the supper-and-boxing establishments like the Bat or the Bucket of Blood, where well-heeled customers paid over the odds for mediocre food before watching a string of young hopeful fighters demolish each other in a makeshift ring between the supper tables. He wined and dined these girls in Soho or Chelsea, and entertained them with the latest cinema releases rather than theatre performances. Occasionally he would pop a couple of them into his sporty little open-topped car and run them down to Skindles at Maidenhead, where they could disport themselves in the Thames-side swimming pool and quaff champagne to their hearts' content without giving him anxieties about being seen by the wrong society types. Bruno had an unerring sense of propriety which his licentious ancestors would have been the first to approve.

Margaret Armstrong hardly fitted into either world. She certainly did not qualify to run with the Respectables, but as his infatuation grew, Bruno was aware she was no more at home with the Fun Girls. She was . . . well, she was Margaret. There was no one quite like her. At first he merely experienced a mild infatuation for her, and spent more time than usual hanging round the nursery, teasing her and idly flirting while she busied herself in preparing the children for their evening appearance in the drawing room before their mother and father.

Then, on an unseasonably warm day early in the spring, he was taking a stroll near the ornamental lake which had been part of the landscaping scheme introduced a couple of centuries before by a follower of Capability Brown. Maugham the game-keeper had said something about the stocks of mallard going down, and Bruno wanted to investigate whether there were any signs that it was either a fox or a poacher. He emerged through a tangle of young birch and almost fell over Margaret, who was sitting gazing dreamily over the water at a busy group of moorhens in process of swimming away from the pagoda island in the middle.

'Bless me if it isn't my favourite nanny!' he said. 'What are you doing, my pretty maid? Have you finally lost patience with your infant charges and confined them to the depths with paving stones tied to them?'

Margaret blushed scarlet and murmured: 'It's my day off – I couldn't take one last week so Lady Clifton said I could have today.'

'And you're spending it all alone here down by the lake, not off shopping or to the cinema?'

'There's no bus into Salisbury until lunchtime, and no one was driving in this morning . . . anyway, it doesn't matter. It's such a lovely day I could sit here for hours.'

'Nonsense! You'll get all damp!' he said decisively, ignoring the fact that she was sitting well clear of the ground on a fallen tree-trunk. 'I'm going for a walk through the Baskerville Wood. How d'you fancy coming with me? I'd enjoy the company.'

Again she blushed. My God, he thought, I've never seen such soft, fair skin. Bet it's like that all over . . . he treated himself to an imaginary image of the satiny flesh in the inner crook of the girl's elbow, and under the rounder parts of the buttocks, and down the cushiony part of her upper thighs . . . The thought was so beguiling that he had to jolt himself back to reality when she rose and said, as if making a major decision, 'Yes, Sir. I'd like that very much.'

The woods were as ravishing as she was, Bruno thought as he watched her while they walked. The young spring leaves had burst forth a couple of weeks earlier, and now formed a broken canopy of green more delicate than the richer tones of summer could ever be. Sparks of sunlight pierced the gaps between the foliage, producing a delightfully chequered brilliance on Margaret's hair and skin. He was reminded compulsively of the fairy princesses who had appeared in the illustrated story books in the nursery of his childhood.

To his faint surprise, the girl proved to be quite bright. In his experience, most young women never had a thought in their heads beyond the next party, holiday or pretty frock. Their greatest accomplishment appeared to be the ability to drive a car if they were rich, and to dance in step in the chorus line if they were not. On balance he tended to look on all women as amusing bird-brains. This one was rather different. She talked fondly but not over-indulgently about her three small charges, and showed quite an impressive knowledge of the countryside for one who had presumably spent most of her childhood in cities.

'I'm surprised you even recognise a greenfinch,' he said,

after she had given him an account of a determined cock finch that insisted on bombarding the nursery windows at regular intervals. 'Most girls of your age don't know a London pigeon from a magpie.'

She smiled. 'Yes, but they usually live in London or somewhere, don't they? Or if they're in country houses, they're too busy at their jobs to notice. It's one of the lovely things about working with the children — I have to take them out into the park here, or up Fenton Hill, as part of my duties. I'd be very stupid if I didn't use my eyes and ears while we were out.'

'I can think of plenty of young women who wouldn't dream of it,' said Clifton.

She was determined not to be flattered. 'Well, the children are very observant, 'specially Lord Henry. They're always at me with questions, so I started looking things up in books to tell them. After that I was surprised how quickly I got to know things just by looking.'

'Whether you think so or not, Miss Armstrong, you are a singular young woman. We must do this again — the sooner the better.' They had done a full circuit of the wood and were about to emerge on to a rise overlooking Fenton Park. As he finished speaking, Bruno reached out, brushed back a loose tendril of the golden hair from her forehead, and kissed her. Her initial gasp of surprise petered out and she responded to the caress almost instantly, eyes closed, willowy body swaying against his. My God, but she got more alluring by the second!

Bruno wrapped his arms around her and kissed her again, this time passionately, pressing open her lips with his tongue and exploring the sweet softness of her mouth.

Eventually he held her away from him. 'I think you need to be taken out for the afternoon,' he said. 'Why waste your time hanging about at Fenton when you only get a full day every couple of weeks?'

She was so scandalised he almost laughed in her face. He wasn't going to have any trouble with this one, he could see that. 'But I couldn't! Lady Clifton would dismiss me on the spot if she knew I'd accepted a lift into town from her own brother-in-law.'

This time he did laugh aloud. 'Nonsense! Of course she wouldn't, not if she thought I was going to Salisbury anyway and you were marooned. You've travelled in the Rolls-Royce before now when Partridge was taking the countess or my brother to the station.'

'Yes, but that was different.' She hardly needed to say that neither the Cliftons nor Partridge had kissed her passionately in Baskerville Wood, or driven her unchaperoned.

'Anyway,' he overrode her objection effortlessly, 'I thought you knew: both Venetia and George are out today. That's why Partridge wasn't available to give you a lift this morning. They've motored down to South Devon to see a kinswoman of ours who's just produced a new infant. Won't be back until late this evening. That's why you're getting up to date with your time off. My sister-in-law won't face the inconvenience of having her children paraded this evening by the nursery-maid instead of you, because she won't be here to see them!

'There you are – you can run in to Salisbury with me with complete impunity. The staff are hardly likely to rush the countess *en masse* when she returns to announce that you were playing truant with me today!'

Back at the house he sent her off up to the nursery suite to get a coat and bag, then strolled into the library with a deceptively casual air. Once inside he made sure the door was firmly closed before telephoning a Salisbury number. 'Hallo, Paddy old chap! I wondered, are you likely to be at home this afternoon? Mmm, races, eh? Thought you might be. Do you think I might – er – *borrow* your main guest room for a couple of hours?'

There was a shout of mirth at the other end of the line as his friend said: 'Really, Bruno, I don't know how you manage it! You do realise it's still well before noon, I suppose?'

'Of course I do! I have to soften up the little victim first, though — you know, spot of lunch, drop of bubbly and all that. Can't take it like one of your damned nags rushing a high fence!'

The two men had done each other similar favours in the past. Patrick Shawcross had a small house of jewel-like perfection overlooking the cathedral green in Salisbury, but no base in London. He was another of the charmed circle who occasionally borrowed Bruno's Jermyn Street chambers, and he often returned the favour by lending Bruno the Salisbury house. Their arrangements invariably involved assignations with attractive women. After the foretaste of Margaret Armstrong's charms Bruno had got in Baskerville Wood just now, he had no intention of leaving anything to chance.

'I'll call at my housekeeper's on the way out and ask her to wait at home this afternoon until you arrive to take the spare set of keys,' said Shawcross. 'Just the usual afterwards — drop them through her letter box on your way back to Fenton Parva, with a small sweetener for the old girl for staying in for you. Do have an entertaining afternoon.'

'Oh, never fear, I intend to! Be lucky at the races.' Grinning broadly, Bruno hung up and went to find Margaret.

Chapter Twenty-four

He gave her lunch at a pretty old farmers' pub on the far side of Salisbury, comfortably outside his family's stamping ground and not the sort of establishment patronised by his smart county friends. Margaret was round-eyed and impressed. She had very seldom eaten in restaurants or cafés and had never been in a public house at all. This one had a snug, small dining room where farmers took each other to celebrate a successful morning at the cattle market, and the food reflected the nature of the clientele. The menu comprised large prime beefsteaks, steak and kidney puddings, oxtail soup and the like. The landlord kept a limited stock of wine for the occasional customer who cared for neither beer nor cider, but generally speaking the two great draught drinks were the mainstay of his sales.

After a large, over-indulgent lunch and enough rough cider to heighten the colour in her cheeks, Bruno took Margaret for a stroll down the bank of a clear brook which gurgled alongside the pub. When they were out of sight of curious eyes, he turned and took her hand. 'I can't think when I had a better time,' he said, at that moment meaning it. 'You're such a breath of fresh air after the usual run of people I meet.'

'I don't even have to say *I* can't think when,' she told him, gazing longingly into his bright eyes. 'I know I *never* had a time like today.' With perfect timing, Bruno leaned forward and kissed her with just the right combination of affection and desire not to frighten her off. As she had in Baskerville Wood, Margaret swayed towards him, incapable of resistance.

'My darling, we can't carry on like this out here — far too public,' he said. 'I know just the place we could go in

Salisbury, where we could have the afternoon to ourselves.'

She followed him as meekly as a lamb, and briefly Bruno wondered if she had any notion what was in store for her. In fact he was doing Margaret an injustice. Since the waltz and the mistletoe-kiss at the servants' ball, she had been dreaming of this moment. No young woman trained in her field was ignorant of the nature of sex and the inevitable results of sexual fulfilment. She had thought about the matter for so long that today's adventure seemed no more than the logical development of what had gone before. She was not frightened or apprehensive. She knew simply that she was deeply in love with this man, and whatever the consequences she must pursue her feelings to their conclusion.

She was somewhat taken aback at the grandeur of the house on the cathedral green. Bruno assumed it was virginal jitters — no one who blushed as readily as Margaret could possibly have sexual experience — but in reality the girl had expected far less. She would not have been at all surprised if he had signed them into some seedy commercial hotel in the trading area of the city, and this miniature palace came as quite a surprise.

Good old Paddy! thought Bruno as his eyes skimmed the note left unobtrusively on the small shelf where the spare key resided. He'd even popped a bottle of bubbly into the refrigerator to speed Bruno's efforts. Clifton wondered if Margaret had ever drunk champagne. Probably not . . . have to watch it, on top of that cider. Didn't want her passing out on him.

He seated her on the sofa in Patrick's drawing room and went in search of the champagne. Margaret gazed around her, bemused at the beautiful and expensive objects which crowded the room. How strange it must be to live like this, able to afford anything you wanted, never expected to share a bedroom, or work when you were exhausted . . . never to do anything against your personal inclination. She shook her head in conscious dismissal of the idea. It was incomprehensible to her.

Clifton sipped half a glass of champagne with her before leaving across, gently taking it from her hand and putting it down on a side table. 'I think I want a kiss more than any more champagne,' he said, folding her into his arms.

Margaret felt no strain, no nervousness. This was the way it should be, had always been meant to be ... she abandoned herself to the pleasure of the embrace and scarcely noticed when he rose, drawing her to her feet after him, and led her up to the blue-painted guest room which overlooked the cathedral green.

Closing the bedroom door, he turned to her and said: 'I want to comb down that lovely hair all around you, and take off all your clothes to see you as you were always intended to be seen.'

Again, the becoming blush. 'I think you'll be disappointed.'

'And I think you're quite mad to say so. Come here at once and I'll prove I'm right.' He led her over to the dressing table and seated her before the mirror, unpinning the coil of hair at her neck and picking up a silver-backed brush from the vanity tray. For a good five minutes, he brushed out the corn-silk tresses, revelling in the springy feel of the healthy hair as it bobbed back into place. 'How does it feel to have a lady's maid?' he whispered, and kissed her neck as he resumed his brushing.

'Ever so much better than if Miss Rodwell was doing it,' she said, eyes twinkling.

After a while he raised her to her feet again, pushed away the stool and began undoing the small pearl buttons down the back of her dress. They fastened it from neck to hem, and when he had finished it remained only to unbuckle her belt for the garment to peel away like the skin off a perfectly ripe peach. Beneath the dress, she wore only crepe-de-chine panties and white cotton stockings. He uttered a gasp of pleasure at the sight of her small, high, round breasts, their flesh creamy-white, the nipples as rosy pink as her cheeks when she blushed. He put out one hand and stroked them with the care of a connoisseur. 'Even lovelier than I expected,' he said, almost to himself.

Bruno slipped the smooth panties down over the long curve of her hips, and she stepped out of them as they fell with a swish round her ankles. A lacy white suspender belt held up the stockings, and he unhooked that, then stooped in front of her to roll the stockings down her legs. Afterwards he ran a finger down the long, smooth length of her thigh and calf. 'I've never seen such long legs,' he said, his mind playing erotic imaginative tricks with what he wanted to do with them.

By now Margaret was in a state of ecstasy. She wound her arms around his neck and whispered 'You'll have to show me, Bruno. I love you, and I'll do anything you want, b-but I don't know how.'

His kiss was pure tenderness now. How often did a man get a beautiful, eager virgin all to himself? 'Don't worry about a thing. I'll look after you.'

And look after her he did. Bruno prided himself on his understanding of women and their erotic needs. He was imaginative enough to know one did not make love to a thirty-five-year-old society woman in the same manner as to a young girl. He was fit, athletic and physically, if not emotionally, sensitive, and he spent the afternoon teaching Margaret more about the satisfaction of sexuality than she was ever to discover from another lover.

He propped her on a mound of pillows, pulled aside the bedclothes and lay down beside her, drawing his lightly splayed fingers from the hollow of her throat down between her breasts, resting momentarily on her flat belly and then sliding on, inexorably, to the deep slit between her thighs with its frame of crisply curled golden hair. Her eyes were closed now, her neck arching back, and she was murmuring unintelligible words of encouragement. Bruno had to fight for self-control. She was almost too good to wait for. This minute he wanted to bury himself in her, slake himself on her . . . and he knew that if he did that, he would never enjoy her so much again.

His fingers moved inside her with perfect control, touching her most secret, sensitive parts, stirring her to a small frenzy, and still he held off too much physical contact. When she was almost frantic, he pressed the length of his body along hers and began kissing her breasts. The pink rosebud nipples flushed darker and stiffened beneath his lips and tongue. She moaned and pulled his head up so that she could scatter tiny kisses all over his face, until he kissed her full on the mouth, pressing his tongue inside her lips in an arousing echo of the way his fingers had pressed inside the lips of her vulva moments before.

'Please, please — do the rest!' she begged. 'I can't wait much more.'

He raised himself over her and eased into her body, still controlled, still gentle. Apart from a small grimace when he first penetrated her, she showed nothing but intense, growing excitement, and now his own desire for her snapped his good intentions. He thrust into her, his initial slow rhythm building rapidly to a frenzy. But he need not have worried about Margaret's reaction. Her arousal had grown with his and he had brought her so close to orgasm before he entered her that now she uttered a low cry, shuddered convulsively against him, then lay still apart from the steady throb of her satisfied body. The effect on him was so electrifying that his own climax followed instantly, and he lay, panting and moaning with satisfaction, against the soft fragrance of her flesh.

They made love twice more that afternoon. In the end Bruno was beginning to wonder what on earth had happened to the middle-aged feeling which had tended to descend on him lately. It certainly didn't seem to operate around Margaret Armstrong. He felt like a randy nineteen-year-old the moment he looked at her.

Eventually, he decided that if they did not leave soon they would bump into Paddy Shawcross as he returned from the races. He ran a bath for Margaret, then padded off downstairs to rescue the champagne, which still had plenty of sparkle left in it. Taking it back upstairs, he poured a glass for Margaret and took it to her in her bath. 'I never thought anything like this would happen to me,' she said, round-eyed again. 'I really do love you, Bruno, and I know there's nothing to be done about it.'

'Nothing to be done about it?' For a moment he was at a loss.

'Well, you know . . . I realise nobody in your position is ever going to whisk me out of the nursery and marry me or anything. As long as I can see you from time to time, it will be all right, I think.'

Hmm, that sounds pretty optimistic, said his baser self. Doesn't sound as if I shall even have difficulty going on playing the field and keeping this little beauty going, as long as I'm careful . . . a warning voice hinted that one day it might prove almost impossible to disentangle himself when he grew tired of her, but he stifled it. Can't have everything, old chap. Let's live for today and let tomorrow take care of itself, eh?

And so Margaret embarked on an affair that lasted for more than three years — three years in which she became less and less content to have only a tiny part of Bruno Clifton, and he spent increasing amounts of time trying to prove to himself that he did not need her.

At first it was wonderful. Margaret still had plenty to keep her occupied, entrusted as she was with the care of a two year old, a three year old and a five year old. If she had any fears that Bruno's interest would fade swiftly, she proved mistaken. Far from limiting his time at Fenton Parva to the minimum necessary for smooth administration of the estate, he seemed to be there almost full-time nowadays, merely snatching the odd few days to catch up with the London social round when Lady Clifton became suspicious of his constant presence.

Without noticing the modification of her own behaviour, Margaret found herself out and about in woods and fields with the children more and more often. Somehow she was always running into their Uncle Bruno, who found the prospect of walking and talking with them irresistible.

The earl was delighted at his younger children's open-air regime. 'Just what the doctor ordered!' he informed Venetia. 'She keeps 'em well wrapped up, so they won't get colds, and they'll be as tough as a whip by the time they're older. Recognising all the birds and animal species, too, and young Henry is better than me on plants already.'

The countess sniffed. 'Well, I suppose it's harmless enough if they grow up spending a lot of time down here . . . she'll hardly be an influence by the time they're old enough for a London social life.'

In later years, Margaret often wondered where the time had gone between 1928 and the end of 1931. It was as if a sparkling necklace of perfect jewel-days had briefly slipped through her hands, then abruptly vanished, leaving only a shadowy memory of a few perfect moments.

In the autumn of 1931, she received the first hint of uncertain days ahead. In her pre-occupation with loving Bruno and looking after the three children, the future had never lain heavy on her mind. Now she was forced to confront it when she lined up the young ones for the evening interlude with their parents, and heard Lady Clifton say to her sister-in-law Laura: 'We're still arguing over the right prep school for Henry. Just can't make up our minds, and of course he'll be going next September.'

September! Had Master Henry really grown so fast? With a lurch Margaret realised it was not merely a matter of losing little Henry's good-natured companionship. When the children were grown, a nanny became superfluous. True, there were the girls, but she required no reminders about the instant transfer to a nursery governess which took place once a family decided the children were ready for education rather than mere nurture. By the end of the summer, Imogen would be six and Claire five. If anything, that was a little old for Imogen to be starting her education. Apprehension closed in on Margaret.

There was worse to come. The following week, for the first time except during his few trips abroad, Bruno failed to arrange a rendezvous with her on her fortnightly day off.

As unobtrusively as possible, she asked the other servants what had happened to him, only to learn he had decided to stay in London this week and part of next. No one knew why and they were all curious. Mister Bruno had spent so much time at Fenton in recent years. Perhaps there was romance in the air, speculated the head housemaid. Margaret bit back the sharp retort which was on the tip of her tongue and merely said, 'Yes, I suppose so . . . the children miss him,' before she drifted away, apparently unconcerned. In her bedroom off the day nursery, she sobbed until no more tears would flow. Maybe she had no concrete news, but her intuition told her she was near the end of everything.

It was not long before the blow fell. Bruno was back at Fenton by the time her half-day came around the following week. Wrapped in a thick coat, Margaret went down to the lake and sat on the old tree trunk where their association had begun, now a special place where both went if no formal meeting had been arranged elsewhere. She was chilly and thinking of giving up the matter as a bad job, when there was a faint rustle of dead leaves and he appeared beside her. Oblivious of time or place, she jumped up and flung her arms around him. He kissed her with all his old tenderness, but then held her away from him. As he began to speak, she put her hand up to his lips in a vain attempt to silence him, but he gently disengaged himself and pulled her down beside him once more on the fallen tree trunk.

'You always knew it wasn't forever, didn't you, darling?' he said, not quite looking her in the eye.

There, it was out. A long sigh escaped Margaret's slightly parted lips. 'I suppose so. I was just starting to believe . . .'

'That it might be all right? Not in our world. At thirty-eight, I'm still *just* respectable as a bachelor-about-town. After that, it's a rather weary performance. And I have the title to think of.'

That stung her. 'The title? But Master Henry will inherit that!'

'Yes, yes . . . of course. If he grows up. There's a tradition of great caution among the English ruling classes. One male heir is simply not enough. If George had fathered two or three sons instead of all those daughters, it might have been different. But in the circumstances, I'm a sort of family insurance to produce alternative male heirs.'

'I see. I don't think I'm going to like what you say next.'

'No, my darling, I'm afraid you're not. I am about to announce my engagement to Sir William Penrose's daughter Madeleine.'

During the conversation, Margaret had felt herself growing colder and colder. Now she began to shiver. 'When?'

'The engagement? Oh, it's to be announced in *The Times* on Monday.'

'No, the marriage. How long?' She was acutely conscious of her almost monosyllabic speech, but powerless to change it.

'Thought it was better to do the whole thing quickly. New Year's Day.'

'I think I'd better go back to the nursery now. I feel cold and there's some sewing . . .'

'But it's your half day!'

She was on her feet, now, and he still perched on the dead tree. She looked down at him incredulously. 'Surely you don't think I could bear to be with you after that?'

'Why not? My darling, we both knew all along parting was inevitable, didn't we? I was going to suggest a really splendid farewell luncheon somewhere next week on your day off, and perhaps a last visit to the house in Salisbury' (in all the years, he had never told her the name of the owner of the house) 'and I thought we could plan it this afternoon.'

Her look was still disbelieving, and unwavering. 'Did you really think my feelings were so — so shallow?' she said, in a tone of wonder. 'After what you just said, you'll never be anything but Mr Bruno or Mr Clifton to me again, and I'm certainly not going off anywhere with you. Now I'm going. The least you can do is leave me with a couple of my dreams unbroken.'

She managed to walk away from the belt of trees, not to break into the wild run her body demanded. Back at the house she locked herself in her room and sat, silent and unmoving, as it grew dark, a piece of handiwork untouched on her lap.

Bruno remained at the lakeside long after she had left him, half sulky, half regretful. Why was life so bloody unfair? Why couldn't a chap organise things so that he could have the lot? He had not been completely candid with Margaret; he had never been that with any woman. It was true that he still found her infinitely exciting as a lover, and enjoyed her quiet, undemanding company more than he would have believed possible. But for the past year or so, he had felt a growing desire to father his own family, instead of having only the second-hand affection of George's children. At heart he was a conformist, and it would never have occurred to him either to marry Margaret or to have children with her out of wedlock and set up an unofficial family somewhere, as many maverick noblemen had done in the past. After their first lovemaking, he had always taken precautions to see she did not become pregnant, and he had no intention of changing that arrangement now.

While he was in this unsettled mood, he had been introduced to Madeleine Penrose. In many respects she and Margaret were physically alike — both tall, graceful and slender, with fair skin and blonde hair. For the first time in his life, Bruno fell in love. He wanted Madeleine, wanted her with him all the time, did not wish to dissemble and keep her on a string like a whole succession of society girls he had known. Whatever his self justifications to Margaret might be, the truth of it was that he had finally met his match. He had proposed to the girl within a month of their first meeting, and she accepted him at once. Margaret might have existed in another time for all she mattered now.

Lady Clifton herself unwittingly administered the *coup de grâce*. After the marriage — which took place, ironically, at St Margaret's, Westminster — the happy couple went off on a long, extravagant honeymoon lasting more than two months. While they were away, Margaret noticed the Elizabethan dower house at Fenton Parva, unoccupied since the earl's mother died there in 1927, was being renovated and redecorated. She uttered a silent prayer of thanks. At least the newly-weds would not be under the same roof as herself. They returned to London two weeks before coming down to Fenton Parva. Margaret assumed the delay was purely to put them back in touch with the capital's social round, but she was wrong.

Madeleine Clifton arrived at her new home in Fenton Parva blushing proudly at the confirmation that she was pregnant.

The countess called Margaret into her private sitting room a couple of days after the couple had installed themselves in the dower house. 'Armstrong,' she said, 'I've been somewhat concerned lately about your future. As the children grow older, I'm sure your own thoughts have turned in the same direction. When Master Henry goes off to prep school in the autumn, it will be more than time for the girls to have a governess. I always felt that a nanny and a governess sharing charges wasn't a satisfactory arrangement. The children never know where their loyalties lie.

'Now, though, the problem seems to have solved itself. Mrs Clifton is expecting a baby at the end of October, and would be delighted to take you as her nanny. So you could supervise the girls while they get used to the governess, then go on to the dower house as soon as the new baby is born. It has a delightful attic floor which they plan to fit up as a nursery suite.' She paused, a receptive, friendly look on her face. 'Well, have you nothing to say?'

'It-it's a bit of a shock, Milady. You know how attached I am to your three . . . I need to think about it.'

As usual in such circumstances, Venetia Clifton's expression turned to irritation. 'It all seems completely straightforward to me. Still, if you're so indecisive about matters . . . come and see me when you have made up your mind.'

There was precious little for Margaret to think over. She

might just have managed to carry on had she been able to go on looking after the three Clifton children, and to have put Bruno and his new wife as far as possible from her mind. But the idea of living in the same house — and the dower house, although spacious, was a cottage compared with Fenton — was utterly unbearable.

Next morning, she went to see the countess. 'I've thought over your kind suggestion, Milady,' she said, 'but I don't think I could carry on here without your children to look after. It wouldn't be the same with this new baby. I'll stay until Master Henry has gone to school and you've settled the girls' governess, but then I must go to a post somewhere else. I hope you'll feel able to give me a good reference.'

Venetia Clifton's face hardened into lines of disapproval, but before she spoke, she forced herself to relax. After all, the girl was a servant, not a slave. She had *some* freedom of movement.

'Very well, Armstrong, but I must say I'm disappointed that you're foolish enough to reject such an opportunity. After all, by the time Mr Bruno's children were out of the nursery, undoubtedly Mary or Ruth would have families and they would have been delighted to employ you. You could have spent your entire working life inside one family.'

Margaret's eyes were downcast, so the countess did not see the flash of pure hatred. And no doubt there wouldn't be any question of my ever having a life of my own, she was thinking. Aloud, she said: 'Yes, Milady, I appreciate that. I still prefer to leave when your children don't need me any longer.'

'Very well, you may go. I shall let you know in good time when we are ready to part with you — time enough for you to find another position, that is. And of course I shall provide a good reference. Until now your behaviour has been exemplary.' The 'until now' managed to imply that Margaret had let down the entire family at the eleventh hour, but she was beyond caring.

It was easy enough for someone as well-qualified as herself to find a well-paid job, and Margaret chose something as far as possible from her beloved Fenton. London was as remote from the rolling Wiltshire countryside as anything she could imagine; the young, fluttery wife of a rich industrialist a most unlikely successor to the Countess of Clifton. And there was no handsome young man lurking around the house ready to break her heart.

The Bartons' nanny had been taken seriously ill and had been forced to leave her job. They were kind enough people, and had not dismissed her, but it seemed unlikely she would ever recover from the rheumatic fever sufficiently to look after two children. Margaret pictured the poor creature with sympathy. What on earth would become of her? Then she shook herself back to reality. What becomes of any of us when we outlive our usefulness? she thought. I'd better save as much as I can from now on. I've no intention of ending up as a charity case in some lord's attic bedrooms, or worse still, in the workhouse.

Not that she felt she had anything on which to spend her money now. She had loved pretty clothes ever since that chilly day in the dress agency when a kindly manageress had practically given her an almost-fashionable coat and dress. But smart clothes were fun only as long as you had somewhere to wear them. From now on, she had decided, her free time would be spent on solitary walks and visits to the cinema. She wanted no more truck with men. Margaret was two months short of her twenty-fourth birthday.

Andrew and Sylvia Barton had two children, a three-year-old boy and a girl of eight months. Mrs Barton was afraid her son, Kitt, would pine for his old nanny, but Margaret was such an appealing girl and her presence so comforting that he quickly forgot the past and settled down with her.

In the end, she had left Fenton Parva much sooner than anticipated. The job offer came up in early July, and the family were almost ready to go off on their annual round of holidays. A nursery governess had been engaged to move in at Fenton immediately after their departure, so that she would appear to the children as a permanent fixture when they came back in September. Margaret had sniffed in contempt at that idea. Why on earth did rich people think their children so stupid? Was it simply that they saw so little of them, they had no means of judging? She knew very well that Henry, Imogen and Claire would be furiously aware of the change and fight it every step of the way. The very thought made her anxious to depart as soon as possible. Much as she loved them, she had suffered too much in recent months to endure the pain of separation from them. Better a quiet departure with them left in ignorance of its permanence.

Lady Clifton had agreed grudgingly that she might be right. The earl took her aside the day before she left, and gave her a parting gift of £75 — ten pounds for every full year of service and five as a bonus and told her they were all sorry to see her go. Then he went off to board the train for Scotland and the grouse moors, and never thought of Margaret again. She managed to avoid Bruno completely.

The Bartons occupied a large, luxurious house in the Boltons, with an enormous garden by London standards. The children were happy and well-behaved, the parents undemanding — at least, by Lady Clifton's standards. Margaret should have been content. She hated every minute. She disliked her flower-papered, airy bedroom, because the was no Fenton Park outside the window; she disliked the dusty smell of late-summer London. She disliked the rush and bustle of the city after the leisurely tempo of country life. And most of all, she disliked the air of informality which prevailed in the Barton household. Margaret held no brief for the system of servants and masters. Privately she detested it. It had, after all, ruined her life. But as long as it existed, she was convinced that only a high level of formality made it bearable. The minute mistress and servants became cronies, trouble lay ahead.

Mrs Barton had different ideas. She was terrified by the thought of being unpopular with anyone, and that included servants, so she asked them to do things where more self-assured women would have issued orders; she apologised before complaining that their work was substandard; and often she conveniently forgot to reprimand them if she caught them being flagrantly dishonest or unconscientious. The house was too well-staffed to show the usual consequences of such mismanagement. In spite of her ineptitude, the furniture remained polished to a high gloss, the table was provided with good meals and the wine cellar maintained in prime condition. But it had far more to do with Andrew Barton's money having bought the best servants than with his wife's ability to manage them.

Everything limped along after a fashion until Christmas. Then Margaret started having trouble with her nursery-maid, a flighty young girl who preferred the idea of a shop job to domestic service. She was constantly late out of bed in the morning, overstayed her time off and did her job with only half her attention. Finally Margaret confronted her and told her she must make up her mind whether she wished to acquire a proper training or leave, because she could not continue as she had been behaving.

The nursery-maid, Susan, looked her over impudently and said: 'It's just a job, Nanny, nothing special, see? They're not paying me enough for that.'

'They're paying you enough for you to put up a better performance than you have to date. Now which is it to be – a bit more work, or dismissal?'

The girl's smile was pure mischief. 'I think you'd better talk to Mrs Barton about that.'

'You know very well Madam will be guided by my view of the matter. That's the way a big staff works.'

'In some houses, maybe. Let's see you try it in this one.' And Susan flounced out of the room without giving Margaret a chance to say anything more.

After lunch three days before Christmas, she went to see Mrs Barton and explain the situation. She knew she was in trouble as soon as she saw her employer begin twisting her fingers into contorted shapes and assuming an anguished expression. When she had finished, she said: 'Well, there it is, Madam. I can't do anything else with her. I'm willing to try again if you give her a real talking-to but I think she'll slip back and in the end you'll have to dismiss her.'

'Oh, Nanny, I couldn't do that! It's Christmas!'

Margaret gazed at her, incredulous. 'Beg your pardon, Ma'am, but what's that got to do with it?'

Sylvia Barton raised agonised eyes to her. 'Oh, my, Nanny, you're so hardhearted! The season of good will and all that. Can't have bad blood in the house at this time of year.'

'Madam, any time of year is much the same to a servant. And with the greatest respect, it's I who have to stand for the nonsense, not you. I object to doing work that should be handled by the maid who's assigned to me, and I won't put up with it.'

'Yes, yes.' Mrs Barton might have been reassuring a fractious child. 'We all understand what a demanding job you have.'

'That's not quite the point, Madam. I'm trained to that job and I'm good at it. But I'm no nursery-maid — haven't been since I was eighteen and I have no intention of doing the maid's job as well as well as my own for no reward.'

'Oh, if it's just a question of *money*, I'm sure we can come to some arrangement . . .'

By now, Margaret was almost stamping with frustration. 'Money has nothing to do with it. I am paid for what I do. But you must make sure Susan works for what she's paid to do, too, or I'll have no authority in my own nursery.'

Mrs Barton attempted to assume a resolute expression, and failed, dismally. 'Very well, Nanny. I shall see what I can do. That will be all.'

Outside the closed door, Margaret muttered: 'See what she can do, indeed! Probably end up sacking me, at this rate!'

That was more or less what it came to, for when she was confronted by Susan's insolent expression, Sylvia Barton's courage failed her, and she embarked on one of her notorious 'I'm sorry to have to bring this up, but . . .' laments which all the servants knew and despised. By the time she had finished, Susan was practically openly yawning, and she certainly had no fear that her livelihood was threatened. Ten minutes later, she bounced back into the day nursery and said: 'Well, Nanny, if that's the worst bogeyman you can turn on me, I'm here for good! Think I'll make us a nice cuppa tea.' With that she disappeared into the nursery kitchen and Margaret silently counted a hundred to try and contain her anger as she heard the girl moving cheerily from sink to stove and back again.

Eventually she rose, went into the bathroom and pressed a cold, wet flannel over her face to calm the burning sensation in her skin. She could not remember ever having been so angry — or so unhappy. Finally she patted her skin dry, straightened her uniform and walked calmly downstairs, tapping decisively on the drawing-room door the second she reached it to prevent her nerve leaving her.

'Ah — Nanny! Come to see if I've talked to Jacobs yet, no doubt. Well, I — '

'I know you have, Madam. I'm afraid it made no difference. If anything, matters are ten times worse. I've come on a different errand. I'm submitting my resignation. I'd prefer to go immediately, but if you insist, I shall stay another week.'

'But Nanny, you can't . . . what will we . . . the children!' A meaningless babble of half-connected phrases tumbled from Mrs Barton's lips.

Margaret was immovable. 'They're your children, Madam, not mine. I was happy to look after them as long as you treated me fairly, but you haven't. I can't continue to work here with that dreadful little girl mucking about all the time, and that's final. Her dismissal is the only thing that would make me stay now.'

'Please, Nanny I couldn't. It's . . .'

Margaret closed her eyes wearily. 'I know, Madam. It's Christmas. Very well, I'll be off a week from today. Now I'd better get back up to the nursery before that girl does any more damage.'

She took the children out for their walk, came home and gave them tea, then dressed them ready to see their parents downstairs before bed. All went smoothly, with Susan having the good sense to keep out of her way and for once to do her job properly. After the children were asleep, Margaret picked at her own supper, finally pushing it aside and going off to her room soon after nine o'clock. She was wearily beginning to undress when she remembered she had received a few Christmas cards by that afternoon's post, and in the fuss over Susan had dumped them on her dressing table without bothering to open them. Might as well make myself really miserable with a few memories of happier times she thought, slitting the first envelope.

It contained a card from the cook at Fenton Parva, wishing her a happy Christmas and hoping she liked her new job. There was also a short note enclosed:

Dear Margaret
I got a letter from Mrs Higgins at the London house the other day, saying your friend Rose has started some smart agency for domestics in New York. Mrs H says it's doing so well Rose can't get enough staff. It is called Best of British and like the name suggests, only takes on good English servants to work in the best American homes. She have asked Mrs Higgins to keep her eye peeled for likely recruits, and she wrote to me on account of that. I thought of you straight off, what with you leaving so suddenly. If you are interested, I have written down the address of the business in New York. Good luck, my dear.

Your friend,
Ada Sutton

For the first time in months, a spontaneous smile burst on to Margaret's face. She glanced up and said: 'Who says I haven't got a guardian angel after all?' Then she went to find a Christmas card she could send to Rose with her request for employment.

When it came, Rose's reply took her completely by surprise.

Dear Margaret,

If only I had known you were not happy, we could have helped each other! I do so hope we can manage that now. I have this wonderful idea for a business — and surprise of surprises — I even found a backer. If the Cliftons knew, I dare say they would kill me. It's Alex Moncreiff, Lady bloody Julia's husband! And he put up the money without any strings attached apart from a straightforward business partnership. Mind you, I don't think I would have objected if he *had* got a few ideas. He is a rather attractive man.

This is turning into a very un-businesslike letter, so I had better get back to the point. We have set up our Best of British operation over here and it is going so well that we are in danger of killing the goose that lays the golden egg. What I mean is, we have so many customers standing in line that we have run out of suitable British staff to fill the positions. That, my dear, is where you come in, if you want to (and I *do* hope you want to).

I can manage to raise the money to open an office in London. I would like you to run it, and to be my partner on the London end as Alex is in New York. It's not a sure-fire success. We could all go broke (except Alex, of course) in the first year, or even in the second. But we could also get rich, and whatever happens, we won't have bossy toffs ordering us about any more. What do you think?

When you have chosen and opened up an office, I want you to advertise for staff interested in working abroad — and nothing but the best. You've had the best training available, so I trust you to spot quality a mile off. There's already a few talent scouts for you to draw on: Mrs Higgins in Belgrave Square; Mrs Sutton in Fenton Parva for a start. The others I have on my books are all London and Birmingham agencies, so they will be off limits to you because they'll (rightly) see you as a poacher.

Please say yes, Mags. You're quiet, and you're a watcher. You probably see more than most of us about what makes people tick, and that will make you good at picking the right candidates. If you can hold the fort until Easter — you and a secretary, that is — you'll get a bit of expert help, because Mrs Higgins retires then and I'm *sure* she will join you full-time. What about it? You only get one chance to live dangerously, you know!

All my love,
Rosie

For the first time in her life, Margaret invested in a transatlantic telegram. It said:

I accept. Where do you want the office?

All love,
Mags

Chapter Twenty-five

Margaret found an office near Baker Street station, convenient for candidates travelling on tube or mainline trains, but smarter than many recruitment agencies in that it was located in a street occupied by a number of medical specialists on the fringe of the Harley Street–Wimpole Street area. It was a perfect set-up for the birth of the enterprise, comprising four rooms – a spacious one in front for use as a waiting area; a central reception space where the secretary would be stationed; and two rooms at the rear, overlooking a pleasant paved terrace. Margaret would occupy one of these, and the other would be used for interviews.

She was measuring up the place for carpets and furniture the morning after signing the lease, when there was a timid tap at the door. Looking up, she was astonished to see Parker, the butler from Fenton Parva. 'Hello, Miss Armstrong, can I come in?' he asked.

'Of course, Mr Parker. What can I do for you? I hardly think you'll be wanting to go off to America.'

'No, not quite . . . but I-I heard about your little – er – enterprise, and I felt I must get in touch. You'll be needing a secretary, perhaps?'

'Of course. I have an advertisement due to run at the end of this week in the *News* and the *Standard*. Why?'

'I don't know whether you're aware of it, but I have a daughter. She's a trained secretary. Her mother and I put aside every penny to send her to the best secretarial school.'

'Well, she must be very much in demand.'

He shook his head dolefully. 'She's been out of work for three months. Nearly at the end of her tether . . . driving her poor mother mad, and I'm not too happy, neither.'

'Whatever went wrong?'

'I hardly like to say . . . seems so − so unlikely, really, but I believe her. Never known her to lie before.' He ground to a halt, clearly too embarrassed to say anything further.

'Come on, Mr Parker, you can tell me. Remember they always used to tease me at Fenton for never being willing to tell anyone what time of day it was?'

He smiled and nodded. 'Yes, of course. It's just so humiliating. She had a couple of jobs, always one step up when she moved on. Then she went to work for this big City solicitor − personal secretary to the senior partner. After she'd been there two months, he − he started a bitta funny business. She wouldn't play − he was a married man and she's a good girl − and finally he really messed her up. Tore her blouse and upset her something awful. Then he gave her the sack.

'She didn't care. She's a sensible type and she said she'd have resigned if he hadn't dismissed her. The trouble was . . .' Words failed him again and Margaret realised what was troubling him.

'He wouldn't give her a good reference,' she finished for him.

Parker nodded miserably. 'And you wouldn't credit the difference it makes. It was only two months, but everybody asks what she was doing then, and if she tells the truth he blackens her character. If she doesn't say anything, they assume all sorts of terrible things about her, and it gets worse with every week that passes. If it goes on much longer, nobody will take her. Would you at least see her?'

'Of course I will! Look, I've only got two chairs and a kettle in here so far, but I'll make us a cup of tea. Then you can go and see the family and tell them. I never asked about your family, but I suppose you've kept them in London all these years?'

'Yes. The wife is a live-out housekeeper, so we've always rented a little flat for her and our girl, and I get up whenever I can. This business has really laid us low, I can tell you!'

'I expect it has! Don't you worry. Even if she doesn't fit

in here, we'll sort out something. I know exactly how she must feel.'

His eyebrows shot up. 'Do you? Do you really? I always wondered if something awful had driven you away from Fenton like that.'

Margaret felt her colour rising and muttered something dismissive, then went to make the tea. Eventually she saw Parker off, having arranged to see his daughter the next day.

Jessica Parker was an ideal choice for the secretarial job — far better qualified than the agency could have afforded without her recent mishap, and a pleasant, likeable girl into the bargain. Margaret could not help reflecting that her chastening experience with the lecherous solicitor had probably stripped her of a little touch of arrogance she might have been developing about her capabilities. Now, though, she was absurdly grateful for a job and agreed to work for a surprisingly modest wage.

A few weeks later, Margaret had already sent thirty recommendations to Rose after intensive interviews in the half-finished offices. By then, though, the place was looking the way they had agreed — far more like professional consulting rooms than a domestic staff agency. There were good carpets on the floor, curtains at the bay windows which overlooked the street, and comfortable country-house-style furniture in the waiting room. The business atmosphere did not descend until one entered the reception and back office areas, and there it was all filing cabinets and functional furniture.

Jessica provided all the back-up skills Margaret lacked. As well as impeccable shorthand and typing, she could arrange a filing system to enable Margaret to find every detail she needed with a minimum of effort. Margaret realised almost immediately that it would have taken at least three months longer to get going, had it not been for Jessica.

Unknown to Margaret, in New York Rose was preparing to stop work and go away to have her baby. Rose wanted no one but Lilian to know — she hardly counted Alex

Moncreiff because she assumed he had only a passing interest in her — and she had no intention of referring to the coming event in a letter to her English partner. One never knew who got to see a letter.

In consequence, she wrote to Margaret on quite another matter as her last act before going on leave:

I shall be away for a while talking to possible employers outside New York about the sort of response we would get if we expanded later in the year. While I am away, do you think you could get in touch with Mrs Higgins? I've had a good idea and I think that together, the two of you could get it off the ground, particularly if this new secretary of yours is as good as you say.

How do you feel about us setting up a training school for our own staff? I know it sounds like biting off more than we can chew, so soon after starting the business, but I'm seriously worried that our supply of recruits will dry up if we don't make sure we keep it steady. As I see it, we would need suitable premises; a couple of first-rate instructors — that's where Mrs H comes in, and you, of course — and good advertising to attract the right sort of people. It means we would get two chances to make a decent profit — one by charging people for their training, the second from our usual finder's fee to employers.

I don't know how long this letter will take to get to you, or what you will think of the idea. I may well have gone off on my trip by the time you have thought it over. When you decide, get in touch with Lilian. She knows all about it — she typed this letter, of course — and I've given her a full set of notes about my ideas on it. If I'm a really lucky girl, you may even have a lot of it in the pipeline by the time I get back. Remember, we only get one try at something this exciting. If we keep our nerve, we can beat them all!

Love, love, love,
Rose

Oh, Rose, am I a miracle worker or something? Margaret wanted to cry out when she saw the letter. A training school . . . advertising . . . instructors . . . fees. How on earth did a very recently ex-nanny set a scale of fees for instruction in advanced domestic skills? Where would she begin looking for a place to conduct the training? How many trainees would they need to make the whole project worthwhile? After ten minutes' panic, she began a two-pronged attack on the problem. She telephoned Mrs Higgins at the Cliftons' Belgrave Square house, and invited her out to lunch. Then she took out a large ring-bound notebook and laid out two columns, one headed PROBLEM, the other headed SOLUTION. Having spent an hour laying out her worst fears on the pad, she called Jessica in and dictated a letter to Lilian Shaw in New York, asking for her opinion and for a copy of the notes Rose had left.

When they had finished the letter and Jessica brought it in to be signed, the secretary said: 'Have you got a few minutes to spare, Miss Armstrong?'

Margaret smiled at the girl. She would never adjust to a well-educated female of almost her own age calling her 'Miss'. 'I should say no, but today has been so hectic, I'd like to do something else for a while. What was it?'

'Just wait there and I'll show you.' Jessica bobbed into her own office and returned moments later, with the air of a successful magician, bearing a silver-plated tray with two glasses and a bottle of excellent sherry. 'You've been so busy you forgot,' she said. 'It's a month to the day since the London branch of Best of British opened its doors. I thought a little celebration was in order.'

Margaret laughed ruefully. 'Only a month? Is it just me, or do you feel we've been in business for centuries, too?'

'I've certainly never been this busy, Miss Armstrong, but I don't think I've ever enjoyed a job so much, either.' She brought the sherry over to Margaret's desk and began to pour it. 'Don't worry about the quality,' she said. 'Dad is a real expert on wines and he'd skin Mum or me alive if we ever went for cheap stuff.'

An hour later, warmed and slightly tipsy from the sherry, Margaret wended her way back to the women's hotel where she had made a temporary home. Perhaps everything was going to progress well after all. They'd certainly been lucky so far.

Later she fell to brooding about Rose, and wondered what on earth had happened to change the shy, almost reclusive maid she had known in England into a human powerhouse of ideas and resourcefulness. Whoever had said 'Go West, young man, and grow up with the country', should have applied the remark to young women as well, if Rose was anything to go by.

Margaret divided most of the following week between interviewing job candidates, and trying to build a strategy for the Best of British training school. Early on, she realised one of her best plans would be to outline what she did *not* want in the establishment. For that she had an awful warning ready at hand: the Parsons Green Centre which had trained her and Rose. Immediately that moved her a considerable way forward. No beginners. It would be fatal to become enmeshed in teaching stupid, semi-literate girls how to sweep floors and mend bedlinen. No wealthy American would import fancy foreign labour for that.

Best of British had to be a sort of Eton of the domestic arts — the place where a first footman or perhaps a senior ship's steward would go to acquire extra polish in order to become a butler in America; where a head kitchen-maid or assistant cook might improve herself sufficiently to plan and prepare a faultless dinner party for twelve. With Rose's supervision, they could even run a short course to prepare applicants for the changed working conditions they would encounter in the USA.

Irrespective of individual ambitions, all trainees would be required to prove they had solid domestic experience, and had achieved an acceptable level of general education. Having successfully raised one's own family might be regarded as suitable domestic experience, which meant they could receive applications from former housewives without much ready cash. There must be some system for training people and charging them later — perhaps an attachment of some of their first year's American earnings? As Margaret enumerated each facet of the new business, more and more questions popped into her mind. She was impatient to meet Mrs Higgins and pick the older woman's brain. With a lifetime of running great houses behind her, Mrs Higgins would doubtless raise five questions for every one which Margaret thought to ask.

When they did meet, Mrs Higgins's advice proved even more valuable than Margaret anticipated. For a start, she came up with the one huge dilemma that had never occurred to the younger woman. 'You'll have to take it out of London, of course,' said Mrs Higgins. 'You'd have to be a millionaire to rent the size of house you'd need to train this lot, and board them as well.'

'Board them? We couldn't do that!'

'We'd have to, silly girl! Practically every senior domestic post involves night work and early morning starts. D'you think we'd get them all coming in about six o'clock and staying around until late evening, then getting on a Number 5 bus to make their way home? Anyway, most of them will be coming straight to us from some domestic appointment. They'll hardly want to be fussing around arranging lodgings for the few weeks they're in training, will they?'

'No, you're right, of course.' Margaret's mind had wandered to something else Mrs Higgins had just said. 'You mentioned a few weeks. I don't know why, but I'd been thinking of a few months.'

'Wouldn't be practical,' said Mrs Higgins. 'It would cost them too much and take too long for them either to save up or pay off in arrears. But apart from that, remember we're not talking about ignorant little girls. These will be people fully trained at all sorts of things around big houses. They'll just need a bitta polishing. I'd say six weeks would be the most we'd want, and that would be cooks, housekeepers and butlers. We can't touch nannies or governesses, of course. You're either fully trained for that in the beginning, or you never get it. No, I'd say two levels. A month for lady's maids, parlour-maids, chauffeurs, companions, valets; six weeks for the really senior jobs. Then we charge them as they go for their board and lodging, and a separate fee for the training. Wouldn't be bad if we could guarantee them a job in America if they complete the course successfully.'

Margaret was staring at her happily. 'You said "we". Rose only said you might . . .'

'Oh, don't take any notice of *her*,' said Mrs Higgins. 'What woman in her right mind would resist a chance like this, particularly at my age?'

'We're never going to get this one off the ground, Mrs H. How could we possibly afford it?'

'Well, for a start, we forget about London. You got to have the office in London. Stands to reason, no one would come to see you anywhere else. But the school? Nothing but trouble. We could get a place to rent outside for next to nothing these days. You've seen all them stories about how the likes of the Cliftons are going broke, what with taxes and things. We find a reasonable-sized country house — doesn't have to be in tip-top condition, neither — and furnish it from sale rooms, and we're in business. Our Rosie's still going to have to come down to earth, though. Either she gets this Moncreiff fellow to cough up a bigger investment, or we wait until the summer to get going. We'll never launch it on a shoestring at this time a year.'

'Will we *ever* manage to launch it, d'you think?'

'Sure of it, love. Once that Rose gets the bit between her teeth, nothing'll stop her. I'm only surprised she's gone to ground now. Thought she'd be issuing instructions to you across the Atlantic, not diving off into the backwoods looking for more customers.'

'Hmm, so did I,' said Margaret. 'I do hope she's all right.'

Rose was as well as could be expected in the circumstances. About a week before her pregnancy came to term, she boarded a Greyhound bus and went off to stay in a

Philadelphia suburb, where a former colleague and girl friend of Lilian was now happily married and bringing up her family with the help of extra income from boarders.

She had agreed to let Rose have the ground floor back double room at her house, a room with a bathroom close by and no steep steps to and from the street. In return for a small extra payment, she had also arranged for Rose to be admitted to a maternity hospital in the neighbourhood where the fees were a fraction of what was charged anywhere in New York. Rose hoped to be in hospital for only a week, but knew both her fragile budget and tight timetable might be devastated by any delays or complications.

Before Rose's departure, Lilian had a long talk on the telephone to her friend Audrey. 'I don't know what to make of her,' she said. 'She acts as if this baby's coming to someone else, not her. She got a bit of a rough deal from the father, and I expect that's what did it, but either way, I think she'll need help when she's had the kid. I'm damned sure she hasn't made up her mind what to do with it yet.'

Audrey, who adored children, was perplexed. 'What's to make up your mind about? You get caught, you have the kid and you love it. Simple as that, provided you got the money to raise it all right, and she seems to have her head screwed on the right way to make it on her own in business.'

'Yes, I know, but you wait until you meet her. She's terribly smart, even all bulging with the baby, beautiful face, perfect manners and a real "your ladyship" English accent, which you shouldn't let fool you. She's been down further than either of us will ever know. You'd think a girl like that, with a clever head on her shoulders as well, could handle anything. But she's got this — this *hurt* look. If you don't get it now, you will when you see her. As if someone had done something really terrible to her that she can't quite believe, and she doesn't know how to protect herself from it happening again. I know I'm explaining it badly, but honest, Audrey, you'll get it straight away when you see her.

'Anyway, she's a lovely kid, and she doesn't have a clue

about what to do over all this. All helpful suggestions gratefully received.'

Audrey tugged at her lip, worrying the problem like a small, fussy terrier. Eventually, she said: 'The Kleins, just down the block from here, have got one kid and can't have another. She had an accident and miscarried her last one, then they had to take everything out. They're dying for another – wouldn't care about it being adopted as long as they could get it young enough. They're quite comfortably off. He owns two little stores that are doing pretty good. I know they'd jump at the chance.'

'Perhaps you should have a little chat about it when you meet our Rosie. I got a feeling adoption might be a bit too drastic for her – too final, if you know what I mean.'

'Yeah, 'course I do. I'd tear anyone apart if they tried to take Marion or Clifford or one of the older ones off me. Leave it with me, honey. I'll straighten her out.'

'I'd be bloody grateful if you did!'

Audrey took to Rose immediately, and set about easing the problems of the coming weeks. 'Everything's arranged,' she announced, fussing over her new boarder with a mug of hot soup within minutes of her arrival from the bus station. 'I'm home all the time caring for my own kids, so there'll be someone here if you need anything when you get out of the hospital. We always treat the boarder in that ground floor back as one a the family, so any time you wanna come out and chat, just you do it. No need to be lonely.' She had the good sense not to pitch in to Rose that evening about her baby's future, merely ensuring the room was warm, the bed turned down and the bathroom towels fresh before she saw her temporary charge off to bed.

Rose was exhausted, both by the journey in her advanced state of pregnancy, and by the sheer weight of work she had accomplished in the past two months in order to create enough time to disappear like this. She had imagined back in New York that she would be endlessly fretting about the state of the business, but the moment the Greyhound left the city behind, it became to her as remote as the waters of the moon, and her mind moved ahead to the vast event which was advancing on her so inexorably.

When Audrey Skelton left her in the pleasant room, she slid luxuriously into the soft bed and waited for sleep to waft her away. Instead, her mind began gently nudging up memories of all that had happened in something less than a year, and before long Rose began to think she would never sleep again. The central thought which cropped up again and again, intruding through visions of a furious Lady Julia, a smiling, sympathetic Alex Moncreiff and the friendly scepticism of Eddie Hansen, was Mark Fletcher-Simms.

Odd, really, she thought, since I never even saw him that day he called on Lady Julia. Nevertheless, she could picture his face, darkening with fury as he realised how he had been deceived — tricked, he would have said — and what a fool he had made of himself by running after a servant-girl in this way, ending up in Georgetown humiliated before a woman of his own class. It never occurred to Rose to doubt that these had been his emotions, or to question Lady Julia's shrivelling account of the entire incident. In normal circumstances, Rose would not have believed the sun was shining on the strength of Lady Julia's assertion. She would have looked outside and confirmed it for herself. Yet here she was, accepting every word the other woman had uttered in a state of blazing fury.

There was a considerable amount which Lady Julia had not told her — like the fact that Fletcher-Simms had asked if he might arrange to see and talk to Rose, in case there was something they could salvage from the mess. Julia had said it was out of the question and that Rose was away for some days. Nor had she mentioned the numerous hints she had dropped that this was not the first time Rose had indulged in disreputable entanglements with men she had 'picked up,' as Lady Julia put it with exaggerated delicacy and pursed lips. By the time Fletcher-Simms left he had been forced to re-classify Rose into a cross between an irresponsible adventuress and a pathological liar — hardly a combination calculated to appeal to a man who until then had thought she was a lovable young woman interested in art and good food.

Not that Rose even had the consolation of knowing he had thought a lot of her, however much her image might now be dented. To her, he was the rich man who had run true to form and abandoned her the moment he discovered something of her origins and had he known more, she thought, he would have run further, faster. What price a drunken father in Shoreditch and a murdered mother in a pauper's grave? It all made the feelings she had for the child in her womb appallingly complex. She had striven ever since leaving Georgetown to dismiss Mark Fletcher-Simms from her mind, and eventually had managed to relegate him permanently to the fantasy figure of their early meetings. Had she thought for a moment that he might prefer the flesh and blood Rose, servant or not, to some illusory blue stocking, she would have been less eager to dismiss him. There had been moments aboard the ocean liner of sheer joy in his company, ecstasy in response to his love-making, pleasure at his unexpected tenderness.

When she dismissed the possibilities which might have arisen from those feelings, in a sense she pre-judged the child too. It would be a disappointment. All Rose's blood relationships had been a disappointment — why should this one be so different? It would be an appalling burden — what would she do with a baby in the next couple of years, undoubtedly the most strenuous her little business would ever face? How would she explain the presence of a baby if a colleague or associate came round to the apartment? The problems jostled at her, quite crowding out the normal anticipation of motherhood and affection. Rose had known so little of that, she had no standards on which to base such feelings. Lacking a foundation for them, she did not even identify them as a maternal urge and discarded them as fast as they arose.

She settled in remarkably quickly with Audrey Skelton and her boisterous family. There was Audrey's husband Joe, a big, genial man who clearly adored his family and whom

Rose found to be excellent company. He was an engineer at a small local plant, and would have been making enough money to keep them comfortably had not both he and Audrey adored children so much they insisted on a houseful. There were five – two girls and three boys – and they shared the timber-frame house's big attic rooms, leaving the rest of the building free for a stream of lodgers, largely construction workers posted away from home for a couple of months, or the pleasanter kind of travelling salesman.

At the centre of it all was Audrey, tiny, bird-like and competent, hardly bigger than a child and yet capable of running the entire household so well that there was never a sign of unwashed linen or badly prepared food. Sometimes, watching her, Rose almost envied the woman. But the feeling wore off quickly enough. She knew she was no earth mother, and that a world like Audrey's would drive her to distraction in days.

Mid-morning on her third day with the Skeltons, she was sharing a pot of coffee in the kitchen with Audrey. The older children were all at school and Marion, at five the baby of the family, was playing with a neighbour's children across the road.

'What sort of plans have you made for after the birth?' Audrey asked her. They had been discussing the cost of buying clothes for new babies, and the question arose naturally rather than being flung at Rose. She stared into her coffee cup for a while before saying: 'I wish I could say I'd made any. I feel guilty about it, to say the least, but it's as if I've been turned to jelly and can't get hold of the problem, somehow. And don't tell me it shouldn't be a problem – I know I should be filled with joy rather than panic!'

Audrey smiled indulgently. 'I wasn't going to say any such thing. Women with a lot more to depend on than you got are apt to be a mite panicky at this stage. Go ahead and have hysterics if you like. I'll handle it.'

'I – it's not that. Funnily enough I'm not too concerned about having a hard time physically at the birth. That's something everyone has to go through. No, I meant I can't come to grips with what to do afterwards.'

Audrey was silent for long enough for Rose to feel fairly relaxed, and said: 'I could probably help, you know. All you have to do is ask . . . or better still, just get it off your chest, what you see as the worst bit.'

'That's easy enough — looking after him, of course! Funny, that, I always think of this baby as "him". I wonder if all mothers do that.'

'Don't think so. Maybe his daddy's still on your mind.'

Rose tossed her head. 'No — and there'd be little point in it if he was. Nothing to be gained from that. Either way, boy or girl, I hardly know what I shall do with the poor kid. I have to get straight back to work afterwards, and the money is so tight there's no question of getting a nanny for him or even a responsible girl from our neighbourhood. I just couldn't afford it.'

'What can you afford?'

'Well, I can afford to keep him — it. You know, food, clothes, shoes — all the day-to-day things a child needs. But when we get on to hired help forget it.'

'You realised what I meant when I said I could help, don't you? I know a really nice couple who already have one child and they'd just love to adopt. The baby would get the best of everything, including a lot of love and attention you might not have time to offer. How about it?'

'I won't say I hadn't thought about that, Audrey, and you've come up with a solution to the one big problem about it — I was put off by the idea of not knowing whether he'd be going to good people. I don't trust adoption agencies any more than I do any other organisation. But if the people came personally recommended, I might think about it . . . only might, mind you.' She considered that for a while, then added: 'And that wouldn't be fair on the couple, would it? I could hardly get them all worked up about having another child of their very own, and then change my mind at the last minute. But it's due any day, and if I don't make some arrangements now . . .' Her voice began to rise as her own nervousness pushed through the tight control she had been exercising, and she began to cry.

'Oh, Audrey, I'm trying to be calm about all this. After all, it's no one's fault but mine. But now it's so close, and I haven't sorted out anything, and oh, God, what shall I do?'

Audrey uncurled from her chair and went to put her arms around Rose as if the girl were a hurt child. 'For a start, you can let me do some a your worrying for you, since there's no big strong man to lean on. I think I can come up with a little idea that'll help.

'What if you had this baby, came back here to Willow Drive after, and stayed as long as you could before going back to New York? You could leave the kid with me for a couple a weeks – you know I take to 'em like a duck to water, and I got so many around already I won't notice another one.'

'Not notice a new baby? Come on, Audrey, even you'd be slowed down by that!'

Audrey grinned. 'Well, not so's you'd notice, anyway. The boarders'd just have to put up with beef stew a bit more often, is all.'

'I still don't see how that would solve things, though, apart from delaying it a bit.'

'Oh, that's just part of it. Once you'd got used to being a mother, and really had a chance to make up your mind, we could talk to the Kleins – that is, if you decided you could part with the child for good. On the other hand, you wouldn't be winding them up and then disappointing them if you kept it, because they'd never get to know you'd considered anything else.'

'Audrey, what would I do without you?' Then Rose's smile faded. 'But what if – what if I *couldn't* give him up?'

'I think we can work on that when the time comes. At least this leaves one possibility for you, without hurting the Kleins.'

'Yes, and bless you for it. Now, I think I'd better go out for a walk before I get chairbound!'

Rose started her contractions at two in the morning three

nights later. Joe Skelton drove her to the nursing home, where she was booked in as Mrs Mark Rush. Ten hours later she gave birth to a big, healthy son. As Rose held him for the first time, smoothing down his little tuft of dark hair and gazing into the unfocused dark-blue eyes, she knew she could never give him up for adoption. As she drifted off into an exhausted but peaceful sleep, her last thought was, but what shall I do with him?

The decision was all but taken out of her hands. By the end of the following week, she was back at the Skeltons' house, feeling slightly wobbly but otherwise much better than she could remember being. Audrey was bottle-feeding Giles (a name Rose had chosen because she knew no one who already laid claim to it) and Joe had just come off shift. 'Whichever way I look at it, you were right to help me delay talking to the Kleins,' she told Audrey. 'I can just about face being away from him, but I couldn't even consider giving him up for good.'

'In that case, I think me an' Joe can help you,' said Audrey. 'Would Philadelphia be too far for you to come and see him?'

Wide-eyed and silent, Rose shook her head.

'Well, then, if you set aside what you'd have spent anyway on his food and clothes an' things each week, and send it to us, we can take care a the little fellow,' she said. 'I'm as hooked on him as you, and I wouldn't ask for anything towards his keep if we didn't already have a house full of our own eating Joe's wages faster than he earns 'em. What d'you think?'

Rose put her face in her hands and burst into tears. 'I don't think anyone has ever done anything so nice for me,' she sobbed.

Joe grinned. 'Then stop blubbering and have a glass a beer to wet the baby's head!' he said.

Chapter Twenty-six

Perhaps Rose's guardian angel decided she deserved some respite after the rigours of recent months; whatever the cause, once she was back in command at Best of British, everything she touched seemed to succeed.

Between them Lilian in New York and Margaret in London had held the fort admirably. Margaret was spending a lot of time house hunting for training premises around the Home Counties; Lilian had turned herself into the epitome of an English lady and was stalking rich prey along Fifth and Park Avenues to add to their already prestigious client list. On her first day back at the office, two fat files awaited Rose. The first contained an up-to-date list of Margaret's London recruits, with full notes on references and professional backgrounds; the second was Lilian's compilation of New York clients – satisfied and still searching – who seemed to have swollen to form an unending queue during Rose's absence.

'Good God, it will take me all this week to wade through this lot, let alone do anything about them,' she told Lilian. 'You must have been worked off your feet.'

'You could say that, but I'm having more fun than I ever had with my clothes on, as my friend Joyce used to say. Listen, Rose, I've been thinking about the catching up you need to do. Why not cut your losses and start afresh with what comes in from today? You trust my judgement now, don't you?'

Rose uttered an indignant snort. 'If I didn't, d'you think I'd have gone off and left my new baby in your hands for over a month . . .?' She blushed and tailed off into silence. Since her return to their apartment the previous Saturday, she had barely mentioned Giles. Lilian had made a couple of attempts to draw her out but had got nowhere. Now they were both embarrassed at Rose's naked revelation that she regarded the business as far more her offspring than she did the child.

Lilian got up impulsively and came round the desk, where she stood with her arm around Rose's shoulder and pressed the younger woman's stiff body close in an attempt to comfort her. 'No need to worry, love. This is Lilian, remember? Whatever you do, you've got your reasons. Just remember I'm on the same side as you.'

After a moment Rose relaxed perceptibly, then clutched gratefully at Lilian's hand. 'Thanks. I really do appreciate that. Some day, maybe, but not now . . .' Her tone took on its old brisk quality again. 'Come on, let's get down to business. You're right about me trusting you, of course. I'll need some sort of update, though. What if I get the inevitable gaggle of society dowagers in here demanding to know why the lady companion and the butler they engaged a month ago hasn't turned up yet?'

'Yes, well I thought of that, too. Look in the back pocket of the New York Clients file. How does that suit you?'

She had prepared a master list of clients and staff, with name, age and present occupation against each potential employee and name, address and special requirements against each client. All carried a starting date, and there was a box at the end of each line to be ticked as each applicant took up the post.

'That's brilliant, Lil! I'm damned glad you were out of work when we met, or I'd never have got into this, but I'll never understand why no one was bright enough to snap you up for all that time.'

Lilian grinned. 'Wrong accent, wrong age and just not quite pretty enough. Simple as that. I'm no old boot, but I'll never be the Mona Lisa, either. What you lack in beauty, you have to make up for in brains, or you go under.' She studied Rose at length, then added: 'Of course, *some* of us have the lot!'

'Get away with you, crawler! I was just going to offer

to buy you a whole tanker full of gin after work tonight, but I may change my mind if you carry on like that.'

'After work . . . that reminds me. You obviously haven't looked in your diary yet.'

Rose shook her head and reached for the big leather-bound book. In the 4.30 pm slot, Lilian had written: 'Alexander Moncreiff — expansion?'

'You get more cryptic every day, Shaw. What the devil does that mean?'

'Exactly what it says. Your sleeping partner was very reserved. Said he was coming up to New York today and spending most of the week here, and that he'd like to see you early on in his visit to discuss expansion plans. It all sounded so cut and dried I thought I must have missed out somewhere along the line when he discussed it with you before.'

Rose shook her head, mystified. 'I haven't seen him since that flying visit he paid us when we finally got off the ground. As I said at the time, he went over the general picture, sounded very pleased about it — particularly when I told him Mags was going to open an English branch — and then rode off into the sunset wishing me Merry Christmas and a prosperous New Year. Haven't seen hide nor hair of him since, though I assume you've been sending him those fortnightly summary sheets we set up.

'Well, well, well! I wonder what he has in mind. The only thing I can think of is my training centre idea, but I can't imagine he'd want to get involved in any more B of B ventures until we've proved ourselves.'

Lilian sniffed. 'You know I feel much the same way. One wrong step now, Rose, and we're all down the tubes. Why not practise walking for a year or two before you try to make the Olympic running team?'

'Stand still and you die — or at least, lose your nerve, which is the next thing to it. I had nine years of being careful and doing what I was told. It got me pregnant and unemployed. Who needs that sort of security?'

There seemed no answer to that, so Lilian went back to

Moncreiff. 'I take it you don't mind meeting him today, anyway,' she said. 'The reason I just mentioned it was that if you're seeing him that late, he may have it in mind to buy *you* a tanker-load of gin, and I don't think he'd welcome me along in that case.

'Lilian, what *are* you suggesting?'

'If you needed me to answer that one, you wouldn't be so arch about it. We'll do the girlish drinkies tomorrow night if you turn out to be free. Tonight, I'll go home and cook something for supper that will keep if you get taken off somewhere terribly swish. Okay?'

'Okay. But I think you've got hold of the wrong end of the stick.'

'We'll see about that when today is over.'

Life had dealt less than kindly with Alexander Moncreiff over the past couple of months. He had never been passionately devoted to Julia Clifton, but most of his friends had married in a similar mood. One did not conduct a civilised existence based on a passionate marriage. Nevertheless he had found her desirable, reasonably amusing, and a pleasant, if superficial companion. More importantly, she was perfectly cast for the role of grande dame, an invaluable talent for one with his plans.

Marriage had adjusted his views a lot. What had looked like clever, spiky humour in a fiancée swiftly turned into shrewishness in a wife. There was no natural courtesy in Julia, no grace in considering the needs of others and in fulfilling them. Her entire existence appeared to be a quest to satisfy the desires of Lady Julia Moncreiff, and to hell with the rest. Alexander was as self-centred as any other rich, good-looking young man, and in other circumstances might have been indifferent to Julia's shortcomings. But he quickly became aware that she could cut swathes through his political ambitions if she grew irritated by anyone from the Brazilian Ambassador to an Italian count. The idea chilled him, but it seemed he was powerless to do anything about it. He had made a cool, calculating choice of wife because he knew divorce was also potentially fatal to his career, and now, rapidly coming to believe he had made the wrong choice, it seemed he was trapped by his own cleverness.

Never a man to waste time on self-recrimination, he had decided to let matters take their course in his marriage. Julia had announced she was pregnant just after Christmas, and it occurred to him that this might mellow her into a more useful proponent of his aims. In the meantime, he would settle down to consolidate family business interests, and pretend — to himself as much as the outside world — that he was indifferent to anything else.

Moncreiff shared some of Rose's attitudes to commerce. He saw no point in embarking on a new venture without doing it wholeheartedly. Looking at the portfolio of investments held by the family, he decided many of them were too dull to be of any interest. His view was unmodified by the fact that the very dullness of the stocks and bonds had preserved the Moncreiffs' prosperity when more daring money was vanishing in the Wall Street Crash of 1929. They had kept so much in Government securities that to envisage them going under, one would have needed to believe that the US Treasury itself was about to be declared bankrupt.

Well, thought Alex, that was all going to change now, and Rose Rush would be one of the first beneficiaries, if she was interested. After that, there were all sorts of fascinating schemes just waiting for the injection of a little judicious venture capital — and he fancied himself as a merchant venturer until he could once again set his sights on becoming President of the USA.

He had been thinking a lot about Rose lately. No wonder her agency was proving so popular with New York's smart set. Rose herself was a walking advertisement for the place. Moncreiff grinned to himself. He would never have guessed Rose was anything but his wife's social equal, had he not met her as Julia's maid. Her language, manners, dress and conversation all pointed in that direction, and it was quite impossible for a cultivated American to imagine someone so accomplished being prepared to work as a maid. Once

New York became familiar with that sort of domestic staff, it was clamouring for more, and given that none of Rose's recruits was brought to the USA without a contract of employment in their possession, there were seldom any problems about work permits.

Rose had spoken the truth when she told Lilian they had barely discussed the training centre in England. But Moncreiff was not the sort of man who needed every point hammered home forcibly. He had picked up enough of the idea to understand its potential, and was fairly sure he had a better grasp of the relatively high cost of setting the place up. Now he had come back to New York with a firm set of business proposals which would stay securely locked in his briefcase if Miss Rush failed to make the appropriate responses.

That need not have worried him. Over coffee in her office, she told him how far her investigations had gone. 'I've drawn up a list of specifications and my associate over in England has done the same,' she said. 'I have a consultant joining Miss Armstrong in a month or two who has a lifetime in this business behind her.' She fought an impulse to giggle at the thought of Margaret's and Mrs Higgins's reactions to being called an associate and a consultant. Kate Higgins would have had to ask how to spell the words – but she was still one of the best in her field. 'Perhaps you'd care to look at it. It explains a lot better than I can across a desk. I'm afraid it adds up to one big sad fact: we can't afford it.'

He picked up the stapled sheets of paper she passed him, and skimmed through the contents. He did not know whether Rose or one of these other women had put it together – he guessed all three had contributed and then Lilian had shaken it into a coherent whole. After a while he looked up at Rose. 'You may be under-capitalised, but it makes a lot more commercial sense than many business plans I've seen,' he told her. 'Have you no assets you could pledge?'

Her laugh held a hint of incredulity. 'Come on, Mr Moncreiff. You know how we started – you staked us!'

'What about the London premises?'

Rose shrugged. 'Leased, and no residual value in fixtures and fittings. What bank is going to finance a couple of women on the basis of a waiting room full of chairs and a nice carpet? We're doing well here, it's true, but how many businesses can you name which make enough in the first half-year to pay the staff, cover the initial investment and hand over a bit of profit to the backer?'

For a moment she thought he had stopped listening. He was bending over a leather briefcase which rested against his chair. 'This is going to need a lot of money, Rose, and I mean a *lot*. It will make the original sum I put up look like peanuts.'

'Then it's certainly out of the question. I doubt if we could raise more than you've already put in.'

'You don't have to raise it. I'm prepared to back you in return for a full partnership. Wait — before you start throwing in objections, I haven't finished. Your associate back in London has to have an incentive and she seems to have burned her boats as enthusiastically as you to go into this. Then there's people like Lilian, and, I suspect, your consultant in England.

'I'm proposing something quite new, because I think it will give all of you the drive to make this thing work. The company will split into four shares — one for me, as backer, one for you, as founder and New York boss, one for Margaret Armstrong for doing the same in London, and the fourth divided equally between your two key Number Two people here and in London. That's Lilian and . . . let me see . . .' he glanced down at her business plan '. . . Kate Higgins. Yours and mine will be the biggest — thirty per cent each — then Miss Armstrong gets twenty per cent and the other two divide the remaining twenty per cent equally between them. How does that sound to you?'

She was staring at him with the air of one who had found her Messiah. 'You'd be prepared to do that for us? You're either a saint or a lunatic!'

Moncreiff's laugh boomed so loudly that Lilian, in the

office outside, glanced up in astonishment. 'Really, Rose, you never fail to surprise me! Anyone else would be buttering me up like mad and you're questioning my sanity! Are you sure you want my backing?'

'I'd like to know exactly why you're doing this. Churlish as it sounds, I've learned the hard way that rich people seldom give anything away. That's how they got rich in the first place. I shall feel happier if there's a logical explanation.'

'Hmm, you have a perfectly valid point. It's not me wanting to be Lord Bountiful. This will be a high-risk venture for a few years yet. No use trying to make people give of their best and go on doing it in the long term for nothing more than a wage packet at the end of the month. When they can see it's their future they're fighting for, it will make all the difference. There, have I explained myself sufficiently?'

'You should be a politician!' He winced at that, but she failed to notice. 'Now,' she added, 'let's talk money.'

Without comment, Moncreiff laid a financial summary on the desk between them. She picked it up and flipped over the first two pages with barely a glance. 'That's what I wanted,' she said, 'to see whether your idea of the bottom line was anywhere near mine.'

'And is it?'

'To within a thousand dollars. That was why I'd almost decided there was no chance of going in on the training side.'

'And now?'

Her grin was feline. 'And now I intend calling in Lilian to tell her she's a partner in a big business, then I'll get her to cable England with the same news for Mags and Kate Higgins.'

'Good God – I never imagined I'd be involved with one female business partner, let alone four!'

'How does it feel?'

'Terrifying. Tomorrow I shall have to go and throw my weight around among all those guys on Wall Street, just to show myself I can still cut the mustard.'

'That's tomorrow. If you're free tonight, I have a suggestion.'

'Suggest away.'

'You can buy Lilian and me dinner, since you're taking over our business.'

'Gold-digger! You're on.'

As she went to get her coat, Rose wondered what she would have done if he had suggested they go without Lilian. She was at a loss for an answer.

It's amazing how much difference a little money makes, Margaret told herself for the tenth time as she bustled around the entrance hall of Midgeley Grange.

The Grange was a cavernous Victorian barn of a place in Hertfordshire, built in the 1850s by a newly ennobled member of the peerage with more money than sense or good taste. 'He certainly got value for his money, if only in the number of bricks they sold him!' Kate Higgins, apparently reading Margaret's mind, had come in behind her. 'Still, let's not look a vulgarian in the wallet, eh? If he hadn't built it so ugly, we'd never have picked it up so cheap. One man's loss is usually another's gain.'

The house had been in reasonably good repair, surprisingly so considering the low asking price on the lease. When Margaret and Kate looked around it, they quickly realised why. No one without the brewer's fortune to back them could have afforded to live in it at all, so there had been no protracted period of decay as a family tried to maintain the place through its long decline. Almost overnight it had passed from the high summer of prosperity to being emptied of its contents and left to stand alone in its rolling acres of parkland.

Margaret had started out with lofty ideals which covered only properties from the Jacobean to the Georgian age. Fenton Parva still represented the ideal in her mind, as it did for anyone who had worked as a servant there.

Kate Higgins soon set her straight. 'You can forget about the early stuff. I worked in a really old house in the early days. It's sheer bloody murder. They didn't even think the way people did later on; there was either no bathrooms at all, or just one for the whole house, so far from all the bedrooms it's worse than not having one.'

'All right, Kate. You've convinced me. But what about the later ones? It would be wonderful to have a training school in one of those beautiful old Georgian places.'

Kate remained unenthusiastic. 'I still don't think it'll work. I know most big country properties are a drag on the market these days, but the ones that *do* shift are exactly what you're talking about. So it would be damned expensive for a start. And that's not all. Remember, we're training experienced people to take a step up in their professions. They'll be going off to the States and from what our Rose says, even the servants have their own posh bathrooms in some of these Park Avenue palaces. Most of the people we train will already know how to run an old-fashioned English mansion and it won't help to be teaching them modern practice in a place that stopped developing about 1800, will it?'

Somewhat wistfully, Margaret put aside her secret dream of creating her very own Fenton where she could imagine herself living an idyllic life with some idealised version of Bruno Clifton. From then on, she was entirely guided by Kate Higgins, whose instinct was impeccable. It was Mrs Higgins who eventually found Midgeley Grange. Margaret had been hunting in the southern Home Counties with growing gloom. Everywhere usable seemed to have been converted to a boys' preparatory school or a nursing home. The other properties were either too rundown for renovation, or too expensive. It was almost five-thirty when she trudged back into the Baker Street office, where Jessica had been doing a brilliant job of holding the fort on the recruiting side.

'Cheer up,' the secretary greeted her, 'Mrs Higgins rang ten minutes ago in a right state. Seems she's found exactly the right place and she wasn't even looking!' Kate had been out to a small village near Baldock, visiting an elderly cousin, another former servant, who was enjoying a well-earned retirement in a tiny cottage there. After lunch they had taken a stroll along the lane behind the back garden, and Mrs Higgins was intrigued by the gingerbread-house lodge cottage at the gates of a winding, overgrown driveway. Her cousin knew the gatekeeper, who had also acted as caretaker of the house and estate since the last owner's departure in 1930.

He was happy to show them around the mansion, although at this stage Kate's cousin cried off and walked back to make the tea. Mrs Higgins eagerly took him up on the offer and spent the next hour plying him with questions about the Grange. By the time she had seen everything, she was convinced this was the place they must have as a training centre.

Her cousin was not on the telephone, but the lodge keeper had one in order to keep in touch with the estate administrators in an emergency. The prospect of leasing the estate was more than enough to persuade him to let her use it, and she contacted the agents before calling Margaret. By the time she and Margaret spoke, she had already arranged a formal accompanied viewing for two days hence, and they had agreed in less than a week to take the property.

Both women shared firm views about the way the finished centre should look. They would need a couple of classrooms, a suite of offices and living accommodation for the trainees. The rest involved no more than using the existing domestic offices for practical training sessions.

'I don't want it looking like classrooms, Kate. Am I wrong?'

'Lord, no. We're talking about grown-ups. Most of them will be quite a bit older than you, and the last time they sat at desks will have been when they were twelve or thirteen. No, I'd like to see them using furniture like the nobs they used to work for and will again, come to that. Give 'em a better sense of their own value, make them feel what it's like to be waited on a bit.

'You know what I mean — someone serving them coffee

and biscuits at eleven o'clock in the morning, and tea in the afternoon. I'm all for nice chairs and little tables scattered about where they can take a few notes if they want, or just relax and listen.'

It took them three months to devise a course timetable, to make the necessary alterations to the Grange, to hire a professional firm to subdue the overgrown garden and to set up a programme of advertisements and circulars to attract applicants. Kate Higgins found a wonderfully disreputable old butler with whom she had worked years before, and who had eventually drunk himself out of top jobs at two great houses. As long as he was left alone with a large wedge of cheese and a couple of bottles of decent port each evening, he functioned marvellously well during the day. He was to take charge of the training for valets, butlers and general manservants. Mrs Higgins herself tackled the general female staff — housekeepers, senior maids and the like — and between them, working to a brief provided from New York by Rose, they set up a 'Get to know what your American employer will expect of you' course.

Just as Margaret was becoming anxious about dealing with the culinary section of the training, they received an application for work abroad from a first-rate country-house cook. At about the same time, Jessica's father, back in London for a few days, ran across a competent male restaurant chef who had tired of the bustle of a big professional kitchen and wanted something more modest. The two of them, Amy Porritt and Tom Ensor, were persuaded to run the cookery courses at Midgeley.

Then Margaret started on the advertising, this time working hand in glove with Rose. They sold the courses as the professional domestic's version of a finishing school, producing a brochure which showed stylish staff bedrooms, spacious kitchens, a vast wine cellar and elegant reception rooms for trainees' use. A comprehensive list of tuition fees was published in the back of the brochure, together with a range of suggestions for finance that included a train now, pay later arrangement. From the beginning, they made much of the fact that they guaranteed a well-paid job in New York to any trainee who completed the course successfully and was awarded the centre's diploma.

Within two months they had received so many applications for training that there was a waiting list. As the first graduates went through the system, eager American employers lapped them up and there was never any difficulty about fulfilling the undertaking to place successful trainees.

It had been hard enough for Rose to accept that she was capable of launching her own successful business. To Margaret Armstrong and Kate Higgins it was well nigh impossible. Kate had come to Best of British with a lifetime's unthinking obedience behind her. It had never occurred to her that much of the time she was using initiative, competence and hard-won wisdom to do her job, and now, in her late fifties, she was discovering her own capabilities for the first time.

Margaret, two generations younger than Mrs Higgins, was nevertheless no Rose Rush. Always diffident about her own ability, it would have never occurred to her to strike out on her own account. Now she found she was good at it, no one was more surprised than she. The combination of realising their own potential and the offer of a permanent share in the business they were building transformed both women, and by the end of their first year, Best of British (London) was as dynamic as the New York parent company.

Chapter Twenty-seven
London, 1936

The last dinner guests had gone. The drawing-room fire still burned high enough to light the room, with the help of a candle sconce on the window sill which was one of Karl Schlegel's favourite symbols of hospitality when guests were expected. Now he and Eleri sat alone on either side of the fire, feet outstretched to catch its full warmth, a fat-bellied coffee pot and a half-empty brandy bottle on the low table between them.

Eleri uttered a sigh of pure contentment. 'Honest, Karl, you'll be the death of me!' she said, in a voice that suggested she could think of no better fate. 'You muffle me up in all this comfort, you magic up the most charming ready-made friends. You give me a free hand to cook the best food I can imagine. What's gonna happen to me the day you fall under a Number 11 bus?'

He chuckled gently and patted his well-filled belly. 'More likely that I shall die of apoplexy, the way you feed me, young woman. Sometimes I wonder if you are not fattening me for Christmas.' He paused momentarily and turned to gaze at her. 'It so happens that you have just joked about something that is worrying me a little. I have started something that cannot be stopped, and I am not getting younger. It would hardly be fair if some day I were no longer here and all this pleasant existence had to stop for you, too.'

Eleri had been joking. She regarded Schlegel as immortal, and could tease him about the way she was treated only because of that assumption. Now, abruptly, a chill passed over her. 'Don't be silly, Karl! Nothing's going to happen to you.'

He made a face. 'Maybe, maybe not. I shall be sixty next year — not old, but no chicken either. I could last until I am eighty. I could die tonight. Whatever happened, you would be totally unprotected.'

Eleri had recovered her equilibrium and was philosophical about the possibility. 'I'll take my chances. Without you, I'd a been some pathetic little mole, messing around underground in some rich people's kitchen, getting nowhere and ignored. When they'd finished with me, or I was no use for anything any more, they'd have chucked me on the scrap heap. If I'd been very lucky, they might have given me a quarter pay as a pension — just enough to keep me on the bread line in an off-season boarding house somewhere unfashionable. If you went tomorrow, I'd have had four years of more fun than I could have imagined before I met you. Which would you rather?'

He plucked at his lower lip. 'An interesting problem. I honestly do not know. What you ignore is that one tends not to miss what one has never enjoyed. The Eleri Jones who cooked for the Cliftons would not have known how it felt to go down Rupert Street buying fruit and vegetables for a meal she had planned simply because she liked it; she would not have known she could sit down at a middle-class dinner table and hold her own with some of the best conversationalists in London; she would have remained unaware of how it felt to learn the art of professional cooking from some of the best chefs in the top restaurants. You understand all these things, hence you will be desolate when they are taken away. And when you are forced to return to what you called mole-like labour, you will remember it with greater bitterness.'

He had got through to her. There was a slightly hollow tone to her laugh. 'Well, nothing's going to change it, is it? So the sooner I forget about what lies ahead, the better.'

'Not necessarily. I gave it much thought. I even thought we might marry . . .'

'Oh Karl — really!' This time her laughter was as rich

and vulgar as ever, and she kicked her stockinged feet in front of her at the absurdity of the whole idea.

'I should be hurt at such a response, you dreadful Welsh creature,' he said.

''Course you shouldn't! You're the best friend I ever had. And I hope I'm the best friend you ever had. I can just see the sorta woman you'd love . . . tall, sorta *drifty*, with lovely clothes and a soft laugh. And she'd have three university degrees and have been up Everest all on her own collecting exotic plants, and the two of you would stay up all night discussing how to free the underprivileged. Do me a favour, Karl. All I wanna do is cook and natter!'

He was staring at her as though she had revealed a vast truth which he had never recognised for himself. Eventually he found his voice and said: 'But even if what you said were true, I have never met such a creature and I am unlikely to at my advanced age.'

'Don't alter the fact that you might, do it? And it don't answer the point that the only person anyone should marry is the one who's meant for them. Ignoring that's responsible for more trouble in this world than anything else — in my opinion, anyway!' she added shamefacedly, just in case he found her views too forceful.

Schlegel smiled fondly at her. 'I could wish some of my intellectual friends had such an understanding of the quirks of human nature. I think it might be of greater value to them than more widely recognised accomplishments.'

'Stop that waffling as soon as you like. It's all very flattering, but it doesn't alter what we were talking about. Getting married is not an answer, Karl. I want to keep you as my best friend.'

He gave an exaggerated sigh. 'Then it has to be my other idea. I had a feeling that one would not go down very well.'

She was on her guard again. 'And what is that, pray?'

'A restaurant. You, my dear, are going to open your own restaurant.'

Eleri gaped at him. He beamed back. 'Can it really be that I have finally succeeded in silencing you?'

She managed to nod, but nothing more. 'What is so odd about the idea?' he said. 'Surely you cannot have imagined that even I was sufficiently greedy to pay for all that training for you in order to eat ever better dinners?'

'N-no – yes . . . oh, I don't think I thought about it at all! I was enjoying it too much and it just crept up on me. But this – Karl, if I got it wrong, I could ruin you.'

Schlegel burst out laughing. 'It would take more than a small bankrupt restaurant to burn out the Schlegel banking fortune. It's been sitting around growing and growing in Switzerland ever since those damned Nazis made it unwise to go on investing in Germany. Why should it stay there forever, and make some distant cousin richer?'

Her eyes were as round as a child's. 'I never knew you were at rich! Why d'you live in Gower Street?'

That set him off into further merriment. 'My dear Eleri! Can you truly imagine me living next door to the likes of the Earl and Countess of Clifton, and spending May on the Riviera, July in Cowes and August on the grouse moor? I should go barking mad – all the time talking about how many birds I had shot down, how many thousands of francs I had won at the casino, whose yacht I had dined on . . . that is no way for a grown man to behave.'

'You know, Karl, all this time, I been thinking you were just special the way you treated me, but you're not, are you? You're one of a kind, and I was lucky enough to find you. P'raps I shouldn't have gone on so much about this dreamy clever woman you should be married to.'

He patted her hand. 'You were right and we both know it. But thank you for the compliment. I value it. Now enough of this mutual admiration! I think we had better make plans for Maison Eleri.'

'Well for a start, that name's out. It's bloody dreadful and the best anyone would expect of it is leek soup and Welsh lamb.'

'Nothing wrong with leek soup and Welsh lamb, the way you cook them, my dear.'

'I know, I know, but if I take you up on this — I only said *if* mind — it'll have to be in some way that uses all you've got people to teach me, not a few meals like Mam never used to cook 'em.'

Eleri's gastronomic education had been continuing ever since she came to work for Schlegel. That first Sunday morning trip to Brick Lane had been one of countless expeditions to explore the flavours and cooking methods of the myriad nationalities which crowded London's slum areas — evenings in Limehouse with bamboo steamer baskets of Chinese vegetables, stir-fried meat and burning hot soups piled high around them; prolonged lunch hours in tiny nameless *trattorie* where muscular Italian women turned out breath-takingly piquant pasta sauces and produced great pots of shin of veal complete with its marrow bones; even traditional English City chop houses where they served huge pork chops with mashed potatoes and schooners of port. All were grist to Karl Schlegel's mill as he taught Eleri Jones how to appreciate not just one cuisine but the food of a whole world.

While he taught her about restaurants when they were out, he drew her into his social circle at home. He had been completely serious in saying he expected his cook to sit down and join in his dinner parties — not all of them, true, he was the first to recognise that some sauces and desserts needed constant watching — but the requirements of food preparation were the only constraints. Apart from that, he expected her to sit with his guests and join in with their conversation. At first she was tongue-tied and embarrassed, but inevitably familiarity and her own naturally extrovert personality did the rest. Within a year she was fast friends with all the regular dinner guests at his house.

After Karl had made her taste the food, he turned to teaching. It was still possible for a promising trainee to buy his or her way into the kitchens of the Savoy or the Ritz — not on an apprenticeship, but to watch the great-name chefs at their preparations for a few days or weeks at a time. Schlegel had financed three such stints for Eleri, who had returned starry-eyed, aching to try out her own version of tournedos Rossini or skate in black butter.

All this time, Karl Schlegel had nursed a secret. He had always yearned to be a chef of genius, but in his eccentric way he was also a realist. He knew he had come too far and explored too many academic disciplines to tie himself to one craft as demanding as that of the chef. Nevertheless he had never shaken off the dream, and when he recognised in Eleri an enthusiasm for food to equal his own, he had consciously begun to prepare her for just such a future. At first he had seen it as setting her up to get a good job should anything happen to him, but gradually, as the realisation grew in him that she was a truly great cook, his ambition for her expanded. In the end it would admit of nothing but that she should have her own restaurant.

Along the way he had learned a great deal about the Welsh girl's character – today he undoubtedly understood her better than anyone else who had ever known her. She was independent and self-willed, and would never accept philanthropy if she sensed that was what it was. And whatever he had in mind for her, Karl constantly told himself, philanthropy had nothing to do with it. It was more in the nature of an experiment – one which involved a dear friend, but an experiment none the less – in seeing whether it was possible to transform the life of someone who had started with nothing, without also transforming their character in the process. So far he was deeply satisfied with his progress. Eleri was better educated, more self-confident and infinitely more skilled than she had been four years earlier, but the qualities which had made him follow her after she smashed the pan at Venetia Clifton's feet remained as steady today as they had been when she was a penniless servant. He loved her, he admired her, and more than anything else he wanted her to succeed in a venture of her own choosing. Now the time had come to reveal his plan, and so far it appeared to be working.

Over the following three weeks they visited a number of restaurants in the Chelsea, Fitzrovia and Hampstead areas, looking for an ideal location. 'Why not Soho?' Eleri asked. 'That seems to be where everyone starts out.'

'Precisely. That's what makes it something of a restaurateur's graveyard, too. All very well if you are planning an orthodox bistro or Italian neighbourhood eating house. Not so good if you are trying a flags-of-all-nations approach like yours. We must find somewhere with a neighbourhood behind it — residents who can talk among themselves and build a reputation for this brilliant young woman who can translate any cuisine into something like perfection.'

'You sure you never tried a career in advertising before we met?' she said.

'You can see what I mean. Now pay attention. All three areas would give you that, though I think perhaps Fitzrovia is too fashionably down-at-heel to generate sufficient profit. Nevertheless, we shall see.'

They had agreed they were looking for a place which would handle around forty-eight covers — more than enough for Eleri to cut her teeth on, but sufficient to show her where her own weaknesses and strengths lay. 'Get this one going, run it well for a year or two, then we review the position and see if you need to expand to new premises,' said Schlegel.

'Or if I should close altogether..'

'Yes, there is that possibility. But how much better to learn it in a modest establishment before too many boats are burned, don't you think?'

'Trouble is, Karl, they're still *your* boats.'

He sighed with exasperation. 'Did you open a savings account, as I suggested, when you came to work for me?'

She nodded, perplexed by the apparent change of subject. 'Very well. How much is in it now, give or take a few pounds? I assure you I am not trying to pry.'

'You soft ha'porth! I know you better than to think that.' She paused, momentarily impressed at her own financial worth, then said: 'Over one hundred and twenty pounds! What d'you think of that? 'Course,' she added hastily, 'it wouldn't be anywhere near that amount if you hadn't been giving me Christmas bonuses and things all the time.'

Inwardly he winced. This girl had been working her fingers to the bone ever since she was in her early teens and she had little over a hundred pounds to show for it. What a society! He put aside the thought and returned to what he had set out to say. 'All right. Since you are so determined that I am the only one who stands to lose, and you do not like it, I will accept a contribution of one hundred pounds of your savings towards your partnership in the business. How does that strike you?' He wanted to laugh with a mixture of merriment and despair when he saw the agonised expression on her face. Like anyone who had laboriously saved a tiny sum, she was as reluctant to risk it as she was to burden him financially. The struggle was mirrored on her face; but almost immediately she appeared to make a decision, and smiled at him. 'That's the best idea you've had all day, Karl. I'll draw it out of the savings account the minute we find a likely place, all right?'

'As you wish, my dear. Now, perhaps we can get down to the real business of the day and find somewhere for you to open this wonderful restaurant.'

During their search for suitable premises, Schlegel was repeatedly impressed by his protégée's grasp of the prerequisites of their new venture. They visited a whole range of establishments, from functioning restaurants for sale as going concerns, to shabby, locked-up shop units which had been out of use for years, some of them never having been restaurants at all. One crisp December morning, they had been to see a succession of such tired, drab little places, none of them remotely suitable, and had retired, disheartened, to reconsider their strategy.

'I still think either of the last two had something going for them,' said Schlegel. You are becoming too demanding, Eleri.'

'No. I'm looking after our money, that's all.'

He fought the desire to smile which always overwhelmed him when she referred to 'our money' or 'our investment', because he knew all too well that her hundred pounds meant more to her than the couple of thousand he would put in if they found suitable premises. 'Tell me why,' he said.

'With the greatest pleasure. That first one: nice size; lousy inside, but that doesn't matter because I wouldn't really like to inherit somebody else's idea of the perfect restaurant kitchen. The trouble is that it looks just like a grocer's shop, and I don't think it could look any different even if we painted the outside sky-blue-pink!'

'And the second?'

'Oh, position, of course. Tucked down the bottom of that hill, who would ever come there? I've never seen this in any books, but I'm sure it's true. If you have to walk *up* the hill to dinner, you're striving after something that's worth having. What fun! Must be good – look how hard we've got to work to get there! But downhill? Doesn't matter on the way in but by the time you climb back up with a belly full of Eleri's heart-stopping food on board, you're on your last legs. All the sense of fun has worn off and you just feel shattered. So that leaves us with the people living in the little side streets just around the restaurant. Not rich enough and not enough of them to keep us going. There you are, I think that's pretty straightforward.'

She smiled like a small, contented tabby cat.

'After that trenchant analysis, Mademoiselle, I think you have earned some lunch. But not up here. It will remind us too much of those drab little failures, I think.'

They had been exploring Hampstead, and now they travelled by bus down to St John's Wood High Street to eat. 'There used to be quite a decent French restaurant along here somewhere,' said Schlegel. 'Haven't been here for years, so perhaps it's closed now . . . but I remember they had a superb cellar at very reasonable prices.'

The restaurant was still there, still open, although Karl said it was far shabbier than it had been when he knew it before. 'I really don't mind, Karl,' she said. 'Ordinary French food is usually so much better than ordinary anyone else's food! Come on. Maybe that wine list is still as good as ever.'

But something was seriously amiss in the little bistro. Most of the customers seemed to be getting what they expected, but two tables had complained. It seemed one party had received some dishes intended for the other, while the correctly ordered portions of food at the second table had been badly prepared. The head waiter, a muscular, well-knit dark young man in a sommelier's apron, was making a valiant attempt to pacify both groups, but there were simply too many dissatisfied customers for one person to deal with. This apparently made no difference to the manager, who was pretending to be busy behind the bar with a sheaf of receipts on a clip-board. The younger man repeatedly cast agonised glances over his shoulder at the manager, mutely calling for help, but the other man obviously knew there was no glory to be gained from the encounter and continued to concentrate on his paperwork.

Eleri was so fascinated by the stalemate that she did not even study the menu, normally her first enthusiastic move whenever she entered a new restaurant. Now she openly eavesdropped on what was going on at the two rebellious tables.

The head waiter soon managed to calm the customers who had merely received the wrong food. He recovered the offending dishes and asked, with infinite courtesy, whether the two people who had ordered them might not prefer a cold first course in order to keep pace with their companions. There would, of course, be a reduction in their bill. Thus pacified, they accepted a fresh choice and got on with their meal. The other table was less amenable.

'These whitebait were old enough to have an annuity when they arrived here!' snapped a tall, thin woman who appeared to be the hostess. 'And as for the escargots! Really, if we'd wanted snails that tasted like that we could have stayed at home in the garden!' There was much more along the same lines.

Still placating, the waiter made small, soothing noises.

'If Madame would permit, I will just taste . . .' He picked up the plate of escargots, took them to an empty table and prised one of the molluscs from its shell. He now had both Eleri's and Schlegel's undivided attention. As he swallowed the snail, he gagged and hastily concealed his reaction, swallowing as if nothing were amiss. But he returned to the table empty-handed.

'You were right to complain, Madame,' he said, the smoothness of the tone giving the lie to his recent disgusted reaction. 'If I may suggest the *soupe à l'oignon*, I can vouch for its quality. There will be no charge.' Without a break in his calming chatter, he removed the offending whitebait too, and swept them away with the snails. Moments later, two *petits marmites* arrived, full of bubbling cheese and onion soup and looking delicious.

But it seemed the young man's troubles were only beginning. After a couple more misplaced or unsatisfactory orders, he disappeared into the kitchen and within moments, the sounds of muffled altercation erupted from the back quarters. While it progressed, Eleri had been looking closely at her surroundings. As the disagreement outside built into a crescendo, she whispered: 'This is the place, Karl – and that's the head waiter!'

She caught Schlegel unawares. 'Eleri – don't be so absurd! We don't even know it's for sale!'

'Don't suppose it is – yet – but at this rate it soon will be. That man is a real pro, and he's being wasted. I bet he'd jump at the chance of a job with a different employer, and he's just what we want.'

Karl beamed at her. 'What *we* want, or what *you* want, dear child? Are you sure you know the difference?'

The tabby cat in her was back, this time bunched up with indignation, fur all pointing in the wrong direction. 'What else would I be interested in except the business?'

'Oh, at your age and state of health, and at his, any number of things!' He made pacifying motions with his hands. 'I'm not making fun, Eleri, really. I think you may be right, even on a professional basis. But make sure you have the motives separate in your own mind, that's all. Otherwise, what you say makes a lot of sense. Perhaps we could . . .'

His further remarks were drowned by the explosion of disagreement out in the kitchen. The swing door exploded open and the dark-haired waiter erupted through it, tearing aside his apron as he came.

'Enough!' he roared at the manager, who almost dropped his clipboard in shock. 'I will not work any longer with that swine! It's a miracle half your customers are not dead!' All over the restaurant, cutlery hit plates as people lost interest in their meals.

'Emil — how dare you?' squeaked the manager. 'I'll see you never work again after this!'

'It would almost be worth it! At least I would no longer be associated with a pigsty!' With that he was gone through the front door, slamming it behind him.

'Karl — for Christ's sake don't let him get away!' said Eleri in a tone that approached desperation. Schlegel took off as though on wings, and managed to catch up with Emil fifty yards down the road.

'Young man — young man, please wait . . . Ah, thank you.' Schlegel drew abreast of the waiter, feeling as if he were about to suffer a heart attack. Between gasps, he began to explain Eleri's plans. The young man regarded him as if he were mad, but Schlegel was beyond caring.

Finally, his enthusiasm seemed to penetrate, and the Frenchman began to listen. He shook his head. 'Please, M'sieur, this has been a dreadful day . . . your plans sound interesting, but my head is whirling. If I give you my address, yes? And if you have a business card, just in case?'

Schlegel heaved a vast sigh of relief. He couldn't possibly have faced Eleri again with no firm contact arranged with this person. They exchanged the information, and the waiter strode off towards St John's Wood station without looking back. Schlegel sighed, shrugged and turned back towards the restaurant.

Chapter Twenty-eight

When he returned to the bistro there appeared to be a riot going on. Two parties who had arrived shortly after Schlegel and Eleri had already left. The group which the waiter had pacified with onion soup was in process of putting on their coats, and the cold hors d'oeuvre group was dithering about what they should do.

The people at the other tables had been well on the way to finishing their lunches and their reactions were more subdued, although Karl noticed no one had picked up spoon or fork to finish the partially consumed food on their plates. The manager was expostulating wildly about the waiter being a little crazy and having deliberately sabotaged the place. No one seemed inclined to believe him.

The tall, skinny woman was the most militant of the protestors. Cutting off the manager's feeble explanations with a chop of her hand that suggested the descent of a guillotine, she snapped: 'Don't be damned absurd, man! Emil was your one remaining asset. If you'd treated him better things wouldn't be in this mess now. He's the only reason we still bother to eat here, I assure you, and since his stay with you appears to be at an end, you won't be seeing us again. Please don't have the effrontery to proffer a bill. I have no intention of paying it!' With that she drew her fur-collared coat tightly about her scrawny form and swept out through the door, her three guests following with somewhat shame-faced expressions.

'She's a sour old cat, but she's right,' murmured Eleri, whose expression showed she was relishing every moment of the drama. 'Let's see how the others go.'

Belatedly, the manager was recovering his scattered wits and it seemed to be dawning on him that any customer who left unhappy now would never return and would most likely gossip to everyone in St John's Wood about what had happened. He approached the cold hors d'oeuvre customers with an air of great diffidence. 'Madam, Messieurs,' he said, 'I cannot apologise sufficiently for this unfortunate incident. If you prefer not to continue with your lunch, perhaps you would accept cognac or liqueurs with my compliments?'

After a murmured consultation, the quartet decided they would, and they accepted the bill which duly arrived for the food and wine they had consumed before the flare-up. But it required no genius to see that they were as unlikely to return as the thin woman's party.

The manager was so hard-pressed in dealing with the constant stream of departures that he had yet to approach Schlegel and Eleri. Eventually, in a brief lull between two sets of customers, Karl called him over and said: 'If you would care to fetch us a bottle of the '28 Meursault, we are quite happy to wait until you are ready for us. Otherwise . . .'

The manager was off like a hare, understanding instantly that 'otherwise' meant 'we go, too'. As they were set fair to being his sole remaining lunchtime trade, he had no wish to lose them. The Meursault arrived and Karl and Eleri sat back to enjoy it. 'Whatever else has suffered, their cellar seems as good as ever,' he said, twirling the rich, bone-dry golden fluid in his glass as he relished its flavour.

'When we get this place, I want the cellar as well,' said Eleri. 'It'll be worth the extra investment — take us years to get anywhere near as good as what's on this list.'

'I keep telling you, we don't even know whether the place would be available.'

She tossed her head. 'After that little display, I reckon the poor sod would practically pay *us* to take it off his hands. Talk about a bunch a blundering incompetents!'

'Does that include your dashing young waiter?'

'It most certainly does not. You only had to look at him to see every move was agony. The thought of having to work in fifth-rate conditions like these when you're a first-rate professional!'

'And I take it you were able to assess his professionalism at a glance.'

'Stop making fun, Karl. You saw as well as I did how he played down that trouble. If only he'd had a bit a backing, he could have stopped that fiasco, but no — they just left him to sink or swim.'

'Well, he appears to have swum — right out of the door.'

She gasped, realising that in the excitement she had forgotten to question Karl on the success of his pursuit. Schlegel grinned at her. 'Don't worry. All is under control.' He fished a piece of paper from his pocket, on which a name and address had been scrawled in spidery French handwriting. 'He has my card, and I have this. Even if we do not come to this restaurant, I think perhaps we can find a place for Monsieur Emil Simon.

'Emil Simon,' said Eleri dreamily. 'What a very nice name . . .'

In the end it was unnecessary for Schlegel to contact Emil Simon. The Frenchman telephoned that evening, apologised for his rudeness earlier in the day and asked whether Karl still wished to speak to him. Karl beamed at the telephone receiver. 'I most certainly do, Monsieur Simon, and I think perhaps we can be of great help to each other. I hope you have not dined yet?'

The Frenchman uttered a bark of laughter. 'After today's display, I am not sure whether I ever wish to eat again, Monsieur!'

'Then we must see about restoring your appetite. Please, if you are not busy, come round to my house and join us for a late dinner. Nothing very grand — we have been out all day and there was no time — but I'm sure you will enjoy it.'

Eleri had made up for the disappointments of lunch — they had settled for a plate of smoked ham and a plain green salad after seeing what else was on offer — by preparing a huge tureen of *moules marinières*, followed by tarragon chicken and straw potatoes. When Karl told her Emil Simon was coming to share it with them, she developed a full-scale attack of panic. 'If I'd known, I'd have done something grander. Karl, this is just a simple family supper! We can't expect a guest . . .'

He broke in: 'If you insist there are many families sitting down in England tonight to a meal like this for family supper, I will know you are deranged!' he told her. 'Stop being so childish. You know without needing me to tell you that a professional appreciates that the skill involved in preparing food like this is every bit as great as in truffled goose!'

She nodded, still on the edge of panic, and disappeared with a muttered excuse, to emerge from her room almost an hour later looking closer to elegance than Karl had ever seen her. She was certainly taking this man seriously . . . could his little Welsh cygnet be growing into a swan at last?

Whatever Eleri's true motives might have been for pursuing Emil Simon, it proved to be a shrewd business move. Between an intermittent flow of extravagant compliments about Eleri's cooking, Simon embarked on a detailed account of the decline of Bistro Victorine. The restaurant was named after the original *patronne*, Victorine Listel. At the beginning, her husband Jean-Claude cooked and Madame presided over the front-of-house.

She had recruited Simon because he was an expert in choosing and storing the better middle-range French wines, and the restaurant's cellar was its weak point. Over five years, the young sommelier had built up an excellent selection of *grandes marques* and little-known treasures from the French vineyards. Victorine's already had a sound reputation for its cuisine. Now its fame spread as customers got to know of the delightful wine list.

'The trouble was that Victorine was a — how do you say it? — one-man band. Oh, Jean-Claude could cook like a dream, but he was a depressive type, always brooding on his own, and unless she was right behind him to keep him going, everything was neglected. They had a son, a few years older than me, but as you often see with the child of a successful parent, he was good at nothing and cared about nothing except to get enough money for horse-races.

'Then Victorine died suddenly. She had just burned herself out, doing everybody else's jobs as well as her own. She had an apoplectic seizure one afternoon just after we had closed, and died with her face in a plate of food.' He made a wry face. 'Appropriate, no?

'After that it was only a matter of months before Jean-Claude went. Funny, you always expect a man like that to be a drunk, but he was not. He never touched alcohol. Perhaps he would have made a more jolly life if he had. He threw himself underneath an underground train. End of story. End of Victorine's. Or at least, it should have been.'

'They did not close down?' Schlegel raised his eyebrows. 'With chef and *patronne* gone, one would imagine there was nothing for which to stay open. Best to close and move elsewhere for a fresh start.'

'Precisely what I said, Monsieur, but Guy, the son, would not listen — he was the manager you saw today, by the way. To close and start again, he would have needed to put all his effort into it and he still liked the horses too much. I kept saying I would supervise the change, but I think he was suspicious of me. Seemed to think I would cheat him if he gave me my head. In the end, I was the only one *not* cheating the stupid man.'

'He seems to have gone on trusting you with the cellar,' said Karl. 'That wine list was every bit as good as I remember, and the Meursault we drank tasted heavenly.'

Simon laughed. 'He would have run that down in time. He did not mind the inexpensive section which makes the bulk of the cellar — that gave him some of his best profits. But the Burgundies and clarets — ah, Monsieur, it made me want to weep. At first it was just that he would not replenish exhausted stock. But then I would find he had sold the odd case of vintage Bordeaux to pay a racecourse debt. You exhaust a cellar very quickly when you play that game.'

Eleri broke in: 'But it wasn't the wine that was causing all the fuss today — it was the standard of the food. I saw your face when you tried that escargot.'

Simon let out a groan of disgust. 'Do not remind me! He got a first-rate chef after his father died, and for a while I thought everything would be all right. But they quarrelled. Guy said the man was using too many of the best ingredients and the bills were too high. The chef walked out and before I knew anything about it, he had taken on that — that criminal! The real sin is that the man can cook, but he is a cheat and a liar. Guy gives him too little money to buy properly, then Michel takes his secret cut, and he has to buy all the rejected provisions at the market in order to get by. Sometimes it is all right — you must know, Mademoiselle, how easy it is to make an onion soup or some oxtails taste acceptable. But snails? Fresh fish? Veal? More and more people complained, more and more stayed away. Profits were next to nothing. Today was worse than it has ever been, but I have no doubt the end will come very soon, now. He cannot hold out much longer.'

Eleri was tentative. 'What are you planning to do?'

He shrugged. 'I have no plans yet. I gave so much of myself to Victorine's — I was just twenty-two when I came there and I am thirty now — that I do not know where to start again, especially after wasting three years there since Victorine died.' He glanced up at Karl, his eyes questioning. 'When you invited me here, Monsieur, you suggested there might be something . . .'

'Indeed, Monsieur Simon. Eleri and I have a small scheme, and we think perhaps you could be just the man to help us get started.'

Eleri's heart vaulted. Karl, I love you! she thought. Thank you, God — I'll never ask for any more favours.

Schlegel was already launching into their restaurant idea, and Simon listened with growing enthusiasm. Finally, Karl said: 'I asked you to join us tonight because I wanted to hear your views about Victorine's as a place to start up. I was only toying with the idea that you might join us. But having listened to you, I think we would like you to do so whether we take Bistro Victorine or not. Are you interested?'

'That, Monsieur, is the understatement of the evening!'

It was well past midnight when Emil Simon left Gower Street. He had given the partners a complete breakdown of the facilities at Victorine's. Karl and Eleri now had a good idea of what they would need to change, of what might survive with a little refurbishment, of the advantages and drawbacks of the St John's Wood area. It all fitted almost too well with what they had in mind. The restaurant provided for fifty covers, had a large, dry cellar and extensive kitchens. There was little local competition − a major reason, Simon believed, why Victorine's had survived so long even under Guy's slapdash mismanagement.

A week after their first visit to the bistro, Karl and Eleri returned there. This time they were the only customers, and Guy looked as if he were on the edge of mental collapse. Judging by the drastically limited menu, he had lost even the dishonest chef about whom Emil had complained so bitterly. None of the dishes listed was beyond the capacity of the average short-order cook: indeed, they tasted as if they had been prepared by one.

Karl and Eleri battled their way through watery soup, stringy steak and a commercial-tasting ice cream, the whole redeemed only by the first-rate bottle of Beaune upon which Schlegel insisted. 'I refuse to permit my stomach to be utterly outraged,' he whispered to Eleri.

When they had forced down the last of the food, Karl called the *patron* over. 'Would you care to sit down and join us in a cognac?' he asked.

Looking amazed, Guy accepted. 'He probably expected the usual brickbats,' murmured Karl as the man went to get the brandy bottle.

They wasted no time. Neither of them wished to while away the afternoon with a man who had run down such a promising business. Both of them wanted to get started at reviving it.

'To judge by your restricted menu today, you have chef trouble,' Karl prompted gently.

'Oh, such as you would scarcely believe, Monsieur!' said the Frenchman. 'No one is reliable these days. No one cares about producing good value for money. It leaves one close to despair. I wonder why I carry on.'

'Then why *do* you?'

Guy peered at him. 'Because one has to live! Besides, my dear parents started this place, and since they have both passed on, I feel I owe it to them to continue in their tradition.'

Schlegel let his gaze linger around the empty tables, taking in the drifts of dust on window sills and the stained checked cloths on the tables. 'It seems to offer a very thin living, if you do not mind my saying so. Do you think your parents would have wanted you to carry on in such circumstances?'

Guy shrugged. 'If there were some alternative, I think I would go tomorrow. But this is not a booming market, Monsieur. I have all my capital tied up in this place. How else could I live?'

'I hear there is more money in the retailing side of food, these days,' said Karl ingenuously. 'And you would certainly have to work shorter hours. Why not sell up and invest in a good delicatessen?'

Eleri almost choked on her coffee. I'd sooner take rat poison than buy a croissant or a pound of salami off that one! she thought.

But Karl knew what he was about. Gently, patiently, he painted a picture of a small, exotic shop, bringing just the right hint of continental exoticism to a pretty side street in Hampstead or Highgate. Guy was clearly taken with the idea. But then he sighed and slapped the table-top with a none-too-clean hand. 'Why do I listen?' he said. 'Of course it would be a good idea but it is a dream, nothing more. I will never sell this place.'

'I might be interested at the right price,' said Karl. 'My niece here is looking for a place of about this size to start her married life.' He flashed Eleri a look which dared her to dispute what he said. 'I cannot afford a fortune, but I might be able to pay you a little over the going rate if you included the contents of your wine cellar − she still has to learn about wine, and it would give her a good start.'

The *patron*'s eyes gleamed with new-found hope. There was an unmistakable greedy tone in his voice as he said: 'It is an excellent cellar, Monsieur. That would raise the price considerably.'

Karl did not bat an eyelid. 'On a very run-down restaurant, which you have said yourself offers no decent prospect of a sale. Come now, don't over-reach yourself. You know as well as I that it is a buyer's market.'

That afternoon, Eleri encountered a Karl Schlegel she had never met before. He was as polite and genial as ever, but dealt with the restaurateur with a relentless persistence which reminded her that he came from successful merchant stock. Finally, they left the restaurant as dusk was falling, with a commitment from Listel to sell them the restaurant.

The moment they turned the corner and were out of sight of Bistro Victorine, Eleri seized Schlegel by the shoulders and capered in front of him as though dancing to the accompaniment of an invisible street organ. 'Oh, you clever, clever man!' she cried. 'We've got it − we've-got-it-we've-got-it-we've-got-it!'

Karl gave her a small, severe shake. 'Eleri − stop it. Stop it at once! You never know if the man has acquaintances who will tell him . . . and all is far from settled. I wish to go through that cellar and make a complete inventory, with Emil's expert valuation behind it, before we proceed any further.'

Her face fell. 'Then you might not meet his price after all?'

'Oh, I don't think you need worry too much on that score. The man is in deep water. He needs a sale. But I do not like or trust him and I know he will try to cheat us. I have arranged to go along and inspect the cellar tomorrow afternoon. I plan to make a full list of all stock, then to get a realistic up-to-date price on it from Emil. After that, an unbreakable legal agreement will be necessary. I do not know if you are fully aware of it, but there is far more value in the cellar than the entire premises, including fixtures and fittings. I have no intention of letting Listel walk off with it.'

Over the following week, Eleri suffered agonies as Schlegel and Simon worked out what was in the cellar and valued it at current prices. By the time they had finished, Simon was furious. 'It is as I thought. He is trying to overcharge you by around fifteen to twenty per cent,' he said. 'If I were you, Karl, I would drop the swine. We can find other premises and build a new cellar from scratch.'

Schlegel shook his head. 'No, I think Eleri has set her heart on Victorine's, and apart from any sentimental attachment she may have developed for the place, I trust her business intuition. I think she can make that place one of London's best restaurants.'

Simon looked at him narrowly. 'Sentimental attachment? I thought the other day was the first time she had been there.'

Schlegel said nothing, merely smiling and nodding. 'Then this — this attachment. What caused it?'

'You cannot guess, my friend? I thought you would only need to look at her to see that.'

Simon blushed deeply. 'But what can such a delightful girl see in me? She is . . . she is—'

'. . . Eleri,' Karl finished for him. 'There is no other way to describe her, for there is no one like her. You are a lucky young man, if you return her warmth.'

A huge, contented smile spread slowly across Emil's face. 'As you say, Karl, I am a lucky man — a very lucky man.'

The Schlegel-Jones-Simon partnership finally overcame Guy Listel's last attempts at rearguard fraud three months later. It was another three months before The Pleasure Dome opened on the site of Victorine's. Only the wine cellar bore any resemblance to the former restaurant.

The following Christmas, Eleri Jones married Emil Simon. Their first son was born in January 1939 and they called him Karl.

Chapter Twenty-nine

By the end of 1938, the training centre was doing so well that it was worthwhile opening a branch in central London. Best of British had become a minor sensation in New York, to the extent where expatriates moving to France and Italy contacted the London office to staff their European properties rather than engaging local help in the areas where they planned to settle. The fees for training courses, which had started as a trickle, became a steady stream as the better sort of servant realised there was a comparative fortune to be made working for Americans.

Margaret Armstrong had gradually grown into the role of successful businesswoman and found she thoroughly enjoyed it. Jessica Parker, now Jessica Eames since she married in 1937, was still her right-hand woman on the recruitment side. Kate Higgins regularly threatened to retire on the grounds that her rheumatism was getting worse, but showed no sign of really wanting to give up her job running the training operation. Margaret herself felt fulfilled and self-confident. She had just one regret: there was no one in her life she could care for and who would care for her more than anyone else.

Sometimes she envied Rose who never seemed even faintly troubled by her lack of attachment to a special man. Margaret had often wondered about Alexander Moncreiff, but nothing appeared to have come of that. Their relationship seemed to stop at business and, perhaps, a tenuous friendship. She sighed. Why was everyone else so good at running their lives and here was she, successful and prosperous, moaning to herself because everything was not quite perfect?

One evening she had stayed on at the office to sort out

some figures. Their services were so much in demand on the Continent that it was beginning to look as if Best of British was starving its American outlet of recruits. As that was still the primary function of the London office, it was up to Margaret to correct the balance.

For a while she was aware of nothing except the columns of figures, the record of placements in the past six months and the forecast of requirements and availability for the coming half-year. Then she realised there was someone in the outer office. She experienced a moment's apprehension. Why on earth had she failed to slip down the catch on the outer door? This part of central London was so quiet after normal business hours that it had never occurred to her. Now here she was with what appeared to be an intruder in the outer office and no way of getting out except to pass through the open arch which connected it to the hallway.

Well, she thought, there's no point in loitering in here with my heart in my mouth. Better get it over with now. She took down her jacket from the hanger in the corner, shrugged it on and reached for her bag. Whoever it was couldn't do *that* much to her. If she screamed, someone passing along towards Marylebone High Street would be bound to hear and come to her assistance.

She opened the door and strode out into the hall with a decisiveness she was far from feeling. What she saw made her weak with relief. It also made her want to shake herself for being so childish about a few noises in the early evening.

There was a man in the waiting room, all right, but he was so eminently respectable no one would ever have taken him for a nosey neighbour, let alone a prowler or burglar. He was wearing a well-cut sports jacket, had neatly cropped sandy-brown hair, and was standing in the middle of the waiting area, thumbing through a magazine. He must have come to register for a job and not realised how late it is, thought Margaret, then irritation overtook her. What a stupid thing for him to do! He must have realised it was too late for normal business. Surely he was capable of ringing the service bell to announce his presence?

Her crossness was directed as much at herself as at the man. She should have been less timid, should have realised sooner that someone was outside . . . the fact that she had not made her react against him in compensation.

'Really, Mr − er—' she began, before realising one could not give someone a piece of one's mind without knowing their name.

He looked up, bright-eyed and enthusiastic. 'Oh, hello! Rowan. Marcus Rowan,' he said.

'Well, Mr Rowan, you do realise how late it is? We try to be as helpful as possible to everyone who calls, but we *do* observe normal business hours. The door was only open because I needed to work late. If you carry on like this, I think you're most unlikely to satisfy any of our American clients.'

He began to respond: 'Actually, I came to . . .' She silenced him with a raised hand and a forbidding look. 'At this time of the evening, I'm afraid I'm indifferent to your reasons for coming here. If you really feel you have something to offer our clients, perhaps you'd care to return tomorrow between nine-thirty in the morning and five-thirty in the afternoon. And now, if you don't mind, I wish to lock up.'

To her consternation, he burst out laughing. 'What I was about to say was that I hadn't come to ask for a job, I'd come to offer one − several, in fact − and it's not Mr Rowan, it's Sir Marcus.'

'Oh . . . oh dear!' Margaret had almost managed to convince herself in recent years that she treated peasant and lord identically, but in her heart she knew it was untrue. She nursed a shamefaced reverence for the aristocracy that only former domestics would understand, and now in her own view she had delivered the ultimate insult − she had mistaken one of them for a servant, and an unemployed servant at that. Her tendency to blush, always her hidden enemy, swept over her now and she felt the rush of hot blood to her face. Damn, damn, damn! she thought. Why should it be like this? He really *isn't* any more important than a butler or valet!

He was still chuckling, but sympathetically rather than mockingly. Finally he said: 'I think introductions are in order. I'm Sir Marcus Rowan, of Chilworth in Gloucestershire. And you?'

Still blushing furiously, she almost whispered: 'Margaret Armstrong. I'm the London principal of Best of British – though you might not have thought so from my performance just now.'

'Nonsense, nonsense – I was most inconsiderate to blunder in here unannounced like that. Truth is, my train was delayed and I didn't think I'd catch anyone at all.'

'But why did you want to, since you live in Gloucestershire? We hardly do anything that would interest you.'

'Ah, well, you see, that's where you're wrong, I hope. I've been in Canada, farming, for a few years. My uncle was the eighth baronet and he was running Chilworth. Old boy dropped dead about three months ago and it took them a while to get hold of me with the news. When I got back here, the stately acres were in a fearful state. He'd let the estate more or less crumble around him. I tidied up matters in Canada and came back – never intended to stay over there once the old boy was gone – and found everything in a terminal mess. He'd either failed to replace his indoor staff as some left over the years, or let others grow so old in service that they were past anything but a bit of light dusting by the time I got home. I decided the only solution was to pension off the handful who were left and re-staff from scratch. Didn't know how to go about it, though, and I certainly didn't want to try training local youngsters up. You have to have an established staff ready to train 'em, don't you, if you do that?'

Margaret nodded, still somewhat bewildered, and said: 'But Sir Marcus, you must know we don't supply the British market at all. Our staff all go to America or to American employers on the Continent.'

'Yes, yes – I realise that all right. But I heard such damned good reports of your people one week when I went down to New York to stay with friends. Thought it was worth a try — you know, as I have need of more than one person. Pity you can't do anything for me. I'd need four or five people and I'd be fully prepared to apply American pay rates and working conditions.'

'Oh — perhaps I was a little hasty. If you care to discuss precisely what you need, I'll see if we can help you after all. Wait a moment. I'll just go and re-open my office . . .'

'I have a far better idea. Why don't we discuss it over a drink. Far less formal than this "Miss Armstrong — Sir Marcus" nonsense, what?'

To her own surprise, Margaret heard herself saying, 'Very well, I'd like that. There's a comfortable pub along the high street if that will do.'

'Lead on, fair lady.'

In the month that followed, Margaret found herself being swept away as easily as she had been by Bruno Clifton. Scarcely a night passed without her confronting her reflection in bathroom or bedroom mirror and ticking it off like an outraged schoolmarm: you're almost twenty-eight years old. You haven't the excuse of youth and innocence any more . . . rich men with titles don't have honourable intentions towards girls like you . . . you never wanted a hole-in-the-corner relationship. Why start now when it caused you such grief before? And so on.

The fact remained that she was thoroughly besotted by Marcus Rowan. He certainly seemed interested in her. Drinks moved on to dinner on their first evening, and he found it necessary to call at the office three times in the next week to enquire about progress. He always insisted his arrival at lunchtime was a coincidence, but added that since he was there, it would be good to eat in company. By the time Margaret had lunched with him on three successive days, Jessica was flashing significant looks at Mrs Higgins, who was spending a lot of time in the Marylebone office while arranging details on the London centre.

The recruitment exercise for Rowan dragged on for a surprisingly long time. He settled for a manservant, a cook-housekeeper and a parlour-maid at first. Then he began wondering about a chauffeur. After that it was a matter of taking advice on the selection of more junior household servants in Gloucestershire.

'Good God, Mags, he's staffing up like an Edwardian nabob — he must be smitten!' said Kate when they went out for lunch together between two of Rowan's supposedly chance visits.

As usual, Margaret blushed bright scarlet. 'He just wants to be sure the estate is properly looked after, that's all.'

'Is it? I could have sworn I'd seen the look he has in his eye before somewhere and it wasn't on any man whose main concern was finding a gaggle of expensive servants.'

'Kate, what are you suggesting?'

'Could it be that our ice maiden has met her match?'

Margaret shook her head. 'Don't be silly! I'm well and truly on the shelf. Sir Marcus will get himself fixed up and then he'll run into some pretty twenty-year-old from a good county family. I'm just a professional adviser.'

Kate snorted her disbelief. 'Yes, I've often noticed professional advisers getting big bunches of carnations from their male customers. Do me a favour, Margaret!'

'All right, I admit I'm keen on him. But I might as well forget about it. I never told you, Kate, but I was . . . involved . . . with Bruno Clifton for ages, and he dropped me. It almost killed me and it was the reason I left the Cliftons. I suppose I really have a lot to thank him for now. I'd never have done any of this with B of B without that to push me. But I couldn't stand it again. It tore me apart. They never really care for our sort — only go after what they can get.'

To her amazement, Kate Higgins took the confession in her stride as if it were an everyday matter. 'That rotten bugger would spoil anyone,' she said. 'I didn't know about you and him, love — you're good at hiding that sorta thing — but he had a name before he was tied up with you, and he's certainly had one since.'

'What d'you mean?'

'Oh, this pretty little feather-brain he married. She was a nice enough kid, and she had all he was supposed to want. But within three months of you leaving Fenton, I heard gossip in London that he was playing the field again. Some men never know when to stop!'

'Well, quite. Are you surprised I'm trying to keep this business with Marcus Rowan impersonal?'

'Yes — 'course I am! One rotten apple doesn't mean the whole barrel is off. To be crude, Bruno Clifton's brains were in his balls. He never thought of anything else for more than five minutes at a stretch. Even had some sorta lovenest flat in St James's, that he shared with his layabout mates. Your Sir Marcus is cut from different cloth.'

'He's not "my" Sir Marcus, Kate.'

'If you believe that, you're too daft to live! He's barmy about you and unless you start doing something about it, he'll think you aren't interested and bugger off. How would you like that?'

'You're developing a very vulgar turn of phrase in your old age.'

'Always had it. Just had to watch me Ps and Qs with the Cliftons and it was easier to cut it out altogether. Nice to be able to say what you think, though . . . like loosening your stays at the end of a long, tiring day. Anyway, young Mags, stop changing the subject and pay a mind to what I say. That chap needs a bit a cosseting, or he'll be off. Then you'll *really* feel sorry for yourself.'

Margaret had plenty of time to contemplate what Kate Higgins had said over the following two weeks. Rowan met her as arranged the day after her lunch with Mrs Higgins, but then he went off to Gloucestershire and she heard nothing from him. The servants they had found for him were already installed at his country house, so apart from sending him the agency's account, she had no professional reason to contact him again. After a week of silence, Margaret began to panic.

Determined not to wear her heart on her sleeve, she went through the motions of a busy social and professional life, but the truth of it was that there was precious little sociability in her days apart from Marcus. She had been upended into business success so quickly that there had been no opportunity to make any social contacts apart from the scattering she hung on to from her domestic days, like Kate. In many respects she was like a young widow or divorcee who had married straight from school and then had been abruptly flung on her own inadequate resources before she had sufficient opportunity to grow up. Now she behaved in a manner very similar to that of the schoolgirl – she began dwelling on her romantic problems, real or imaginary, and, obligingly, they instantly achieved melodramatic proportions.

At heart, though, Margaret was a sensible girl and after a day or two of brooding, she decided she must stop being spineless. The following morning she put on her smartest suit and when she arrived at the office instructed Jessica to reserve a table for one at the Savoy Grill. When your courage is failing, that's the time to do something you thought you could never pull off, she told herself. She left Baker Street by taxi at 12.45, remaining enigmatic with Jessica about the nature of her luncheon engagement. At least I'm the only one who will ever know it's just me, myself and I! she reflected ruefully.

At first she enjoyed herself more than it had ever occurred to her she would. The Savoy did not exist to humiliate but to cosset its guests. Margaret was treated as little less than a VIP, and the early stages of luncheon were accomplished in a whirl of cocktails, tiny, delicious bite-size hors d'oeuvres and a general air of being pampered. She was sipping the last of the smokey white wine the waiter had recommended to accompany the prosciutto and peach which comprised her first course, when she glanced up and almost choked at what she saw. On the far side of the room, out of direct line of vision thanks to a decorative column, Marcus Rowan was helping an unspeakably glamorous woman to a seat.

Margaret's first impulse was to get up and run. So this was what he was doing when he didn't see her! So much for all those rosy daydreams . . . so much for all Kate Higgins's encouragement. Once a silly housemaid, always a silly housemaid! Anyone would think she'd never had the chance to learn better. Margaret began fumbling for her bag. Pay. Get out. Get away. Anywhere but here. Another minute and she'd choke. But a chilly little voice inside slowed her down. Do stop being so childish, it said. Since when has there been a law against men seeing pretty women? What does he owe you? For heaven's sake learn how to conduct yourself with confidence in public. You're not a child any longer.

No, she wasn't. She was an adult, who had just encountered disappointment, certainly, but had not witnessed the end of the world. Now was the time to learn to control her feelings, not after weeping for four hours alone that night. Margaret sat it out, though the delicious food had turned to ashes in her mouth.

Nevertheless, she *did* weep that night, though not for four hours. She was already deeply involved with Marcus Rowan and would have liked it to go deeper still. Now it appeared that door was closed. She dragged into the office next day, hoping against hope there might be a message, but there was nothing.

She suffered increasingly throughout the following week. Why, oh why, had she taken it for granted that his unmarried status meant he planned to remain a bachelor? What could be more logical on his taking up his inheritance than for him to staff up the estate before arranging the wedding? That was obviously his intended bride — she was so beautiful . . . what had made Margaret imagine she could ever compete in such stakes? Finally, when the following Thursday arrived without further word from him, she took matters into her own hands and telephoned him. Better to be put out of her misery formally than go on like this.

'Ah, just the lady I wanted to talk to!' he said. 'You'll have a large account for me, I think. Rather than post it, perhaps you'd be free to deliver it in person and stay over from Friday to Monday? I thought I'd invite a few people over . . . you know, give the new staff their baptism of fire and all that . . . There's a good train getting in at Cirencester just after five-thirty on Friday. How about that? All right? Look forward to seeing you.'

And that was that. Why am I in such a state? she asked herself. He was so bright and breezy he's obviously just organising a casual house party and he's included me as an afterthought. I'm probably a bit of a curiosity — the only independent business woman he knows . . . Her mind went on working in circles for the following twenty-four hours.

At Cirencester station the next afternoon, she craned her neck to see him. Where could he be? She had missed him terribly in the couple of weeks since they last met . . . her shoulders slumped with the disappointment of seeing Jenkins, the chauffeur she had found for Rowan, instead of her host himself.

'Sir Marcus's compliments, Miss Armstrong, and he said please forgive him for not coming himself. He's making a few last-minute preparations for the weekend.'

Of course, he would be, she thought, disconsolate that she probably would not get him to herself throughout the three days. All those guests everywhere, possibly one of them about to become the special woman in his life . . . She sat in the back of the luxurious car, watching the wintry Cotswold landscape without pleasure.

It was completely dark when they arrived at Chilworth. Lamplight glowed in the uncurtained window of the lodge cottage, and as the gate-keeper shut the seventeenth-century wrought-iron gates behind them, her heart gave a skip of anticipation. Even if I see him at a distance, she thought, at least I'll *see* him. It's been such an age . . . oh, Marcus, why didn't I let you know I was interested before it was too late?

Clearly someone at the manor was listening for the crunch of car tyres on gravel, because the oak-panelled front door was thrown open as the car stopped outside. Bobbing and smiling, the new housekeeper showed Margaret into the hall. It was a dream of a house, one which made Fenton look like an upstart. The hall was covered in Jacobean linenfold panelling from wainscot to ceiling — although the Rowan title went back a mere two centuries, they had been Gloucestershire gentry since the 1400s — and solid, age-blackened doors gave promise of immaculately maintained rooms beyond them. If this was what Sir Marcus had meant when he said his uncle had run the place down, his own standards must be ridiculously high, thought Margaret.

Mrs Walker led her across to one of the doors, knocked discreetly and opened it in response to some command unheard by Margaret. As she stepped forward, the intoxicating scent of winter greenery swept over her. The room was decorated with branches of evergreen and great swatches of chrysanthemum. Marcus Rowan leaped to his feet and almost bounded across to her, taking both her hands in his.

The housekeeper seemed to have disappeared without trace. Marcus led her to the fireside, still gripping her hands. 'I don't understand,' she said, 'where are all the other guests?'

'I'm afraid I was dissembling. Faint heart never won fair lady and all that.'

'Whatever do you mean?'

'Well, dammit all, I seemed not to be getting anywhere with you in London, and in the end I thought I may as well pack it in. If I'd gone on I'd have had more servants at Chilworth than there were people living in the village. So I threw in the towel and came back down here to sulk. Trouble was, I still couldn't get you out of my mind, so when you rang I invented a house party. I'm afraid you're it, Margaret. I've been chivvying the staff to turn the place into love's young dream ever since your call.'

He stood back and regarded her hopefully. 'Do say you're not cross. If it's the wrong thing to do, I'll drive you back into Cirencester, we'll dine together and I'll get Jenkins to drive you back to London at the end of the evening.'

Suddenly Margaret found it hard to breathe. 'And if I'm *not* cross?'

'Well, I thought you might stay, and I really do have some people coming over to dinner tomorrow evening. Thought we might make it the occasion to announce our engagement.'

It isn't really happening, she thought, it can't be . . . no one does anything this romantic any more . . . She closed her eyes for long seconds, and when she opened them again, the logs still crackled in the fireplace and the flowers and foliage still emitted their intoxicating smell. Marcus Rowan was regarding her as if she were the most precious object in the world. She closed her eyes again and swayed towards him. His arms closed around her and he kissed her, deep, confident and loving. 'I hope that means yes,' he eventually murmured.

'With all my heart and a bit more,' said Margaret, and reached out to embrace him again. This time, stepping back from him, she stumbled slightly against a low polished table, and gasped sharply as she glanced down at it. It bore a portrait photograph of her unknown rival from the Savoy. 'Wh—who's that?' she asked faintly, her finger quivering as she pointed at the hated image.

'Oh, you'll meet her for yourself shortly! That's my bossy big sister. You'll love her — everyone else does — and I met her in town last week to tell her of my evil intentions for you. She's thrilled. Hope you don't mind a ready-made family . . .'

'I can't think of anything I'd like better,' Margaret murmured almost inaudibly.

Chapter Thirty
London, 1945

Really, the lengths some people feel they have to go to for a bit of pleasure! thought Jane, as she stood looking around the latest addition to The Eros Club. It was the brainchild of one of her regulars, who had promised he would bring along at least two large parties a month if she installed it. The room was something straight out of a schoolboy fantasy of Gay Nineties Paris, with draped pink satin ceiling, heavy gilded chandeliers, lush deep-pile carpets and groups of chaises longues piled with oriental cushions, disposed about low tables designed for banqueting. There was a small stage for the live sex show they always seemed to want when they came in groups, and even a pocket-handkerchief-sized dance floor. Jane's club had long ago acquired a reputation for its dance partners who performed stark naked.

'There's gonna be more complaints of indigestion than I ever heard in my life after that lot have had a few evenings eating lying on their sides and then humping the girls,' she murmured gloomily. 'Why can't they just do it in bed like sensible people?'

Still, there was money to be made from it — lots of money. Dave Summers had made a fortune in scrap metal during the war and now it was over he looked set to make another in black market goods. There were plenty like him and more of them were finding their way to Jane's than ever before. Nothing like a good war for boosting the entertainment industry, she thought.

Sometimes Jane felt she should pinch herself to make sure she was really living her life and not dreaming it. Even fifteen years on, she often slid into unwelcome reminiscences of her days as a maid, and the remaining shreds of the conventional girl she had once been rose up to persuade her the rest was mere illusion. In fact, it was hard to imagine a life further removed from her existence as an employee of the Cliftons.

The one thing missing from her life in recent years had been Gavin Lange, and even now she frequently felt his absence as a great gnawing ache which nothing could soothe. Without question, Gavin had been the making of her. Their partnership had blossomed into profound friendship within months of their setting up home together. Each trusted the other more than anyone else they had ever met. Furthermore, their relationship had proved as profitable on a business level as it had emotionally. Gavin's homosexuality even removed the one potential area of friction — after James Teal, Jane had decided it would be a long time before she wanted sexual involvement with another man.

In time her sensuality had begun to re-awaken, and she had embarked on the occasional love affair. But the nature of her occupation prevented her from taking sex seriously, and inevitably the flirtations did not develop beyond a few weeks of passion which quickly cooled. At the end of each short affair, Jane turned gratefully back to Gavin, with his unfailing good sense, his comforting presence and unquestioning loyalty. She treated him in much the same way listening to his confidences about this or that lover; commiserating over a betrayal; protecting him from discarded boyfriends.

Their business partnership had worked even better than Gerry Hamilton had prophesied. After they had extracted Jane from her involvement with James Teal, she settled down in Gavin's flat and went to work again. Both of them were pleasantly surprised to discover within a couple of months that there was no need any longer for her to patrol the streets around Piccadilly. Once her presence was noticed around his club, there was a steady stream of interested enquiries about her from male customers.

Part of the explanation lay in the picture she and Lange

presented together. They were so good-looking, and set each other off to such visible advantage, that men who might not have glanced at Jane in the street found themselves scarcely able to take their eyes off her. By their first Christmas together, Jane was conducting all her business from the club and the flat. It made life infinitely easier, by protecting her from the unwelcome attention of pimps who would inevitably have approached her had she remained on the streets, and, even more importantly, from James Teal.

He did not return to the club after the first altercation with Lange, partly out of care for what remained of his reputation, but largely because his ego found it impossible to confront the reality that he had been defeated by a mere nightclub entertainer. Jane arrived there with Lange each evening, and left with him when it closed, unless she had already gone back to their flat escorted by that evening's last customer.

She herself was surprised by the ease with which she took to such a disreputable job. During her brief spell in Soho, she had never quite overcome her distaste for selling sex. She never understood why, but Teal appeared to have cured her of all that. If that was the way some men carried on even with women they professed to love, she reflected, there was nothing particularly honourable about it. Far better to run the whole thing on a businesslike basis, remain detached and make a good living from it than to be abused and robbed into the bargain. It did not suit her to consider that Teal was a dangerous lunatic and could hardly be regarded as typical of the male population.

Jane quickly became accustomed to earning more money in a week as a prostitute than she had in a year as a maid. She found it far less repellent to take off her clothes and have sex with a man than she had to kneel on a doorstep with a scrubbing brush and a bucket of greasy water, and if her profession occasionally did depress her, she was invariably able to cheer herself with the purchase of an expensive new hat or bottle of scent.

And above all there was Gavin. They both made a point

of leaving Sundays free, and stayed in bed late before going off somewhere expensive for lunch. Within a few months, Jane had bought herself a small, open car, and on Sunday afternoons they would drive to Brighton or somewhere picturesque along the Thames Valley. In the evening they would gossip companionably, covering everything from their personal secrets to dreams for the future. Their first year brought them closer than any married couple and most lovers. After three years they were more intimate than ever, and between them were also earning a great deal of money. That was when they went into a much bigger partnership than either had previously envisaged.

Gavin had gone on to a party after seeing Jane back to the flat one night. When he came in next morning, she was sitting at her dressing table, peering with dissatisfaction at her reflection in the triple mirror as she brushed her thick red-gold hair. Lange peeped around the door, waved and said: 'Good morning, princess! How is . . . ah! By the look on your face I need hardly ask. Don't tell me you're cross because you only got one trick last night!'

'Stop being bloody clever. It's too early and I'm depressed.'

'Now what have you got to be depressed about on such a beautiful morning?'

'Beautiful morning, nothing! That's what's depressing me. Gavin, that sun is showing up every line on my face!'

He roared with laughter. 'You're joking! You're barely twenty-three years old.'

'It's not your age — it's the way you make your living. All those men are beginning to show in my face, Gavin.'

Abruptly, he stopped laughing and moved further into the room, stopping behind her and examining her face intently in the mirror. Eventually, he said, 'Hmm, I believe I understand what you mean — but that's nothing to do with ageing.'

'Is that supposed to make me feel better?'

'Of course it doesn't — I know that. But it *does* mean

you can do something about it. You can't do anything much about ageing.'

'Come on then, clever-clogs, what's the answer?'

'Time to move into management, old girl. Your days on the production line are over.'

'Do talk sense. I don't understand a word you're saying.'

'Why not? It's simple enough. I've been playing with the idea for some time. This was bound to happen sooner or later, and I was hoping it would come up before you began looking worn. Well it has. You still look perfect.'

'So what's the big idea?'

'You and I are going into a new line, that's what, with a little venture that combines the most enjoyable sins imaginable – good food, excellent booze, beautiful girls and a little discreet gambling. We can't fail.'

'Oh yes we can! That sort a thing eats money.'

'In that case, perhaps you'd care to tell me how Ma Meyrick made so much out of it. One week a doctor's impoverished widow on the South Coast, the next a nightclub proprietress – and within a couple of years all her daughters married off to peers of the realm.'

'Yeah, and if I recall correctly, a couple of jail sentences in between and dead in her early fifties.'

'We all have to go some time, darling.'

She glared at him for a few seconds, attempting to be cross, then surrendered with a half-despairing laugh. 'All right – convince me we can pay for it and if you do that, we'll give it a try.'

Given the right product, Gavin was a born salesman. Now he went about his new project with missionary zeal, approaching two compulsive gamblers he knew with a suggestion that they might like to back a very slightly illegal casino; planting the thought in the mind of a few wealthy, drunken insomniacs that it would be very convenient to have a secret anything-goes watering hole in the heart of Mayfair; mentioning to the more notorious womanisers of his acquaintance that shortly there might be a private establishment where all the girls would be as glamorous as

Jane Ellis. In next to no time he had an impressive list of backers willing to add their contributions to his and Jane's savings.

After that they went property-hunting, and found the sort of place they wanted available on an absurdly slack lease in a Mayfair side street. The peer who owned the freehold had retired to his country seat in a state of terminal financial embarrassment and was willing to take more or less the first offer he received on the property.

They went into business after minimal alterations, promising themselves they would renovate as they began making a profit. The money was not long in coming.

Over the next three years they converted a decaying mansion from little more than a glorified brothel with a bar and a card room attached to a ground-floor casino, bar and restaurant, above which were fifteen of the most opulent suites in London, many equipped for the playing out of fantasies – from the Arabian Nights to a most ungodly convent.

The one theme with which Jane would have no truck was violence. The memory of James Teal would never fade and she had no intention of creating conditions in which other men might treat girls in a similar manner. 'There's plenty of ways to have fun with a girl that don't involve beating the shit out of her,' she informed Gavin by way explanation.

Their contacts were sufficiently important for them to remain safe from unwelcome police attention, at the price of generous bribes and a free anything-goes night for those who fancied it once a year close to Christmas. An air of superficial respectability was maintained by the fitting out of what had been the ground-floor front hall and morning room of the private house as a small bistro called Maison Jeanette. Jane made sure the prices were a little too high, the menu somewhat dull and the food just too mediocre to attract a regular clienèle. They wanted no bona fide gourmets impeding the real business of The Eros Club, which occupied the rest of the building behind the panelling at the rear of the bistro.

The odd inquisitive diner was told the men who came and went in the course of the evening were members of a select private dining club which met upstairs but was run independently of Jeanette's. No, the *patronne* had no idea where they might contact the membership committee, but anyway she understood the waiting list was over-subscribed and closed for the foreseeable future. People stayed away from Jeanette's in droves and members packed The Eros every night. Gavin and Jane had hit on a very profitable venture.

'If you go on like this, you'll be so rich I shall have to marry you for your money,' he teased her one night as they checked over the place at closing time.

Jane smiled back, only half joking, and said: 'I might accept you at that.'

'What an odd couple we would make!'

'I'll bet you we'd be a couple who stayed together long after all the big romances had petered out..'

Tenderly, he drew a finger down her cheek. 'You may be right at that.'

'Right? I'm so sure of myself I'll have a bet on it with you. A hundred quid says we'll still be together ten years from now, and looking forward to another twenty.'

'Done! By then some Adonis will have snapped you up and you won't regard me as anything more than a friend you used to know.'

'You're wrong, Gavin. I promise you're wrong.'

He merely laughed, reached into his wallet and took out a handful of banknotes. 'I just happen to have been to the bank today . . . races tomorrow, remember? I have a hundred. Let's stake it now.' He opened a cupboard under the bar counter and produced a small porcelain pig moneybox which Gerry had given Jane as a good luck present when she and Gavin started The Eros. Then he folded the crackling five-pound notes into individual slips like fire spills and posted them one by one through the slot in the top. 'Now you,' he said, holding out the container.

'Gavin, I was joking! You can't . . .'

He grinned. 'Don't tell me you haven't got it. I know there's a careful little Welsh girl tucked inside that smooth surface, convinced disaster is around the corner. You'll have a hundred somewhere.'

'All right, then, you're on! Wait a minute.' Jane disappeared into the small office behind the bar and returned moments later with a bundle of ten-pound notes. 'Not as crisp and new as yours, but neither of us objects too much to dirty money, do we? There we are — there's mine.' And she followed his example, squeezing the folded paper through the slot.

'Who'll hold the stake?' she said.

'The one man we trust as much as each other, of course — Gerry. I'll hand it over to him tomorrow for reclamation in ten years . . . or will it be twenty?'

'Let's go for ten. I think we'll both accept it as permanent after that.'

Lange put the piggy bank carefully on the bar counter. 'And now, bed. We both have a busy day tomorrow.'

They had converted the top floor of the house into a suite worthy of the Dorchester, with a big bedroom, adjoining dressing room and bathroom for each of them opening from opposite sides of a drawing room which ran the length of the building. Although neither of them cooked more than once a month, there was a tiny kitchen and an intimate small dining room. Each bedroom had its own door opening directly on to the corridor which ran to the passenger lift at the end of the landing, and there was a staircase inside the suite which enabled them to go down to street level and through a back exit without going through club premises.

Now Gavin escorted her up in the lift and they said affectionate good nights outside the drawing room. Deep down, neither had any doubt that they would still be together in 1948, or even 1968. In the event, they were parted sooner than either would have believed possible. Now, seven years later, Jane still recalled every detail as if it had happened yesterday.

The Eros operated on a members-only basis. It was far

too risky to run such a club as they did some of the raffish establishments off Bond Street and Regent Street. They did not need more customers, and the potential risk was enormous. The police were all right – those who worked the Mayfair beat had a lot to lose if The Eros went out of business – but the gutter press and the self-proclaimed guardians of public morality were quite another matter. Both Jane and Gavin knew how easy it was to fall foul of either. It was not worth the transient profit of a couple of temporary memberships.

Guests were different. Jane was almost as uncomfortable about them as she was about what she termed the doorstep merchants, but she knew no one would patronise a club where they could not bring their friends as guests for a riotous evening out. Nevertheless, she was right to be fearful.

A group of happy businessmen had retired to what were universally known as the hospitality suites. They had block-booked four of the most exotic rooms, and six of them had retired armed with champagne and accompanied by Jane's most luscious girls. She had just finished seeing everyone was settled in and attending to special requests. As she returned to the club floor she was chuckling silently and thinking that at times her job resembled that of a restaurant manageress rather than a madam. The idea amused her so much that she was not really paying attention to the clients who thronged the downstairs bar area. A large glass of champagne would go down a treat now, she thought, strolling across to the bar.

She waited until the barman had finished mixing a couple of exotic cocktails, then said: 'Large glass a the Widow, please Joe, when you're ready.'

'Perhaps you'd care to put it on our bill?' The voice struck ice into her heart. She did not even need to turn her head to know who had spoken. Slowly, slowly, as if her world was winding down, she turned her head in the direction of the voice. James Teal was sitting on the high stool beside the bar.

The silence extended forever. Then, as if someone else

were speaking through her lips, she said: 'We don't allow scum in here. How did you get in?'

His face, already grim when he first addressed her, abruptly took on the terrifying expression she had last seen when he beat her to a state of unconsciousness. 'You'll regret saying that until the end of your days,' he said, in a tone he might have used to comment on the warmth of the day. His eyes had the flat, mad look she had learned to dread.

'Who are you with?' she said, her voice still cold as winter.

His eyes were unchanged, though he sounded normal enough. 'Since you ask, I'm the guest of one of your exalted members. I am so-o-o grateful. I looked everywhere, you know. It was strange. You seemed to disappear without trace. In the end I put it on a high shelf. Knew I'd get up there eventually . . . and hey presto! I did.'

'You know your trouble, James? You think small. I bet you looked for me! You looked for me down the Dilly, then p'raps you tried Greek Street or the Haymarket. Then p'raps Ma Meyrick's. Wouldn't go near Gavin, would you? He made you look too small. Just about the right size . . .'

Teal's smile was straight from Hell. 'Ah, but you see, I found out about your dear Gavin. So much for the immaculate profile and the big muscular frame . . . he's as queer as rocking-horse shit!'

Jane clenched her fists in an effort not to hit him. 'You think what he does is queer? *You?* Don't make me laugh – he's as normal as a bank clerk compared to you!'

'You may think that, but who'd believe a tuppenny tart when she said a man of my class had been behaving badly?'

'Behaving badly? That's like saying Crippen behaved badly!'

He leaned towards her, almost whispering now. 'Forget about that. I know something else about your delightful partner – he's not British.'

'Oh, give the customer a coconut! In spite of what the Fascists say, not being British is still legal.'

'Not if you're in this country without the proper papers.

And, my dear girl, he is. I know. Some nice little friends of mine have checked.'

Jane had developed an unusual degree of self-control since her earlier contact with Teal, but he was straining it now. She felt the colour drain from her face, and knew it gave the lie to her uncaring laugh. 'And what d'you think you can do with that?'

'Oh, Jane, come now! You're a bright girl. You don't need me to tell you the wolves are at the door for the likes of him.'

'Meaning?'

'Meaning, my sweet, that it would be the work of a moment for me to tell Special Branch about Gavin Lange's somewhat unorthodox claim to British citizenship. He'd be on the first tramp steamer to Hamburg, and our German friends have a tougher line with poofs than we do.'

'Not even you would do that.'

'But my dear, why not? I love my country. I don't want it polluted by that sort of filth. If we don't have leaders with the guts to do something about them, their own countrymen do.'

'They're not his countrymen! He's British.'

'Hmm, I think the Home Office would find that hard to believe. I don't know quite how they'd classify him, but at a guess it would come somewhere between stateless citizen and German illegal immigrant.'

She changed tack. 'There must be a price, Jimmy. There always was with you.'

'A price for what?'

'For leaving Gavin alone.'

'Oh, I hadn't really considered it. I was thinking of my duty as a good citizen.'

'Like fuck you were! What's the price tag?'

'What else could it be? You, of course.'

Then she knew she was finished. 'I — I don't understand.'

'I think you do, Janie dear. I've inherited the old ancestral pile since our paths last crossed. I want you up there for a few days . . . holiday . . . if you can understand *that*.'

There was cold sweat on her palms and behind her knees. She felt the hair standing erect on her neck. She knew what he had in mind and she also knew it was her one — slight — chance of saving Lange. As she opened her mouth to answer him, another voice cut through the conversation.

'I think you had better leave now, *sir*. You are annoying the lady.'

The flat, basilisk stare shifted momentarily from Jane to Gavin, who had approached them unnoticed as their intense conversation progressed.

'If I were you, Lange, I'd be careful — very careful. Your future depends on this.'

'If it means survival at the expense of Jane's suffering, let us dispense with such nonsense,' said Gavin. 'I want you to go — now. What might or might not happen tomorrow is of no concern to you.' And before Teal could say anything else, Lange had applied the most unobtrusive armlock Jane had ever seen, and marched him out of the bar.

Minutes later he returned, looking as if he had done no more than see a drunk off the premises. As he rejoined Jane, he leaned over Charles Lovering, who had signed Teal in, and murmured: 'Don't bring him again, Charlie — he upsets the ladies.' Then he picked up the champagne which had been discharging its bubbles unnoticed in front of Jane for the past ten minutes, and said: 'Drink up. If this is my last night in England, I want to drown a lot more before we close.'

Jane spent almost an hour pleading with Lange to let her ask Lovering to put her back in touch with James Teal. 'It's not too late, Gavin. I'll get over whatever he has in mind for me, you know how tough I am. I can't bear to lose you.'

He merely laughed. 'You have little understanding of the psychology of blackmailers, do you? Even if you survived this country-house nightmare he seems to have planned for you, do you really think that would be enough? He would then come back to London, inform on me anyway, and attempt to take my place at this club. It's sad, Jane, but accept it. We all lose sometimes. This looks like my turn.'

'But there's every chance you won't survive it.'

'Death is not optional, my dear. It's simply that some of us last longer than others. Besides, I'm quite a survivor. They don't guarantee to arrest the likes of me back in Germany, you know. I might actually manage to avoid them.'

'Yeah. And I'm riding a solid gold push-bike! What are the chances of us hiding you?'

He made an irritable gesture. 'Forget about that! I could just about tolerate being a fugitive in Germany. But in my own country? Never. They can take me from my home and treat me as a civilised human being, not a criminal on the run.'

Three days later, that was exactly what they did. Two large men in plain raincoats arrived at The Eros, identified themselves as Special Branch, and gave Gavin twenty minutes to pack a bag. Jane saw him down to the street entrance and embraced him as if she never wanted to let him go. He kissed her, then said, very quietly against the muffling thickness of her hair: 'Attend to Teal for me. That is all I ask. And remember: if I can, I shall come back.' He stood away from her, holding her at arm's length, and said: 'We still have that bet outstanding. It would be nice if you won it.'

Jane had never thought of herself as a criminal. In her view she was a working woman who ran a business efficiently and provided a range of services for which people were prepared to pay considerable sums of money. No one suffered by what she did and often she thought they benefited. In all her life she committed only one act which went against the pattern.

The club membership included some very rough diamonds. Although many of them were noblemen and industrial millionaires of long standing, there was a fair sprinkling of flashier types who had made money quickly during the 1930s and were determined to spend as much as they could before their luck ran out. Without asking questions about precisely what they did, Jane understood well enough that they belonged to the true underworld rather than to café society.

After she had spent a day or two grieving for Gavin and hoping against hope that he would return, she accepted he must have been deported and went to see Gerry Hamilton. Gerry had been away for a few days' holiday and had no idea what had happened between Teal and his two friends at the club. Jane had barely begun to explain when he was half way out of his chair, ready to go seeking vengeance. Jane pressed him back into his seat. 'No you don't. The swine isn't getting away with a thumping this time. I want to stop him for good. Hell isn't hot enough to make up for what he's done to Gavin.'

'I'm with you there, love, and I still want to be in on it. Just point me in the right direction.'

She shook her head. 'I want him wiped off the face of the earth, and neither of us could do that with a prayer of saving our own necks. We need professionals.'

'Are you saying what I think you're saying?'

'Yeah — not just for Gavin. For all those tormented little girls an' all.'

'What d'you want me to do?'

She produced a typewritten list. 'Just pick out a couple of names for me, Gerry, that's all. Then forget this conversation ever took place.'

He glanced down the list. It was the membership roll of The Eros. 'Why foul your own doorstep?

'There are other ways of looking at that one. All the fellas on that list like me and get on well with me. Most of them owe me the odd favour. I want a few who wouldn't turn a hair at the thought of getting the Honourable James bumped off, and wouldn't have any tricky ideas about telling anybody.'

'Oh, that's easy enough. There are two pros on that list who work direct, and at least five blokes who have the contacts. If I were you, I'd go for the ones with the contacts. You never know when the do-it-yourself boys will run short a cash and come leaning on you for a little bit of hush money.'

'That's my boy. Now you're taking it seriously.'

He sorted out three names for her — men she knew quite well, all of whom owed her favours of one sort or another. 'D'you want me to make the approach?' asked Gerry.

'Do I, buggery! I want to get every ounce of satisfaction out a this.' That evening Jane sat down at her private telephone an hour before the club opened, and rang the first man on the list, inviting him to supper and making it clear she wanted to discuss a business matter. The last thing she wanted was to end up being chased around the drawing room as she tried to plan her revenge on Teal.

Denis Haynes turned out to be the answer to her problem. She had no need to contact the other two members. She told Haynes what she wanted and he chuckled grimly as she finished. 'Nice to have someone willing to pay for a little job I'd probably a done for nothing,' he said.

Jane looked at him questioningly. 'It's all right, Janie love, no big mystery. Nothing really personal to me, neither, or he'd a been removed a long time ago. Nah, it's just that he cut up a pretty little brass one a my boys was very keen on. She was never the same again, and neither was poor old Tony. I don't think blokes like Teal should be running around loose.'

'Me, neither, so let's see he isn't for much longer, shall we? I'll pay well. It will be worth it.'

'Say no more. You'll get a phone call to let you know the job's been completed. For obvious reasons the caller won't be very specific, but you'll get the general drift.'

'Fine. Oh, and Denis — please see it hurts the bastard as much as possible.'

The call came in the early hours of the morning a week later. Jane had closed the club for the night and was already asleep. She groped for the phone, forlornly hoping in her drowsy state that it was Gavin come home. A flat East London voice said: 'Some people don't take proper care a their cars, do they. Bad accident tonight, vehicle went somersaulting off the road down by the side a Clifton suspension bridge. Should think the driver'll look as if someone broke every bone in his body when they get 'im out. G'night.'

There was a click and the telephone went dead. The story made the London evening papers next day. James Teal, described as 'The Playboy Peer', had apparently drunk too much at a friend's supper party and had careered off a West Country road in his high-powered car, plunging into the Avon Gorge and killing himself instantly. The *Evening Standard* report added with relish that the police surgeon said he had never seen such extensive injuries. The immense length of the drop to the gorge bottom must have been responsible.

Jane went over to her drinks cupboard and mixed herself a large gin and tonic, which she raised to a silver-framed photograph of Gavin before tasting it, and saying aloud: 'That one was for you, love.'

After that, as she often told herself, there seemed little to do except keep on carrying on. Eventually a postcard came for her, postmarked Hamburg some time earlier that month. It said: 'No one locked me up yet, but give them time! Love G.'

She did not hear from him again.

The years that followed were a time of unparalleled prosperity for Jane. First soldiers, then successful black marketeers, poured into London and The Eros was consistently full of people who spent as if there were no tomorrow. It was such a popular place, and soon acquired such a mythic reputation, that she did not even need to relax the rule about proper membership. She could have filled the place night after night – and did – with men whose names appeared regularly on the membership list. They tended to come and go nowadays more frequently than they had pre-war, but as long as they went on paying, she was indifferent to their fate.

It was not that Jane lacked humanity: she had a vast reserve of it locked inside her. But life had taught her that very few people were prepared to give without the hope of making some profit in return, and that too often those who were fell on hard times. Gavin was her perennial example. Her only way of handling what had happened to him was to close her mind completely to what was happening within Germany.

She was unenthusiastic about the war in general, and remained aloof as long as discussions amounted to no more than *Boys' Own Paper*-style discussions of who had the best generals and the most effective aircraft. It was different if anyone decided they wanted to talk about the brutality of Nazism within Germany. Jane's regulars quickly learned that if they wished to keep on her good side, they saved such discussions for somewhere other than The Eros Club.

As the war drew to its close, she managed to remain curiously detached thanks to this attitude. The number of uniformed members around the club gradually waned and the loud-suited, newly rich spivs proliferated. But in Jane's view a war profiteer was no worse than any other sort of pirate, and in her thirty years she had yet to encounter a clean, noble way of making money. VE Day came and went, and Jane laboured on at her club, changing it to satisfy the ever more exotic tastes of her clientèle, skilfully dodging any but the most emotionally superficial romantic encounters, and generally laying up for herself a secure future.

She tried never to stop and think where and with whom such a future would be spent. There was Gerry Hamilton – dear, lovable Gerry, a true friend if ever she had one. But her rapport with him was different from her ease with Gavin, and she knew instinctively that eventually close contact would push them apart.

Much further back, she remembered Eddie Anderton – lovely cuddly Eddie, the man who had given her the guts to go on the game without making it seem like the lowest way to make a living. Eddie was still around, fabulously rich these days, but he must be coming up to his sixties already, and Jane had no intention of retiring from her business for a long time yet. Even if he still remembered her as fondly as she did him, he would be doddering or dead by the time she chose to settle.

At this point in her musings, Jane invariably grew sorry for herself. Thirty years old, countless affairs behind her, and still no sign of anyone with whom she wanted to share her life. And dear God, what if they did! she thought to herself as she stood looking at the Gay-Nineties-out-of-Roman-Banquet room she had just tailor-made to the request of some common-as-muck war profiteer. They'd take one look at what she had created and run screaming from her life.

She switched out the lights and left the garish new room, moving back through the club's main bar on her way to her private lift. Of course, there was one man who wouldn't react like that; one man who had helped her set it up, who could sit and laugh with her about the essential silliness of it all . . . Gavin Lange. That made her simultaneously angry and upset. 'Silly bitch!' she said. 'Gavin was queer — hardly right as your lover.' And Gavin is also dead, probably by some horrible method, too, whispered the hateful voice which sometimes came to haunt her. It did not happen often these days. She had shut herself off too thoroughly from the effects of the war in Europe. But even Jane's resolve was not quite capable of excluding all knowledge of what had been going on.

She slammed through the bar, where Joe the head barman was polishing glasses and setting up ready for that evening. 'I've had enough of this place today, Joe,' she told him. 'I'm off to the pictures — they've got something funny on at the Curzon, I think. If there's anything really urgent, tell 'em I'll be back before nine.'

It was a good frothy Cary Grant comedy. As Jane found her seat, the advertisements were drawing to a close. She settled in as the titles over the newsreel began running, and felt vaguely uneasy. She had managed to avoid the ten-minute Movietone and Pathé Gazette films since early in the war, for much the same reason as she discouraged war talk at the club. You're taking all this a bit far, she told herself. The war's been over for months — you won't see anything that rubs your nose in what happened to Gavin . . .

And then, there it was. The usual falsely optimistic, theatrical voice of the news commentator said: 'And here we have the latest pastime for debs: driving Land Rovers, setting up feeding depots and running first aid stations. They're the newest volunteers for relief work at the Displaced Persons' camps the Allies have opened all over Europe to rehabilitate refugees and concentration camp victims before they begin the long hard struggle to put their lives back together again . . .'

The cameras had started with close-ups of a group of upper-class English girls, their fashionable haircuts swept back under scarves, once-elegant fingernails chipped from unaccustomed work at changing jeep tyres or unloading trucks. One of them grinned wearily as the camera picked up a framed photograph on the desk of her at a debs' ball, wearing a sequined gown and with her blonde hair tumbling in healthy waves over snowy shoulders. Now the shoulders were covered by rough fatigues and the blonde colouring was already growing out of the few strands of hair that escaped the scarf.

The shots which followed showed male and female volunteers from all over Europe and America, manning a vast fenced area which stretched as far as the eye could see. Grotesque, skeletal caricatures of human beings were sitting, standing or shuffling about within the compound, some still wearing the striped prison pyjamas which even Jane recognised as concentration camp standard issue. Momentarily the camera held a man, not old, but lined like an octogenarian by starvation and pain. On his left breast was a crudely sewn patch of plain cloth.

'Last reminder of a dreadful system which not only sorted out the so-called Master Race from inferior types, but also graded the types into different categories and colour coded them to make administration easier,' said the commentator, the inhumanity of the practices he was describing modifying even his plummy tones. 'Jews were given one colour, gypsies another. There were even special colours allocated to mental patients and homosexuals.'

Jane could stand no more. Oh, Christ – Gavin! Gavin like that, reduced from the fastidious blond god she had known to a trembling heap of smelly rags mumbling over a cup of vegetable broth! It was too much . . . Blindly she got up and blundered out of the cinema, hastening back to The Eros to hide herself from the world. What could she do? Could she ever forget what had happened, ever be healed of the wound?

Back in her suite, she had a couple of stiff drinks which calmed her a little, but they did nothing to ease the pain. She had been sitting quietly, staring at the photograph of Gavin, when Joe rang her on the internal phone. 'I know you said only urgent calls, Jane, but it's Gerry Hamilton. You always like to see him and he is asking for you particularly.'

'Yes, of course, Joe, you did the right thing. Send him up – he knows the way.'

When Gerry arrived he was carrying a small overnight bag. 'Just brought a couple of bits and pieces around, Jane. They're things of yours that have been in the flat for years, but I've decided to move on, and—'

'You've what?'

He smiled. 'Glad to see someone doesn't want me to go! It's okay, not permanently. I just got fed up with London looking like one big bombsite and a job came up in Brighton for six months. I'm taking it, giving up the flat, and getting a new place when I come back, that's all. I just didn't know what to do about these few bits and pieces.'

'That's a relief! I thought I was seeing you off for good. Let's see what you've got.'

Most of it was not worth hanging on to and consisted of small keepsakes Jane had collected to remind her of longpast days at the seaside or a nightclub. Then, rather uneasy at provoking sad memories, Gerry added: 'There was one other thing . . . I hardly like to raise it, after all that happened, but I think it might be quite a lot of cash. Remember asking me to be stakeholder?'

As he spoke, he produced the little porcelain piggy-bank which contained the betting money for her wager with Gavin that they would survive at least ten years together. Jane reached out almost hesitantly and took the pig. She cupped it in her hands and as she looked down at it, the tears began coursing unchecked down her cheeks.

'Oh, bloody hell, Gerry, that settles it! I know he's probably been dead for years, but something inside me says he isn't and I shall never be happy unless I find out. I'm going to look for him.'

Hamilton stared at her incredulously. 'Come on, Jane, we're both too old to believe in fairies! Where would you start looking?'

She sniffed, her weeping already almost forgotten now she had a possible course of action. 'Newsreel . . . I saw a newsreel this evening showing a DP camp with a bunch of English roses helping out. Wherever they can go, so can I.'

'Oh, I don't doubt it. But have you any idea how many of those camps there are in Germany and Poland? They're scattered right across Eastern Europe, and the Russians aren't letting any British do-gooders into their sector. You can't just take pot luck.'

'Oh, yes I can! Well, not *quite* pot luck. This place has been coining it ever since 1939 and half of it's Gavin's share. I'm going to spread a bit of it about and see what I find out. As our mam used to say: "Cast your bread upon the waters." '

Gerry regarded her with something like awe. 'Well, love,' he finally said, 'if anyone can do it, you can.'

Chapter Thirty-one

The intrusive sound of the big diesel engine scaled down and stopped. There was the sound of army boots making contact with hard ground, then the lorry door slammed. Seconds later, the tailgate bolts of the truck squealed in protest as they were disengaged.

The human cargo of the transport cringed in the back of the waggon. They were all too accustomed to such journeys ending in confrontations with bloodthirsty dogs and savage, whipwielding guards. Now, though, there were friendly, if bewildered, GI faces outside, and no dogs anywhere. Gradually the cringing group of passengers untangled themselves from their fearful embrace and shuffled towards the tailgate.

'Come on, fellas,' said the driver, 'we're all friends here. No need to worry about us.' His co-driver nudged him and he said, 'Ah – sorry – forgot.' The co-driver translated and the pathetic passengers came blinking out into the sunlight.

'Maybe it's all right after all, Gavin,' said Lange's friend. 'Perhaps we were wrong and it's not a trick.'

Gavin merely shrugged. 'Trick or no trick, we have no choice. Let's go.'

Peter Chekov jumped feebly from the back of the vehicle, straightened with difficulty and looked around him. 'Oh, no! It *is* a trick, Gavin! There's a fence – dogs – they're no different . . .' He set off at a staggering run across the bare patch of ground where the lorries were unloading.

Two GIs came forward to restrain him. 'Hey, hold on, now!' said one. 'No one's gonna hurt ya. Just medical precautions, that's all.'

Chekov made no reply beyond a high, thin shriek. He

went on running until his feeble strength gave out, then collapsed, sobbing, on the ground. Gavin, still in the truck, glared down at the soldier. 'Clever boy,' he said. 'Why shoot him when you can frighten him to death?'

The soldier, bewildered, turned on him. 'Just what have you guys got against us? We're here to help you, honest. We let you outa that hell-hole, remember?'

'Sure, to move us into another one. You expect gratitude?' Gavin lacked the will to run. He sat down on the back of the truck and watched, detached, as his travelling companions disembarked. Eventually he was the only one left. The GI came back.

'Come on, now. What's the point of staying perched up there? We got food and medical supplies over at Base. You'll get a shower and fresh clothes.'

'We heard that before. Guess what came through the shower heads,' said Gavin.

The soldier turned pale, but held his ground. 'I know you feel bad, but this is for real. We're only here to set you free.'

'Then how come that nice new tall fence?'

'I don't like that any more than you do. The truth of it is that there was everything from cholera to diphtheria inside that camp. You all gotta get a medical and some shots, then we'll process you through to a decent DP camp en route for home. The wire is strictly temporary.'

'DP camp? What's a DP?'

'Displaced person, o' course. All of you — there's nothing left out there. You wouldn't believe it.'

'If you had seen what I have in the past few years, you would believe anything, soldier boy. I am not a displaced person. I am British.'

'That's as may be. It'll all be sorted out in the next week or so. Come on, now, get down. You guys have been through enough. I don't want to do anything else to you.'

'Okay. It couldn't be worse, wherever you are taking me.'

It seemed that many of the former internees did not share Gavin's view. By the time he got through the gates of the temporary camp, Chekov was wandering about just inside, crooning to himself in a tone akin to madness. Lange hurried to him and put an arm around his shoulders. 'Come on, Peter. The worst is over. We can pull through this.'

His friend raised calloused hands to cover his tear-streaked face. 'You, maybe,' he moaned, 'not me. One fence too many, Gavin. Just one fence too many . . .' He turned away from Lange and wandered towards the wire.

'Hey, you!' yelled a guard in the watch tower. 'Geddaway from there! Those wires are electrified!'

Oh, no – not now! thought Gavin. Don't let him go now, after all this . . . With his last strength he lurched forward behind Chekov, intent on stopping the other man's mindless progress towards the fence. As he ran, his worn-out left boot caught on a stone and he stumbled, falling full-length at the base of the watch tower. The impact with the ground knocked the air out of his lungs, and for a moment he lay, panting, where he had fallen. Then, realising Chekov was still moving, he forced himself to his feet and started forward again. 'Peter – wait! You don't understand . . .'

But his friend was deaf to intercession. Lange was still a good ten feet behind him as he reached the wire. Chekov stretched out his arms like a child embracing his mother. His claw-thin fingers clutched the fence. There was a sizzling noise and a faint smell of roasting meat. Chekov's back made an obscene concave curve and his ribcage thrust forward parallel with his hands. Somewhere, a guard threw a switch to cut the current and Chekov's lifeless form slumped back on to the ground. By now Gavin had reached him. He was dead, his face blank, his eyes closed.

Lange cradled Peter on his lap, his body racked by huge, dry sobs. Seconds later, the first guard reached him and leaned over the pair, gently touching Gavin's shoulder. 'We couldn't stop him – honest – how were we to know?'

Gavin flung aside the comforting hand. 'Touch me again and I'll tear your arm off,' he said.

The soldier retreated and moments later was explaining at length to another GI what had happened. 'Don't they understand *anything*?' he said. 'We can't just set 'em loose

— they'd infect half the population. It's not as if . . .'

A long shadow fell across them. 'It's not as if anything, you mindless bastard,' said Lange. 'Have you the faintest idea what we've been through since we came to Buchenwald? You don't take a man from behind one fence to put him behind another — not when he's endured what happened to us.'

The load of guilt was too much for the soldier. 'Look, I didn't write the script! I'm just here trying to help . . . you'll be outa this in a few days. Until then you gotta handle it any way you can.'

He was exceptionally tall, and was looking Lange directly in the eye. Gavin returned his gaze unflinchingly, then said: 'You will be shipping out as many dead as alive by then. Not from cholera, but from the wire. Surely you learned enough from those beasts to realise you can keep people in with a non-lethal charge?' Then he turned and walked away.

The relief team were working flat out, sorting piles of clean clothing, making up food parcels, contacting would-be host families who had agreed to open their homes to a refugee for a few months. Two days earlier, a Movietone News camera crew had come to film these plucky English girls doing their bit to help the reconstruction of Europe after the worst war in human history. The film would be showing this week in cinemas throughout the United Kingdom. Much had been made of the fact that three of this particular relief team were London debutantes, who had cut short their elegant fingernails and cropped their Veronica Lake hairstyles in order to shed any social butterfly image that might still stick to them. Jane Ellis laughed to herself at that bit. She wondered how many of her former clients, well-heeled businessmen from Coventry and Nottingham and Leeds, would start out of their seats in the one-and-nines in horrified recognition of the Mayfair madam who had arranged such gratifying sex for them the last time they were in town. They had probably been wondering where she had gone. Now they'd know — Buchenwald.

After seeing the news bulletin at the Curzon, she had started work from the only point she could identify – voluntary relief work. What had started as a personal crusade for Jane had turned into something else. When she volunteered to go out in one of the relief teams, it had been because she saw no quicker way of cutting through the red tape in her attempt to find Gavin Lange. She still did not know whether he was still alive, and no one was likely to pay her any attention if she joined the ranks of well-heeled foreigners who were combing the ruins of Europe in search of those they had loved before the war. She had spread a lot of money about, seeking information about a tall, slender blond man of English origin, but without immediate results.

At the same time, she had set out to mimic the activities of the young women she had seen on the screen. Within weeks, her attitude had changed, as she realised that the newsreel which had set her off on her quest had been a bland shadow of terrible reality. When she saw for herself the scarred children and crippled adults, she began to realise she had a bigger debt to pay than merely finding Gavin again. Whatever suffering she had endured in her life was nothing compared with the least they had undergone. Now she worked flat out for eighteen hours in every twenty-four, attempting to solve some of the basic problems and give them some hope of a new life.

Buchenwald was the third back-up unit where she had worked, and by far the worst. The Anglo-American military detachments who ran the temporary accommodation near the original concentration camp were experiencing appalling problems. They were losing almost as many ex-prisoners as the Germans had disposed of in the last days of their tyranny. Some simply seemed to give up. Some were so sick from the diseases they had caught or with which they had been deliberately infected, that they died within days. But most disquieting was the growing roll of internees who simply walked on to the electrified wire boundary fence and committed suicide.

Jane had heard gossip about this strange phenomenon

since a couple of days after her arrival. But she had no direct contact with it until she came into the office at eight o'clock one morning to find a perplexed young American major talking to Deborah Walker, the girl who shared her office.

She listened to him in silence for a while, then said: 'Hasn't anyone suggested an explanation yet?'

'No, Ma'am. We're completely fazed by it.'

'This might seem like a stupid question, but why do you lock them up behind electrified fences? I thought you were supposed to have liberated them.'

'I don't like it any more than you seem to, but those are our orders. It's not for long — two weeks at most, less for a lot of them — but we have to be sure they're not carrying infectious diseases, and they have to be de-loused and cleaned up. Trouble is, they're mostly in such bad mental shape they'd just go wandering off if we didn't confine them, so the powers that be decided on the wire.'

'But *electrified* wire?' said Deborah.

'Yeah, I know. We tried the ordinary sort. They seemed to think it was their duty to escape, and over they went, by the dozen. That's when the current was connected.'

Jane was livid. 'And it didn't occur to any of your top brass that people too desperate to understand they were out of a concentration camp wouldn't be put off by the risk of electrocution! Dear God, what a way to run an army!'

'It wasn't just us!' he said indignantly. 'Your officers were just as hot on it.'

'Oh, I'm sure they were! Bet they made lots of noises about knowing what was good for them. Doesn't seem to have kept the poor sods alive, though.'

The major had the grace to blush. 'No, I realise that. I – it's mainly why I'm here. I was wondering if any of you girls might feel like volunteering to go and — sort of — *explain* to these guys . . .' as he finished speaking he took an instinctive step backwards and raised one arm defensively. 'I know how dangerous it is — you could pick up just about anything . . .'

'Balls!' Deborah was already on her feet, heading for the

hook where her jacket hung. 'I'm in – how about you, Janie?'

'Try going without me. Major, I can assure you I've got no intention of catching cholera, diphtheria or anything else. I'll just add a drop more gin to my drinking water to sterilise it in future. Come on, you started this. Show us where to go.'

As his Jeep trundled over the uneven ground outside the temporary camp, Major Schwarz explained: 'I hate to ask you people in the support organisations, but the poor devils won't look at anyone in military uniform, let alone listen to them. It's a waste of time for us to try and tell 'em anything. You're just about our last hope. I don't think I can bear to see many more of the poor bastards burn themselves up on that wire.'

Jane was staring at him with an expression that stopped just short of awe. 'Didn't it occur to any of you that if you *had* to electrify the wire, a mild current would dissuade them? Even if they kept jumping on it, at least it wouldn't kill them.'

'Funny you should say that, ma'am. There was a guy today said the same thing – kept insisting, and the wire had just killed his buddy, so it was hard to tell him to shut up.'

For some reason she never understood, bells rang inside Jane's head.

'Where was he?' she asked, tonelessly.

'Ah, somewhere in the camp I'm taking you to. You girls been inside. You know how big the perimeter is . . . I dunno which sector he's in.'

'Major, I want to find that man. Locate him for me, and I'll solve every problem you have – it's a promise. Now, where did you see him?'

Dusk was closing in as they got to the western perimeter of the fence. Gavin was still holding on to Chekov's stiffening body. For some reason it seemed to be his last contact with reality. He was vaguely aware of a vehicle approaching somewhere to the rear. Not more questions . . .

more trouble . . . more stupid people asking for answers that were self-evident.

Very gently, he laid aside Chekov's corpse. 'Sleep well, old friend,' he murmured, 'and leave a space for me.' Then he got up and started the longest walk of his life, towards the wire perimeter fence. As he went, he said, over and over, 'It couldn't be worse. It couldn't be worse . . .'

The tall fence grew closer. Eventually, the first strands were only a yard or so from his outstretched hands. He uttered a huge sigh. Why had he held on so long? What was the point? Peace after stormy seas, that was what he needed. He started to pace out the last few strides, then suddenly his advance was barred by a large open motor vehicle which squealed to a halt between him and the fence. Damn! He'd have to find another section. Like an automaton, he wheeled and started moving further along the boundary.

Somewhere deep in his memory, a familiar voice was calling him. 'Gavin — Gavin, don't you remember? It's me, Janie. Gavin! Wake up!'

Wake up? Was it Sunday morning and had he overslept one of their outings again? He tried to gather his scattered wits. No . . . this wasn't a sunny flat in London. It was hell, and it was Germany. His mind was playing tricks, tricks it hadn't wished on him for a couple of years at least.

But wait — this was no trick. He'd never seen Jane in military fatigues. If she was wearing them now, she must be *here*. Even his fevered dreams did not extend that far. Lange stopped his zombie-like advance on the wire and blinked hard, several times, to clear his vision. No, she was still there. 'Is it you? Is it really you?' he asked, staring down at the frantic, diminutive figure in front of him.

'Oh, yes, Gavin — yes, yes, yes! Please recognise me! I've come to take you home.'

'Easy, lady. No promises you can't keep, remember?' said the major, uneasy at their familiarity.

'Fuck off,' said Jane. 'Gavin, grab hold a my hand. Now come with me. We're going home. Home, d'you hear? Don't worry about anything any more.'

'You can't do that,' said Major Schwarz.

'And I said fuck off!' retorted Jane.

A week later they were married at military headquarters, a necessary precaution to ensure the validity of Gavin's papers. Within three months The Eros Club was permanently closed down, its backers paid off. The owners had decided to forsake the city for a farm in rural Wales. Jane Ellis had won her bet on a ten-year union and cemented it by becoming Mrs Jane Lange, a sheep farmer's wife in rural Breconshire.

Chapter Thirty-two

Rose was generally so thoroughly content that she was afraid to admit it to herself. In the late 1930s and early 1940s, Best of British went from strength to strength, expanding from its New York base to service much of the north-eastern seaboard. When Britain went to war with Germany, the firm received a huge boost of recruits determined to get out of Europe before the real trouble started, and when the flood dried up, she hit on a new plan. She opened a Best of British training school in upstate New York, with a day training centre in New York City, and set up training for American domestics in the techniques of service as taught in England. It took off as satisfactorily as her earlier ventures and soon she was purring contentedly over her latest brainchild.

She even managed to persuade Kate Higgins to come to New York and run the establishments. She had tried to persuade Margaret, too, but her friend, now Lady Rowan, was determined to stay on in England and help the war effort. She seemed to feel the fact her husband was on active service with the Eighth Army in the Western Desert obliged her to take up some patriotic enterprise of her own. Rose shrugged and returned to her business. Margaret had changed a lot since she settled down to being a country gentlewoman.

At this stage in her musings, Rose usually started to feel vaguely uncomfortable at her lack of dependence on any man. Every magazine she read, every lightweight novel, told her she should feel incomplete without the man of her heart; but she felt anything but that. Her business and cultural interests filled her life. Even her son Giles seemed to have no real place in her heart. He was an attractive little boy whom she enjoyed seeing on her regular trips to

Philadelphia. In fact, by the early 1940s her various interests were doing well enough for her to afford a nanny, so that the boy could live with her in New York. Rose told herself she rejected such a plan because it would have separated Giles from his beloved foster parents, but in fact she felt safer, less vulnerable, living in her own world bounded by purely business relationships.

Lilian Shaw remained the one friend who spanned both worlds, and she had nothing but support for Rose's attitude. 'No use asking me to tell you you're doing the wrong thing,' she responded on one occasion. 'Some people get so badly hurt early on in life that it's a miracle they stitch together anything at all. I don't pry, but I get the impression you're like that. And if I may say so, lovey, you made a bloody fine job of picking up the pieces.'

Once, and only once, did Rose think the walls of her ivory tower might be breached by true involvement. She had always had a soft spot for Alexander Moncreiff, partly because of his trust and generosity early in their business partnership; partly because she somehow felt she would be scoring over Lady Julia if ever she had an affair with him. She knew he was interested in her, because he always made sure he saw far more of her than was necessary for business when he came to New York.

Moncreiff had been elected to Congress in 1938, and was playing a far greater part in politics than business by the time the European war broke out. His particular interest was foreign policy, and he spent a lot of time out of America on fact-finding missions and sponsored trips. Rose always suspected the main reason was that his marriage had soured irretrievably.

He was in New York in mid-November 1941, on a flying visit before making his way to San Francisco and thence to the Pacific. He was one of a group of congressmen and businessmen who were visiting US establishments in the Hawaiian islands.

He dined with Rose the night before he left, and returned with her to her apartment for drinks afterwards.

They sat companionably together over old brandy, and talked about whether or not it was inevitable that America would go into the war as President Roosevelt clearly wanted them to.

'You must feel a bit nervous, junketing around the world at a time like this when anything could happen to you,' said Rose.

He shook his head. 'Nothing to hold me here. I imagine it's fairly obvious that Julia and I have had nothing in common for years now. Marriages of convenience are all very well, but when they go wrong there's no cement to hold them together.'

'I don't think love matches have too good a record on that score, either,' said Rose.

'That depends entirely on the object of one's affections.' He was gazing at her when he spoke, his meaning unmistakable.

Astonished at his intensity, Rose pressed a hand to her breast and said: 'Don't tell me you mean me, Alex?'

'What else would I be saying? The trouble with you is you're so tied up with that business, you never see anything else. I've been trying to tell you for years.'

'But I don't – don't . . .'

'Don't feel anything in return?' He shrugged, trying to smile. 'Can't be helped, I suppose. I'm too used to getting my own way.'

'No. I was going to say I don't think I've ever considered it. I'm extremely fond of you – and that's no put-down. I could never give myself easily. It's something I'd have to think about . . .'

He was beaming now. 'That's the best news I've heard this year! Never thought I had a prayer. Don't worry, Rose, I won't push. I shall be away until a few days before Christmas. If I may, I'll come and see you on my way back to Washington. Perhaps you'll have had time to think by then. In the meantime, I'll keep my fingers crossed.'

When she saw him to the door, he kissed her, taking care merely to brush her forehead with his lips. 'You really are the most beautiful woman,' he said. 'Keep yourself safe until I come back.'

She watched as he walked to the lift and waved to her as the door closed behind him, wondering how she would react when she had time to think over what he had said.

Two weeks later, the Japanese bombed the main American naval base at Pearl Harbor in Honolulu. Alexander Moncreiff, part of a delegation visiting the base, was killed along with a colleague by a stray bomb discharged by a departing plane.

At first Rose was paralysed with grief, then she began to analyse her feelings and to wonder how much was regret that a good friend was gone rather than mourning for a dead lover. She had certainly decided she would indulge in some sort of affair with Moncreiff, but had not thought the matter out further. Now it was never going to happen. Might-have-beens had their painful side, it was true, but reality was usually far tougher. She mourned privately for Moncreiff and publicly went on with her well-ordered life.

She never failed to be surprised at the speed with which time passed. Her absorption in business was far from all-consuming. She had developed her pleasure in learning French and Italian, and as soon as the war ended began visiting Europe to see the sights and improve her languages. Her early use of galleries as an excuse to meet men had endured to become a true passion, and she spent long, happy hours in New York looking at some of the wonderful exhibitions which always seemed to be coming to the city.

The 1940s trickled away almost unnoticed, Kate Higgins's final retirement standing as the one real milestone. Margaret Rowan continued to run the English operations for Best of British — largely from her beautiful Cotswold mansion. To her sorrow, Margaret had remained childless, but she was so happy with Marcus Rowan that it was far from the tragedy it might otherwise have been. Rose felt curiously remote from it all. Marriage, housekeeping and related tasks seemed worlds away from all she knew.

Her son Giles grew into a tall, vigorous young man who

worshipped his foster-father, Joe Skelton. Joe trained him as a mechanic and engineer, and when Giles reached the age of twenty-one, Rose insisted on financing him and Joe in their own small engineering business. It was all managed affectionately and suited everyone concerned, but Rose knew she became more of an outsider each day to the Skelton ménage. When she had fled to their home to find refuge while having an illegitimate child, she had been living even more precariously than they. The family had lent her its strength then, but now she was a rich, independent woman from a world they did not begin to understand. She saw Giles less and less often and rejoiced in his ability to do well in the business with Joe.

As the 1950s advanced, she grew increasingly conscious that something was lacking in her life, and try as she might to sort it out, she seemed incapable of finding an answer. A figure from her remote past proved to be the trigger of a solution.

Rose sometimes awoke from a crazy dream which she started getting after she first read *Alice's Adventures in Wonderland*. In her version of the dream, she was Alice and the White Rabbit was Mark Fletcher-Simms, who instead of dashing about complaining that he was late for an appointment with the Red Queen, endlessly pursued her through city streets and along the decks of an ocean liner. While it made her uneasy, it did nothing worse, because its symbolism was so childishly obvious. He really did seem to pursue her through life, although more by chance than anything else, and even after his disastrous appearance in the Moncreiffs' Georgetown house she could hardly blame him. Once it even occurred to her that his arrival on the scene had brought a change for the better in her fortunes.

The first week of October 1957 turned out to be full of reunions with her past. It started with a profile in *Time* magazine, which lionised Rose as the ultimate rags-to-riches success story, now queening it in New York. The piece was published the day before Rose's encounter with Alexandra Moncreiff, and although neither woman mentioned it, Rose was profoundly conscious that the girl had read it before seeing her. So, it seemed, had someone else who was familiar with her past.

As she returned to the office from lunch with Jim Austerlitz, her secretary said: 'There's a man waiting in reception for you, Miss Rush. I told him your diary is full but he said he was an old friend from England and wanted to wait until I was able to check with you personally.'

Rose made a sceptical face. 'I didn't know I'd any old male friends from England. What's his name?'

'Fletcher-Simms, Miss Rush. Mark Fletcher-Simms.'

'Good God! That is a surprise. When am I seeing that chap who wants three people for his Tuscan villa?'

'Three forty-five, Miss Rush.'

'Okay, let's give Fletcher-Simms half an hour. It's been a very long time . . .'

Mark was as sleek and smooth as ever. His tanned face was lightly lined under the eyes and around the mouth, and his hair was silver, but she would have known him anywhere. He came into her office with a somewhat sheepish smile, greeting her with: 'I hate to look like a celebrity hunter, but I couldn't resist coming to present my compliments. I saw the piece in *Time*.'

'Are you living over here now, then?'

'Dear me, no! I'm sure I should have run across you before now if I had been. No, I'm here researching a book on American painters in the 1920s, and just happened to see the article.'

'Has it taken you twenty-odd years to forgive me for lying to you, or for being a servant?'

'There was nothing to forgive,' he said, looking genuinely bewildered. 'I was prepared to track you down wherever you'd gone, and beg you to marry me, but then that dreadful Moncreiff woman told me you'd been coming to America with her to avoid a scandal you got yourself into in England, and I gave up.'

'Say that again. I seem to have missed something.'

'You know, getting pregnant over there. I can see no

lady's maid in London at that time would have been permitted to get away with it. I must say it was damned brave of you to risk coming to America to strike out on your own.'

'But I wasn't . . . I didn't . . .'

He was beginning to look puzzled. His confusion enabled Rose to gather her scattered wits, and to realise that a full confession now would solve nothing. This man had fathered a son on her about whom he knew nothing. He thought she had been pregnant by someone else and that was the only reason he had never come looking for her. How could she tell him their son was a grease monkey in a little workshop in Pennsylvania? How could she disillusion him about the waste of those years he might have been married to her?

'Rose? Rose, where have you gone?' Fletcher-Simms was saying teasingly. 'Surely I can't have conjured up that many memories?'

'You'd be surprised, Mark. Tell me about yourself. Did you stop chasing mysterious girls in galleries and settle down in the end?'

'Oh, yes. It had its ups and downs, but on balance it worked. My wife died in a car accident a couple of years ago, but I have two terrific children − boy and girl.' He grinned. 'The girl's called Rose.'

'You old sentimentalist! I must say, whenever you turn up in my life, things start happening.'

'Not this time, I think. We're both getting rather middle-aged for things to happen to us.'

They talked on for a while, then he got up to leave. 'I hope life has given you at least some of what you wanted, my beautiful girl,' he said. 'Things would have been very different if I'd managed to hold on to you.'

'I'm sure they would have been, but we'll never know now whether that was for good or ill, will we?' She got up and kissed him tenderly, then he left her to prepare for her business appointment.

For the rest of the day Rose's mind was flitting away from what she was supposed to be doing, and pecking at her memories of Fletcher-Simms. Why was she so restless? Was it the thought of the life they might have had?

Quite suddenly, Rose knew what it was, and knew, too, what had been vaguely amiss in her life recently. She needed a sense of continuity and it was completely missing. The last high-powered client came and went and she sat doodling idly on the blotter in front of her. The intercom let out an intrusive burp and she asked her secretary with some irritation what was amiss.

'It's the young lady who came after a post earlier today, Miss Rush,' said the secretary. 'She's just come back into the office and asked if there's any chance of you seeing her before you leave. I told her I thought it most unlikely, but . . .'

'No, Giselle, send her in. I'm sure it won't take long,' said Rose, feeling the adrenalin begin to pump again at the idea of a new confrontation with this formidable young woman.

She seemed to see Alexandra Moncreiff with different eyes as the girl came back into the office. Why, she thought, it's like looking at myself at that age with a good dose of arrogance splashed on top. Why didn't I see it before? Outwardly, Rose showed no signs of feeling disturbed. Inwardly, she was seething with a growing sense of identification with this spoiled young creature. All she said was: 'I thought we had covered everything this morning, Miss Moncreiff, but if I can be of further assistance . . .?'

Alexandra squared her shoulders and forced herself to be polite. 'Yes, there is,' she said. 'I was unforgivable this morning. My behaviour was disgraceful. Please try to excuse me because I was so nervous. I've been walking around thinking about it all day, and I just realised half an hour ago what I wanted to do. I think perhaps you might consider it.'

'Tell me more.'

'Everything you said about me was true. I'd be terrible as a servant — and that's not a mark of disrespect for servants. It's taken me all today to realise how tactful they have to be — how awful it is always to have to put other people first when you know they're no better than you, but they just have more money.'

Elation leaped inside Rose. It's a miracle she can even see that far, she thought. There's hope for this girl yet. 'And where did that lead you?' she asked.

'I—I think I could learn a lot about running a business like this by doing a job for a while. And I got to wondering if I took one of those horror assignments you have, and stuck it out for six months to a year, would you consider using me afterwards to help out here in headquarters?'

Rose grinned broadly. 'My dear girl! If you were able to keep the Australian horror happy for up to a year, I'd take you on immediately afterwards as my personal assistant. If you proved capable at that, you could look forward to helping run the joint!'

Alexandra shook her head. 'Let's see if I can even crawl before I learn to walk or run, shall we? Arrange the interviews for the Australian job and I promise to stick with it, if there's any chance of working directly for you afterwards. It was pure jealousy that made me behave so badly today, and the best way to handle jealousy is to prove to yourself that you can do the same things as the person who has what you want.'

'Hmm, that should keep me watching my back.'

For the first time, Alexandra gave her a really warm smile. 'Oh, I don't think so. I think this is the first time anyone has given me a chance to make it on my own. It's quite a thought.'

On her way home that evening, Rose found it difficult to keep a smile off her lips. Alexander had arranged for his share of the company to revert to her in the event of his death or bankruptcy. He had seen it as a business provision, and had not expected to be cut down so early. But now there was a logical heir to the firm, and one Rose could regard as her own successor, too. But the girl would get her share only if she earned it. Even now, the self-contained, private Rose Rush had her own secrets. If Alexandra fell down on the job, the company remained in Rose's hands. If the girl made good, they would share a prosperous future in Best of British.

But she isn't your flesh and blood, said a warning voice inside her. Aloud, Rose answered it: 'Joe Rush was, and look what he did to me! Give me strangers any time!' Her car drew up at the kerb and swept her away towards her comfortably private apartment.

Chapter Thirty-three
June 1970

'I still think it was insane to leave them there all on their own. Good God, man, thirty bedrooms and two restaurants? It wouldn't surprise me if the poor buggers had run off and left it all!'

Emil laughed easily. 'That's my Eleri — never throw away a dramatic moment when you can use it to the full.'

'Well, if you're going to be insulting!'

'You know better than that. I wouldn't want you any different — you light up my life, Madame Simon.'

Immediately she softened. 'Sweet-talker! You'd better mean it. And if anything have gone wrong, don't think I won't *still* hold it against you!'

'You may declare a vendetta on me if it has. But I have never felt safer in my life. You really should have faith in your own offspring.'

'If I didn't have faith in them, believe me it would have taken more than you to shoe-horn me off to Jamaica for a month. Now for God's sake, gerra move on. I may have gone off and left them to it, but I'll bust a gut if I don't get back soon and see how they're coping.'

The years had dealt kindly with the Simons, both physically and materially. At sixty, Eleri still had the appealing look of a slightly overfed tabby kitten. Her face was remarkably free of lines and her hair retained much of its bright brown buoyancy. She always put it down to thirty-odd years of happiness and hard work with Emil. His once dark hair was greying now, and half a lifetime of Eleri's incomparable food had thickened his waistline slightly, but beyond that he, too, retained the look of the young man she had fallen in love with.

The Pleasure Dome had prospered beyond their wildest dreams, doing remarkably well during the war when Eleri went over almost completely to a menu of game and fish, neither of which was rationed. By the time the days of post-war prosperity arrived, they were so well-established that nothing could stop them. At regular intervals, new Pleasure Domes opened – Chelsea in 1953; Carlos Place – still Eleri's special baby because of its top address – in 1955; Walton Street in 1959. A Fulham branch followed in 1964, just in time to catch the first well-heeled Sloane Rangers as they moved in and began gentrifying the area.

By the time Islington and Hampstead had been added to the chain, the Simons were looking for a fresh challenge. So far they had succeeded by working to a foolproof formula. When a new branch started up, Eleri forsook the one where she had been cooking and moved on to the new restaurant. They never considered a new venture unless they had heard on the grapevine that there was a first-rate chef available. Emil would make a series of scouting trips to France to pick up a sommelier with a potential to equal his own as a young man, and to find at least one good waiter. 'Englishmen do many things well, but service jobs are not among them,' he was fond of telling Eleri. He attracted the French staff with the temptation of good wages and civilised working conditions – neither being common factors in the profession at other establishments.

There followed at least a week of full-scale rehearsals of preparing menus, tasting them and checking the logistics of the new restaurant. Once they opened, Eleri stayed in charge of the kitchen for at least a month, then left the new chef to get on with it. After that, neither she nor Emil interfered. The chef and sommelier ran their own small kingdom, and as long as they accounted satisfactorily for themselves at the weekly staff meetings, were allowed as much freedom as they wanted. As a result, both the Simons received a steady stream of requests, suggestions and proposed innovations which were seldom less than useful and sometimes made a lot of money.

Eleri did not cook permanently at any restaurant in the chain. 'It's a young woman's game,' she said, 'and I like my time off too much for that.' Instead she kept her hand in by acting as substitute chef whenever one of them went on holiday. The rest of the time, she and Emil were kept busy by the day-to-day tasks of management. It was a full, satisfying life, but by the late 1960s they were both confirmed innovators who knew they did not wish to expand their restaurant business any further.

'We're the wrong sort of restaurant for the City,' said Eleri after lengthy discussion of the possibilities of expansion. 'Much as I hate to say it, Emil, I think we've taken up every bit of London we want to cover. What do we do next?'

He shrugged. 'Start a few branches around the outer suburbs, perhaps?' But his tone lacked enthusiasm. Neither of them needed to state the arguments against the development, lack of personal control and over-extension of resources heading the list. 'I know,' he added. 'It is too much you and me, is it not? Without us, it would fall to pieces.'

'You and me . . .' Eleri was tapping her pencil against her teeth. 'Dear God, we ent arf stupid sometimes! Those poor kids of ours are probably frothing at the mouth to have a go and we don't give 'em a look-in! I think it's more than time we started.'

'What are you talking about, woman? They're all doing what they want. We cannot simply uproot them.'

'Can't we, then? Just watch me! If I know our lot, they just been waiting for us to ask!'

They had four children, three sons and a daughter. Karl, the eldest, was twenty-nine. With his parents and a godfather like Karl Schlegel, it had been inevitable that he would go into the restaurant business. Karl had been cooking before he was seven, and was better than most gifted amateurs before he reached his teens. That did not prevent his mother from demanding he got the best training available. 'Karl Schlegel got it for me through the back door,' she told Emil.

'*This* Karl is going to France and you're finding one of the top Michelin chefs to train him.'

Karl, supremely talented, with a gentle smile, his mother's slightly rolypoly shape and his father's irresistible charm, completed a training crowned with awards for every young chef's competition the French restaurant profession could devise. He returned to England in the early 1960s, just as the explosion of interest in good food was becoming a mass preoccupation instead of an elitist pursuit, and worked for a couple of years in the Chelsea Pleasure Dome. He was the only chef whom Eleri ever admitted was better than herself. In 1966 he had astonished the whole family, married one of the most glamorous photographic models in the business, and decamped from London to open a harbourside restaurant of his own in Devon.

Marianne, the second child, was as much a natural to the catering trade as Karl, but she had no ambitions to rival her mother and brother as a cook. 'Two's quite enough,' she had said, when the question of earning a living had come up. Turning to her father, she added: 'I know you like to show me off as a champion cook, but really I'll never be more than a dabbler compared with these two, and you know it. Even you're hard put to it to compliment me on my omelettes!'

But she had stayed in the family trade, none the less, going into management and training in Switzerland at the best hotel school in the world. From Switzerland, she had gone to France and then to a couple of the most exclusive millionaire developments in the West Indies, where she had quickly risen to general manager of a top hotel group. Recently Eleri had taken to worrying about Marianne. 'I know something is wrong,' she told Emil. 'Her letters are . . . sort of brittle, somehow. Mark my words, there's a man in it, and a man who's let her down.'

Emil was perplexed by the whole business. He trusted Eleri's intuition but he himself would not have gathered any such impression from his daughter's spiky, amusing letters. When Eleri embarked on her ingenuous 'Why didn't we think of involving the children?' routine, he began wondering, though, whether the whole strategy might not be an elaborate ploy of his wife's to bring her favourite child back to a happier life.

Then there was Nick. Nick was made to be a maître d'hotel. He was so handsome that although he was her son, a glance at him sometimes took Eleri's breath away. His effect on female diners was predictably devastating. Nick had trained with his father, and was the one second-generation Simon who seemed set to stay with the restaurant chain for good. Now that Emil's main function was general management, Nick chose and bought the wines, did a similar back-up job on the sommelier side to Eleri's chef stand-in service during staff holidays, and generally acted as his parents' right-hand man. The big hotel restaurants made regular attempts to head-hunt him, but Nick was a happy man, with a job he enjoyed, parents he adored and a constant stream of female admirers waiting for encouragement. Who needed the Connaught?

Adam was the youngest, and the only Simon who had shown no interest in following the family business. What he did share with the rest was a desire to earn his living with his hands rather than in an academic field. But where Karl or Eleri used butter and meat as their raw materials, Adam used fine woods. He had trained as a furniture maker, and now ran his own small shop in Pimlico, producing exquisite limited-edition chairs, tables and screens. In the last year he had also been developing an interest in architectural restoration, an offshoot of the furniture and textile renovation techniques he had learned as a student.

It was Adam who sowed the first seeds of the expansion idea in Eleri's mind. He arrived for dinner with his parents one evening, clutching a handful of glossy magazines he had picked up at the local newsagent's on his way from the shop to their Chelsea house. As Emil busied himself pouring glasses of Rainwater Madeira, he thumbed through a couple. He abruptly stopped his idle page-turning with a gasp of pleasure as his father approached him with the wine.

Emil grinned at him. 'Can my philistine son have finally developed an interest in the great vintages?' he asked.

Adam shook his head impatiently. 'Look at this, Pa. Isn't it perfect?'

Emil looked down at the open copy of *Country Life*, which showed a black and white photograph of an elegant but unexceptional mansion on the For Sale pages. 'I confess it would not have made me hold my breath,' he said, 'but to each his own. What is so special about it?'

Adam, glowing with enthusiasm, proceeded to tell him. 'The external stonework; the proportion of the windows; the – the sheer *unity* of the design! Can't you see? It's as perfect of its kind as one of Maman's dinners?'

Emil looked over his shoulder with exaggerated caution and pressed a finger to his lips. 'Shh! She might hear you! She would spill your blood if she heard you compare her food to a pile of old masonry!'

'A pile of old masonry! I'm the one who'll be shedding blood if you say anything else like that. I'm telling you, Pa, that is architectural perfection!'

'But it appears to be falling down.'

'So is Stonehenge, but what a place. I'd give every penny I own to get my hands on that and restore it from end to end – refurnish it with genuine old stuff and some special pieces of my own . . . oh, man, what a dream!'

'I have fathered a tribe of lunatics. It would cost a fortune.'

'Of course it would . . . but what if you persuaded someone to treat it as an investment?'

'Who would invest in a crumbling pile of masonry?'

'I keep telling you, Pa, it wouldn't be crumbling when I'd finished with it! And I know exactly the sort of people who'd invest. Wait – I'll show you.' He delved into the rest of the magazines, eventually producing one called *Design For Living*. Opening it at a lavish full-colour double-page spread, he said: 'That's what it could be – and then some!'

Emil sucked air noisily over his teeth. 'Adam, it would

cost enough to finance another chain of restaurants. It's out of the question!'

'Is it? Read between the lines of that feature. You're a pro. You'll be able to guess what they're making out of that place. I could make you something even better.'

The article was about an Elizabethan manor house in Hampshire, half derelict when its hotelier owner had snapped it up a few years ago, now one of the fairy tales of the up-market leisure business. 'Look at it, Pa,' said Adam, eyes shining. 'Surely I don't need to tell you the next great leap in the catering business is going to be country-house hotels?'

Then Emil uttered the sentence he had been regretting ever since. 'But none of us knows anything about running a country-house hotel!'

'What did you just say?' Eleri had materialised in the doorway and was looking at them both with the light of battle in her eye.

'Nothing, my dearest – nothing of any importance . . .'

She sailed into the room and snatched the magazine from Adam's hands, beginning to scan the pictures and copy as she did so. When she looked up again, Emil knew he was beaten. '*Iesu Mawr*!' she murmured. 'I remember dear old Karl once telling me about some Prussian general who looked at London and said. "What a place to loot!" Well, now – what a place to loot!'

There was an even bigger incentive ahead to her empire-building instincts. Emil handed over the copy of *Country Life*. 'He wants to buy this place and convert it,' he said by way of explanation. Eleri, only half listening because she was day-dreaming about the renovated mansion in the first magazine, glanced down at the monochrome picture.

Beneath the illustration was the summary of the property's features, under the headline:

For sale as a whole or
in four lots
FENTON PARVA HOUSE, FENTON, WILTSHIRE

Eleri looked up at her husband and son. 'I don't care what it costs – we're having it!' she told them.

Since then, the world seemed to have gone mad. Emil was French peasant through and through. In the past he had always financed each new restaurant with the profits from the one before. They had opened the most expensive Pleasure Dome – Carlos Place – only because Karl Schlegel had died that year and had left them a considerable legacy. Apart from Karl's initial investment, which he had insisted was a wedding gift, they had always been self-financed.

Now they seemed to be mortgaged to everyone. In fact their indebtedness was excessive only in Emil's cautious imagination. They prepared a business plan with meticulous care and there was no question of the Pleasure Dome chain failing to provide sufficient collateral. The restaurants not only provided a backing; they retained sufficient residual value to cushion each branch against any temporary setbacks in the trade.

It still made Emil tremble to see the sort of bills incurred by timber treatment and roof replacement on a building like Fenton, which had been neglected since the war. In the end, Adam's patience snapped and he ordered his father out until at least the basic work was finished. In the meantime, Eleri was dragooning the rest of her family into line in support of the enterprise.

Now, two years later, she still found it hard to believe that everything had worked so well. Nick was no problem. He was happy to work anywhere if he had control of the cellar and his family were within easy reach. He and Emil quickly reached an agreement that they would divide responsibility between them for the first year for restaurant chain and hotel, deciding at the end of the period on a permanent arrangement.

Eleri's instinct that all was not well with Marianne proved well-founded. When she telephoned her daughter in Trinidad and tried to find a tactful way of raising the possibility of getting her back to run an English hotel, the girl almost knocked her down in the rush to accept.

'Hang on, now, love,' she said at last. 'I don't want to make you feel family responsibilities are dragging you away from such a wonderful job. Are you sure about this?'

The silence went on so long she thought they had been disconnected, then her daughter uttered a small sob, hastily suppressed, and said: 'Oh, Maman – you have no idea how much I want to come home! What I'd give for a rainy English afternoon.'

Eleri glanced out of the window, which was swamped with a stream of autumn raindrops. 'Ah, well,' she said, 'I s'pose there's no accounting for taste!'

The biggest surprise of all was Karl. Never a great letter-writer, he had always telephoned once or twice a week to keep them up to date with news. The calls had tailed off somewhat during the summer, but Emil and Eleri had put that down to the busy holiday period and staff shortages. It was not until Emil wrote to outline their proposals for Fenton that they realised they had failed to notice what trouble their eldest son was in.

The day he received their letter, Karl was on the telephone. 'I couldn't bother you before, Pa, but I think you will save our lives if we come in with you.'

'Now wait a minute,' said Emil. 'God knows how long it will be before we show a profit, if ever. You have a restaurant which is talked about in all the best guides, you live in a beautiful place and you have a settled life. This is very uncertain.'

'I wish I recognised the picture you're drawing,' said Karl. 'The guides tell you what it's like in summer. We're in a lousy position in the winter, and we don't make enough between June and September to carry us the rest of the year. We've no space for rooms, so we can't offer people off-season weekends. Result: no profit. We live in a lovely place, and we eat like princes, but otherwise we're being driven crazy with worry.'

Emil went to tell Eleri about the conversation. She beamed her tabby cat grin and said: 'Everybody else have got a *batterie de cuisine*. Ours is beginning to look like a *batterie de famille*!

Once the family were lined up behind him, Emil felt much more secure. As their preparations progressed, he grew calmer and Eleri became increasingly hysterical. Finally, by the end of the winter of 1970, they were ready to start promotional work. That was when Emil told Eleri he was taking her away for the pre-opening month and not letting her near the hotel until it was on its feet.

'We have a bunch of the most competent, trustworthy children anyone could wish for,' he said. 'There is no point in our doing this if we are going to steal all their thunder. You know as well as I do that they can handle it. We will go away and swim and sunbathe and when we return, you can put on a gorgeous evening gown and help to welcome the first guests. No arguments. This is the start of their reign, not ours. Give them their fun.'

So they had gone off. For a week, Eleri had been in the Caribbean only physically. Her mind was far away, in the fold of a Wiltshire valley. Then, inevitably, her pleasure in Emil's company, the beauty of a place she had only dreamed of before, and even the prospect of going home to find a family gathered around her as they had been in childhood, combined to make her relax and enjoy herself. Until they reached Heathrow on their return, she was positively regal.

After that it was different. All the way down the M4 she was bubbling on the edge of hysteria. Emil steered the big Jaguar up the oh, so familiar drive at Fenton Parva, and they swept around the first curve beside the lake. Eleri murmured: 'First time I came up here, I was next to the chauffeur and the old dragon of a retired nanny was telling me I really wouldn't mind spending my time scrubbing saucepans and skinning hares.'

'Do you feel different now?' asked Emil.

'That swimming pool.' She gestured at one of Adam's more dramatic additions. 'I look at that, and I know that the meek shall inherit the Earth.'

The sentiment sounded so odd in the circumstances that

Emil glanced up at her, laughing his disbelief, and almost steered them into the ditch beside the drive. 'Careful!' Eleri grabbed the wheel and corrected the steering. 'I don't wanna miss this bit.' The big car cleared the bend and the immaculately restored house lay basking in the late afternoon sunshine. 'Looka that,' said Eleri. 'I feel as if I been waiting for that sight all my life.'

The first lady of Fenton Parva had come home, and she knew, from now on, everything would be all right.

More Compulsive Fiction from Headline:

MADEMOISELLE

A rags to riches saga
in the bestselling tradition
of A WOMAN OF
SUBSTANCE

MERLE JONES

Legendary designer Alouette Doré, queen of the fashion business for most of the century, has always avoided giving interviews about her past. But, now in her nineties, she wants to set the record straight. And the story Mademoiselle has to tell is a remarkable one . . .

Escaping from her drab existence as a shop assistant, Alouette joins the household of an aristocratic playboy and here the seeds of her future career take root. For her harsh convent upbringing has at least taught her skill with the needle and it is this that will make her fortune.

She starts by opening a hat shop, and soon her original creations adorn the heads of the stylish society ladies in her circle. Then she designs a range of daringly imaginative clothes and her reputation as the new queen of fashion is assured.

But Alouette's fame and fortune sometimes come at the expense of her personal happiness and, at the end of her rich and varied life, Mademoiselle comes to question whether she has paid too dearly for her success . . .

FICTION/SAGA   0 7472 3124 9

More Compelling Fiction from Headline:

MERLE JONES

KINGMAKER

The engrossing new saga from the author of *Mademoiselle*

The sins of the mothers...

From the day she is widowed, pregnant with her only child, Marged Richmond has only one man in her life – her son Henry. Determined to found a dynasty of Richmonds who will conquer the commercial world, she works and schemes to turn Henry into a gentleman. And when he threatens to ruin all her plans by falling in love with the wrong girl, Marged takes ruthless steps to put a stop to his infatuation – steps that set in train a sequence of events that dogs the family as surely as a witch's curse.

Despite his material success – which in the next generation culminates in a magnificent West End emporium, a byword for luxury – Henry has to weather repeated tragedy and eventually his children's children inherit a crumbling empire in a world of all too rapid change...

In the bestselling tradition of early Susan Howatch, *Kingmaker* is the story of the devastating effects of one woman's ambition on the succeeding generations. Moving from the beautiful Welsh countryside to the grimy Manchester slums and the luxury of top London society, it confirms Merle Jones as a talented and absorbing storyteller.

Don't miss *Mademoiselle* by Merle Jones, also from
HEADLINE

FICTION/SAGA   0 7472 3319 5

A selection of bestsellers from Headline

FICTION

RINGS	Ruth Walker	£4.99 □
THERE IS A SEASON	Elizabeth Murphy	£4.99 □
THE COVENANT OF THE FLAME	David Morrell	£4.99 □
THE SUMMER OF THE DANES	Ellis Peters	£6.99 □
DIAMOND HARD	Andrew MacAllan	£4.99 □
FLOWERS IN THE BLOOD	Gay Courter	£4.99 □
A PRIDE OF SISTERS	Evelyn Hood	£4.99 □
A PROFESSIONAL WOMAN	Tessa Barclay	£4.99 □
ONE RAINY NIGHT	Richard Laymon	£4.99 □
SUMMER OF NIGHT	Dan Simmons	£4.99 □

NON-FICTION

MEMORIES OF GASCONY	Pierre Koffmann	£6.99 □
THE JOY OF SPORT		£4.99 □
THE UFO ENCYCLOPEDIA	John Spencer	£6.99 □

SCIENCE FICTION AND FANTASY

THE OTHER SINBAD	Craig Shaw Gardner	£4.50 □
OTHERSYDE	J Michael Straczynski	£4.99 □
THE BOY FROM THE BURREN	Sheila Gilluly	£4.99 □
FELIMID'S HOMECOMING: Bard V	Keith Taylor	£3.99 □

All Headline books are available at your local bookshop or newsagent, or can be ordered direct from the publisher. Just tick the titles you want and fill in the form below. Prices and availability subject to change without notice.

Headline Book Publishing PLC, Cash Sales Department, PO Box 11, Falmouth, Cornwall, TR10 9EN, England.

Please enclose a cheque or postal order to the value of the cover price and allow the following for postage and packing:
UK & BFPO: £1.00 for the first book, 50p for the second book and 30p for each additional book ordered up to a maximum charge of £3.00
OVERSEAS & EIRE: £2.00 for the first book, £1.00 for the second book and 50p for each additional book.

Name ....

Address ....

....

....